A WILDERNESS GIFT

Over the brave's shoulder, de Tonti saw a moving figure in the shadows beneath the tree. It was a woman quietly watching the proceedings without a ghost of emotion on her extraordinary face.

"My chief has ordered me to make fitting restitution for my error. This woman was the best I could think of," Walking Many Mountains said, turning slightly to include her with a gesture of his hand. "Her name is Weeononka—in your language that means Fleet Woman."

De Tonti continued walking, shaking his head, avoiding any glimpse of her. He had been shocked by her beauty, her eyes daring to peruse him unlike any Indian woman he'd seen so far. But what trouble she'd be on the expedition. La Salle would kill him, or worse, dismiss him, leaving him at large in the wilderness. He flared at the Iroquois. "I don't want her. Now leave me alone."

"Very well, then," said Walking Many Mountains, dropping back, but he stopped de Tonti short when he said, "But Weeononka is from the Arkansas. . . ."

RIVER OF DESTINY

RIVER OF DESTINY

Pat Winter

BANTAM BOOKS
TORONTO • NEW YORK • LONDON • SYDNEY • AUCKLAND

RIVER OF DESTINY

A Bantam Book / August 1986

Map by Ray Lundgren

ISBN 0-553-25869-9

Published simultaneously in the United States and Canada

Bantam Books are published by Bantam Books, Inc. Its trademark,
consisting of the words "Bantam Books" and the portrayal of a
rooster, is Registered in U.S. Patent and Trademark Office and in
other countries. Marca Registrada. Bantam Books, Inc., 666 Fifth
Avenue, New York, New York 10103.

PRINTED IN THE UNITED STATES OF AMERICA

O   0 9 8 7 6 5 4 3 2 1

In memory of my Arkansas daddy
Curtis Lenore Cooper

This is a retelling of the legends of Petit Jean Mountain. It's not pure history. It's a story woven in the blank spaces between the lines of journals, letters, and histories, intended to enliven interest in events too long forgotten, and to illuminate remarkable lives long unsung in the history of Arkansas. Of that name alone there are more than fifty variations. For clarity I've used modern American spellings except in a few special cases such as the word *Mech-a-si-pi*. The Quapaw words are speculations based on Sioux, the linguistic parent of the Quapaw dialect.

Chapter 31 is a quote from the English translation of the 1693 "Memoirs of Henri de Tonti," in *Historical Collections of Louisiana*. Other primary sources are English translations of the memoirs and letters of La Salle, St. Cosme, Penicaut, Hennepin, and Joutel, from whom I quote La Salle's letter to de Tonti, which La Salle's brother either secured before the explorer's death or forged afterward on his stationery. The firsthand description of La Salle's last hours, as well as his note to de Tonti in Chapter 32, is quoted from Joutel. Principal texts used are George Catlin's *American Indians*, published in 1830, and Frances Parkman's *La Salle and the Discovery of the Great West*, 1897, from which are quoted La Salle's commission from Louis XVI in Chapter 16, and his letter commending de Tonti in Chapter 24.

For invaluable contributions, grateful thanks to Joelle Dobrow, Carla West, Robert Hoskins, Lydia Galton, and especially Patrick O'Connor.

Pat Winter
Hideout Mountain, Arkansas

THE MISSISSIPPI RIVER VALLEY
AT THE
TIME OF DE TONTI'S TRAVELS
(from a French 18th century map)

LAKE SUPERIOR

CHIPPEWA NATION

Michillimackinac Island

SIOUX NATION

LAKE HURON

Chicagou River

LAKE MICHIGAN

NEW FRANCE

Detroit

Fort Crevecoeur
(Broken Heart)

LAKE ERIE

ERIE NATION

ILLINOIS NATION

Illinois River

Ft. St. Louis

Mississippi River

IROQUOIS NATION

Wabash River

Missouri River

Cumberland River

OSAGE NATION

BRITISH VIRGINIA

SHAWNEE NATION

Arkansas or Tonti River

Tennessee River

CHEROKEE NATION

CAROLINA

Kappa   Chisca

CHICKASAW NATION

Appalachian Mountains

QUAPAW NATION

Chickasaw Bluffs

Osotony

CHOCTAW NATION

MUSKOGEE NATION

CREEK NATION

ALABAMA NATION

SPANISH FLORIDA

Natchez

MOBILIAN NATION

Red River

TAENSAS NATION

St. Augustine

Mobile Bay

GULF OF MEXICO

I

WEEONONKA

WERONIKA

1

Bad weather was on the wind. The girl could smell it. All her snares were empty. The rabbits could smell it too and burrowed deeper to live off their fat awhile longer until the bad wind changed to normal springtime.

Over this ridge lay one more trap she'd put out late yesterday in a thicket of shriveled blackberries. She nocked an arrow to her short bow as she stalked that last snare. If it was sprung, her quarry would be waiting alive and unwounded. If the trap was empty, she'd eat only journeycake again tonight. No animals were moving, not even birds. Around her the land seemed to hold its breath between gusts of wind and suspended seasons. The land didn't have a name in those days. People didn't own it. The land owned the people, who regarded their northern mountains and southern river valley as the Great Mother, adored and feared and too full of mystery to be called anything except wonderful.

But lesser beings need names.

To remember their ancient exodus her people called themselves "the ones who drifted downstream."

When Weeon'onka came to spend her sixteenth winter alone on this mountain to find her own name, the nation was known simply as Drifted Downstream, or *Ugaxpa*, in the Siouxan language. Frenchmen soon to come would not hear the music in *Ugaxpa* and would soften it to *Arkansas* when speaking of the land and *Quapaw* when speaking of the people.

Weeon'onka was a lowland Quapaw who had lived the past ten winters with her late mother's mountain tribe, the Osage. She walked tall by Quapaw standards but was about average among the Osage, who were generally bigger than their southern cousins. Raven-haired and willowy in a dress of gray-colored skins, she blended with the forest. Her skin had the high color of rubbed cedar; her eyes were as dark and quick as minnows in cold creek water. Though she traversed a steep humus skirt of rough mountainside, she didn't leave a mark, not even a moccasin print, and made no more noise than a dry

3

branch in the wind that carried the smell of a freak Crow Moon snowfall.

The last snare held a rabbit. Meat! she thought in anticipation but put the bow back into her travel bag when she saw it was quite a small rabbit peering up at her with fear-glazed eyes. She was so hungry for meat even this skinny snowtail looked appetizing. Her supply of jerky had run out two sunrises ago in the second moon of her *tanka y'ante inati*—the time when a girl went off to live alone until she had a naming vision. On three different nights she burned moon blood in the cave's shadowed back reaches and drank the black drink that was supposed to put her into a naming trance. Three times the vision drink had made her sick, three times she had had no vision. She hadn't brought enough food from her relatives' lodge to stay up here in Mother's caves much longer, yet she'd lose face if she returned to the Osage camp without her adult name.

It was a bad turn of events, which had laid her spirit low. She slipped her hand into the basket snare, grasping the pulsing warmth of the little creature who would make, when mated to a soup of wild garlic, cattail tubers, and dried blueberries, a sparse but delicious stew. Her spirit lifted with the imagined meat-cooking aroma as she took the bony doe out by the scruff.

Her thumb felt for fragile neck bones beneath the fur. The rabbit did not fight; it was paralyzed by the stalking fear. Weeon'onka was just about to snap its neck as she'd expertly done without sentiment hundreds of times before, when she felt rabbit babies under belly fur like wet hickory nuts in a sack. Her fingers probed: four, six, nine in all, ready to be born.

"Well, Mother, you've chosen to play a joke on your daughter," she whispered. It could create very bad *wa kon* to take a pregnant kill. Convention grudgingly allowed it in extreme hunger with extensive cleansing rituals but something in the hopeful quiver of the rabbit's whiskers stayed Weeon-onka's hand. She made the mistake of looking into the creature's eyes, where she saw her own small hopes reflected.

"Not much for us to eat out here today, eh, sister?"

The rabbit hungrily investigated her salty fingertips as Weeon'onka sat on a fallen oak. She took from her parfleche bag a lumpy journeycake, which she began to shave with a fine flint knife. The cake was made of many things: dried berries, persimmon, amaranth seed, cornmeal, piñon nuts, hickory meat, and bear suet, all held together with honey and bleached acorn flour. The starving rabbit took the offering and begged for more.

"Go away before I change my mind," Weeon'onka advised, her stomach growling as she nudged the creature away with her moccasin toe. Not exactly morose but neither with a singing heart, she munched on the rest of the journeycake. Her lost stew hopped away, suddenly remembering to be frightened.

Maybe I've offended *wesa*, Weeon'onka thought. The wind died after a little fit. It was so quiet she imagined she might hear her manitou, the snake, whispering secrets. "Maybe I'll just name myself," she decided out loud when *wesa* didn't answer. She looked around, letting her eyes search for something that suggested a good woman's name. What I really need, she thought, is a *sign*.

A foreign sound shattered the stillness, the distinct cry of an Osage warrior calling "Weeon'onka—" many times up the echoing mountainside and drawing closer each time, *"Hau!"*

She stood in silent shock: It was unthinkable that a man would approach this area sacred to the Mother and set aside exclusively for girls in ritual isolation. Yet there was the familiar masculine voice calling again.

It was Game Dancer. Of all the men in the village, why would he interrupt her ritual? That he was so close at this moment made her legs feel hot, made her ears tingle. Before her *tanka y'ante inati* a girl was free to take any lover, but after her woman-naming she was expected to put away childish play and settle down with one husband. Of all her lovers Weeon'-onka liked Game Dancer best and he made it clear to everyone in the Osage community that he wanted her, too. All that stood between their digging the foundation for an earthlodge was this, her *tanka y'ante inati*. Why would he risk polluting it?

She left the open blueberry meadow for cedar cover on the ridge. The great bowl of land swept southward before her, ringed by ageless eroded blue ridges and deep gray hollows. The wind had scraped away any low clouds, leaving only a high silver ceiling shot with the cold white circle of the sun. Half a day's walk down this draw lay the Osage village. Her eyes scanned the trail of littered boulders shaggy with green moss, the only color in the otherwise unadorned wood. She couldn't see the interloper but from the direction of his last call he had to be on the path just below this approach to the caves, in the brow of the mountain. She waited, tensing, for some further sign from him.

Soon a purposefully blackened puff of woodsmoke rose above a line of bare hickories. It scattered immediately but after the conventional pause of five breaths another oily smokeball broke against the wind. It was the signal for attention. Well, she thought, at least he wasn't coming any closer. But she wasn't ready to surrender to his impertinence, though her body ached to wrap itself around him. Two moons with no pleasure made her hungry in more than the belly.

After a polite silence his voice called again, "Dancing Buck says come home."

She crept closer to his position, circling wide to approach downwind of him. Her bow was ready. To his credit, he had stopped just outside the sacred precincts. But it was an outrage anyway. It was her duty to be furious with him. Now she was near enough to smell his acrid fire. Her nipples were hard, her eyes bright with desire that intensified as she stalked the mighty hunter who was now her prey.

Her woman's bow was half as tall as his but of the same resilient yellow wood for which this region was famous. It might be a diminutive weapon, but at this range it was deadly accurate. Drawing down from a favorably high position she could have sent a fire-hardened arrow in one ear and out the other before the man knew what hit him, mighty warrior or not.

So when instead she put it precisely one hand's width to the right in a knobby old dogwood, it had the effect of drawing his immediate wide-eyed attention. The arrow twanged in the hollow silence between them. He looked up. She was silhouetted against the sky's diffuse glare. She had expertly managed to be not only downwind but also between him and the sun. She had outstalked the stalker, and even though they were entirely alone, the warrior was chagrined that he'd been outmaneuvered by this impudent girl who nervelessly aimed another arrow at his right eye.

Unable to believe she'd really follow through on her threat but bound by honor nonetheless, he defiantly threw off the buffalo robe to reveal his polished chest and showed open, empty hands. "I am a warrior ready to die," he announced, but his eyes were twinkling.

Game Dancer was tall even by Osage standards and dressed

for travel, that was, hardly at all. It delighted her to see the hang of his loincloth was disturbed. He acknowledged her observation with a sensual smile. His meticulously plucked scalp was shiny with oil, his lifelong manicuring of it producing the perfect Osage standard of male beauty. He wore none of the usual paint on his head and had taken most of the feathers and other clan decorations from his scalplock. He wore only a modest bunch of feathers in each earhole. Here and there his skin was tattooed with significant signs and healed battle scars. He carried a thunderous headknocker on a waist thong, a bow of finest local wood, and a bulging quiver across his back.

Truly magnificent, she thought, and she was most fortunate to have his attention. But the game had gone on long enough. She relaxed the bow. "Why did you come here?" she asked as she descended the ledge while he watched beside the dogwood where her arrow still trembled.

"To take you back."

"I'm not ready to go back." She yanked the arrow from the tree, regarded its hot point briefly, then put it in the parfleche.

"It's not a matter for debate."

"Surely you can be patient a little longer."

"Our father wishes it," he said, using an honorific title for the Osage civil chief. Dancing Buck was considered the male parent of the whole village.

"And you don't?" Weeon'onka laid her palm on the hot skin beneath his neck. His heart was pounding just like hers.

"No—I mean, I want you to come home too," he said quickly, grabbing her wrist but pressing only lightly with his thumb on her own drumming pulse. He favored her with another smile that promised pleasure. "But I'm here on his wish."

She twisted her hand from his and rubbed it while she talked. "Why would he trouble over this insignificant person?"

He shrugged.

"I can't leave before I get my name."

"Dancing Buck says out of respect for him you should come immediately."

"Not until I get my name." But she knew it was inevitable. A summons from Dancing Buck could not be ignored.

He retrieved the bear robe from the ground.

"What have you there?" she inquired.

"What?"

"That object in your belt, what is it?"

"Nothing. A foreign trinket."

"Foreign guests are in the village?"

"A raven from the south." Couriers between friendly nations were called "ravens."

She stepped closer to see the object but he moved defensively aside to adjust his robe.

"*Hopo, hopo*," he said, meaning, "Let's go," but when he turned again she was gone as though she'd melted into the wide shale plateau. In a bound he was after the only trace of her, a pebble rolling down the ridge. His powerful legs moved at a steep angle to the line of cedars. Once on the ridge he paused, scanning laterally for any sign. He glanced in the direction of the forbidden twin caves that were like sightless sockets in the limestone face. He was very close to violating taboo. If she went left toward the brow, he would not follow. There was nothing in the physical world this warrior feared, but the dark mysteries of those places gave him the chills. And unexpectedly burning sexual desire, a gift from the Mother's proximity as well as the girl's. He could feel her presence like a touch on his thigh. A twig snapped to the right. He whirled around, angry at her for teasing. Maybe she'd gone crazy up here all by herself, he thought as he dashed after the shadow moving to the right through the cedars away from the holy caves. A creek tumbled beyond the evergreens. One wet moccasin print stained a rock pointing toward another cedar grove.

He ran her to ground panting and scratching not ten paces ahead with a leap and a tackle. They rolled together against a mossy bank.

Aroused by the chase and finally in each other's arms, lovemaking followed as inevitably as the creek followed the ravine downhill. They had pleasured each other many times before but never as finely as they did that late afternoon. The sun broke briefly through. They stripped to their tattoos to soak up the beautiful warmth, making love sitting facing each other in the traditional "twin rowers in a small canoe" position, legs entwined. He lay her back and began the wordless, mindless chant men sing to women. Suddenly she was swept upward against him as he knelt, then stood with a great cry of ecstasy. She'd never experienced anything like it but was old enough to have heard stories about the life force shooting from the ground through a man and woman joined and completely in tune with each other. She had never realized she'd be uplifted so completely that her toes dangled off the ground. Game Dancer was so pleasured, he was laughing softly, eyes closed as his body sought balance by pivoting. Weeon'onka clamped her legs behind his back and held on. Slowly at first, then gaining speed, he swung her around as her arms slipped from his neck and down his arms until their clasped hands tied them firmly together. Like children they squealed with delight as they twirled around and around, her long loose hair a wing behind her. But even Game Dancer's powerful body tired after a while. Still joined sweetly at hips and hands, he let her down and dropped, panting on her. Neither would break the bond but held on as ardor subsided. This seemed to her to have been a wordless ceremony. She watched him for some sign that he took it the same way, but he was reticent. It was he who pulled away. He lay back as the clouds moved in and the wind cooled them.

After passion waned, she began to look doubtfully at the brooding mountain. It wasn't the act of love that might profane this place; to the Mother sex was a religious celebration.

It was the male presence this close to Her caves that might offend. Even Weeon'onka wasn't sure if she had led him far enough away. When he saw her concern, they dressed quickly without speaking and started back down the ridge. Weeon'onka couldn't resist one more look back.

What was to become of her without a woman's name, she privately wondered, settling into pace with the warrior. At first he talked casually with her, as if he had something to say but couldn't say it. He grew silent as they neared the village. The sheen that desire had rubbed on them in the afternoon turned frosty by evening, when their breaths began fogging and the first unseasonable snowflakes stuck to their eyelashes.

Nobody stirred outside the cozy earthlodges scattered along the meadow pass. Game Dancer silently signaled the lookout when they passed his concealed position and hurried on to the central cabin. Dancing Buck greeted them formally and with unusual honor.

With their own hands his wife, sister, and youngest daughter fed Game Dancer and Weeon'onka small delicacies and made polite small talk while the men smoked. Weeon'onka was possessed by thoughts of food but silenced any requests for seconds when she saw her lover suddenly ask to be excused. Buck nodded as if this had been prearranged, and the young man left the lodge without further comment, refusing to catch Weeon'onka's eye.

Chief Dancing Buck turned his craggy face toward the girl while his women settled along the back bed ledge, giving her in effect a private audience. Weeon'onka couldn't have been more astounded. "Why am I suddenly given this unprecedented honor?" she asked.

Buck puffed on his long feathered pipe before he replied. "You have an opportunity to benefit not only this village but also your father's people."

So, she thought, the raven from the south was from the Quapaw. She waited for him to continue. "Your aunt's husband wishes you to go there and be his second wife."

"My uncle?" She only vaguely remembered the man whom she'd last seen in her sixth winter. "But my aunt is still living."

"And wishes you to be her husband's second wife. I know it's strange even for Quapaw, but such things were done in the days of the great wanderings. It's your choice, of course, but it would strengthen the alliance between us if I let you go. As a gesture of goodwill, you see."

"But Game Dancer and I—" Then she realized. "He knew about this, didn't he?"

Buck nodded. "Your uncle paid him the bride price."

"The foreign trinket!" So that was why he wouldn't talk about it, why he'd acted so shy with her. Then he'd compounded the outrage by making love as though nothing had changed.

"I wasn't party to their bargain. I only know Game Dancer will no longer court you."

Weeon'onka felt a shaft of white hot anguish rush from the soles of her feet to her forehead. The backwash of anger boiled in every part of her but she kept it inside, so all that showed was a deepening of her color as the shadow of bitter understanding crossed her face. Her scalp tingled with rage that someone she trusted had deceived her after trading her for something so valueless. This, on top of having no woman name, was more lost face than she could bear. People would whisper behind her back. They'd act polite and shut her out as an object of pity.

Chief Buck himself felt sorry for her when he saw this realization cloud her beautiful face. Buck was too smart to get between a man and a woman, but he was disappointed in the warrior. He'd specifically assigned Game Dancer to go after her so they would have private time for him to make it right between them. But he could see Game Dancer had not told her anything. At least now it was likely the girl would go, rather than stay and be humiliated by his rejection.

"I cannot go," she said miserably. "I shouldn't have left the mountain." She was fighting back tears. Buck's wife, sisters, and daughters beyond the fire watched, entranced by her ordeal. The expectant glistening of their eyes made her determined not to give in to their morbid curiosity by acting like a weakling. She willed her voice to be stronger. "I still don't have my woman name." It was a terrible confession. They'd never heard of anyone, male or female, failing to get a name from the isolation ritual.

Buck frowned. But someone else chuckled. The sound was unexpected, breaking the mood somewhat as a shadow moved nearby. His ancient elder sister sidled up to Buck to whisper in his ear. The old man's face brightened; he wished only to satisfy everyone. Besides, the girl had his sympathy: she must have her woman name before marriage. His sister, who often counseled him, had just suggested a solution that was unorthodox, but well within his power as official father of the village. It was his province to name newborns; she was his first adult. While his sister nodded encouragement beside him, he placed his tattooed hands on Weeon'onka's hair. "Whoever named you Fleet Girl had wisdom. There are very few persons who take the name at birth they'll keep throughout life. Weeon'onka you were born and Weeononka you remain." He accented her name differently the second time; thus, she became Fleet Woman.

The sister scurried close to her, muttering a ritual chant, eyes bright with appropriate sisterly emotions. She daubed red earth and oil from a cold clam shell into Weeononka's partline. This was the conclusion of the ceremony that would have been given for her after the naming vision. The paint cooled her anger and enlivened her scalp as though her head had been symbolically opened for a new, larger identity.

"This is a sign of special destiny," Dancing Buck pronounced, taking a long draw on the pipe. Then he did something which shocked even his sister. He handed the pipe, reserved exclusively for himself and male guests, to the girl. She hesitated only a moment, then, with a look that said she appreciated the gesture, she reverently accepted the calumet. After a careful but unflinching pull on the pipe, she handed it

back to him. She began to choke as the unfamiliar fumes
expanded in her lungs. Tears brimmed her eyes but she was
determined not to lose the smoke. She saw him encouraging
her and she found a way to let smoke trickle in a fine stream
from her nostrils the way she'd seen the warriors do it.
Privately she decided that was all she'd ever need of the awful
nippowoc but she smiled with pride because she had been
invited to share smoke with this esteemed person. Buck's wise
old sister clapped her hands while the others looked in open-
mouthed wonder at something they'd never seen before. Fleet
Woman smoking would be the subject of gossip long after she
left the next morning to fulfill her special destiny.

2

Weeononka and three others traveled east through the
deeply eroded misty mountains that white people would
someday call the Ozarks. The second day they broached a long
southward spine where the spot to turn south had long been
marked with red clay and bear grease paint. They'd camped
the first night beneath the massive limestone overhang marked
with the symbols for day and river—of how many days travel it
was to the Nigestai, which flowed into the Mech-a-si-pi. The
ridge dropped immediately toward the great river's wide
floodplain, and by the third day on the trail Weeononka missed
the mountains. She kept looking back but the forest was so
thick with creepers and fat-bottomed trees she could no longer
catch a glimpse of the highlands. As she and the other three
descended, they had also moved from cold weather to humid.
"Don't waste time looking backward, Weeononka," Crow
Sister said. The older Osage woman preceded the girl on the
path along the western bank of this river, swatting flies with a
feather fan. In front of her on the narrow trace was Game
Dancer, and following behind was the Quapaw raven, Three
Crows Flying, who carried Weeononka's belongings with a
trumpline across his forehead. She had never had anyone carry
her bundles and she caught herself several times about to ask if
she might lighten his load. Crow Sister had seen the impulse,
and had reminded her that his chief had set him this task and it
wasn't her place to shame him by offering her small help.

"Don't worry, I hear a certain chief eats only the fat brides," Crow Sister joked, dropping back to walk beside the girl now that the path widened. "They say a certain chief is still a virile man even though he has forty and nine winters."

Weeononka wished the woman would be quiet. She was mortified by Game Dancer's escort anyway. Since she had discovered his deceit, she'd felt scalded by him. She tried to catch his eye, hoping to hear his explanation, but he was aloof, expecting her wrath but not courting it. Crow Sister insisted on calling attention to the humiliating situation but Weeononka was determined not to let her joking relative, who, by tradition, had the right to say anything to Weeononka, make her angry. Instead she thought about what Crow Sister implied. It was true. She was concerned that she was being married off to some old man who wouldn't be able to give her children.

She looked at the woman, who was grinning at her with tannin-stained teeth. Crow Sister was an expert hide tanner and wore the brown teeth like a badge.

"It is said a certain chief has many sons," Crow Sister added after a while.

Weeononka couldn't miss this gesture toward her in the presence of the man she would rather have been marrying. But this Osage warrior, Game Dancer, was silently ignoring their women's conversation. He considered himself honorable in accepting the foreign weapon from the Quapaw chief through the raven as intermediary. It was a fair trade. He had been wanting one of the strange weapons that spat small medicine balls with fire. Three Crows Flying told him it was made by white men, a story this warrior preferred to disbelieve until he had further proof. He'd been hearing of these white men for some time. He had yet to see one for himself.

Still, the weapon was a wonder to behold. The conniving Quapaw had not told him how to work this weapon, however—that would be the second part of the agreement, fulfilled when he brought this girl to the round lodge of the Quapaw chief.

Game Dancer was aware that Weeononka was eyeing him. Her questioning gaze made him restless and he refused to allow his eyes to rest on this most desirable woman. He really did hate to lose her, he thought. She was the most beautiful woman in his village. He tried not to look at her, at her deep

strange eyes, her perfect cheeks like doeskin. He caught a
glimpse of the vermillion paint in the partline of her glossy
black hair, which she chose to wear loose in the manner of the
Quapaw, who braided their hair up in coils about the ears only
when a girl became a wife. He felt the stab of her resentment,
believing that even if he reneged on his deal with the Quapaw
chief, she would never again respect him.

It felt suddenly good to be free of such a spiteful woman.
Still, he couldn't look at her directly. Why did she keep trying
to force him to meet her gaze? Didn't she know that was
unseemly?

"And they say he is very wealthy, this certain Quapaw
chief," Crow Sister was saying.

"So don't mourn what might have been with some ordinary
person." She stopped walking and whispered something
behind her palm into the ear of the younger woman. They
laughed softly and continued walking with their arms linked
together. Game Dancer's face felt hot when he passed them on
the trace. He called back sharply to the Quapaw warrior about
his bringing up the rear too slowly.

What were they giggling about? Game Dancer wondered as
he took up the trail before them as nominal head of the party.
He silently cursed the cloud of gnats around his face, but was
too proud to let it show that they worried him.

He was mortified that Crow Sister might be impugning him
to Weeononka to make her cherished girl feel better about
having to go to the Quapaws. Game Dancer was wrong,
though his guess was in the right direction: her whisper was
about the reputed girth of the sex of a certain Quapaw chief.

Up ahead the creek bent in its approach to the greater river
the Quapaw called Nigestai, which a short distance further
south joined the greatest river of them all, the Mech-a-si-pi.
They approached the bank, where they paused as Game
Dancer prepared a ritual; it was a tradition. Just as the people
thanked any animal they killed, they also soothed the spirits
thought to be living in moving water.

This was a floodland region with few rocks and no hills. But
this trading path was an old one; the Quapaw, despite the
occasional hostilities that were bound to happen between a
people of the low country and those of the high, were in a loose
alliance supported by numerous family ties with their cousins,
the Osage.

Just this side of the river bend lay a quagmire of blackberries
turning pink on a swamp of vine, totally impassable. The path

wound around this gigantic chief of blackberry patches but the path was overhung here and there with uncontrolled growth. Game Dancer stopped short with a gesture to the others as he surveyed the morass of thorny vine. He made the hand sign for snake. He could smell the copperheads, an acrid, heavy medicine odor.

Snakes loved blackberries. There were few things Crow Sister was afraid of, but a snake was one creature she avoided. She made an involuntary grimace, drawing back at Game Dancer's warning and the smell that wafted from the berry-patch. Weeononka, on the other hand, liked snakes: their smooth shiny scales, their graceful motion. The snake was her totem animal and so held no fear for her, though she showed them respect.

All four stood there, frozen in the moment—the burdened warrior, Game Dancer, Crow Sister, and Weeononka—each in his or her own way trying to identify that sound as if the sun itself with innumerable fingers were strumming the air. They looked around at each other, simultaneously recognizing the light song.

It was Weeononka who identified it in the silent speech of the hands; she touched her right index finger to the tip of her dusty rose tongue, the sign for sweet, and made the sign for good, a hand gesture sweeping out, level with the heart.

She started to speak, but Game Dancer silenced her, wary of some other sound his tracker's ears could distinguish under the bees' hum. After a few strained moments in which nobody moved, Game Dancer relaxed and signaled they could continue on the path.

"I would very much like to collect some honey as a wedding gift for my husband-to-be," Weeononka said to nobody in particular.

"It would take too long," replied the hunter, glad to be in control, to be telling this unseemly woman what to do. "We're supposed to be at the river village by sundown." He gestured at the sun. "He dies soon," he added, frowning seriously so as to head off any opposition because the sun himself was on his side.

"But," she continued, "it would require only a pause to find that honey—it's over in that big gum stump." He didn't need this woman to tell him the location of the honeycomb. A curtain of bees hung above the lightning-struck stump over in the direct middle of the berry thicket. It was so full, a great goutte of honey oozed from a crack.

"Think how good honey would be tonight," Crow Sister offered, smacking her lips.

"The credit would go to you, Game Dancer, for bringing in what is surely the largest honeycomb this woman has ever imagined to the chief, your friend and fellow bargainer."

He couldn't miss the barb hidden inside her logic but he didn't wish to be goaded into pausing.

"I'll bet you . . ." Weeononka said softly to him alone, ". . . a new quill-beaded quiver that you cannot get us honey without a single bee sting." She saw him hesitate, having never passed up a wager before; that was why he was named Game Dancer.

In the moment of his hesitation, Weeononka pulled a bladder from her equipment pack. She already had it out so that he would have a place to put the honey.

Three Crows Flying freed himself of his burden and stood watching with the women as Game Dancer took up a long stick to poke away the vipers that might be lurking under the thorny bushes. He moved very quietly through the bees, making such deliberate movements he didn't stir them up. He reached out to test the footing of the ancient, blackened stump. Just as his hand touched the mossy bark, an arrow he immediately identified as that of his enemy the Chickasaw parted the air with a high-pitched whir and pinned his hand dead center to the bee gum.

"What Osage skinhead dares to steal this honey?" demanded the Chickasaw warrior in Osage, a common language of trade. He stepped from concealment with a crystal-studded head-knocker ready to swing, two ominously tattooed companions just behind him.

So far Game Dancer had made no sound. When the arrow pierced his hand he hardly flinched; now he reached with his other hand to extract it.

"Don't move."

Game Dancer stayed his hand. The leader moved closer to him while the other two walked with grim casualness toward the women and Three Crows Flying. Game Dancer observed with fascination that the enemy warrior held one of the strange weapons, kin to the one he had hidden in the folds of the buffalo skin on his back. The odds were that this one wasn't waiting to be told how to fire it, as Game Dancer was, so he held back any hostile impulses until he could find a more advantageous position. He just hoped this rascal would not search his buffalo skin. How he would hate to lose the foreign weapon now that he had given up so much for it. Game Dancer leveled a glare at the short warrior from the eastern tribe that had been enemies of the Osage for as long as anyone could remember. Except for loincloths made of river oyster shells he and his friends were naked, with bands of blue and black tattoos around their limbs like bracelets. His long hair twisted in a ropelike turban around his face. A single white plume shot out from the crown of his pointed head. His forehead was artificially flattened and high. The Chickasaw flattened the heads of their babies on their cradleboards because they thought the effect beautiful. The Osage liked to flatten the backs of their babies' heads, but they left the front to be shaped as nature directed. Game Dancer considered the warrior before him exceedingly ugly and barbaric. "Nothing on this side of the Great River belongs to Chickasaw, worm eater," he said, slinging drops of blood from his hand.

"Is not my aim excellent? Direct hit at a distance of ten runs."

The bow he displayed was of course of Osage bow wood, the only wood anyone cared to use for the purpose. The irony was not lost on the Osage warrior, who broke off the feathered end of the arrow that pierced his hand, contemptuously spat on the Chickasaw feathers, and threw them to the ground. He slid his palm from the shaft without any indication of pain and without taking his eye from the Chickasaw, who watched the insulting gesture with a smug pout on his thick lips. The other two Chickasaw were binding the women's hands behind their backs; Three Crows Flying was already bound.

"I repeat, nothing on this side of the Great River belongs to Chickasaw—"

At that moment Three Crows Flying, hands still tied but footloose, made a break for the jungle. Because the two Chickasaw warriors were busy tying the women's hands, the Quapaw's bolt caught them off guard.

Three Crows Flying had not been named for nothing. His running ability was legendary on this side of the river. That's why the Quapaw chief used him as courier.

The Chickasaw leader was furious, though he was careful not to let his aim with the foreign weapon waver. He spoke harshly with tightened lips to the larger of his men. Game Dancer spoke very little Chickasaw but he could guess what was said because the fellow took out after Three Crows Flying.

Game Dancer didn't hide his satisfaction. The shorter-legged Chickasaw hadn't a chance to catch up with the runner, who would reach his home village in a short time. The Quapaw chief would send out a war party for the girl, without question, as well as to honor his alliance with the Osage. Besides, he would not miss a chance for hearty battle with their mutual enemy, the Chickasaw.

The Chickasaw leader returned his full attention to Game Dancer. He spoke in a tone of voice that implied there was nothing of consequence in the escape of a mere Quapaw. "We are looking out for our new white allies," the warrior replied, holding out his free hand, obviously demanding the Osage's weapons. Game Dancer handed over his headknocker, bow, and full quiver, reflecting on this interesting disclosure. So, there really were white people about. It wasn't just a story. Game Dancer hoped he had the opportunity to see one of these white persons. He'd once seen an albino from the Taencas tribe and he wondered if these white people had pink rabbit eyes like that one had. Imagine, he thought, a whole tribe of white people, not just a single unusual freak. That would be something to talk about around the winter fire, in the traditional season for storytelling.

The Chickasaw motioned with his fingers for more weapons: Game Dancer grudgingly handed over his two knives with a bloody hand, praying to the spirit of the red paint that the Chickasaw wouldn't think a foreign weapon similar to his own might be hidden in the buffalo robe.

What was bothering Game Dancer was why these enemies had not simply killed them for their scalps in traditional animosity. The second warrior led the two women to stand beside Game Dancer. The leader said something disparaging to his man. The warrior hung his head in shame. Game Dancer caught only a couple of words, something about losing a slave and he would be held responsible by . . . here was a strange word Game Dancer couldn't make out. Something unpronounceable, like Mag-Quac.

Well, at least now it was obvious why they hadn't been killed outright. Crow Sister made a small whimpering sound and the warrior slapped her shoulder. His leader uttered a sharp bark and something about "not damaging the trade goods." Chagrined, the warrior backed off.

The leader made a quick gesture, one hand swirling, then pointed to Game Dancer. The brave whipped out another cord and proceeded to tie the Osage's arms behind his back after inserting a thick branch in the bend of his elbows. The warrior looked back at his leader, who gestured at his man and at the bee gum. The fellow proceeded to approach the honeycomb. The leader then pointed eastward with his own massive head-knocker studded with small sharp fragments of flint, indicating that Game Dancer should proceed along the path in front of him.

There was nothing to do but comply. No more words were exchanged, only universal hand gestures as they left the Chickasaw gathering honey in Weeononka's buffalo bladder, which he had picked up from where she had dropped it.

Weeononka started to speak but the lead warrior glared her into silence, then in single file they took up the path, leaving the honey-gathering warrior to do his work alone.

She handsigned: "That is my wedding dress." She had worked two entire winters quill-beading her wedding dress of softest mulberry bark. There had never been a wedding dress like it, all the women of the Osage village agreed. She added one word, "Please."

"If you speak again, woman, I will cut out your tongue to feed to my dog," said the leader in a calm voice. He stared at her until she dropped her eyes in the manner he expected. To Game Dancer he said as they started walking, "Why do you Osage let your women be so impudent?"

In this particular case Game Dancer agreed, but he showed no compliance. It was true that Osage women were the most independent and outspoken of any tribe's females hereabouts. To the males of other tribes this eccentricity was much discussed because it was rumored that such an upbringing made for a hot woman. The question among the rumor mongers was, was it worth it?

It was a short journey to the river called Nigestai, or Red. The Chickasaw had set up a camp on the northern bank near its confluence with the Mech-a-si-pi. In this camp was built a large pen woven from stout branches. Inside were several other western-bank people, some wounded, all hungry-looking and dirty. One old man was bleeding from a wound on his thigh. Weeononka counted three men, including the old one, and six women, one with a very small baby at her breast. Even in this fading light Weeononka could see that the child had been hurt. There was a large ugly bruise on its tiny face. The mother seemed to be having trouble getting the infant to take her nipple. She fussed with the child, crooning in what sounded like Taencas, the language of a people of the western riverbank whom the Quapaw had displaced when they migrated here several generations ago.

It was into this pen that Weeononka, Crow Sister, and Game Dancer were rudely directed. Then their captors ambled off to join their fellows around a fire, where they were laughing in loud voices, drinking from odd brown containers in the company of the strangest human being Weeononka had ever seen.

This creature was oddly dressed, partly in leather clothing, partly in something else. Even in the firelight it was plain to see he had a deeply rounded chest, like the mightiest bowman, that glinted of metal. Weeononka tried to get a better glimpse of this marvel. His costume was also extraordinary for having parts of red material that was very attractive and unlike anything she knew, having never seen woven cloth before. Even stranger, he had orange hair all over his face. At first it looked as though he were wearing a mask. She had never seen a beard and mustache before. Every man she'd ever seen, Quapaw, Osage, and any males of tribes that traded with them, plucked out what little facial hair they grew. Even more startling was a matching thatch of curly hair on his head in the unbelievable color of pipestone.

This white man took up a conversation, partly in his own language and partly in Chickasaw, with the warrior who had captured Game Dancer's party. The white man screamed, eyes bulging, at the Chickasaw, who took this abuse with some dignity.

"No women!" he screamed, shaking a thick fist toward the cage where Weeononka and Game Dancer watched. "Only strong men can work the Indes cane fields to make our rum!" He hugged a bottle and pointed at Game Dancer. "Warriors, understand? Strong men, not women. You want rum, get me men to make it!" Eventually his spleen was vented, because he went back over to the fire and drank from one of the brown containers.

The sun was dying. Night brought a host of stinging insects that appeared to know the humans in the pen were fair game. They descended on the unfortunate captives, a gray blanket of small sharp thorns, even through the bear grease.

Weeononka and Game Dancer watched the celebration that grew louder and more raucous as the sky grew darker.

Overhead spread the great tent of stars, campfires of the ancestors, Weeononka had been taught as a child. She never believed that story, but she wondered what the stars were, twinkling up there like stationary fireflies. "What tribe do you suppose the weird one is from?" she finally asked Game Dancer.

"I think it's one of the white men I've been hearing about. I think he is one of what the lead warrior called a . . . a Mag-Quac." He twisted his tongue around the word, trying as nearly as he could remember to reproduce what the Chickasaw warrior had said.

"What an ugly human being."

"Red hair. It's enough to make one puke."

"Do you think they intend to feed us or eat us?" Weeononka asked wryly. She knew full well why they had been put in the human cage. Crow Sister moaned a little at her bad joke.

"Don't worry," Weeononka said soothingly. "I was only joking."

Game Dancer didn't answer. He stood with his huge arms still bound, but leaning against the bars of their cage, sereptitiously testing its strength.

A single guard lounged nearby, but he appeared more interested in watching the party near the bonfire than keeping an eye on his charges.

The white man was dancing now to the gleeful shouts of the Chickasaw braves. Soon they joined him, laughing and hooting. The red hair and beard of the fellow formed another kind of torch in the firelight, flapping like a pennant on a war lance. The ugly white man sang in his equally ugly language, a hawking screech that sounded to Weeononka's ears like the yelp of a kicked dog.

Behind her, one of the captive women began sobbing. When Weeononka looked around, she saw it was the young mother. The baby wasn't moving. The woman keened into the night breeze. Weeononka joined her. The girl eyed her gratefully above her song. But Weeononka was without comfort. A cold dread crept upon her, as though she had wandered into some kind of warning but couldn't clearly read the signs. The grieving mother cut short her death wail; the singing of the warriors and the red-haired white man drowned out her cries anyway. Far into the night the warriors staggered around.

Game Dancer was grimly reminded of his own drunkenness at the green corn festival. He had vowed never again to drink

anything that would make him act like that. Weeononka saw
the look on his face and wondered what he was thinking. He
glanced at the guard, who wasn't paying any attention to the
captives. It seemed everyone in the cage slept except Weeononka and Game Dancer, though Weeononka didn't see how
they were able to under such circumstances. Her skin itched
to be free of the confinement. All she could think about was
getting free. It didn't matter if she died in the attempt. This
cage was making her want to scream; she could not bear being
held like this. She hoped Game Dancer would decide it was
the right time. He made a small motion with his chin, and
Weeononka, who had been intently watching him for a sign,
moved as if relieving a cramp to sit with her back to his.

She quickly began to untie his bonds. Her nimble fingers
took no longer than a few seconds to free the knots. But Game
Dancer did not immediately move his hands, keeping them
bent behind him as if they were still tied against the stick.
Then he untied her bonds in the same quiet manner and she
imitated his pretense of still being bound.

It was not the right time yet, his eyes told her when he
finished and leaned against the bars. She signed resignedly,
stifling the scream for freedom that was rising in her. Soon,
soon, she silently begged. He appeared to understand;
bondage was intolerable for him, too. What she couldn't know
was that he was delighted to find this streak in her. He was a
little more sorry he had traded her away. She would probably
have made a strong wife, a warrior wife and the mother of
fighting sons. He, too, sighed and looked away lest she see this
in him and take it for weakness.

Sometime afterward, the warrior who had gone after Three
Crows Flying returned alone. Game Dancer and Weeononka
exchanged pleased glances. Together they watched the party
continue. Later they saw the white man direct one of the
dancers to relieve the guard. He did so with a grudging word
to the other, who quickly joined the men at the fire. The white
man was furious at the warrior who returned empty-handed.
He strutted about, yelling in a strained slurred voice. He
seemed to be trying to provoke the warriors into some kind of
game.

As Weeononka and Game Dancer watched, captive audience that they were, the white man started pounding his metal
chest, slapping it to produce a ringing noise. The warriors

apparently didn't want to play his game and tried to slink out of it. But the white man caught one of them by the arm and bade him pick up his bow and quiver. It was obvious the white man was ignorant of the universal sign language as he struggled to make his wants known with crude gestures. He seemed to think that by yelling his language he might make himself better understood. But he managed to make it known that he wanted the Chickasaw warrior to aim and shoot arrows at him, striking him in his wonderful metal chest.

Weeononka was so surprised she covered her mouth. The warrior went a few paces off and took aim. Then to the amazement of herself and Game Dancer, the warrior sent several potentially fatal arrows at the white man. They bounced off his glinting chest and provoked no response from him but laughter. The other warriors watched but did not seem as awed by this spectacle as the newcomers.

Truly, Weeononka thought, these white people have powerful medicine able to turn away arrows with their metal skins. Even though they looked like people, they were different from ordinary people. She looked at Game Dancer, who also seemed impressed by the show. How can we fight such mighty enemies? her eyes asked him, but his return glance was enigmatic. He was plotting their escape, not asking such foolish questions, Weeononka realized. Game Dancer didn't care if they were supernatural beings; he'd fight them to the death anyway.

Weeononka felt ashamed that she was curious to see more of the white man's marvels. It was childish, she knew, but she couldn't help it; they were fascinating. She wanted to touch this metal skin with her own fingers, to see how it grew on them. How wonderful it would be, she thought, to have metal skin shining like the sun himself. Now the white man gestured at the warriors, protected by nothing more than painted symbols, that he wanted to aim his fire-throwing weapon at them. They shrank back, not laughing at his joke as he did in great guffaws. This seemed to make his point for him, that his weaponry and defense were better than theirs. They acquiesced with the way they stood around the white man, though Weeononka thought it must hurt their pride to be bested by such a crude person no matter how much *wa kon* he possessed.

The drinking and singing continued. A smiling moon rose over the forest. They could hear the Nigestai River's murmur

under a chorus of tree frogs and night birds. Weeononka
sagged down against the bars but was unable to approach
sleep. She saw Game Dancer's eyes glinting in the light of the
fire, still waiting for the right time. He saw her watching him
and aimed a knowing smile at her. She nodded, understanding
that they would move together when that right time came. It
pleased her that he was planning with her. She could almost
forgive him for trading her away. As she sat there, she
pondered what he had done, and concluded after some time
that he really had had no choice. It was her uncle's right to
claim her. The Osage was only honoring the alliance. His own
chief had probably advised him that he could do nothing but
give her up.

But still, he should have told her before their lovemaking.
The way he had done it wasn't clean.

Presently a couple of the drunk warriors ambled toward the
pen, engaged in a friendly argument. Weeononka could not
translate because she did not speak Chickasaw but she
thoroughly understood. They were deciding who would get
her first. By the time the two had arrived at the pen gate,
Game Dancer and Weeononka had risen to their feet without
any notice by the two Chickasaw. The shorter of the two said
something that the other considered gravely, swaying a little.
Then his heavily tattooed face cracked in a smile and he
nodded hugely. He bent over and picked up three short sticks.
He held them in his closed fist while the other uttered a short
guttural word, apparently calling the throw. The first man
threw the sticks on the ground while closing his eyes. Together
the two looked at the pattern. Evidently the larger man won
the bet, because he laughed, clapping the other on the
shoulder and saying something that was probably, "Don't
worry, you can have her after I finish."

Weeononka tensed as she turned to the gate that the winner
was opening. She caught the look in Game Dancer's eye. Now
was the right time.

3

The river could only murmur accompaniment for the prisoners but darkness was their ally as the loser of the bet lounged against the bars of the cage—a grave mistake since even as the winner motioned for Weeononka to follow him out of the cage, Game Dancer had moved with deadly swiftness. He put the stick that had bound him through the bars and under the chin of the hapless young warrior before Weeononka emerged from the pen. The loser was pinned against the cage choking silently to death, even standing, should any of his friends glance over. Even the lazy guard didn't notice the futile little spasms in the loser's legs as he died standing, held that way by the stick lodged between the bars and across his throat.

Meanwhile, Weeononka kept the winner busy with her eyes. There was just enough light from the dying fire for him to see them flash at him. She smiled as he reached out to fondle her breasts.

It was the last thing he ever did. Game Dancer moved behind him with one of the rawhide thongs that had bound his hands and garroted the man as he smiled back at the girl. But this action roused the guard who was holding one of the firesticks. Game Dancer reached around the fellow's neck and broke it with a sure twist of his massive arm, catching the foreign weapon as the man fell.

Weeononka roused Crow Sister, untying her hands. Then together, with no words and few gestures they began to wake the other captives. They stole from the cage one by one, each looking back over a shoulder at the celebrants, who were still singing drunkenly near the dying fire. Only the young mother refused to move. Weeononka tried to get her up, but mourning had stupefied the girl. She gazed with round crazy eyes at her benefactress as though she did not realize she could go free. Her arms seemed to have no muscle tone; the dead baby rolled from her lap without her notice as Weeononka tried to help her stand.

Game Dancer reached back into the cage and touched Weeononka's shoulder. She looked up, stricken at her failure to rouse the young mother but she hurried after him and Crow

Sister on his signal. They were deep into the forest when they heard the shouts of the men behind them. The moon had set so it was cave-dark as they circled back around the slave catchers' camp. They followed the Nigestai upstream and westward, where they knew the Quapaw village of Osotony was located. From time to time they could hear shouts and shots from the Chickasaw and their white man but they were far ahead of the pursuers.

It wasn't long before they heard another sound ahead, the music of war drums and Quapaw war chants. Game Dancer had been right—the Quapaw chief wouldn't miss a chance to get his niece back and take a few Chickasaw scalps at the same time.

To Weeononka the sounds ahead meant something else. Now for sure she would part with Game Dancer. Their little time together, which had sweetened him for her and, she was sure, herself for him, was over. She was taking the last steps of her girlhood, headed toward her husband-to-be. Weeononka wondered what her future was going to be as she followed Game Dancer along the last small distance to her new life. She wished she and this warrior could just keep on walking forever beyond duty and obligation into a future of their own making.

Crow Sister evidently sensed this mood in Weeononka. In a quiet gesture of affection she stepped beside the younger woman. She took her hand and squeezed it.

Soon a Quapaw warrior who had been stealthily following them stepped onto the riverbank trail. Game Dancer had been aware that an advance scout from the village was dogging them; this was customary. The two warriors exchanged hand-signs. It was not the duty of this sentry to question but merely to accompany them back to the village, where the chief would find out how they came to be here. The sentry gestured that he would be their escort, and again they took up the dark trail.

Hand in hand, behind the shadow of Game Dancer and the sentry, the two women entered the firelit camp of the maddened Quapaw, who had turned out to every man and woman to watch the painted warriors dance around the fire in preparation for war. Even the little children had caught war fever. They were dancing wildly in their own small circles, imitating their elders with miniature but functional knives hacking at imaginary enemies. A couple of the older boys made their play more real with a mouse. They had disem-boweled the rodent and were dancing around it screaming chants like their fathers near a bonfire.

"Ay-yi!" cried a woman in an arresting voice. Later Weeon-onka learned that the voice belonged to her husband's first wife, The Blossum. It had been so long she didn't recognize her father's sister. Her eerie call halted the drums and the dancing as if a supernatural event had taken place. Everyone in the village, man, woman, child, and wildly painted warrior, turned to see the sentry with his raised headknocker enter with the three thought even now to be in Chickasaw clutches.

There was a moment of shocked silence as it became obvious the reasons for going on the warpath had just appeared.

Weeononka would never forget the scene if she lived to be a hundred—the firelight on the sweating and painted faces, the breeze that rushed into the silence to replace the abandoned sound that had ceased with their arrival, the treefrog song in the bush. Then a beautiful warrior with white hair and a youthful face stepped out of the throng of dancers and walked toward her. Not toward Game Dancer, as would have been the custom, one warrior to another, but to Weeononka. It was a singular honor, especially considering that this man was peace chief and medicine man of this village, Man-Who-Stands-in-the-Middle, Weeononka's uncle by marriage to The Blossum. She vaguely recalled him from childhood when she had lived here before her parents' deaths. He did not have white hair then and so he looked different from her memory. But she was surprised to see that despite the white hair he looked very young. He held out his hands to her. They were strong and hard, not the hands of an old man. His eyes were dancing and everyone, at least four hundred souls, listened for his word. "Daughter of my brother, it is truly you. Welcome, beloved child. We were afraid for your life."

Then, graciously, he turned to Game Dancer and said, "Surely you've performed a great deed because we have been told by our faithful runner, Three Crows Flying, that the Chickasaw and a white monster had captured you and were eating you for dinner."

Game Dancer laughed. Three Crows Flying stepped from among the dancers, sweat running in rivulets down his red-painted naked body, and laughed with Game Dancer. The villagers laughed and cheered, excitedly talking all at once, as the chief led the three to the great pavilion where tribal matters were discussed. Tonight, because of the heat, the skin sides had been raised on the pavilion. A section of the roof had been removed to allow smoke from the council fire to rise up into the night.

Behind him followed another chief of the tribe, who scowled as Man-Who- motioned for food and water to be brought while the three settled down on buffalo robes to rest and refresh themselves.

The scowling chief, a man in his late hardened forties with a deep scar across his nose, stayed close to an entourage of the most experienced warriors. They exchanged looks with him and among themselves that spoke much of displeasure.

Man-Who-Stands-in-the-Middle gestured toward the rubbed-shiny post standing near the fire. "Will you do our pole the honor of counting coup upon it?"

Game Dancer walked with formal pride to the pole and slapped it with his hand. Its hollow cavity produced an echoing boom that brought everyone to expectant attention.

A young male medicine assistant removed a painted buffalo robe from the calumet stand. The sacred pipe was lodged on two carved forked poles, and rested on an elaborately painted buffalo skull. The peace chief reverently took up the calumet. With great ceremony, for this one was known for his scrupulous ritual conduct, he lit the pipe with a coal his punctilious assistant had waiting in a hollowed stone. Man-Who- handed it first to his oldest counselors. These elders had naturally settled into their usual positions in a loose circle around the peace chief and his guest. Weeononka and Crow Sister sat just behind this elder circle as was fitting for women, and of course they did not smoke the calumet. But women of the village offered them food and damp skins to wipe sweat from their faces.

The calumet passed around the old men unpainted for war, through Man-Who-'s hands to his war chief. There was a moment of intense silent communication between the two men but at length the war chief took and smoked the pipe then politely gave it back to the peace chief. He in turn handed it to Game Dancer, who took one long draw on the sacred pipe and dutifully gave it back to his host, who took its smoke into his lungs.

This was all normal preliminary. Around them everyone settled down to hear the story that Game Dancer proceeded to tell in great detail and with appropriate gestures reenacting the adventure. Game Dancer, even though an Osage, was well known here because he had served as a raven between his chief and this one many times in the past. He was known for his storytelling and he made it good. Everyone hung on his words. Little children whimpered, fleeing into their mothers' laps when he recounted the appearance of the monstrous white man with hair of fire. Despite the fact that she had been there, Weeononka got bumpy-flesh when he spoke of the impervious chest of metal on the white man. Of all they'd heard of the white spirits, this was the most amazing to the Quapaw. That whites had parts of metal was the biggest *wa kon* even the oldest among them could remember hearing about. She remembered how the Chickasaw arrows fell impotently against the chest of metal and wished fervently again that she had been able to see this marvel closer and touch it with her own hands.

When Game Dancer had finished the story, Man-Who-Stands-in-the-Middle rose to make a little speech. "My people. Tonight we really have good reason to thank our manitous. Not only are our friends restored to us without any harm but now we can wash the red paint off and let it take the place of our blood." He raised his arms to the irregular patches of sky that could be seen through the smoke, full of brilliant stars. "We can put aside our weapons and think no more of war."

It was a formal pronouncement but it was clear that not all in the assembly agreed.

The war chief stood up among his young men and stepped forward. "My honored brother, Man-Who-Stands-in-the-Middle," he said with great dignity. "We always listen to your wise words. Even the sky listens to you tonight. But the stars weep to hear what a mighty chief tells his people." This was the proper way for him to ask to speak. Man-Who- held continual civil and ceremonial power while the war chief was elected only for a particular battle.

"Honored brother, say what you have to say," replied the peace chief coolly, stepping back to give the war chief the speaker's position.

"My warriors: You have not taken on the red paint in vain. Even though our little sister has been restored to us we must go and teach these Chickasaw that they have no business on our side of the Great River. Let the preparation continue, that

we may teach these sons of worm eaters a lesson that their
grandsons will remember."

A great cheer rose up among the warriors, who had been
less spirited since their reason for fighting had apparently been
removed.

"But why carry on a thing for which there is no reason?"
asked the peace chief.

"How do we know that tomorrow these Chickasaw criminals
won't come here to take us slaves for their white master as they
tried to do with our friends here?"

"Let us postpone the action, then."

A hoarse grumble rose among the painted warriors. One
even dared to shake his lance, causing the shells on its tip to
rattle.

"I say we have had good signs about this battle. Let's not
waste them!" The warriors cheered the war chief at this point
with much lance rattling and with drumming of headknockers
on the hard-packed ground of the council floor.

A breeze blew into the pavilion, singing against the poles
that held up the hide roof. A blast of smoke downdrafted,
giving strange shadows to the flickering firelight. Man-Who-
Stands-in-the-Middle was silent for a time after this display. It
was clear that every sign was a portent to him. He looked
around catching the eye of several of the most mature and
experienced braves. Each of them gave some sign of agreement with One Thunder Turtle.

Finally he looked at his wife, The Blossum, the woman who
had cried out. He was asking her for an opinion here; they had
discussed the raid privately and she agreed that they were ill
prepared to do battle with the more numerous Chickasaw.
However, as mother of the tribe, she spoke not only for herself
but for the other women when she answered, "Husband, I do
you honor always but only five of our wives want to take a
chance on further people catching. Most of the wives agree
with One Thunder Turtle and say go after the enemy before he
eats us from the toes up."

The women murmured approval as The Blossum dropped
her eyes. She was sorry to have to refute her husband publicly
even though they both had seen it coming.

But the peace chief stood his ground. He gave One Thunder
Turtle a look that said so, underscored with an emphatic
handsign: "Let us cool off before we walk into the unknown."

The war chief grabbed up a handful of small kindling sticks

from the woodpile and shook them at the peace chief. "Let wood decide," he said, the traditional request for a straw vote.

Man-Who- nodded assent. The war chief moved around the circle of warriors, holding out the twigs. As he walked slowly among them, each warrior took one of the sticks and stood there holding it in full view. One or two of the most vehement stuck the twig into the decoration on their war club then stood mutely still with the club held in the attitude of attack.

One Thunder Turtle offered Man-Who- the last twig.

The peace chief seemed to sag a little then he drew himself up. His own war paint was smeared now, streaked with his sweat. He had considerable power in council, and of course concerning everything *wa kon*. But after a war chief had been elected, he remained war chief until a battle was done or until a majority vote canceled it. But that was a rare thing since the warriors believed it egregious *wa kon* to paint and fast for battle and then not draw enemy blood. All this was traditional, but he would try one more attempt at reason.

"All of you know I believe in the tradition of fighting for honor. But in this case I believe we are not fighting a traditional enemy. If these whites truly possess greater *wa kon* than the Osotony, if they have the tricks to use their metal weapons, then I say they'll destroy every one of us." But he knew they didn't believe him; he had not been able to prove to them that the metal weapon he possessed was useful.

He stood for a moment in eye dialogue with One Thunder Turtle. Sweat from their earlier exertions and clashing wills could almost be heard oozing from their naked bodies. Behind One Thunder Turtle stood the supporting walls of painted fierce faces demanding to fight by their very alignment in close ranks.

Man-Who- took the twig and snapped it in two, signifying that he was willing to abide by the majority but that he was divided. It was his right to withhold from actual battle but he would not go that far in his opposition now since he was already painted and therefore committed.

This was what the people were waiting for. There rose from the women, children, and old men a roar of approval. Their one great voice had spoken. The drums started again. The nondancers moved back so the dance could continue. It would do so deep into the night.

One Thunder Turtle was instructing a young warrior to take the traditional red-painted club over into enemy territory.

There he would lay the club on a well-trod path beneath a significant tree and carve arrows into the bark. This would be the time-honored way of engaging the enemy.

But Game Dancer told One Thunder Turtle that he thought in this case it was a bad idea.

One Thunder Turtle was vastly conservative by nature. He had not survived all those battles without following well-tried procedures. He was shocked that this Osage would suggest he break tradition.

"Your civil chief is right, my friend," warned Game Dancer. "The Chickasaw have learned new ways of fighting from these white spirits. These spirits do not honor the old ways. They don't honor the brave dead by feasting on them. They want only to take slaves, for what unknown purpose this mere hunter cannot fathom. Don't give them the honor of a warning."

One Thunder Turtle conferred with his lieutenants about this grave alteration of tradition. There was a mixed reaction. Some of the young ones wanted to take a chance. But most of the older warriors were equally horrified at the suggestion to breach tradition.

"But I tell you they have already broken tradition by using the firesticks. We are not bound if they are not bound," Game Dancer reasoned.

"But if we offend the *wa kon* of the red paint we will not have a chance to win the battle," replied One Thunder Turtle.

The young warrior with the painted war club stood between them. And as each man spoke, his eyes were drawn toward that man, back and forth by their rhetoric. The other warriors and their women in the shadows watched as intently the political spectacle of public debate that they expected from these two men.

A very old man, tall and bony under his leathery skin, stepped into the discussion. Formerly a great warrior himself, now retired to council, this old man's name was Many Trees Singing because of his renown as a woodsman. He had already girdled several trees down by the river, which these warriors would hollow into sleek ten-man bateaux. He was famous as a chooser of trees for particular uses—cypress for canoes, yellowwood for bows, and hickory for arrows and ball game rackets. His name referred to his talent for picking the right tree for each particular purpose by its song. He was so revered he was allowed to wear buffalo horns on his headdress, the

only man in the village to do so at this time. Many Trees
Singing was uncle to One Thunder Turtle but in these matters
that had nothing to do with his counsel. He said, "My
children, listen to my solution: Do not give away your fighting
advantage in this case since tradition has already been broken
by the Chickasaw using white allies. But don't stoop to the
level of these Chickasaw, whom we know to be barbarians
anyway. Uphold tradition by carrying the painted war club
before you as you approach the battle. In this way will you
satisfy both needs."

One Thunder Turtle and the men behind him seemed
agreeable.

Game Dancer demurred, stepping back, since he had no
cause here but was merely giving a friendly warning. As he did
so, something off to one side behind the chief's lodge caught
his eye. He squinted; the firelight was bright but whatever it
was beyond the lodge was in shadow.

"We would be honored if our Osage brother would take on
the red paint with us," said One Thunder Turtle. A murmur of
assent buzzed behind him. Game Dancer's prowess was well
regarded.

Game Dancer heard his name and drew his attention from
the animal—for surely that was what it was. There seemed to
be no danger. A couple of people and a child were near the
creature, which appeared to be fastened with a rope to a post
behind the chief's lodge.

But Man-Who-Stands-in-the-Middle stepped in. "There is a
more important task for this Osage brother. To make a truly
successful attack on the Chickasaw in their homeland we need
more than our number of warriors. I propose to send Game
Dancer back to his mountain chief with a message of alliance so
that his chief may help us put down a menace to all the people
of the Nigestai valley."

One Thunder Turtle was about to say his men did not need
the assistance of a group of merchants to help them wage war.
The Osage were more famous for trading than battle, though
later they would earn a different reputation protecting their
Ozarks from white intruders.

Man-Who- caught the eye of the war chief; something
seemed to be settled between them. Actually their positions
left them most often at odds; this was an old game for both of
them, which went back even to their boyhoods. Man-Who-
warned with a mere look that the Osage was an ear for his chief
so no insult should be implied.

So One Thunder Turtle did not speak.

Man-Who- clapped Game Dancer on the back. "Perhaps you can give more information to these men about this white spirit since they will be opposing him soon."

Game Dancer nodded but he couldn't help glancing quickly at the strange white animal on four legs, which had now moved to the length of its rope so that firelight illuminated it. The creature was placidly munching on a tuft of grass.

Man-Who- caught the glance. "Later I will take you over and show you my *cabay*. Besides, there is another matter I wish to discuss with you in private."

"Is that what it's called, *cabay*?"

"It's from the whites. I won it in a gamble with some Caddo." With a friendly pat on Game Dancer's shoulder, Man-Who-Stands-in-the-Middle walked away from the knot of warriors. He looked around and saw Weeononka, whom he took by the hand, leading her to the entrance of the largest of the loaf-shaped lodges to the right of the council pavilion where a lovely but frail woman had been watching the proceedings from a raised platform covered with luxuriant furs.

Without words he gave Weeononka's hand to his wife, who smiled benevolently, motioning for the girl to sit beside her. She saw the chief's wife had knobby, swollen wrist and ankle joints, signs of the crooked-bone. Weeononka could not miss the glance of deep devotion that passed between The Blossum and Man-Who-Stands-in-the-Middle; her heart sank, for truly this man loved this woman and would have no love to give to anyone else. But why then, Weeononka pondered, would he be taking a second wife?

"Weeononka, welcome," said The Blossum as her husband rejoined the dancers. "Here," she added, patting the fur robe with a twisted hand, "sit closer so that I may speak with you. We have much to discuss, you and I, eh, little sister?"

4

"I have no doubt these are men of metal, little sister," said the sachem, confirming what Weeononka had already decided about the white men. The sachem was really Man-Who-Stands-in-the-Middle, who was both chief and medicine man of this village. In the person of the sachem, he wore a mask made of a mummified alligator's face and eagle feathers. He had many masks, one for every role a chief must play. One was a helmet of soft white egret feathers. He had loaned that mask to Game Dancer so he could play a role later, and now, in the alligator-eagle guise he spoke with Weeononka, whom he had taken as second wife that afternoon in a simple ceremony that almost got lost amid the tribe's busy preparations to send off a war party. He had approached her with a leg of venison, and as ancient tradition instructed, she replied by giving him an ear of corn. This was done out on the dancing ground, well within sight of several village elders, who nodded approvingly.

Now they were married. The warriors had taken time out from their preparations for a celebratory smoke and to escort the bridegroom to the new lodge where Weeononka waited inside. She had observed all the amenities, The Blossum acting as her instructor. Now on the evening of their wedding day, Man-Who- was with her in the new little lodge the village woman had hastily built next to the one he shared with The Blossum. Normally two or three families lived in one lodge, except for the chiefs, war and civil, who were honored with their own private houses. She had prepared the meal, and now dutifully sat before it on folded legs under a beautiful new mulberry-bark dress, waiting to serve her husband every morsel from her hand to his mouth as the custom dictated.

But in the place of the joy she should be feeling, Weeononka went about her duties without much heart. Her worst fears had been confirmed. Here sat her husband before her and he was not going to stay the night.

She knew it. When these people called her Little Sister, that's exactly what they meant. She sighed as her new husband spoke through the cumbersome mask. He was going to use her as counsel, train her to be his medicine assistant, his formal wife with visiting dignitaries, and probably little else. She'd known it from the moment she caught the look of adoration he gave his true wife.

"Once I thought they could transform themselves by superior *wa kon* into four-legged animals from the neck down. But now I know they merely use animals they call *cabay*." He scooted closer to her on the eating mat. "The elders and most of the people of the village want me to get rid of my *cabay*. They think it's bad *wa kon*."

She had seen the strange animal tethered over in a round fenced area where Game Dancer had himself seen the creature for the first time. Man-Who- kept a guard on the *cabay* all the time.

"You're supposed to be able to ride it," he said, "but nobody has been able to stay on this one's back. I tried and it nearly killed me. That's why the people want me to get rid of it."

"Well," she replied, "if they use animals, then maybe these whites are just men after all. Maybe they've found some way to get metal skin, maybe they paint it on the way we paint on colored earths."

He shook his head. "I don't know. I just don't know."

Weeononka thought for a while then said, "But you can guess. What do you think—are these white persons human people, ghosts, or manitou?"

The alligator mask made a negative wiggle. "Our Sioux cousins call them spirits. Who knows? What do you think now that you've seen one?"

"I don't know if they're spirits or not, but whatever they are, it's mighty *wa kon*," she answered, thinking of the hideous white man and his marvelous metal skin. "Other than their metal, they seem to be just human beings. Not particularly good ones, from what I've seen."

"But what human being has metal skin? The people think they must be spirits," said the man inside the alligator mask.

"But they don't act exactly as one would expect *wa nough hgee* to act. You must know more about them than this woman . . . husband . . ." How she wished he would throw off the mask and make her his wife but she knew in her soul, from her manitou, the serpent *wesa*, that he would never be her husband.

"You must be wondering what has happened to you, girl," said Man-Who-Stands-in-the-Middle after watching her vacant reaction. She was not interested in the white men or their magic.

She looked down at her hands, not wishing to offend him with the truth of his surmise—that she was selfishly wondering what was going to happen to her.

He realized he was jumping ahead, not taking into account a young woman's interests. It would take time to turn her thoughts toward the politics of tribal concerns. But this one was serious-minded, had been even in childhood, when her parents lived in this village with her. She had always seemed older than her winters. And here she was even now, emotionally distant from the subject at hand, the subject that was occupying all his chieftainly thoughts as well as those of the entire tribe, and yet she was discoursing wisely upon that subject. She would make a fine chief woman, he thought. Very smart. Maybe too smart. He hoped she'd be so eager a wife, she wouldn't figure out the feather helmet right away.

Weeononka's private thoughts were full of reciprocal respect for this man, too. How she admired his directness, aimed at her with the leader's natural assumption of being obeyed. Oh, what a wonderful wife she could make for this man, if he would only let her, she reflected. She longed to stroke his beautiful white hair, which he wore long and tied in strands. Unlike the Osage, the Quapaw men did not pluck their heads bald except for scalplock. They wore it in the manner of the Crow and other western tribes—long, braided, twisted, and decorated. His silver braids showed beneath the mask. She thought this man's hair must be as soft as corn tassles, it was so shiny.

She wanted to touch the braid ends, but dared not. If only she could take up her beading just to have something to do with her hands. The quiver for Game Dancer was nearly finished. Since the women had done everything to prepare her household, including building the lodge itself, she had taken up the quiver project to conceal her nervousness at everything that was happening around her that vitally concerned her life to come, but over which she had no control.

Game Dancer was planning to leave the next dawn, and Weeononka was pressed to finish the last decorations on the present. Well, she privately sighed; she would have little to do tonight after her husband left her. At least she would have time to finish Game Dancer's quiver, and she wouldn't be sleeping late in the morning after her wedding night—as a regular bride would—so she could find a way to present it to him before he left.

Man-Who- wearily removed the mask. He was supposed, by tradition, to make love with her with that mask on. The alligator chief was an ancient spirit that had terrified the ancestors of the Quapaw when they first came to this country. This tradition was supposed to guard against the monster, and Man-Who- staunchly defended tradition. However, in privacy, he might be less meticulous. He lounged back on the furs The Blossum had given Weeononka.

Every woman in the village dutifully contributed an item

each—a perfect household down to beautifully incised pottery in the distinctive dark red clay of the region. Man-Who- took a dainty flake of food from a clay platter and munched politely as he spoke. "What has happened is that my wife is dying and she and the elders of my village have forced me to take on a younger wife to take over my own's duties when she's gone. In doing this they have conspired against me to take away—" He caught himself in an outburst of emotion not suitable for a chief to demonstrate. "They prevented me from taking certain privileges due a husband of a chief woman."

This told her nothing new but to have it so bluntly laid out stunned Weeononka, who was more used to subtleties. "A privilege my own mother exercised?"

He seemed surprised. "Then you know about her death?"

Weeononka had little sadness connected with her parents' deaths. She had lived with her relative, Crow Sister, a loving substitute mother for so long she barely recalled her real parents. She had learned of their sad end only recently, so it had not been a childhood memory for her. "I told you Crow Sister did her duty teaching me. I know my mother voluntarily followed my father into death."

"As it is my right to follow The Blossum. Because of this marriage, however, I won't be able to abide by that tradition." His look clearly stated that his life would be over when The Blossum died.

"They've done this because my husband is so valuable a leader the tribe cannot lose him."

He smiled genuinely at her but shook his head.

"They've done this because I'm the only one here who has seen these white people. They're afraid and think I can somehow save them from any injury the whites are rumored to practice against us." He looked tired and resigned to his fate of having to go on living.

Weeononka caught a glimpse of the anguish this man was feeling. Here he was, trying to discharge his duties to the tribe at a time of crisis while the only person he loved was withering away before his eyes.

"I saw that her joints are swollen with the crooked-bone. I didn't know people died from that."

"She's dying from something else. She grows weaker every moon."

"Surely your great medicine—"

"Nobody's medicine has been able to help."

Weeononka touched his hand. He patted her hand firmly but without the slightest indication of passion.

"This cannot be a happy situation for a young woman who surely wants many children."

Her look revealed her ardent agreement.

"You will have children."

She did not ask how that was going to be accomplished when her husband was not planning to sleep in her lodge. But she did not want to challenge him, so all she said was, "This is all strange custom for me."

"It will all become clear. Meanwhile, listen to everything The Blossom or I say. We are all evading ritual issues which the counsel continues to ponder." He stood and stretched, preparing to take his leave as she knew he would.

"Before you say goodnight, my husband, I have one request."

"Yes, little sister?"

"Since this is a marriage in form only, would it not be better if we gave this lodge to a family, perhaps the wife and children of a great hunter or warrior who has fallen. I could move in with The Blossom. I could help while you're gone, and here I feel . . . lonely."

"She does need someone with her all the time now." He nodded to himself. "I'll speak to her, and when I leave with the war party tomorrow you may move in with her if she agrees. I think she will. Did you know it was she who chose you for my second wife?"

Weeononka smiled but she didn't feel happy. She hoped her hurt didn't show, since this was meant only as the highest honor to her. Probably the mother of every eligible girl in the village had hoped her daughter would be chosen. "Thank you, husband . . . uncle . . ."

"You should always refer to me as husband, especially if any of the elders is present."

She nodded, standing with him.

He leaned over and kissed her forehead as a father would a daughter's. "Goodnight, little sister."

"Please—" she blurted.

He had been about to leave but he turned again at the distress in her voice.

"Please, husband. My name is Weeononka. I do not wish to offend. But I am no longer a girl." She had already explained about her unconventional woman-naming.

"Of course, I shouldn't refer to you as my sister—the elders would feel I wasn't carrying out my promise with heart." He touched her shoulders with each hand. "Weeononka it is, then." He picked up his mask but turned back once more, smiling, "The Blossum's arms hurt and I must massage them for her. But, later, after you've put out your little fire, your husband will return to you."

Before she could speak he was gone. After a while she took up Game Dancer's quiver to finish beading it. Then she smothered the fire and listened to the darkness. Presently she saw the flap of her lodge lift against the glow of night, then close as someone entered. It smelled like Man-Who-Stands-in-the-Middle, and felt like him, but it was too dark to see. She satisfied her desire to touch his wonderful hair glowing moonlike in the dark, and though she had expected it to be soft, she was startled that it · was as soft, as smooth as . . . feathers. When she tried to speak, he put his mouth on hers and would not let her utter another word.

5

In the newest morning light Game Dancer handed the foreign medicine ball spitter to Man-Who-Stands-in-the-Middle. He had already discreetly returned the feather helmet. The two men stood facing each other on the Quapaw dancing ground a little apart from the fifty or so warriors who stood unmoving, awaiting the word to move out. Even though they were patiently disciplined, willing to stand like this all day if commanded to do so, there was a thick miasma of intent about the war band, a pulsating aroma of menace that rose like a mist toward the brilliant sky.

"Perhaps it can aid you in the coming fight," Game Dancer said. He was the only one of the assembled warriors not displayed for battle. Instead of the honored red paint of war, his body was smeared with common bear grease to keep off flies on his journey. He looked tame in comparison to the others, and the contrast filled him with undeserved chagrin.

The Quapaw chief took the wooden and metal weapon he had given the Osage in exchange for the woman. "Thank you, Game Dancer, for all you've done for us."

He gave the weapon to one of his lieutenants without comment. The fellow put it away in his own travel pack then stepped back into the group.

"I would ask, however," Game Dancer continued, "that you teach me how to fire it as you promised in our bargain." He made a gesture indicating Weeononka, who stood as patiently as the warriors, waiting until the formal goodbyes were made so that she could give Game Dancer the quiver.

Man-Who- looked distinctly uncomfortable at the request. "I'm afraid that is not an easy promise to keep, my friend."

Game Dancer asked why with his eyes.

"You see, the medicine ball spitter must have medicine balls to spit." He looked up at the taller Osage with frustration in his eyes.

"You mean you made this promise, as part of the bargain that I bring you the girl, when you knew you could not fulfill it?"

"Of course not. At the time I made the promise I had some of the round metal. Now, I do not. But the weapon also takes a kind of powder I haven't learned the secret of making. I do have plenty of this powder, which I am happy to share with you." He produced a worked buffalo horn from a travel bundle slung over his shoulder, opened the wooden plug at its narrow end, and poured some of the powder into a depression in the weapon. Without words he showed the other man how it was done.

"And one needs the round metal? Nothing else will work?"

"Not that I have been able to guess. But you can catch a white man and you will find him with as many of the objects as you wish to take. But you have to catch a white man first."

"I was hoping you'd be able to help me use this," Game Dancer said as he removed the weapon he'd taken from the Chickasaw. The Quapaw chief took it and looked it over. It was similar to his own but larger with a narrower and longer barrel, the difference between British and French manufacture. He gave it back to the Osage.

"A fine thing it is, too. I hope you can figure out a way to make it work." He pointed to the barrel. "I think this one will require smaller medicine balls than the ones I used in learning to fire my own . . . pistol. This is what they call it, 'pistol.' The larger variety they call 'musket.' The Sioux, who have had more experience with the white men, call all the medicine ball spitters *mon za wa kon*."

Game Dancer repeated the new words as he took the powder horn offered by the chief.

"One reason we wish to pursue the Chickasaw enemy is your report that they travel with a white man. I hope to catch him and roast his toes to make him tell me the secret of making the medicine balls. White men are too few and hard to catch. It would be better not to have to depend on them at all for the round metal."

Game Dancer gave a guttural affirmative to this as he put his confiscated pistol and the powder horn into his own pack.

"But now that you've given me back the weapon, I am shamed because I have given you nothing," the chief continued.

Game Dancer shrugged. "My visit here has not been unpleasant."

Man-Who- smiled, recognizing a reference to the previous night. Because he was going to war, and fasting for it, he could not have shared Weeononka's blanket in any case, though he would always prefer The Blossum's to any other. He was indebted to Game Dancer for helping him the night before; he must give him some kind of present. He'd been thinking about this since his talk with Weeononka. "No, I have a fine gift for you. But first, because I know you're a modest man and might refuse, you must assure me you'll accept this gift."

"Sometimes a gift can be a curse," Game Dancer said wryly.

"Not this one. I have seen you looking at my *cabay*."

Ever since he first saw the creature, Game Dancer had been fascinated by it. Though it had a reputation as a terror that no man could ride, he found the horse as docile as a pup tethered out in the sweet grass. He'd spent many hours since he had come to this village watching the creature.

"A most remarkable animal. They say the Spanish ride them," the chief explained. "Like the weapons, though, the horse requires a trick I haven't mastered. But with my own eyes I've seen the Caddo on similar animals so I know they can be ridden."

Such a thing sounded funny to Game Dancer. Sometimes a hunter would leap upon the back of a buffalo for sport but other than that, the concept of riding an animal was new to him so he asked, "For what purpose?"

"Why, to move very fast, of course. With these eyes I have seen the Caddo move as swiftly as the west wind," the chief explained, using handsign to supplement the strange concept. "But I have failed to stay on its back. You are a man of strength and wisdom. Maybe you can succeed where I failed." He appraised Game Dancer's growing delight. "How would you like to have this fine *cabay*?"

Game Dancer grinned largely. Man-Who- clapped him on the back and walked to the boy who had brought the *cabay* up behind the throng of people as the chief had ordered. The villagers parted for him as he strode forward and took the rawhide that bridled the animal.

Whatever its evil reputation, the magnificent *cabay* allowed itself to be led among the people with a gentleness of spirit that caused a murmur to rise. They had seen it throw every man in camp at least once.

Man-Who-Stands-in-the-Middle handed the reins to Game Dancer, who carefully patted the horse's haunch, expecting the demon to turn. But it only nuzzled him. "Seems tame enough."

"That's true as long as you merely lead it or feed it." He rubbed his own backside. "I can testify to its terrible temper. A Caddo told me the horse was not tamed when it was a baby, so now it can never be tamed."

The *cabay* tried to find a treat in Game Dancer's hands. So gentle was the creature that it had become spoiled by the village children, who brought it tasty roots and honey cakes.

"Does it have a name?"

"No. I decided that it could not be named if it could not be mastered."

Game Dancer nodded approval. He slapped the great arched neck. The horse had a pleasing aroma. "I shall accept your honorable present and name him when I have mastered him, then," Game Dancer said proudly so that all could hear.

The chief nodded. He took Game Dancer's right hand and rubbed it into the red war paint on his own chest. Then he laid the Osage's hand on the *cabay's* flank. "This, then, is Game Dancer's *cabay*. Let all know it by this sign."

The people shouted their approval. Man-Who- was satisfied that his action served two purposes, always something to strive for. Personally he didn't like the *cabay;* it seemed to him a spoiled creature that had taken face from him by throwing him rudely on his butt. He had hoped when he first acquired the horse from the Caddo chief that it would bring him prestige. But it took too much to feed it in the winter and Man-Who- was glad to be rid of it and win approval from his village at the same time. Out of the corner of his eye he saw two of the elders nodding their heads with his decision. "Tell your

estimable chief Dancing Buck that the Quapaw go to fight our
mutual enemies," said the chief in a tone of oration, gesturing
toward the war chief and assembled braves behind him.

Game Dancer nodded curtly.

"Tell him that his assistance will ensure victory for us all,
that there is none but the Quapaw standing against these old
enemies and their new monstrous allies. The Tunica and
Caddo will be led off like dogs. Other river people will flee into
the bush rather than face the white men and their weapons
that spit fire and metal. Only the fearless Quapaw dare to stop
these invaders." He made no reference to the fact that the
Quapaw themselves were invaders here not a hundred winters
ago. They were standing on ground where once a Taencas band
had lived before the Quapaw drove them out.

Game Dancer wished privately that the chief would forgo
this repetition of requests he had already privately given the
Osage to take to his chief in the mountains. To Game Dancer
this harangue only lost him more face because of his own
failure to be painted for battle? Despite its importance, his task
as raven held far less honor than that of the lowest Quapaw
warrior ready for the fight.

He knew Man-Who-Stands-in-the-Middle wasn't speaking
to him but was actually bolstering his men with an implied
promise of help from the mountain tribe.

"Tell your chief that we'll expect his war party to join us at
the bluffs this side of the Great River on the first quarter of
Grass Moon." It was now past half Crow Moon about twenty
sunrises from the date he requested. That was enough time for
Game Dancer to return to the Osage camp, and if he could
convince his chief to march immediately south, a war party
might make it by first quarter Grass Moon. "With his
assistance we will take canoes over and strike into the heart of
the Chickasaw!" His voice had grown louder as he spoke these
words. He raised his fist as a signal to his men.

They answered him in one mighty voice with an ominously
rumbled war cry that swelled to piercing intensity and finally
broke into the multitude of individual men's voices, whooping
and cawing their desire to be at the enemy's throat. Their
outcry lasted only a few moments. In respectful silence they
once again stood awaiting the order to disperse.

With a fierce smile Man-Who- turned to his warriors, every
able man in the village except for the handful who would stay

behind to guard here. He looked each warrior in the eye and they returned the intense stare. Then he gestured to One Thunder Turtle with a strong nod. He in turn gave the signal to the others and they began trotting off into the forest, keeping their silent ranks. They had said their goodbyes to their families when they earlier had left their individual lodges. It was traditional that a war party was not to be feted upon departure. To treat it otherwise was to draw the attention of evil spirits, who might bring bad fortune for the combatants. The village must proceed as if this were an ordinary morning, completely ignoring the departing warriors.

Some women were walking to the river. One of them, a young pregnant wife, glanced shyly back. One of the younger warriors last in rank and waiting to follow his seniors into the wood shuffled his feet and hoped that his wife's indiscretion in breaking the taboo had not been witnessed.

But theirs was not the only infraction of tradition.

The chief cast a longing glance at The Blossum, who was sitting on the pallet outside her lodge, watching the proceedings with a keen eye. Neither made a gesture, but Weeononka saw them exchange that look again, the look that completely shut her out, in fact, shut out the whole world except these united two. Weeononka was still amazed that he could make such wonderful love with her last night, and yet be so devoted to The Blossum. Indeed, this was a mighty medicine warrior.

The exchange was as brief as it was intense. The chief trotted after his men. Only Weeononka had seen his exchange with his wife. But Game Dancer had seen Weeononka. She looked at him and knew immediately that he'd been watching her, probably had seen her witness the chieftain's forbidden conjugal farewell.

Crow Sister walked out of the lodge where she'd been staying, a small travel bundle on her back, arms and face greased, her feather fan ready to swat flies. Weeononka and she had not spent much time together since their arrival in this village. Weeononka was sorry for that, sorry she was saying goodbye to the woman who had been the only mother she remembered. She saw Crow Sister felt the loss, too. Silently they embraced. Then Crow Sister seemed to understand the girl had something to say to the Osage warrior who stood waiting beside them. The older woman left Weeononka's side to say goodbye to The Blossum and thank her for the village's hospitality.

Game Dancer, still holding his horse's reins, had only to pivot in his moccasined feet to confront Weeononka. She held the quiver out to him. He looked at it a moment then said, "But I failed to get the honey without a sting." As though he needed to prove it to her, he showed her his scabbed hand where the Chickasaw arrow had pierced him.

"But you would have won the bet had it not been for the Chickasaw. And it was my fault they caught us. If I hadn't teased you with the wager, we would not have stopped. Besides, your old quiver is falling apart."

She gestured that he should take the new one.

"It's beautiful," he said, examining the quill beads that made up the intricate geometrical design meaning "flying very straight." This was Weeononka's specialty, beadwork with hollow dyed and cut porcupine quills. "It's the finest *o ju ah* I've ever seen," he said with genuine appreciation for the labor involved. But he wondered why she had given him this splendid gift when he had made a trade that insulted her. "Why?" he asked, unable to look her in the eye. She had thought about that, too. She just knew she wanted to give him something; maybe it was to leave him with some memory of her or just to say that she was parting without hating him. "I forgive you," she replied after a while. "I realized when you gave the foreign trinket back that you did what you did because Dancing Buck requested it. I don't blame you for doing your duty." He saw the sadness in her eyes that said there was more. "I just wonder why you didn't tell me, why you made love on the mountain as if it were all still the same."

He shook his head. "I'm sorry. You're just . . . I mean . . . when I saw you in the sun like that . . . I wanted you, that's all." He shrugged. "I'm sorry to lose you," he finished softly, barely brushing his fingers against hers.

This gave her small comfort. She nodded, unable to say more. He wondered how she could be sad catching so fine a husband as this Quapaw chief. She would surely outlive his sickly old wife and have a good life with him for many seasons. "Thank you," he said, unslinging his old quiver; as if demonstrating the truth of her words, the strap broke, spilling his arrows on the Quapaw dancing ground. He and the enigmatic woman he had traded for a pistol he gave away bent reflexively together to retrieve them. Their hands touched momentarily as they put the arrows into the new bag. He left the old one where it lay at their feet as they stood, also together. "I wish you many sons and daughters. Man-Who-Stands-in-the-Middle is a renowned warrior and a fine man." He wished she would not look at him so intently. Would she never learn to use the discreet downcast eyes of a modest woman? What was she trying to say with this impudent glance? Did she suspect the favor Game Dancer had performed for his host last night?

"I know he'll be a good husband to you, Weeononka," he said to fill the vacant silence between them. He was trying to determine what she might know for sure. "He's very lucky, this Quapaw chief," the Osage nervously added, looking for the bridle he'd dropped. The horse had not taken off but contentedly munched on a tuft of parched grass that managed a tortured existence on the dancing ground.

She wondered what he was complimenting her about. Lucky to be getting a wife who could so skillfully bead porcupine quills, or something else? Game Dancer surmised she did not suspect the identity of her late-night visitor. Good. That's the way the chief wanted it to be, Game Dancer thought as he stepped back.

Crow Sister took his movement for the signal that it was time to leave, and walked from The Blossum, who hadn't missed a thing.

"Goodbye, my friend," Weeononka said to Crow Sister. They embraced again and Crow Sister whispered a goodbye that only she could hear.

"*Ho ke che wa,*" Weeononka answered, meaning farewell.

"Come and see me often. I want to know my grandchildren." Crow Sister smiled but there was a strange look in her eye, which Weeononka could not interpret. In fact, there was one person who had seen who entered and who left Weeononka's lodge the preceding night. However, this was not the time or place to inquire about such a matter. Crow Sister quickly turned and walked with Game Dancer from the compound.

It was already warm even though the sun hadn't yet crested the tall treetops of the jungle. A bird was singing its heart out nearby. A couple of little boys playing at war darted by with their toy bows close enough to Weeononka to ruffle her skirt. The larger of the two saw Game Dancer's discarded quiver in the dust. He grabbed it on the run, but Weeononka was quicker. She caught it from his hand and he was too shy to argue with this strange woman he knew belonged to his powerful medicine chief.

The boys ran off.

Weeononka regarded the ratty old quiver, limp and insignificant without its contents, tattered and shiny from long use.

The women were singing on their return from fetching water. Another bird's song joined the first, and tentative fingers of sunlight slanted through the forest from the east.

Weeononka stood alone on the dancing ground touching the torn strap of Game Dancer's quiver, not knowing quite what to do with it but utterly certain she could not throw it away or give it to a child to playfully destroy. She felt a little foolish hanging on to the useless old thing. Suddenly self-conscious, she looked around to see if she had been observed. There were the bright eyes of The Blossum shining in concentrated attention. What emotions hid behind that glance? Weeononka wondered.

In the same gesture she had first used to summon Weeononka, her aunt patted the bed with twisted fingers. The two women had spoken very little, yet now their lives were as intricately woven together as the reeds of a basket. How did she feel about this younger woman she'd personally chosen to take her place, about all the events that had happened in so few days?

It was time to find out.

6

Days flowed by like the Great River.

Full Crow Moon came and went, and the dark of Grass Moon approached. Runners had twice returned to the Quapaw village with no news to report. The Chickasaw enemy had not been engaged, had not even been seen. The war party, which was hollowing canoes on this side of the river, waited for the Osage to join them for the big raid into enemy territory on the other side in a few days.

In this state of anticipation and suspended action the thatched village of women, children, and old men went sleepily about its business of life. Weeononka fit right in, of course, this once being her home, but she had forgotten how hot it could get in the lowland spring. It seemed strange to have left a late snow less than a moon ago. One unusually muggy afternoon Weeononka was trying to survive the heat, watching The Blossum cook *sagamite*, lowland fashion. In her home village up in the mountains she had often enough prepared the dish of cornmeal, meat, and whatever else was available. The usual method was to put the ingredients into a vessel, either a clay pot or a watertight basket, and then drop in red-hot stones until the mixture cooked thick. Any bones, feathers, or other debris boiled to the top, where they could be scooped off.

But here in the lowlands there were few stones to use as boiling rocks. Weeononka had seen small twisted pieces of hard clay and now she witnessed how they were used by the lowlanders in place of boiling rocks. The clay was thrown into a fire and heated until it was hot enough, then thrown into the cooking pot in place of a rock.

She watched The Blossum get the *sagamite* to a good simmer, and they talked for a while about how different nations accomplished the same things using different materials.

"People are smart all over," said the older woman, stirring the *sagamite* with a wooden ladle in her crooked hand, then using the ladle to lift out feathers from a small quail she'd been aging. "I don't know why some people think they're superior, but they do. Human nature, I guess."

"The Quapaw think they're superior to the Chickasaw."

"Enemies have to make up stories about each other to give them reason to kill. No doubt the Chickasaw think we're inferior. That's why they can wage war on us."

"Do they really eat worms?"

The Blossum laughed gently over her cooking pot. The aroma of the *sagamite* wafted on the breeze to the pallet where Weeononka lay just outside the lodge doorway. It was too hot to cook inside. "They eat mussels from the river. I suppose they are some kind of worm." She chuckled to herself.

"Why do they mash their babies' heads in front?"

"It's an old custom among many southern tribes. I never figured out why it's done. Tradition, I suppose. My husband . . ." she looked up shyly at the younger woman. "That is, our husband says it comes from farther south where the people practice all sorts of barbarities, human sacrifice, even killing babies on top of great man-made mountains, like the mounds south of here, only bigger, and made of stone. He says they cut out the babies' living hearts and fling them into the fire while the children are still screaming. He says they paint pictures of these sacrifices and are very proud that they make so many each moon."

Weeononka was very pleased The Blossum had included her but she growled an obscenity against anyone who'd sacrifice a baby. "Even the Chickasaw don't eat babies," she said, and laughed with The Blossum. Ritual cannibalism of enemies caught in battles was practiced by every tribe, even sedate Quapaw and Osage. But it was a local tradition that none were as barbaric as the Chickasaw.

They were silent together for a while when The Blossum finally said, "Did our husband please you the night before he left us?"

Weeononka glowed back at her, "Oh, yes. He's wonderful!"

"Indeed. What I have always told him. Keep reminding him of it, my dear, when he returns."

"He seems so young, yet he's a grayhair."

"During the great wanderings his grandfather married a Mandan woman. White hair sometimes comes early to that nation."

"He prefers your lodge to mine."

"I'm an old habit."

"Much more than a habit, I think."

The Blossum sighed, saying much without words about her relationship with the man.

Her friendly frankness encouraged the younger to say more to her aunt than she might have so soon. "I was surprised when he returned to me that night."

"But you couldn't be left alone on your marriage night."

"He came to me only out of duty."

The Blossum looked at her a long time before replying, "Duty isn't a bad thing. It's not second best. In time you'll grow to see that attention to duty as an ennobling thing. Because you don't have to do it, you see, unless you choose it. Someday after I'm gone all this will be your duty," she said, indicating much more than this one lodge. Weeononka knew that inside on a special bone pedestal was the clan's sacred bundle, symbolic of the tribe's unity. So when The Blossum gestured at the lodge, it was that larger idea she meant. "Your duty will be to keep the sacred bundle safe. It's the material heart of the Osotony and as long as it rests here, the people will prosper."

"I may be pregnant."

"But that's wonderful," she exclaimed. "That's even better!" She reached over and patted Weeononka's hand with her own twisted fingers. "The people will love you even more if you bear Man-Who-'s child."

"But . . ."

"What's the matter with you—you should be happy—and the first time! It happened that way with me, too, with our first son. We have four, all grown into fine men with wives and children in their own lodges."

"Well . . ."

"Tell me, what's wrong?"

"I don't know . . ."

"Don't know what, girl? That you are pregnant or not?"

"No. I'm sure I am." She had been ready to ask The Blossum where the isolation hut was, expecting her moon blood days ago. But it hadn't come yet.

"Well, tell me, then, what's wrong?"

"It's difficult to speak of."

The Blossum waited, watching her intently.

"To tell you I must impugn our husband's honor."

The Blossum still waited.

"I don't think it was Man-Who-Stands-in-the-Middle who slept with me that night."

The other woman was unreadably silent.

"I think he had another warrior take his place."

"There is no doubt that our husband joined you after he left me," said The Blossum, but she wouldn't look at Weeononka.

"I think it was Game Dancer."

"Surely you would know the difference. The hair alone . . ."

"I think it was Game Dancer wearing a ceremonial feather headdress."

The Blossum gave her supper a good stir then sampled a taste on the ladle. "This *sagamite* is ready to eat, but it's too hot. I'm tired of staying in this one spot. Would you mind walking slowly down to the river with an old woman?"

"Well?" said Weeononka as she helped The Blossum to rise.

"Well what?"

"Did he stay with you that night or not?"

"I sleep very soundly, especially after a massage from our husband. You will learn he is a man of many talents."

"So, you aren't going to tell me."

"I tell you that our husband did not sleep in my bed the night of your marriage."

"I think it is not fitting that the mother of a tribe divides her tongue in half."

"Hand me that basket. If we're going to the river we may as well collect some blackberries."

Weeononka took up the basket and together the two women walked from the dusty compound down through the communal corn field that encircled the village. Several young women were giving their time to the Corn Mother, wearing nothing but slim loincloths as they bent over their buffalo-pelvis hoes. They saw The Blossom and waved to her but didn't break the lilting song they sang as they weeded the maize plants. It was very good *wa kon* for the Mother of the village to visit the field, and the tillers were joyous to see her now. Knowing the significance of her presence, The Blossom stooped to touch the strong young corn sprouts. She rubbed the delicate fronds in her gnarled fingers then smelled them meticulously. "A good crop this season. Mother has blessed us with just the right amount of rain and sun—we'll have the green corn festival soon." She examined the interior of a leaf but it was too soon for the tiny ears to have formed. "I knew it would be a good season when Man-Who- agreed to bring you here. We obviously have Mother's goodwill or she would not have let you get pregnant so quickly."

"Mother is usually fair to her children," Weeononka replied coolly. "We human beings should emulate her."

But The Blossom would not be baited. She stood slowly and continued along the path to the sand banks of the slow-moving river.

"Please tell me, Blossom. A woman needs to know."

"But it doesn't matter, really, does it?" The Blossom looked at her wryly. She knew of course that Man-Who- had paid Game Dancer the bride price. "You and he weren't strangers."

"That was before . . ."

"All you need to know is that our husband was with you."

"At least give me some sign."

"Tell me why it matters to you."

"It just does, that's all."

"Why? You think if it were Game Dancer that would mean he still cares about you?"

"You don't have to worry. "I'll be faithful to Man-Who-Stands-in-the-Middle."

The Blossom's face softened. "I know, dear Weeononka. What a confusion we've put into your young life."

"Tell me. I just want to know for sure."

But The Blossum was stubbornly silent.

They filled the berry basket quickly. The sweet aroma of honey locust filled the air. But it was hot. They sat down to rest and cool off beneath one of the white-blossomed trees that leaned over the bank of the sluggish river. The Nigestai was calm now, almost clear. Its waters were low because there had not been much rain that spring when it was usually cresting with flood. This same peaceful stream would transform into a muddy roaring monster that ate its banks when the rain came.

The old woman said quietly, without provocation, "I'll wager your child will be a lucky one."

Weeononka grinned, recognizing a reference to Game Dancer's love of a gamble. "Thank you," she said, and together they walked slowly back up to the village, Weeononka carrying the heavy basket, gladly letting The Blossum lean on her where the path was steep.

The young wife who had looked back gave birth a few sunrises later. Because it was an easy birth the midwife waited until the sun was nearly up before she called The Blossum. Normally Man-Who-Stands-in-the-Middle would have named the baby. But in his absence, The Blossum was expected to perform the important ritual that would ensure a long, prosperous, and happy life for the newborn *okee o eet e ka*, little warrior, for the child was a boy.

The young assistant, whose name was Buffalo Fleece, knelt just outside the chief's lodge. She scratched on the doorposts until a sleepy-eyed Weeononka awoke to the strange earthy smell, of newly burst birth water and blood, that wafted in with the assistant.

"Tell *wa kon wee on* that she has a new Quapaw to launch upon the river of life," said Buffalo Fleece. "Spirit woman" was one of the many titles held by The Blossum.

"I think she just got to sleep," Weeononka responded in a whisper. "She had a painful night."

The midwife assistant shrugged. "The *okee o eet e ka* is a beautiful baby. It would be a sadness if he were not properly named." Weeononka had seen such an attitude in the people, who assumed they owned their chief and his wife. They never failed to demand everything from them. Weeononka had lived amid this tradition all her life, yet had never seen it from this perspective before.

Buffalo Fleece backed away from the chief's doorway but the strangely beguiling aroma of new birth lingered on. It was only a fleeting moment, but Weeononka knew at that moment she was truly pregnant; the private doubts she had had were gone. She stretched. The sun was not up, but it was already hot.

It wasn't even Sprouting Moon, yet it was already as hot as the mountains during Heat Moon. What would it be like deeper into the summer? Today would be a scorcher, she thought as she crawled on all fours to the raised sleeping platform where The Blossum lay in blessed slumber, away at least for a little time from the pain that racked her bones.

"Mother . . ." she called softly. As she stoked the fire from the night coals, Weeononka began idly thinking of names that would be apt for a little boy born today. She heard a bird call echo from the forest; the air was so still she could clearly hear the current of the Nigestai flowing nearby on its way to the Great River. What did these peaceful signs portend for the newborn? It certainly wasn't her duty to be thinking along these lines. But as The Blossum groggily stirred, the first thing she said, sniffing the air profusely, was, "What would be a good name for a little warrior born on such a hot day?"

Weeononka started, feeling awe for the old woman's ability to know the unknown. "That is big *wa kon*, to know what has happened before you are told."

"Doesn't take any magic for me to know that someone, probably the woman of the most advanced pregnancy in this village, has just given birth. The midwife who helped her labor was just here. I have smelled it many times before. See? No magic. Always look to the practical cause before you make it *wa kon*, girl. Ah—there is so much to teach you, I don't know where to begin. If Man-Who- had done as I wished, you would have been here two winters ago."

Weeononka poured her some leftover tea from a clay pitcher, hoping the sassafras and chamomile would help The Blossum's pain. As usual, she never complained, but Weeononka could tell the older woman was aching from the slow movements she made climbing from her sleeping platform.

Gratefully The Blossum took the polished buffalo horn of tea and quietly sipped it, her knobby legs and poor crooked feet dangling from her bed.

"But you knew it was a boy. Surely that was *wa kon*?"

"What would be the first explanation?"

"You overheard . . ." Weeononka liked the whole idea of

wa kon but didn't want to be told there was a scarcity of this
wonderful thing, or let go of the possibility that this woman
could teach it to her.

"Yes. That's how I knew." She regarded the young woman
briefly. "There is very little *wa kon* left in the world. Most of
the time, things, even strange things, can be explained
without it."

Weeononka wanted there to be more *wa kon* in the world
than this elder sister implied, so she answered a little
petulantly, "You don't want me to honor your wisdom."

"Honor your own wisdom." The Blossom drained the cup.

Both were silent for a time. Finally Weeononka said quietly,
"How about Hawk Dark Moon." She thought it was a hawk she
had heard. She wasn't used to the strange echo of these regions
close to the river.

The Blossom regarded the suggestion for a time as she
finished sipping the tea. She set aside the cup and began to
pull on her skirt—it was too hot to wear much else, so like the
younger women of the village during these warm days, she
didn't wear a shirt. Despite her crippled extremities, The
Blossom still had beautiful breasts. She stood and stretched as
best her crippled bones permitted.

"Hawk Dark Moon it is, then," she said, looking for her
walking stick.

"You mean it's a good enough name?"

"It's a beautiful, apt name."

"But I've never named anyone before," Weeononka protested, thinking of her own failure to name herself. "I'm not *wa
kon*."

"You are now."

The Blossom was exasperated that the stick was perversely
gone, as it so often seemed to be these days when she needed
it more and more.

Weeononka searched with her. "Where did you have it last?"

"If I knew that, I wouldn't be looking."

"Ah—here it is—" Weeononka said, finding it beneath The
Blossom's bed.

"*Wa kon* is a funny thing," The Blossom continued even
though the sun was close to rising. It was considered very bad
medicine if a newborn went unnamed after its circle cleared
the horizon. It was a short walk down to the sandbar, the most
open spot in the area for viewing the sun and the traditional
spot to name babies. But The Blossom moved slowly, so there

was every reason to get on with the ceremony. Through the raised flap in The Blossum's hand, Weeononka could see Buffalo Fleece standing outside, impatiently looking at the sky.

"You either have it or you don't, but sometimes people have it and don't know it." Then she added as an afterthought, "But usually one catches on."

"But how do you know when you have it?"

"You named a baby didn't you? That can only be done by a person with *wa kon*."

"But I made it up. I listened to my head talking."

"That right there is very big medicine. People who listen to their head and truly follow are often possessors of enough *wa kon* so that other people see it in them and let them lead." To herself she mumbled, "Though it's an awful burden sometimes."

"But—"

"Would you have me waste such a fine name? We'll talk about this later. Don't let it cause you grief. Just listen to your own *wa kon*." With that she was gone, the buffalo hide flapping softly against the doorpost.

So it was that Weeononka, but not The Blossum, was in camp when the Chickasaw struck.

7

Weeononka, inside the lodge straightening the sleeping platforms, heard a dog bark. It suddenly stopped, choked off. She stood with an unfolded buffalo robe in her hands, listening. There had been a strange pitch to the bark. She dropped the robe and walked to the opening where she had turned back the flap to air the lodge.

Outside, the camp was deathly still. The council pavilion was empty; a thin string of smoke from a perpetual fire rose up through the ceiling flap undisturbed by any breeze. At this moment nobody was in sight, not even the old men whose sole duty was to perpetuate the fire at the ends of three logs. Children could be heard playing unseen somewhere far to the left and presently a small child, little older than a toddler, crept onto the hard ground chasing something scuttling in the dust. The child giggled and reached for the insect or lizard, whatever it was.

What Weeononka saw next was impossible. The child flew up into the air with an astonished look on his little face. A moment passed before she realized a naked tattooed man with long feathers in his topknot ran behind the child. What had lifted the baby impossibly off the ground was the blunt ham of a war club swung with casual skill. She heard the child's head pop. He was suddenly spread on the ground with a flock of the tattooed warriors looming behind him, whooping, hacking, and, she could now see by the smoke that already had one lodge, burning anything in their path. Within three blinks she saw three other children run nearby, only to be struck down. The war club was the favorite among these jungle hunters from the eastern bank of the Mech-a-si-pi. She heard a woman's scream cut off like the dog's that started it all.

But carnage didn't appear to be all they had in mind. She saw beyond the wall of wavering smoke a line of the eldest children, mostly boys. This afternoon one of the elders had a group of them off in the meadow completing some lesson on trapping small game. She didn't see the elder anywhere about, but the oldest boys were among the children already tied together with rope nooses around their necks like a string of fowl, hands bound behind their backs. Weeononka shivered, remembering the position of her own hands not so long ago. The body never forgets, she thought.

Suddenly a marauding warrior appeared, laughing, backing out of a smoldering lodge. He was quickly followed by one of the women, mother of two of the teenage boys, and wife to one of the war chief's lieutenants. The woman came out screaming, her husband's hunting knife in her hands, slashing at the stumbling Chickasaw, who wasn't taking her seriously. But when she snagged him, the sight of his own blood frenzied him. He flew in despite the hacking knife the woman used to good account, and struck her. She slumped to the ground. The brave threw open her legs and plowed into her first with his own body, then with his war club. She never woke up.

The muggy day made their fires stubborn. They threw on bladders of bear grease and pine sap, creating several infernos that finally joined. Through all this, which had so far lasted only the time it took to walk the few paces to the river, Weeononka was looking about for some route of escape. The chief's lodge sat rather by itself behind the council pavilion, which was now a wall of flames as the dry bark on the roof ignited. Even if someone had wanted to come here from the rest of the village, they would have had to circle around to avoid the flames.

But there were too many Chickasaw who would see her if she merely ran out the door. All she could do was leave by the back of the lodge. She tore through a stack of provender in baskets along the back wall unused for sleeping. Presently she succeeded in tunneling through the stored food and rolled buffalo skins The Blossum had stacked so neatly. She ran a tight household with everything efficiently stored by priority of use. Weeononka demolished the work of months in her wild push to the outside. The wall was made of tightly woven rushes and river clay daubed with pitch. She found a cooking knife and proceeded to hack and pry her way through the fibrous wall. She looked over her shoulder where the frame of the lodge door revealed new scenes of horror beyond the pavilion. But so far this lodge was out of the main line of attack, which seemed to have come from the northeast. As she worked at the crawlhole, she concluded that the enemy must have reconnoitered the Quapaw canoe camp, circled around, and hit the village left defended only by a handful of guards. How long have they been watching us? she wondered, thinking of the many times in the past few sunrises when she had been alone in the forest collecting roots to make bead dyes, or down by the river with a couple of women. It might have happened anytime.

But it was happening now, she reminded herself. She heard new screams outside nearer than before as the enemy found hiding victims. The warriors were frenzied as if they had been held back from fighting for a long while before this moment when their leader unleashed them like a pack of starved wolves.

Her knuckles were bleeding now but she had penetrated the wall. She pushed her foot against the bark planks and pushed with all her might. Her leg went through the splintered wood too easily. She left flesh behind. She had been wearing only a low pair of soft doeskin slippers that didn't protect her legs. But she kicked again, unmindful of the pain.

Lacy sunlight shining on the back wall of the lodge broke through her clawed exit but as she was about to escape she cast another glance just to make sure she was still unobserved. Fury progressed outside but so far none of the attackers approached this lodge. Satisfied she had a chance, she started to scramble through when her eye fell on the Osotony Quapaw sacred bundle leaning in its traditional place of honor above Man-Who-'s sleeping platform. The Blossum's words came back to her. This was the material heart of the people, this sacred collection of things that marked the clan's long journey down the river and eventual settlement on this land. Individual Osotony would live and die but as long as the bundle was intact the Osotony would survive. The survivors of this attack would need the bundle to have the heart to begin again.

But she knew she mustn't be burdened with it in a belly scramble through the woods. She hated to have to leave it but couldn't take it with her. Furtively she looked around; this lodge would no doubt be vandalized, probably burned. Her eye was suddenly caught by the flat stone The Blossum used to cover her below-ground cache of tubers and seedcorn. Without further reflection Weeononka dragged away the rock and threw the vegetables out of the deep dry hole. She grabbed the sacred bundle from its buffalo bone pedestal, thrust it into the pit and pulled the cover back into place. If The Blossum survived, she would come back here and find it. With great satisfaction Weeononka slung bedding over the cache to hide it, then, convinced the sacred bundle just might go unnoticed, she returned to the opening she'd put into the back wall.

Very soon she was crawling out into sunlight filtered by the trees that marked the border of high-ground forest. Not daring to expose herself by standing up to run, she continued slithering across the weedy ground, through the now empty corral area where her husband had kept the horse he'd given to Game Dancer. Water weeds grew high along the branchlet that creased the rise beyond the corral, but she snaked her way along the ground unmindful of what she might encounter. She looked down at the side slit of her skirt: On her exposed thigh the tattoo of her manitou *wesa* glistened with sweat. It seemed to have a life of its own. She thanked the snake for helping her see the way to safety and like the snake she slid on her belly through the trickling water. The screams were farther away now. From the protection of the tall grass she paused to glance back. All the lodges burned briskly as the flames touched pitch in the foundations.

The line of captives had grown longer. At least twenty-five youngsters were roped together. She saw that none of these was injured, and even as she watched, she saw a Chickasaw kill

a fine young boy who surely would have been spared if he had
not been obviously bleeding.

The sight weakened her neck. She dropped her head on her
wrists and cried without making a sound. Chewing gently on
the nearest part of her hand, she continued to watch what was
happening, unable to turn from it even though she would have
given anything to be able to do so. But by its very excess the
scene was fascinating. Knots of warriors were beginning to
cluster as the number of potential victims decreased. Chants
were breaking out among them as they went about collecting
scalp tokens from the fallen and the dying. The feast of the
dead, the meal of victims the Chickasaw believed would
impart vitality, would soon follow. This was something she did
not want to witness. But she dared not leave what seemed like
the safest spot she had gained, until darkness could protect a
move.

The chanting grew louder, bringing memories of another
night she had watched these same warriors dance. They were
drinking the white man's drink again. So far she had not seen
the white man himself, but this alone inspired her to imagine
his presence.

She watched them torch everything left in the village,
including a couple of old villagers found hiding under overturned corn baskets. Before long she saw in the firelight the
Chickasaw war party leader who had captured her before. He
appeared furious at the braves when he interrupted their
victory celebration. Though she did not know his language,
she could tell by his gestures that he was unhappy with the
prisoners—they were probably too young. The eldest male
among them had only seventeen winters. The Chickasaw chief
probably wanted to know why none of the men who were
guarding the village was among the captives. He must be
shaming them, by the looks on their faces, that it's easy to catch
children but more difficult to catch armed warriors. Then he
abruptly gestured in her direction. She realized with a
creeping chill that this man wanted to know about the lodge
she had vacated, the biggest one; why was it still standing and
where were its occupants?

He ordered several braves to distribute themselves behind
that lodge. As she watched his hand gestures and caught his
meaning, Weeononka almost panicked. She caught herself,
heart pounding, already scrambling to her feet to make a dash
for it. But sense overcame her or maybe, she'd reflect later, it

was her manitou advising her to quiet wisdom. Whatever, she dropped back to her belly, almost knocking herself breathless, and began to crawl in the direction of the sheltering forest.

She was wearing only a short leather skirt but at least it was some protection—her only bedroll tonight, her only leggings against briars on the run tomorrow. Slithering along the wet grass and loamy earth she thought again of *wesa*. Do you ever break the eggs inside your body when you travel along like this? she asked her manitou. As always, her manitou never answered, except to give her good ideas when she needed them.

She wondered about the baby. Was it like manitou, unable to speak, but able to hear her? What are you thinking, little baby, as I slap you along in this bumpy manner? she thought as she maneuvered across a gravel outcrop. It was dark now, without a moon. The tree frogs had taken over the air with their many voices. Weeononka didn't rush, but her persistent quiet meander covered ground. Somewhere off in the near remove she saw torchglow, heard men speaking gruffly to each other. She froze, a bug on a leaf, a frog under the egret's legs, hoping her dark form would blend with the darkness. Every once in a while she would slowly ease her body forward. In this way she gained the forest perimeter while they were still searching over in another direction.

She was beginning to feel safer. But with her own life seeming less in danger, her staggered mind began to throw memories of carnage around behind her eyes. She wretched into the damp ground covered with leaves and smelling of warm fungus. She cooled on her back, her stomach settling, but her mind still racing with images of death. The fires still burned. She heard the leader call to his men, saying something she didn't understand, something that sounded fatigued. Maybe they'd give up. Then she heard the leader haranguing his soldiers. He may have turned in her direction, or perhaps the breeze threw his voice nearer, but he sounded not ten paces away.

Heavy with fatigue she began crawling again anyway. She could smell the forest around her now. All was darkness and in that darkness was sanctuary. She felt small legs crawl across her hands as she plodded along, herself a crawling creature. She moved through moisture and drank cool spring water.

Far overhead through the shivering canopy of dark tree crowns she saw the lance points of the stars. Still she crawled,

unable now to stop since she had set herself with such
determination on this course. She imagined herself not only a
winding snake, belly-bubbled and full of eggs, but also a
wandering buffalo on her four stout legs searching forever for
the perfect green grass of buffalo dreams. She was a mother
panther crying petulantly for her kittens to come to teat
because her milk was full and already giving in great silver
drops. She was the little rabbit mother she'd snared not so
long ago, watching for the one who set the snare. She was
deer, she was beaver, she was all four-legged creatures running
from the predator into the arms of the forest. But by then she
was mindless and so when she crawled against the Chickasaw
leader he laughed with his men at her foolishness when she
tried to push away his legs, thinking they were saplings. She
looked mutely up at this grimly laughing tree. In the torchlight
he recognized her face from the time before. He jerked back
her head with a hank of hair in his fist to see her better then
muttered a guttural affirmation in his own language. Then for
her benefit, as though he were calling coup on an enemy and
he wanted that enemy to know it, he said in Osage, "Yes, this is
the one I want."

From somewhere deep inside she managed to glare at him.

He spat on her and pulled her hair again, then forced her
head down. "Get your evil eye off me, woman!" He saw her
trying to watch him as one of his men tied her hands behind
her back. "I said lower your eyes—" He raised his hand to
strike her, but she quickly averted her glance and he held
back.

One of his men must have asked something about her,
because the leader answered first in his language and then in
hers, "Yes, this is the bitch who killed my son."

8

The slave catchers had moved their camp downstream. It
was larger now with several human cages, all full. Weeononka
noticed that there were very few woman. She saw some of the
Quapaw braves but most of the prisoners looked like Taencas
or Tunica. There was also a line of prisoners bound together
and tethered between two large trees. The slave catchers tied
the Osotony boys among this gang.

They kept her separate. As soon as they arrived at the camp, they tied her to a tree off to herself near a hastily built lean-to she later learned belonged to the red-haired white man she'd seen earlier. She was given a jug of water and fed once a day but other than that for the first two days they left her alone. Even the fierce Chickasaw chief who had earlier spoken so harshly to her left her to herself. It gave her wormy dread for him to look at her, though. A couple of times she found him watching her from afar, arms across his chest. She couldn't interpret the message of his face and was glad not to have to. At least he left her alone.

But she was sure it was only a temporary respite. Evidently the white man had given orders about her. There was no comfort in that surmise. Bands of the Chickasaw went off from time to time and often brought back one or two prisoners. They were obviously snatching lone warriors whom they would not be able even to touch without the white man's weapon. But the white man was ominously absent. In and around the hut, which everyone avoided, she saw foreign objects. Her tree was too near this fearsome territory for herself not to be part of it. She could only await his arrival.

She decided that the Quapaw had crossed the river; otherwise one of their scouts surely would have found this large noisy encampment. Though she was kept from the center of activity, she perceived that the Chickasaw braves were disgruntled, but it wasn't until her third day in the camp when the white man returned that she found out why.

He came accompanied by the Chickasaw leader and two prisoners. Weeononka saw with a sinking heart that one of those bound was One Thunder Turtle. The other was Man-Who-Stands-in-the-Middle. Surely only the white man's firearms could help the Chickasaw take two of the region's most famous chiefs. The two Quapaw stood while the white man and the Chickasaw argued in the white man's language sprinkled with Chickasaw words.

Weeononka felt tears streak her cheeks before she was aware she was crying. She wanted to call out to her husband, who stood with his head hanging, hands tied behind his back around a branch through the bend of his arms. After a few moments of argument with the red-faced, furious white man, the Chickasaw chieftain walked away. He took Man-Who- and One Thunder Turtle with him toward a tree not too far from Weeononka's and tied the peace chief there. He found another tree on the other side of the white man's hut: there he tied One Thunder Turtle. Because these two were leaders, he wanted them separate from the other prisoners.

It was near dusk. The Chickasaw warriors already had a cooking fire going. They passed around the brown containers Weeononka had now grown to associate with their drunkenness. When darkness fell and when the warriors were making enough noise not to bother with their captives, she called over to her husband. He may have passed out. His body hung against its bonds but he woke quickly enough at the sound of her voice. Their positions were about ten paces apart, close enough to converse without attracting attention.

Her husband cried out when he recognized her voice. She told him quickly, omitting grim details, about the attack. She said it was possible The Blossum and some of the women and children survived because they were down on the river naming the new baby.

Man-Who- shook his head. "Unfortunate little warrior. His father was killed in the ambush that captured me." He said the Quapaw warriors probably didn't even know yet that their two chiefs were prisoners and confirmed her suspicion that the slave catchers were picking off single scouts or hunters simply by the superiority of the guns. She commented on the displeasure of the Chickasaw warriors.

"You know why," he said ominously.

She suspected but didn't want to think of the reason. The traditional mode of war was to take slaves only to replace Chickasaw who died in battle. A war party always brought back some healthy slaves to replace the fallen. Women of the dead had first choice of such captives, who were adopted into the tribe, often with full tribal privileges. Anyone else captured was tortured for the entertainment of the tribe and the benefit of the victim's manitou. It was considered the highest honor for a warrior to die in this manner.

"They're mad at the white man who wants only living captives," Man-Who- continued.

This didn't make any sense. No tribe could need this many replacements; why would someone want so many extra people? "Why?"

"I don't know exactly how but it has something to do with what they're drinking." He was quiet for a time, then said, "Remember when I said the white men were made of metal?

Well, I was wrong. I thought they were superior, but now I know these whites have even less *wa kon* than red people."

She regarded the scene of celebration near the fire, a reenactment of her first night among these slave catchers. The Chickasaw were chanting louder and louder, and to Weeononka's ears, they sounded definitely hostile.

"What are they going to do with us?"

"I think they plan to march us to their allies the Iroquois."

This struck a cold note in her. Weeononka had grown up with that one word signifying all that could be evil among human beings. Iroquois. Of all the known humans the Iroquois were the most inhuman. They killed to make everyone who survived an Iroquois. Those who joined their league lived. Any resistors died. It was the Iroquois from whom the early Quapaw fled along with other Sioux-speaking tribes who were the descendants of the original forest people of the middle continent. The Iroquois were the eternal human predators who wiped out entire tribes such as the Huron, who were their own relatives. Their very name could inspire nightmares born out of old stories told around the campfires when Winter-maker stalked the forest in tall white moccasins.

Man-Who-Stands-in-the-Middle listened with interest to the growing intensity of the warriors' chants. "Feel the night, Weeononka. Something very *wa kon* is about to happen."

Weeononka, taking a little comfort from the fact that he'd remembered to call her by her name, nevertheless felt a chill. When she said this, he answered sadly, "There is so much I was going to teach you. My only regret is that I didn't bring you to the Osotony Quapaw long ago as The Blossum wished."

Without thinking, Weeononka replied quickly, "And my only regret is that I never knew my husband."

He appeared surprised.

"But how can you say this? Your husband returned to you the night of your marriage even though he was preparing for war. For you your husband broke his fast."

"No. My husband, being a warrior of great honor, was true to his fast."

"Impudent woman," he said, but without rancor.

"But the night isn't over. We may yet have a chance to continue our lives . . ." she said, hoping she could inspire him to escape. But he seemed so tired, so beaten down.

The fire across the way flamed higher. She saw in the new light that her husband had been hurt; blood matted his white hair. He didn't look to her as if he could focus.

The warriors grew louder now as the night deepened. When the white man walked nearby, two braves blocked his way. His hand fell to his pistol but the Chickasaw leader intervened to translate the warriors' demand.

Man-Who- translated for Weeononka. "He says the Makac does not know the way of the Chickasaw. The Chickasaw do not gather human dogs as pets for anyone. There is no honor in this. . . ."

The Chickasaw said a long string of phrases Man-Who-interpreted simply as, "There must be a feast of the dead." He looked steadily at her across the space between them. "Little wife, I have an idea that might at least save you. I feel great *wa kon* here and I think I can make it work for us if you can go through it with me."

Weeononka shuddered. She could not feel her hands tied behind her back. She was cold down to the marrow in her bones with the implication here; her numb hands tingled as blood coursed through her with a chill that raised the flesh of her arms and back.

"He says that the men will no longer gather people for Makac unless they are allowed their tradition."

The white man didn't say anything for a while. He glared at the braves, who didn't blink. He pulled out his pistol and began inspecting its parts as a threat. The Chickasaw leader moved close to him, speaking softly so that none could hear.

"I don't understand, husband."

"Did you really mean it—that you wanted your husband tonight?"

"Yes, but—"

"Then follow my words with great care. What we will do is dangerous. It is a high thin ledge above a deep canyon. But I am going to give you enough *wa kon* to keep these Chickasaw a respectful distance from you after . . ." Ominously, he did not finish the thought.

The men by the fire were still, watching their leader confront the hideous white man they all hated but who could hold them off with his awesome firestick.

The white man and the leader conferred in private for a while then in apparent disgust the Makac turned away and strode toward Weeononka. Her heart pounded as he approached but she saw she was frightened for nothing. He didn't even look her way. He went inside his hut. Presently a weird glow showed around the hide that served as a door.

Man-Who- said Makac had a *wa kon*, a spirit light in there that allowed him to have a little sun burning all night long.

That was an amazing thing Weeononka would have liked to see. Wonders of the white man never ceased.

"What did they decide that made him so mad?" she asked.

Man-Who- regarded the Chickasaw leader, who was conferring with his warriors. They listened then cheered as a single man. Man-Who- let his bleeding head roll a little on his shoulder so that he could see her. "Makac says they can have one prisoner to feast on," he replied with great calm. "But it must be one already wounded, for Makac cannot get his price on wounded slaves."

Her husband's idea was clearer. Before she could reply he called out to the warriors. "Honor me with the ceremony!"

His voice arrested them, then they cheered agreement. Already the two warriors who had confronted Makac were walking toward her husband with grim smiles on their faces.

"If you ever see The Blossom again, tell her I always swore I'd follow her but I never expected her to have to follow me," said her husband as one of the Chickasaw untied him. He slumped a little when the bonds loosened. The Chickasaw leader walked up to him as the other two respectfully helped him to stand.

"My son," said the Chickasaw, using the honorific title, "you will be honored tonight as only the Chickasaw can honor a warrior." There wasn't a trace of sarcasm in his voice. He was bestowing his profession's highest honor on another warrior. It was an ancient tradition, ancient enough for all the known tribes to practice though some like the Quapaw didn't indulge in it often.

"My heart sings with anticipation," replied Man-Who-Stands-in-the-Middle, drawing himself up proudly. His tribe might have had current scruples against torture and ritual cannibalism but the ceremony was part of his people's venerable tradition. He was joyous that he would not be made a slave and that he was being granted his heart's desire, to be with The Blossom as quickly as possible, forever. He did not believe she had survived the Chickasaw attack on the village as Weeononka suggested. A warrior, he was more cynical than the girl who was softened by hope.

The Chickasaw made him a small polite bow. "Your servants await you," he said, motioning to his men to proceed.

Man-Who-Stands-in-the-Middle looked over at his young

wife straining against her bonds. He could barely see her from here. He was sorry she would have to witness his pain, but knew she would be proud of his courage. As a warrior he had been waiting all his life for this moment. He could tell that she was not going to scream; she was smart and headstrong, but she would know not to damage the *wa kon* of his upcoming performance with disharmonic noises.

She'd save her mourning song until after his death song. This was the proper way.

Meanwhile he could make sure some of the *wa kon* he stirred tonight settled on her head. Man-Who- said, "My father," using the warrior's formal address in response to the Chickasaw's own, which implied that he was being adopted into the tribe. "I have been told the Chickasaw were honorable warriors. Dare I hope they will grant a last request?"

The Chickasaw was taken aback, but he nodded with a look of puzzlement on his tattooed face. "If the request is within reason."

Her husband regarded Weeononka again. "This girl was mated to me while I was fasting to meet the honorable opponent," he said diplomatically. "I regret only that I did not get a chance to bring her to blanket."

The Chickasaw laughed heartily. A couple of his men who also spoke Quapaw echoed his good cheer, and were already nodding their heads. The spectacle of the life force so close to the death force was too good to miss. The Chickasaw leader gestured for them to untie the Quapaw's hands. Now, as the speakers of Quapaw translated for the others, a mighty cheer rose up among them. The prisoners on the line were restless, unsure if this turn of events boded well for their own situation.

Over by the fire someone threw down a buffalo robe. Man-Who- swayed unsteadily before her while the warrior untied her hands. She was speechless with terror. What if he had miscalculated and they all descended upon her?

Her husband saw her flat-faced distress. "Don't worry. I'm going to give them the mightiest *wa kon* they've ever seen at the stake tonight. My manitou is calling me—hear it?" He cocked his bleeding head, listening to the wind in the trees by the river. He had a frightening smile on his face. She was astonished to see his manhood stiffening beneath his loincloth. How could he be full of desire at this moment when he faced the torture pole? The Blossum was right; this was some man.

The Quapaw chief knew the reaction of desire to life-and-death situations. Many times before a battle he'd found his passion high; that's why warriors fasted from sex, to build their energy. Unlike her, he wasn't surprised that sex and death were linked.

He took her hands in his and spoke briefly, "Such a thing as we are going to do is powerful, woman." He led her to the robe. Very tenderly, despite the watching eyes and the mounting male excitement that left the air heavy, he knelt before her and began to stroke her face and hair. She was not as able to ignore the watching eyes. "This has nothing to do with them," he whispered, gently turning her face away from the audience, forcing her to see only himself. "This has only to do with us."

"I've never come to blanket before onlookers."

"Think of it as the green corn festival."

"But then everyone is doing it."

"This is a sacred blanket, Weeononka," he answered. His hands unlaced her soft mulberry bark skirt and slipped it over her head.

The fire snapped. A wind whipped it up, drying sweat from her naked body and replacing it with prickling delight as his fingers brushed her here and there, raising her flesh.

"We are the only two humans in the world," he whispered in her ear. "We are the first man and the first woman formed out of chaos. There is none to watch us except the Mother and the stars."

The watching eyes did diminish with Man-Who- so close like this. Above them the stars were brilliant. He laid her back on the robe, not taking his loving eyes from hers while he removed his loincloth. She saw for the first time the tattoo of his manitou, the crane, on his right thigh. A great sigh rose up around them; he was a well-formed man the others envied. The watching warriors knew the connection between the life *wa kon* and the death *wa kon* but to watch the phenomenon taking place before their very eyes was a rare and astonishing event.

All but the enraged white man felt this awe. He had been peeking out from the flap of his hut. Now he ran screaming in fury toward the fire. But the Chickasaw leader stopped him, admonishing him that he should not interfere with the sacred ritual in progress. The warriors underscored the threat by shaking their war clubs. With a curse the white man strode off toward the river.

Weeononka had not even been aware of this; her husband
held her so tenderly. He was in no hurry but was determined
to taste the pleasure of her pleasure to the last sip. She caught
the strong beam of affection from his eyes. He could make this
wa kon, she realized. All she had to do was follow his lead.
They sat face to face rocking back and forth, twin rowers in a
small canoe.

The watchers began a slow mounting chant behind them. It
was as if every onlooker was submerging his own *aneh* into
Man-Who-'s personality. The chant punctuated his thrusts as
he began teasing her with penetration. Over on the slave rope
the few women present were coupling as best they could with
their nearest partners. There was no rape involved. They were
simply stirred by the event, like the public excitement of the
corn festival, which all tribes celebrated. There was no frenzy
to the scene. Most of the watchers merely chanted, using their
spears or headknockers to beat time to the rhythm of the two
principal dancers. But the life force came up through the soles
of their feet from the pounded earth, swelling their sex. The
women on the slave rope were untied.

The warriors cheered in unison when Weeononka cried out,
and urged Man-Who- to complete the ritual with his own
pleasure. Her husband collapsed upon her shoulder. His
breathing was ragged with more than spent passion. She
smoothed back his hair; the wound on his head was seeping a
trickle of blood. His eyes were unnaturally dilated. He didn't
seem to be able to focus on her. "Your nipples are very brown,
woman. The color of the earth. I bet you're pregnant."

She nodded, looking down at her breast smeared with some
of his blood.

"And you say your husband did not come to you that night!
Have you any doubts now?"

She mumbled no, kissing his neck and face while he tried to
rise, wanting to hold on to him all night. They had lived their
entire life together in these few moments. Now it was over.
She knew their time together was finished.

Two warriors loomed behind her husband, helping him to
stand. They led him to another buffalo robe on the other side
of the fire, where the delighted hosts bathed him and fed him a
ritual meal. Another tenderly wiped the blood from his
forehead and hair and salved his wound with bear grease.
Others were digging a hole, into which they placed a heavy
cedar tree trunk with all the branches hacked off.

The Chickasaw leader helped her to replace her clothes then assisted her to walk back to the tree where he bound her hands. He didn't look at her, but hurriedly fastened the knot. Before, he had seemed to hate her. Now he treated her respectfully. Silently she thanked her husband because surely he had given her *wa kon* that others could see.

Without a word he left her and returned to the torture pole, where they were preparing Man-Who- for the final ceremony.

"No!" called out a strong masculine voice. Weeononka recognized it as One Thunder Turtle, who formally addressed the Chickasaw leader. "I waited until my honored chief had his pleasure, but now I must protest that it is I, a war chief, who should be given the honor of the feast and not the peace chief!"

The Chickasaw hesitated.

"Nonsense," replied Man-Who-, steadied by his two guards. "There is no question that it is I who deserve the ceremony."

"But this man is not a professional warrior," yelled the old fighter, stepping as far out from the tree as his bonds would allow. "He is a talker—he would make women out of us all." One Thunder Turtle used an old expression, that is, "one against war," since women did not engage in battle.

"But this is ridiculous," replied Man-Who-, "I am this man's civil chief. I outrank him."

"And you are only slightly wounded," remarked the Chickasaw chieftain to One Thunder Turtle.

"While I am hurt so badly my vision is affected," said Man-Who-. "I think I am going blind. Not even that stupid white man wants a blind slave."

The Chickasaw chief snickered, looking guiltily about for the white man, who would not have understood Quapaw even if he had been listening. Weeononka realized that the awful white man had cowed the Chickasaw warrior. What a shameful thing to witness, she thought, hating the white man even more.

"This is an outrage—I call on the wood to decide!" bellowed One Thunder Turtle.

The Chickasaw warriors were thrilled that their games had taken this dramatic turn—to have two chiefs debating for the position of honored guest at the torture ritual was a heightened excitement that made their hearts beat faster. They would be able to make side bets, gambling being one of their favorite sports.

"Let them game, let them game—" urged the warriors. The chieftain could only comply with his men's request.

So it was that One Thunder Turtle with his escort of guards sat cross-legged on the packed dance ground in front of the torture pole after the intended victim's ordeal had been stayed a second time that night, facing off against his old opponent for the last time.

"Must you turn everything into a debate?" growled Man-Who-, weary, his head aching, his sight fuzzy and wishing to get on with it. He knew his old friend had no desire to die at this time. He was merely carrying through a chance to argue.

"Why not? It was boring over there with you getting all the attention," replied One Thunder Turtle. One of the Chickasaw on his guard handed him a fistful of carved sticks.

"You stand in my path, Snapper," Man-Who- chided, using a childhood nickname that referred to the way the war chief was named. "And like the turtle, you never let go."

"Not till the thunder rolls!" The war chief laughed.

"Must you always oppose me?"

"Someone has to keep you in line, Whitey," he said, using Man-Who-'s own nickname among the braves.

The Chickasaw, who loved this intensity more than eating, let them gamble a long time, three out of four rounds. One Thunder Turtle was caught cheating by Man-Who-. He demanded a default. But the Chickasaw had too much riding on the throw to let it go like that and so the two men played another round with two wins each.

Man-Who-Stands-in-the-Middle won the tiebreaker.

Weeononka groaned; but she knew it had been inevitable.

The guards escorted One Thunder Turtle back to the prisoners, making doubly sure his bonds were secure. After more ceremony the chieftain led Man-Who- to the torture pole and tied him there. Each warrior with growing hilarity began to gather branches from the ground around the Quapaw chief, who had begun his death song. It filled the forest so that the night creatures fell silent.

It started simply with their knives. Weeononka couldn't see exactly what they were doing, but she could tell by the strained interruptions of her husband's song that it was something terrible.

But the song continued. The Chickasaw leader addressed the Quapaw several times in ritual words, adding knife strokes to the others' as they began to chant along with the victim. His song often deteriorated into screams but he kept up the chant that he had been practicing all his life.

Weeononka knew that the Chickasaw were paying the highest honor to her husband by thus allowing him this death. She had of course seen this ritual performed before, but it had always been with a stranger as central performer and not someone she knew. She tried to not hear her husband's song but as the night deepened, the song elongated into a blood-chilling keen that could not be ignored. She knew Man-Who-Stands-in-the-Middle was strong. He would probably last all night. Weeononka was consoled that this warrior's death at least saved this proud man from being hamstrung and made a slave for some foreigners.

His song thanked his manitou for a long life with many sons and many scalps taken in honorable battle. He sang of his first vision quest when he drank the sacred black drink and went into trance, finding out for the first time that his destiny was to lead the Osotony Quapaw. He sang of his first buffalo kill, his first woman, his first son.

They were taking off his skin in thin strips. Weeononka tried not to look, but couldn't help it once or twice. He was glistening scarlet in the firelight, only his face still flesh. It was an awesome, glorious death song, and she was so proud of him. She wished The Blossum and the other people of the village could know how bravely their headman was leaving them. Surely with such a magnificent death song he would be walking the starry Path of Ghosts with his ancestors very soon. The ancestors themselves surely could hear the terrible music and must be bending over this very moment to listen from their star platforms.

The hosts heated delicate French metal hatchet heads until they glowed red on a chain, then hung them as a necklace around his neck. Man-Who-Stands-in-the-Middle screamed his grateful appreciation to them for startling his soul, which had been sleeping.

The air was full of his cooked aroma. Weeononka would never smell meat cooking again without thinking of her magnificent husband and the great death song he would leave as a legacy. She could tell all the warriors of the Chickasaw as well as the boys from Osotony tied up between the trees were amazed and inspired by Man-Who-'s masterful performance.

He would be remembered into many generations, this night being the subject of numberless future stories each of these witnesses would relate.

"My mother thanks you, dear brothers, for giving me this fire," he screamed when they began on his feet. Much, much later the torturers were growing faint from their exhausting labors but the man who stood in the middle of their throng begged them for more. The Quapaw over on the slave rope chanted a counterpoint to him, stamping the ground to keep time.

A nearly half moon rose over the Mech-a-si-pi's purple bluffs, which white men would continue to call after the Chickasaw into ten generations. Man-Who- still chanted, though now in a flat monotone uninterrupted by anything done to him. He was long beyond feeling. He saw his manitou, a single white crane in the eastern sky where He-Who-Rises approached. None present was aware that he had decided to die only when the sun shone on him.

The man on the stake found some reservoir of strength untouched by agony and renewed the death song in a louder voice. The warriors administering the rites shook their heads in disbelief. None among them had seen so long-hearted a man.

But inside the hut the white man made a loud noise of his own, a mighty swearword. He rampaged through the deerskin flap and stood there staring in the direction of the fire.

"I can't bear any more, you God-damned savages—" He walked around hitting one fist against the other, saying single words with great force.

Weeononka guessed it was some kind of a prayer because often he would cast his eyes toward the sky as if asking for something there. She could see that he had stuffed his ears with rags and wore a great furry cap. Even so, at a new-pitched wail from Man-Who-, he tried to stop his hearing with his hands at each ear. He saw her as if for the first time. Growling his one word prayers he roughly untied her and pulled her into the hut where he proceeded crudely to assault her. None of the warriors would have touched her, considering that her *wa kon* was too powerful. But the white man was ignorant. Outside, the few who had seen him take her into the hut considered him a mad fool for getting so close to the *wa kon* woman.

He didn't unbind her hands, which were still behind her back. She tried to gesture that he should untie her; if he was determined, then at least she could make it more pleasant. But he seemed to be unaware she had a face, so intent was he on the rest of her. It was interesting to see the chest of metal up close. She studied it for a time, wishing her hands were free so she could touch it. Indeed there was a small *wa kon* light burning by some mysterious process over there, a small pale shaft with a thin flame. This was her first candle. She wanted to ask the white man many things, but he disregarded her. She lay back, letting her mind float up and out. She made no noise but in her heart she sang with her husband, who continued his music outside.

"Got no hair," the smelly white man muttered, expressing the whites' main amazement at Indian anatomy, "Got no goddamn crotch hair—" Then he gasped and pushed off her, choking on a repeated word. She had no idea what he was saying as she sat up and watched him. Then she saw him pointing at her thigh where the tattoo of *wesa* curved across her muscle.

"Snake, snake, snake!" he said, backing away as he pulled up his britches.

The man outside pierced the night with another scream.

The white man tried to cover his ears again, apparently having abandoned the idea of taking this snake woman. She was greatly relieved, but why was he acting so crazy about the ritual outside? One would think it was himself on the pole. Surely he could hear as she could the beauty in the song, the courage not to yield to pain but to make it music. But the white man appeared unaware of this level of beauty in the death song.

The man tried to bury his head in a pile of furs, burrowing like a dog. She couldn't help beginning to laugh though she caught herself lest she insult him.

But he had seen her smile and it infuriated him. "Animal!" he spat as he stood. "Laughing while that's going on—" And he slugged her senseless, grabbed his long gun, and left the hut.

She groggily got to her feet. Her jaw hurt, but not as if it were broken. She could move it, though painfully. She caught a glimpse of the white man departing with his musket. By the time she left the hut, he was almost ready to fire. The warriors had not seen him but very soon they would. He wasn't aiming for stealth but blatantly advanced with his weapon pointed at the head of the man who screamed his song.

9

Makac the white man shot Man-Who-Stands-in-the-Middle in the temple, ending his magnificent death song far too soon.

The Chickasaw warriors around him were so shocked at the impiety it took a long second for the deed to register, then they fell on him with the intention of tearing him apart. Only the intervention of the Chickasaw leader prevented it. Even the prisoners on the sidelines made disparaging noises at the stupidity of the dishonorable act.

Weeononka, staggering from the hut, had seen what was going to happen but was powerless to prevent it. She started when the gun discharged. This was the closest she'd been to one of the weapons put to its singular use. Despite her respect for the tradition, in her deepest heart she was glad her husband's suffering was over, honor or no honor. But she knew this was not the way Man-Who- would have wanted it. He had been way beyond pain and had probably been interrupted in the middle of a magnificent vision.

This was the moment when she should have simply walked away. In the confusion she could easily have wandered off, but the ringing in her ears and the blow she had just received numbed her. By the time she recovered her senses, the Chickasaw leader approached her and led her to the torture post. He said in her language that the remarkable dead man so strongly impressed the Chickasaw with his courage they wished to give him a warrior's burial. Would she as his wife like to prepare his body?

She was joyous at the opportunity, knowing that most of the time torture victims were given no more burial than the stew pot. The Chickasaw, ignoring the imprecations the white man continued to heap upon them, helped her cut the body down. They brought her a fine buffalo hide in which to shroud it, bear grease, and *wa kon* paint with which to put on the proper designs. The Chickasaw leader even gave her some precious *nippowoc*, which she had smoked such a short time ago with Dancing Buck, to sprinkle over the remains. She wished she had time to make him a death suit and moccasins beaded on the soles in magic designs to guide his feet on the right path. The traditional words would have to suffice. She whispered in his ear using his name for the last time, "Walk toward the setting sun, Man-Who-Stands-in-the-Middle, and don't look back."

The Chickasaw had been so impressed with his extraordinary death song, each gave of his own store of sacred eagle feathers. Weeononka arranged them in a fan she placed in his hands before wrapping the buffalo hide around him. A warrior helped her sew it into a tight cocoon.

By that time it was nearly noon, the traditional hour of burial so the soul of the deceased could follow the sun to the western country where it went every night.

Other Chickasaw had untethered four of the strongest prisoners to dig a grave. The Quapaw warriors begged for the honor. Sioux relatives of the Quapaw who lived on the Great Plains put their dead to mummify on platforms, then buried all who died every few winters in a communal grave. But in this damp climate where mummification was impossible the Quapaw and other local tribes buried their dead in the ground.

The body was not simply lowered into the red earth. The men built a cedar platform above the grave floor. Riverbank reeds were spread on this platform before the warriors lowered the body. In time the grave bed would decompose, lowering him farther into the arms of the Mother of all.

When all this was done Weeononka began her mourning song. The several women on the slave rope wailed with her while the men, prisoners, and guards stood respectfully listening.

All except the white man, who cursed them all in his strident tongue, calling on his manitou to damn them. The sound of her song infuriated Makac but he dared not interfere further. It was a piercing song that should have ended with her knifing off her hair or the end joint of one of her fingers. But the white man wouldn't allow her a blade, and when she tried to batter her hand with a rock, Makac made the Chickasaw stop her. Makac had plans to sell her to pay his passage away from this terrible country; a disfigured woman wouldn't bring the highest price.

The chieftain tied her to the tree again but with grave politeness. "I blamed you for the death of my son," he said softly to her, "because he was going to you when your friend strangled him on the bars of the cage. But today I forgive you and will take no revenge because I have seen you were the wife of a great man."

"Thank you," she whispered, hoarse from her song and silently thanking her husband for his astute calculation of *wa kon*.

Thereafter this man whose name she never learned always made sure she had the best morsels of food and the freshest water. He made sure it was he who tied her bonds, securing the sinew so that it didn't cut off her blood. In the next few weeks of the slave march to Iroquois country she owed this man her life more than once because he intervened on her behalf with Makac, who would have abused her because of her husband's death. He called her ugly-sounding names and never came near her again. She was certain his hostility would have erupted into violence if the Chickasaw leader hadn't sternly warned him. He might use her, he might eventually sell her, but as long as she was under Chickasaw guard, he would not harm her. The Chickasaw told the white man in his own language that if Makac broke this taboo, he, the chieftain, would not be able to prevent his soldiers from continuing the interrupted ritual upon the person of Makac. They were already betting that the white man did not have near the staying power of the Quapaw.

Even with his awesome weapon Makac didn't dare test the Chickasaw on the subject of the Quapaw woman. At first he threw her evil glances but later just ignored her.

So it was that after an uneventful journey northeastward through the great brooding forests of the continent's heartland, through districts where no tribe lived, across blue mountains and wooded valleys, over streams as small as baby spit and rivers as wide as lakes, Weeononka came to be among the Iroquois.

She was five months pregnant in Thunder Moon when the slave catchers and their fatigued line of trade goods entered the great Iroquois village. The delighted Iroquois chieftains took charge of the slaves, whom they were to escort farther east to white slave traders. Makac told them through his Chickasaw interpreter that his people, Englishmen on the coast of the Great Sea, would pay them in fine hatchets, cooking pots, and wampum beads. This people highly prized European glass beads in long woven strands that helped one to remember complicated prayers, verbal history, and ceremonial procedures.

The red-haired Makac, who declared his undying hatred for all things Indian, left with the party taking the slaves to his countrymen on the Atlantic coast, vowing to make only one last journey into the country of southern savages. He would not, he said, come back even once again but for the contract he'd signed for a quota of heartland savages to work the sugarcane fields of the Caribbean Islands. One more trip to the country of the Arkansas would fulfill his quota. The last thing he did before leaving, after partaking of Iroquois hospitality and the calumet ceremony, was to sell Weeononka to a young brave who had not taken his eyes off her since the moment of her arrival. This warrior paid for Weeononka with a packet of medium-grade beaver pelts. He was shy; he wouldn't touch her. He beckoned her to follow him, her hands still bound behind her. She felt she could sleep for days but was suddenly alert to what might happen. This after all was homeland of the dreaded Iroquois, human monsters, who ate other tribes for sport. There was no telling how many of the old stories were true and how many were the product of vanquished Quapaw imaginations.

She was about to find out on this dusty late summer evening with the heart of the great tribe throbbing around her. Delicious smells wafted from a thousand firesides. The sky was fast running to indigo in various shades of mauve and purple. There was a whisper of coolness on the smoky air, a hint of Winter-maker's advance. The upcoming Hunting Moon was the month when the trees turned color.

This village near the great inland sea the whites would call Lake Superior was headquarters of one of the wealthiest and most powerful bands in the Iroquois League. Weeononka and her new owner walked through the smoke-laden air of autumn. Most of the inhabitants were home in their own lodges at this time of evening but without warning a strange person almost walked into Weeononka, startling her so much she cried out. This odd person beamed a smile at her and apologized in a strange musical language. She watched him walk away, bent and apparently engrossed in his own thoughts.

"Who?" she asked her new owner with her eyes.

"He's our blackrobe, Brother Martin. Nobody pays him any attention. I don't know why the mothers let him live here."

"A man in a dress?" she questioned, but the Iroquois seemed short-tempered on the subject and urged her on without answering. His mind was on this woman, not a crazy

priest. His staunch Iroquois heart swelled when he looked at
the southern woman from the tribe called "the downstream
people." She was no more beautiful than women of his own
people, but there was something about her that beguiled him.
Her eyes were so large and expressive, her body so supple
especially in pregnancy. He ached with wanting her but she
gave him only stony looks. He knew that for now he would
have to be patient. Grandmother would know how to bring her
around, make a good Iroquois of her. Surely she would grow to
appreciate him. Already he was holder of twenty scalp tassels,
which he was wearing now on his jacket with great pride. His
war chief had honored him twice with dog feasts, and it was
said that he'd be a war chief before too long even though he
had only ten and nine winters. He knew the Quapaw didn't
honor war as much as the Iroquois: no tribe did. But he was
confident that this desirable woman would come to regard him
as a suitable husband. She was more spirited than the usual
girls he'd seen from southern tribes. He was sure she'd like the
honored position of women among the Iroquois.

He had heard from the Chickasaw that she had been wife to
a great man. Now she would be wife to an even greater man.
These were the thoughts that filled the head of the proud
young warrior called Walking Many Mountains, son of the first
daughter of the reverend mother Cornsilk Weaver.

The women had already harvested the last of the corn,
which Weeononka later learned was planted on an earlier cycle
here. Rustling husks draped each longhouse. One could not
walk through a household without brushing against the
shimmering harvest hanging on poles so tightly packed that
the house itself seemed to be Mother Corn's body in the
earthly form of dusty golden kernels in crisp husk dresses. The
presence of the life force was so strong here Weeononka almost
fainted. The aroma of months of winter provender was a
sensual perfume that assaulted her nostrils with the smell of
meals yet uncooked but possible, of thousands of small cakes,
big soups, pots of *sagamite*, hard loaves of traveling-bread
boiled and cooled, sliced and run with honey on a cold night
by a warm fire many moons in the dark winter future.

Whatever terror this place held for her at least there would
be enough food. When she first went to live with the Osage
after her parents' death, there had been one hard winter she'd
never forget. That season had come unusually early to the
Osage village, killing the harvest before it could be brought in.

The proud Osage had starved, old persons and babies being the hardest hit. Weeononka could remember one horrible night of frenzied hunger in Crow Sister's household when she secretly tried to eat the shriveled sole of an old moccasin.

Her adopted tribe had been for the most part prosperous but she would never forget that winter of famine. Ever since, this harvest season was an especially happy time for her because its labors promised the winter store.

She might be a slave here, might be treated with expected abuse, might be forced to look all the time at the ground. But at least there would be enough to eat. As she entered the fireside of the warrior who had bought her, she was comforted by this thought, that she and the child would not starve. But she was ready for anything when the warrior's old grandmother seated on a plush buffalo robe crooked a leathery finger in her direction, and aimed one authoritative syllable at her grandson. He untied Weeononka's hands and took a seat to one side. He was extremely deferential to this old woman, Weeononka observed out of the corner of her eye as she approached the matriarch.

Cornsilk Weaver pointed to a spot on the robe where the "guest" should be seated. Immediately a young girl brought shell cups full of steaming sassafras tea to both the warrior and his new slave. Weeononka didn't speak a word of this language, but they shared universal hand signals with which Grandmother tendered the observation that the southern woman before her was pregnant.

Weeononka nodded. She made the sign for five moons. Grandmother nodded then fell into a deep observation that attempted to peel off Weeononka's *aneh*, or personality, layer by layer.

But Weeononka held her ground and held the crone's eye, resisting the idea that she might be a witch of some peculiarly nasty Iroquois breed. She reminded herself that this was just an old woman, not to be feared but, like any old person, to be respected. She couldn't know it then, but would later, that this wrinkled crone was a political force among her tribe. The Iroquois honored the mother above all else. Their social arrangements were entirely based on the mother's lineage. Even the sagacious senators who made up the Iroquois League held their positions on the pleasure of certain women like this one sitting in utter silence on the buffalo robe.

For a long time they sat like that, Weeononka in a discreet

waiting posture though she was aching to sleep, and the old woman watching her with steely intensity. Around them waited the large extended family, called a "fireside," of this particular longhouse. In all, this fireside included about twenty-five or thirty adults though there were some visitors present this evening. Even the little children were still as Grandmother perused this stranger her son had brought into their midst.

Weeononka lost all sense of time with the old woman's eye on her. She had no doubt that this silent interview could go on all night. The shadows deepened. Birds called in the forest. A dog barked.

It dragged on. The family around them began to stir, to go about its nightly business of cleaning up after eating, getting children ready for slumber. Down the length of both sides of the longhouse ran a wooden bench. Bundles were stored beneath it. The women were removing sleeping robes. The men were lounging back languidly puffing their pipes, watching the grandmother put the new woman through the test. The lodge was smoky, somewhat stuffy with the many smells of human habitations without windows. To stay awake, Weeononka reviewed all that had transpired to bring her to this place. When she finished this review, she went over the burial procedures celebrated at her husband's death. She was sorry his weapons had not been buried with him. How would he hunt game in the sun's country without his bow or headknocker? Maybe his spirit would become confused in the strange country of his burial, away from the souls of other Quapaw. Would he lie in his lonely grave forever, never to be reburied at the thirtieth moon with other Quapaw bones?

And what effect would Makac's terrible medicine ball in his head have on the dead man's journey with the sun? But her husband had been such an extraordinary man and his death song so honorable maybe his ancestors would help him. She recalled how she had dreaded being with him before she knew him. Now she was exceedingly sorry she had not had more time with him. Was this wisdom, she wondered, or only regret?

During all this mental exercise Weeononka was careful not to think her husband's name lest it call him even now from his path with the sun. She felt the new man's eyes on her; that look was unmistakable. Inwardly she groaned. She felt nothing for this man. When will I find a man going in my own direction? she wondered.

This one was young, shy for all his arrogance, and not at all unpleasant to look upon. She wondered why the Iroquois and the Osage had so many styles in common even though they lived far away from each other. Just like Game Dancer, this man wore his hair plucked except for the bristle of a scalplock running from his widow's peak to the back of his neck. It was even decorated with feathers and strands of painted hair the way Game Dancer adorned his scalplock. Maybe the Osage, like the Sioux and the Quapaw, had fought the formidable Iroquois, and being less warlike than that tribe, had adopted the style of the conqueror. No man wanted to look like a loser, she reflected, thinking of Game Dancer's pride. This man had that same pride.

But thinking of Game Dancer only made her want him, not this callow imitation. She wanted to go home to the mountains, find Game Dancer, and continue what she had begun with him. She wanted to raise their son with his father. On the slave trail she had a dream that she was carrying a son.

There hadn't been a sachem around with whom she could discuss that dream, and parts of it were hard to understand. In the dream the baby lay in a cradle made from the moon, but clouds swelled around the cradle. She desperately hoped that someone here among the Iroquois could help her interpret that disturbing vision.

The old woman's eyes blinked, her only movement for a long time.

Weeononka decided she would stay here at least until after the birth. She calculated that would be sometime early in Hunger Moon, the month the whites called February. A bad birthing moon but here among all this wonderful corn it could be good. There was something about the old woman's face that promised great wisdom. Around her withered neck hung thick ropes of wampum beads. The design afforded the old woman a memorizing device for a great deal of knowledge to judge by the size of the white and purple strands. This was the first Weeononka had seen of the imported beads. This was her area of expertise, the making and working of beads. But she was used to dyed sectioned porcupine quills. These were something else entirely. She craved to handle the wampum, to let her fingers define the texture of this new material, glass, which was unknown among her people, in fact unknown among most of the American tribes, whose fascination for it would cost them so much.

84 PAT WINTER

This was something beautiful from the white men.

The old woman fingered the wampum ropes at this moment. What prayer was she silently reciting as her dry skin fondled the slick glass for which so high a price must be paid to the Europeans? This was something to learn about. Like any craftsman Weeononka was beguiled by a new material for her art. She saw the beads in many designs, her own tribe's principal way of picturing past events. She was only vaguely aware of the Iroquois use of beads as memory aids.

Even with things to learn from these people, however, Weeononka knew she would someday take the opportunity to go home. Once they accepted her they would lose face if she tried to leave. They would kill her if they caught her trying to escape. She'd have to try anyway. But until spring, about Grass Moon, she would stay here, bide her time, grow in strength and wisdom. Her legs were going to sleep so she shifted slightly as she drifted into a trance. She emptied her mind of all thoughts, made herself into a scoured bowl into which anything could be poured.

Cornsilk Weaver was waiting for some sign. This woman was strange, strong-willed. Maybe she was too strong and would cause dissension among the other women of the fireside. But the Weaver knew her beloved grandson wanted this one; she liked to give him what he wanted, since he was her favorite. She saw the girl shift position and the tattoo on her thigh for the first time. A snake! This indeed was a sign—the word *Iroquois* meant "snake," and here was a woman with that powerful symbol on her leg. Obviously it was her manitou. To Cornsilk Weaver this could only mean her destiny had brought thi: woman here.

As soon as she reached that perfect place of trance, Weeononka knew without doubt that this grandmother was going to see her worth; she'd wait all night and all the nights of the next moon if she had to, to demonstrate her worthiness. That attitude would impress the reverend mother Cornsilk Weaver. Weeononka thought she heard an actual click as she and the grandmother found each other in that place of *wa kon,* of absolutely coincidental thought where each knew the other immediately.

The old woman began uncoiling her long rope of wampum from her neck. Without a word between them, Walking Many Mountains moved closer to her in an attitude of expectancy. This was evidently a special event because the gathering of family and friends around them leaned closer, quieted children, took last sips of tea. This group was settling down to listen.

Cornsilk Weaver began to speak in the measured tones of memorized poetry, a sweet rocking song that lasted a long time into the night. Children went to sleep while their elders heard the many stanzas of the creation myth they had heard so many times before. But to Weeononka this particular version of the story of the beginning was new, and the grandmother's sonorous voice was pleasant to the ear. As the woman spoke, the grandson translated what she said with extraordinary grace into handtalk. It took a long time to relate, but in brief this is what Cornsilk Weaver said:

"Before anything, before trees, rocks or men, Earth-holder, greatest of the ancient ones, lived on the sky floor. Beside his lodge grew his white tree of light, which he tended with loving care. There was peace among the ancient ones.

"Earth-holder loved his wife, Flowers in Bloom. But the evil shooting star, White-Tail Dragon, put suspicion in his mind concerning her fidelity. The enraged Earth-holder flew about, tearing up everything, including his tree of white light. The light flowers withered as he yanked the great plant out of heaven by its roots, thereby creating a great rift between upper and lower. He threw his sobbing wife into that hole and she fell down and down through the darkness. Ancient ones who had the souls of birds caught her on their backs and took her down slowly. Ancient ones who lived in the dark waters brought up mud from the bottom of things to give the woman a place to stand. Soon after she touched dry land, she gave birth to a daughter, who many seasons later mated with a man of the turtle people. She died giving birth to twin sons but lives on as the moon. Her sons were Teharonhiawagon and Tawiskaron. Their grandmother, the original mother who was thrown from heaven, took the boys in and raised them. The first, who was beautiful and kind, she hated because she had been told he was last born and so was responsible for the death of her daughter. The second, who was crippled and ugly, the grandmother favored. But his heart was evil, and later when his older brother began to create human beings and all the other creatures, the second brother created monsters.

"Thus good and evil came into the world at the same time and so it is today." She leaned back, obviously finished. "But," she continued, her fingers having moved down the thick bead strand as long as a man, "the balance between good and evil is up to each of us."

Here she paused. Walking Many Mountains relaxed, loosening up his shoulders and arms, which had not been still for the long history. But he quickly resumed his handsign translating when she spoke again.

"The ancient ones cradled the pregnant woman's fall from heaven, and the sea beings gave her earth to stand on." She swiveled stiffly as she asked her family, "Can we do any less than the ancient ones, I ask you?"

The people answered empathetically, no. The young warrior's handsigns weren't necessary. Weeononka and her child would be accepted here. At least for now, this was a place of sanctuary.

II

HENRI DE TONTI

10

In early 1678 while kings haggled over peace after a long mean war, a young Franco-Italian officer found himself marking time in a Spanish gravel quarry a league off Sicily's northern coast. He and the other fifty-six prisoners of war on this yellow bone of an island were left in the open with a minimal guard because nobody cared if they pickaxed each other or jumped the high ragged cliffs to deadly freedom. There was a single harsh law here: Each day the prisoners must make one pile of gravel as tall as El Comandante.

El Comandante strolled casually as he did every evening in his glinting tin vest and pointed helmet to inspect the day's work. The low sun lengthened his already long shadow. He was tall, more than a fathom, taller than the previous commandant. This new man had been here only a short time, but long enough for the prisoners to know how much sulphuric limestone must be broken to make a Comandante-high pile of acceptably uniform gravel. However, the weather made each day's production a game of chance. The pile was unstable. A gust of wind or just the contrariness of wounded stone could trigger small but significant avalanches.

So it was with suspenseful interest that everyone in camp observed El Comandante's sunset ritual. The aromas of pork-belly gruel and black bread laced the air. Heat waves still simmered from the pit where the prisoners leaned on their tool handles, waiting with growling stomachs to see if today's fickle pile would hold its peak. If it did, they'd be fed. If the pile was not high enough, they would not eat tonight and would have to finish two piles tomorrow.

Among the war-wounded who broke roughcut into finer gravel was this particular black-haired French officer drinking a trickle from a waterbag. He was bearded as were all the prisoners, naked to the waist and too swarthy to be pure Frenchman, his right arm missing halfway to the elbow. Next to him still holding the handles of a wheelbarrow was an older native Frenchman with grizzled hair and a painful sunburn except for a mariner's tan. "We go to sleep hungry again

89

tonight, *mon capitaine*," the old man groaned. Twice this week the pile had failed inspection.

Captain Henri de Tonti wiped his mouth with the back of his hand. "I haven't seen him cheat yet," he replied, offering his *aide de camp* a drink. The former commandant used to tease the prisoners.

"What does it matter?" Sabat said, taking a sip. "If starvation doesn't get us the heat will."

"We are not going to die here."

"Yes, sir," Sabat replied scowling, and though he rarely ventured into sarcasm, indicated with a nod the far sails out on the water. "We'll just wave in those fishermen and be on our way tonight to your New World."

Going to the New World was de Tonti's dream, one he shared with fellow prisoners to keep up their spirits as well as his own. At Sabat's suggestion he couldn't resist a glance at the shimmering western horizon where he dreamed destiny called him. Movement caught his eye: The waterboy who used to be a drummer in de Tonti's marine regiment was cresting the narrow path that descended to the island's only fresh water spring. Across his thin shoulders he hauled a wooden yoke slung with two sloshing buckets.

El Comandante terminated his inspection with a scowl, ominously shaking his head so that his long mustachios brushed his black doublet collar. It was true; the pile had shifted. Even now a trickle of gravel ate away the blunt pinnacle. One vast community groan swelled from the prisoners.

"He kicked it!" The dust-hoarse scream came from the waterboy shedding his yoke, plunging forward past de Tonti, who called his name and tried to stop him. But the lad was crazed strong with hunger and expected the former commandant's habit of cruelty. "I saw you kick it, you son of—"

El Comandante turned in his tracks as a thick explosion cracked the air. The boy dropped instantly to the dust with a terrible wound in his chest while the nearest guard reloaded his massive old-fashioned blunderbuss.

De Tonti bent to hear the boy whisper, "We *will* go to the New World, won't we, *mon capitaine*?" De Tonti had shared his dream with anyone who would listen.

"I promise you," he replied in hoarse despair as he watched life fade from the boy's eyes.

The guard gestured with an articulate muzzle at a burly

prisoner, a French sympathizer from Spanish Corsica, to help the one-armed captain pitch the boy's body into the sea. A few of the prisoners crossed themselves as El Comandante said in passable French, "Like yourselves, I do not wish to be here, but nonetheless, here I am. Every Saturday afternoon a royal barge arrives to take away a new quota of seven piles of gravel. My predecessor didn't take the quota seriously. That is why he's no longer with us. I take the quota very seriously, gentlemen, and so will you. This is a humiliating command for myself, a soldier, but while it is mine it will be obeyed by a gentleman. I do not kick the pile. Meditate upon my words as you rest for tomorrow's labor."

The prisoners turned in a muttering herd to the deep bowl of the quarry.

"*Con su permiso, Señor Comandante!*" de Tonti called firmly, freezing everyone, pretending he didn't see the guns swing toward him as he walked toward El Comandante. The captain was confident after hearing his speech that this man was no monster, just a soldier accomplishing his mission. He also recognized in the man's pronunciation the accent of the cold western Pyrenees.

"Because El Comandante is new to the Mediterranean," he continued in Spanish, "he may not know how one must adjust to the climate here."

He stopped a good dozen paces from El Comandante, whose whole face narrowed, eyes drawn closer to his arrow of a nose above the bow of lip hair.

"Now that it's getting hotter," de Tonti continued in French as one sensible man to another, "we must begin work earlier each day, take a longer midday break, and finish in the cooler evening hours."

"And the men will do as you say?"

"They will do as they must," de Tonti replied, glancing around at them. What he was actually proposing was an hour and a half more work each day but spread over more time. Most of the prisoners were Mediterranean veterans so they nodded vigorously in favor of the *siesta*.

"And this will guarantee my quota?"

"*Señor*, with a schedule that takes the heat into account you can easily have eight loads each week." The prisoners agreed.

El Comandante felt pinned by the crippled Frenchman's commanding golden eyes as well as his logic. He knew he must make a show of power lest the prisoners and even his own

troops consider him a weakling, especially if he allowed
himself to be publicly bested by a one-armed inmate. "And
who will be their waterboy?" The garrison used an ancient
rain-fed cistern on the isle's highest point but the prisoners
were required to haul their own water from the precipitous
spring. The water run wasn't as physically difficult as breaking
rocks by main force, but it was a task reserved for the lowest
ranking among the prisoners because of the closeness of that
ledge to eternity. It would be even more dangerous in the
gloaming of twilight.

"I will," de Tonti said in a clear voice all the men could hear.
The prisoners sent up an affirmative cheer as the guards
glanced at their superior. El Comandante felt this impudent
Frenchman had won some face at his own expense, but he was
tempted by that bonus pile of gravel. He hesitated, then
shrugged his permission.

De Tonti, under every eye in the compound, turned toward
the water buckets, which lay where the waterboy had dropped
them. Sabat almost cried out to see his captain so abased
struggling under the yoke. The Corsican who had helped him
with the dead boy shucked his own shirt and stuffed it between
the yoke and the captain's shoulders. De Tonti nodded his
thanks and called back, "We'll have the pile by sunset!" as he
trotted gracefully down the incline.

They worked until the pile was high enough by the señor's
own grudging witness then threw down their tools again and
pressed close to the mess buckets with almost festive camara-
derie. But Sabat hung toward the end of the lines scanning the
cliffreach for his commander. Finally when everyone had
eaten, de Tonti returned from a last water run. Most of the
men were sunk into exhausted slumber but several came to
him with their cups and respectful thanks. He used the dregs
of a bucket to wash dust from his face and beard then gratefully
took the wooden bowl of gruel Sabat had saved for him.

Sabat silently watched him wolf down the vile meal,
thinking how highly he regarded this man he'd long served.
But Sabat's loyalty had turned to undaunted love in their last
battle at Messina when de Tonti's right hand was lost as he
redeployed a sizzling Spanish grenade that would have killed
Sabat and several other men including the dead drummer boy.
He was glad de Tonti couldn't remember that awful night when
the old servant hacked off his own long seabraid to use as a
tourniquet to keep de Tonti from bleeding to death. While de

Tonti madly intermixed a long conversation with Jesus Christ with Neapolitan lovesongs, Sabat had cauterized his arm in the smoldering coals of incinerated flour sacks in the ruins of a bakery—hit in several direct cannon volleys before the Frenchman anchored in the harbor found its Spanish powder magazine target half a block away. De Tonti had lost every memory of it all. Sabat accepted his own keen recall as punishment for costing the captain so much.

Now, six months since that battle, these thoughts flitted through the old servant's mind as he watched de Tonti balance the bowl with the arm's scarred stump. He was learning to use what was left with considerable skill, unaffected by self-consciousness or embarrassment—no modesty was possible in this place where few days passed without someone's agonized death. It brought a lump to Sabat's throat to see how bravely his captain took the mutilation, how he didn't let it dim his hope.

It made Sabat ashamed of his own bitter hopelessness. He was thinking he'd gladly die for this man, follow him into hell itself if necessary.

Last light was fading from the west. De Tonti chanced to glance up, and caught the dour look of bitter recall on his servant's features. With a wink he forced Sabat to grin.

Both were silent in the suddenly purple night until de Tonti licked the bowl clean. Hunger still gnawed at his insides, and his shoulders were aching as he tried to find a position of relative comfort upwind of the jumbled, stinking, snoring bodies in the pit. Overhead the hard stars seemed to be signals from ships in the hot black ocean of night.

"To see you like that—" Sabat started to agonize, but his captain interrupted him gently to say there had been a purpose in volunteering for water duty. "I found us a boat down there," he whispered into Sabat's fuzzy ear. He had spied it when he threw the boy's body into the sea. It was similar to the small coral-fishermen they'd seen on the open water, evidently wrecked during some forgotten storm and never salvaged from this forbidden shore, which had been a prison since Viking days. The boat had no mast and only a splintered fragment of its rudder. But despite one large puncture in the keel above the waterline he was sure the sleek little vessel was seaworthy. The eyes painted on the keel for luck had seemed to brighten with anticipation of escaping its own prison on the rocks; however, this inspiration de Tonti did not tell his servant but kept to himself.

There were no guards out here at night. The other prisoners were too deeply asleep from bone-crushing fatigue to wonder about two of their fellows who crept toward the shallow latrine to one side of the quarry.

They heard a sound and froze, but continued on without challenge when the sound lengthened into a double moan of grunting pleasure.

De Tonti grabbed two shovels when they passed the current dig, handed one to Sabat, and held the other as he started down the fragile ledge. Slowly and carefully he guided his night-blind servant down along the rough slope he had earlier memorized.

They found the hull right side up in a spray-dashed crevice, and just as they began to launch it, a deep voice with a Spanish accent crystallized the beat of their hearts. "Let me go with you—"

At first de Tonti thought it was El Comandante gaming with them but then he saw the shadow detach itself from the deeper blackness. It was the Corsican who had padded the yoke for de Tonti. "I am André De Arcos and I am very strong."

The two Frenchmen almost collapsed in relief while De Arcos explained that he too had spotted the boat down here. With his great strength they easily launched their little shell. They caught the tide away from the craggy shore and before long were bobbing beyond the swell. Once they nearly broke back against the rocks but De Arco and Sabat at the shovel oars saved them. In the stern de Tonti fought with the broken rudder. Soon they caught the current, which swept northwest around the island. By the time a sickle moon rose behind them they had made headway toward the hulking tip of Sardinia.

They settled into a rowing pace, and in the manner of strangers cast suddenly and dangerously together, talked about their lives. After a while Sabat slumped snoring over his oar, and de Tonti and De Arcos tangented off into philosophy. Very soon, de Tonti knew that there was more to the man than what De Arcos presented himself to be—a minor bondservant to the Duke De Arcos who'd been conscripted under fire to defend a dockside countinghouse. Because De Arcos had refused to shoot the French soldiers jumping from their galleys to the docks, he was thrown into prison with them. De Tonti, who knew what it was like to be treated as a foreigner, didn't blame this young Jew for changing his name to survive a hostile regime. And that he was wise enough and daring enough to select the name of the ruling Spanish duke in the region lured de Tonti into a long leisurely conversation counterpointed by the benevolent rocking water.

"My father was a butcher," De Arcos was saying after the moon had set. He flexed his huge arms and laughed. "A pious man, and a scrupulous butcher. I learned much from him."

"Not piety, I suspect," de Tonti remarked.

"For nineteen years of my life," De Arcos rambled, "I lived papa's life, saying the prayers, obeying the tradition. The morning papa died, I did not say the prayer. The sky did not fall; nothing was changed. I never said the prayers again."

De Tonti shrugged knowingly. So far neither man had even hinted at Judaism, a virtual crime in several kingdoms, especially Spain, and only grudgingly tolerated in France. De Tonti related his own private apostasy, more dangerous in France than being a Jew, as dawn stained the eastern quadrant.

Finally, all discourse exhausted, De Arcos set aside the oar, giving in to sleep. De Tonti fell into a numb zone somewhere between trance and true slumber, slumped with the others in dumb fatigue in the bilge water, so that later, none of the three men heard the Spanish voice hailing them from an approaching galley, nor felt in the new morning light the lowering of its inevitable shadow like a gull dropping on a jellyfish. Swiftly following its shadow, the galley slid alongside their little craft. The sound of wooden oars scraping their hull brought de Tonti to eye-bursting attention. The next thing he knew he was looking up the flared hexagonal barrel of a Spanish blunderbuss while De Arcos and Sabat came awake beside him. The three expected death to come in a blinding explosion as they involuntarily flinched back from the awful bore.

But that was not meant to be. One of El Comandante's hardest men brusquely ordered them to climb aboard, and although they were treated like so much raw meat, flung into the hold to await their fates, they were not physically harmed or even so much as chained to the oars with the galley slaves. The guards were strangely unabusive an hour later as they climbed back into scorching daylight to the escort of muskets. The smell of sulphur was strong after the freshness of the sea. Even de Tonti's optimism withered at the sight of that island where, scarcely an hour after dawn, heat waves already shimmered above the sere yellow pit.

But they did not return to the quarry. Without explanation they were put into a cool, clean garrison cell where they waited only a short time before El Comandante himself visited with a pen and paper he shoved at de Tonti. "Make your mark."

The captain awkwardly scrawled his name, writing left-handed for the first time and certain he had just illegibly signed his own death warrant. He would have read the official-looking words but the officer withdrew the paper to sprinkle it with sand as de Tonti looked up with the question burning in his gold eyes. "When is it to be, then?" he asked in Spanish, knowing full well that the traditional hour was sunrise.

"You mean when are we going to shoot you?"

There flashed in de Tonti's mind a recollection that a common Spanish method was the surprise garrote. Instinctively he glanced over his shoulder.

The officer laughed almost politely. "We only went after your sorry hide to trade for someone worth the trouble."

"A hostage exchange?" de Tonti said, with hope billowing in him like the west wind in the sails of the ship that would surely take him to the New World.

"You must be worth something—that fairy king of yours traded us a governor's son."

11

About the exchange de Tonti learned very little. Three weeks later, from the rail of a French galley, he and Sabat watched the island sink into the south while Europe grew larger to the hazy north.

On the garrison wall at Marseilles he did not find his name among the dead, missing, or court-martialed. In the press of the mustering out, his command was nonexistent, no orders arrived through usual channels, and it appeared that he was neither dead nor alive to his commanders but was suspended in bureaucratic limbo where armies lose soldiers more often than in battle.

Ministry of Marine orders finally found him, through civilian clerks, a formal and unconventional billeting: unspecified temporary duty at the garrison in Paris. Attached to the orders was a startling wax-sealed envelope. Inside was what must have been an exhaustive list of coffeehouses scattered throughout sprawling Paris. Imbibing the harsh New World concoction had at first been scandalous. Preachers had ranted against it and several coffee sellers had been imprisoned. When it took the king's fancy, however, it became the rage of the city. To visit every one of the cafés would take the better part of a day.

Beneath the list an aggressive hand commanded him to "Find La Salle at . . ." He knew the exploits of the already legendary Canadian who had gone farther into the great western wilderness of New France than any white man. La Salle's name pulsed through the Court, famous then infamous as his adventures lost favor among the Jesuits who had the king's ear. Such gossip trickled down through military echelons, rousing old men to reminisce about adventures and young men to seek new ones.

A secretary's initials ended the list but the command was signed by a nobleman known to be a direct line to and from the king. De Tonti and Sabat stared at it in the press of soldiers, each straining to see the posting wall where their urgent questions would be answered: Will I go home? Will I be part of the mop-up? Am I alive or dead?

The nobleman's name put a chill of pleasure into the captain. It meant he was no longer consigned to oblivion. Sabat noticed the effect on his master's face, and would have asked, but de Tonti hustled them immediately into a crowded coach express to Paris. He had only one blurred memory of the rattling journey. People, even the few women he'd seen on the streets, seemed to be wearing drabber clothing than when he had left home.

De Tonti spent his first day back in the capital looking for the man who could help him fulfill his dream.

When de Tonti had begun his search that morning, the sun had been shining. Now in late evening it was raining hard enough to wash the filth from the center gutter of the street where he found the last coffeehouse on his list.

Under a great floppy-brimmed felt hat he had retrieved from his garrison locker, he drew the layers of his old-fashioned Roquelare cape around him and hurried down the sloping alley. He had the cobbles all to himself. There were none of the usual sedan-chair taxis on the street. It was so bad

a night even the beggars stayed home. He jumped the flooded
gutter with a mariner's grace and took six steps down to the
basement door of *Le Café Turc*.

He was about to push through the doorway when a lean left
arm patterned with distended veins reached out of the inky
shadows to block his way. De Tonti was instantly galvanized,
hand on sword hilt as a hooded male voice heavy with more
than spiritual menace, whispered, "End this foolish search for
the sake of your immortal soul."

De Tonti stepped backward, for the first time since his
release drawing the short blade for serious purposes.

The body attached to the threatening arm moved in the
darkness. De Tonti knew another blade was now positioned
but the adversary hesitated, as if more words might be
enough: "Stay away from La Salle—"

De Tonti lunged in fury. He'd been imprisoned too long to
tolerate a lien on his free actions. The enemy whirled—de
Tonti felt the swirl of the other's cloak but it was too dark to
see.

He leaped up the steps and onto the glistening street, where
there was just enough glow from the café transom to see the
shadow swordsman emerge along the same path. They harried
each other up the alley's slope for a few minutes, long enough
for de Tonti to test his mettle. Though the adversary fought
with the conventional long and short blade in right and left
hand, he was not in de Tonti's league. Probably used to
sneaking up on unsuspecting victims at night, de Tonti decided
in contempt. In less than a minute he had divested the cowled
swordsman of his short sticker, and drawn first blood in the
process. "Tell me who sent you—" he commanded, hardly out
of breath, his cutlass caressing the fellow's clavicle. All to be
seen of the loser's features were round eyes. From the cowl
came a mumbled prayer in Latin. The bloodied hand made a
feeble cross. De Tonti caught a glimpse of blue tattoo on the
wrist, then in a desperate feint the beaten foe tried to push his
way past on de Tonti's right. Perhaps he'd been aware the
captain wasn't using his right hand, or perhaps that way offered
the deepest shadows in which to melt.

They scuffled. De Tonti felt a heel glance off his thigh; the
misplaced attempt to cold-cock brought the caped figure to his
knees. The sword clattered to the cobbles and rolled in a
skewed arc across the slope. Now, where any other warrior
would offer his chest and hope for mercy, this one made a

clumsy but powerful dash against de Tonti's right side. There was nothing to do but dispatch him.

He heard the parting of the flesh, the whoosh of air from a pierced lung, the groan of awareness that the body's precincts had been invaded.

Again, as every time, de Tonti felt the old sad empathy steal over his bones. He loved the fight but hated the kill.

The figure slumped against the weapon that impaled him. De Tonti eased the dead weight down, hearing the last sigh escape. The cowl fell back to reveal a face that told of nothing but hard living, twisted thoughts, and inclement weather. De Tonti looked again at the tattooed hand. A small cross with radiations around it bisected the back of the wrist.

The captain stood after wiping the blade on the dead man's coarse clothing. He replaced it and looked around to see if the duel had been witnessed. The last thing he wished to encounter was civil authority at this awkward point in his life.

The alley was silent and rain-sprinkled. A burst of male voices came from the café. De Tonti stepped away from the corpse, still expecting to confront a witness, perhaps one of the fellow's friends waiting to back him up.

He took one last glance over his shoulder as he returned to the café door then pushed through into a single low-ceilinged room that appeared to stretch into smoky infinity. The place was reminiscent of a huge tent with richly patterned rugs on the walls, full of tobacco fumes and the dull gleam of fire and candlelight off brass.

De Tonti gave the room a soldier's hard reconnaissance before proceeding. His entry brought in a swirl of fresh air that went unnoticed by a knot of well-dressed men tied up by intense conversation near a hearth. An old man in a battered fez scurried up to him to take his order but de Tonti shook his head. The waiter, who was definitely not Turkish, left him alone.

The captain used his feathered hat to brush raindrops from his cape and leather baldric that held a cutlass and a graceful Brescian pistol. He slapped the fine old hat against his thigh then replaced it on his black hair tied unfashionably back in a seaman's braid.

In stylish contrast the king's guard officers and minor courtiers by the fire shook their elaborate wiglocks in a growing argument. One voice dominated the others. A fat pillar hid the speaker but de Tonti had a sudden intuition that this dominant voice belonged to the man he'd been looking for all day.

"Indubitably, gentlemen," the voice continued, "I tell you that in a situation where a man might have the chance to choose between king or church, it would be neither for that man."

This shocked the eight other men around the speaker.

"But how," said one of the dandies, whose mustache—no doubt in imitation of the king's—was the merest of lines on his contemptuously curled lip. "How can you advocate this . . . this . . ." He struggled to find the word to communicate his ire. "This cupidinous individualism when you yourself plan to ask for the king's patronage to find this legendary river of yours."

De Tonti positioned himself behind the pillar, where he was in shadow but where he could watch the first man. The man sighed heavily; his long white clay pipe had gone out and he looked as though that worried him more than the question. Finally he deigned to answer as he rose from the chair to tong a coal from the fire, "I simply say that I cannot do honor to His Majesty's service unless I serve myself first."

Clearly the eight gentlemen were too shocked to respond. Jourdain glanced at one of his fellows as if to say, See, what did I tell you? The fellow spat into the fire.

"I say the first master of a man must be himself," continued the orator, whom de Tonti by now was certain to be none other than the visionary Canadian explorer, René Robert Cavelier, Sieur de La Salle. He held the coal to his pipe, sucked heavily until he had his flame, then tossed the brand back into the fireplace.

The one who had spat sniffed into a lace handkerchief, stood with elaborate design, and walked away as if too scandalized to remain in such traitorous company. When he passed de Tonti's pillar, he left a wake of heavy perfume that turned the captain's empty stomach. He fought down his gorge: he had not eaten since this morning's early garrison mess. He'd spent all his time tracking down La Salle, who was now puffing on his pipe, ignoring the one who threaded his brocade way among the empty tables and out the door past de Tonti, who tensed, waiting for a cry of alarm when the departed officer stumbled over the dead man in the gutter. But none came. He relaxed somewhat, feeling damp air from beyond the door as it closed. This place was stuffy. What he mainly wanted to do was leave it, find a tavern where men did not perfume themselves, sit down to a bottle of good Orleans wine, and enjoy his first night home in eight long years.

He leaned against the pillar and listened with the remaining gentlemen as La Salle continued.

"I advocate nothing more than the natural order of humankind," he explained with an air of superiority de Tonti suspected could raise the hackles of a mummified saint.

La Salle was an imperious, large-boned man in his late thirties gone a little soft around the middle but true to his Norman stock in stature. He was, however, pale. De Tonti somehow expected a sun-blackened ruffian. Unlike the other gentlemen, the Canadian was not wearing a wig. The hairline of the aristocratically high brow was clearly visible. The notorious adventurer didn't sport any hint of a mustache as if by his personal appearance he anticipated gentlemen's fashion to come. Louis XIV's own lip hair was said to be scantier after each visit by the royal barber.

De Tonti himself preferred to keep the full though neatly trimmed mustache and beard he'd grown in prison though he was aware that his choice relegated him to the ranks of the hopelessly unfashionable. The truth was de Tonti was beyond such amenities. He had forged a tough pride about the marks his experience had placed on his appearance, a pride that helped him survive with sanity. How, he wondered, could a man who'd been through what he had care for fashion? There had been a time during his cadet days when silk socks and brass buttons seemed important. He was lifetimes away from such concerns. In his mind he heard his mother's voice admonishing him for letting adversity lower the standards of the gentleman she had raised him to be.

". . . and I have a perfect argument for my case," La Salle was saying.

De Tonti shook off reverie. It bothered him that his mind sometimes wandered. He figured it was a symptom of imprisonment.

"Why are Frenchmen going to the New World?" La Salle asked, obviously wanting an audience, not an answer. He puffed his pipe with studied indifference and strolled among the seated men. "For a king's glory? Well, that may be His Majesty's motive in sending us but he's not going personally and his glory means little to ordinary men. You might say we go to the New World to save heathen souls. It's true a few clerics are throwing themselves against the savage soul. A few Jesuits." None could miss the tone in his voice when he pronounced that word. "But that's not the reason we nonclerics go into the wilderness." It was well known La Salle had been educated by the monks of Loyola but had left their order because he wouldn't submit to their rules on self-abasement.

"For profit, you might say." La Salle continued to answer his own rhetorical question. He set down his pipe. "Of course that's the only true reason. But what motivates that profit? What are Frenchmen buying here that we bring from the New World?"

La Salle was pacing in de Tonti's direction without appearing to have a destination. "What pushes otherwise sensible men to leave the most civilized place on earth and tramp off to expose themselves to a hostile jungle where unnamed animals, savage cannibals, and malign diseases attack them? What could possibly be valuable enough to lure us? Gold? Precious jewels? Spices?" He turned suddenly back to face his primary audience and answered himself emphatically, "No!" He glanced unexpectedly with hazel eyes back into the shadows where de Tonti had placed himself. Behind what he had supposed to be the dark security of the pillar de Tonti was aware that La Salle was observing him.

"I'll tell you what motivates us—it's the ordinary Frenchman's desire to own a fine, feathered beaver fur hat. A fine hat something like this one—"

It happened very fast. Before de Tonti could react, La Salle snatched the black beaver with natural plume off the captain's head. De Tonti detected no malice in the Canadian's action. He'd already turned away to continue his lecture, but de Tonti felt singled out. He'd considered himself the hunter and La Salle the hunted. He chided himself that he let himself be taken off guard.

For La Salle's part he'd been informed from high places that a young soldier would seek him out. He'd seen de Tonti standing in the shadows. Now the explorer had to find out if the slightly bedraggled owner of this hat was that soldier.

"And a fine hat this is," he was saying as he examined the band with the diligence of the stingiest ragpicker. "I myself may have collected the very fur that went into this impressive piece of headgear."

Jourdain was about to speak but La Salle, who seemed to be taking fire from an inner vision, stopped him. "A little of the peculiar history of the beaver fur hat. Any of you, even Monsieur Jourdain, would be proud to own a splendid hat like this, but I wonder. Would you be so anxious to place this thing on your noble heads if you knew what it took to make it?" Jourdain bit his lip in fury at being hushed like a naughty schoolboy.

The Canadian twirled the hat on his finger. "The fur of the beaver is the best in the world for making felt. The Indians wear their robes with the fur next to their bodies." He waved the hat at Jourdain. "It is that fur, rubbed free of the coarse outer hairs by those greasy, filthy savage bodies which makes quality felt." He paused, letting this sink in. Jourdain pulled back as though the hat were excrement. "There's no better way yet discovered by civilized men to get felt fur. Traders buy pelts the Indians have worn—the longer, the better. Of course the savages think they're putting one over on us ignorant white men by unloading old worn robes for marvelous glass beads and iron cooking pots."

De Tonti saw that La Salle liked throwing his insults at this pompous gathering. With a final twirl La Salle tossed the hat back to its owner. To catch it de Tonti was forced to step into the light and the direct scrutiny of the man he'd come to scrutinize. He knew immediately he'd been maneuvered to do so by the Canadian.

A couple of members of the audience were past disgust. The officer in the blue and silver uniform of the king's own guard had taken off his own hat and was looking at it as if he might vomit.

"For such vanity do we go to the New World," La Salle concluded like a lawyer summing up his case. "If that isn't pandering to"—and here he imitated perfectly Jourdain's rather high pitched voice—"cupidinous individualism, then pray, gentlemen, tell me what is."

This last comment was directed at Jourdain, who attempted to answer only to be cut off a second time. "For their own selfish reasons do men accomplish glorious deeds. I only advocate that we admit it, be proud of it, and pretend nothing more noble."

"Outrageous!" sputtered Jourdain. He had his hand on his saber hilt. "For what's to keep individual men from running amok in your savage country?"

"Monsieur de La Salle," sneered the guard officer before La Salle could reply, "your philosophy is weak in the knees."

"And I suggest, monsieur," La Salle responded with a politeness that would have etched glass, "that you are weak in the head." The guard bristled.

Jourdain stood. "I have heard quite enough." He sniffed deprecatingly. "I should have expected nothing better from you, a man who left the holy teachings for his own greedy pursuits."

"If my pursuits were merely greedy, I would have stayed on my Canadian estate which nets me twenty thousand *livres* a year."

"I suppose," interjected the guard, "that China will be your reward."

This heightened the color in La Salle's face: *La Chine* was the sarcastic name his detractors called his Montreal estate. He used his stare like a thrown grenade; he let it have its impact before replying. "There is a mighty river," he began with oily civility and deadly calm, "that flows from the northern wastes in the country of the Sioux. We don't know where it empties, this river the Indians call the Mech-a-si-pi. But there is a small chance that it flows into the Gulf of California, part of New Spain, you may remember. In such a case, then, my expedition to find the river's mouth would indeed lead to the discovery of a southwest passage to China."

"This is the fantasy you bring before the king?" Jourdain asked incredulously.

The guard officer snorted a chuckle. La Salle's face turned ugly. Everyone bolted to his feet.

De Tonti's neck hair was standing for the second time tonight. The flintlock pistol in his baldric was not his favorite weapon and was too crass a device to be part of the traditional gentleman's attire. He was the only man in the room so armed.

"Oh, no, no—" interjected another voice, a new one in the charged atmosphere. It was the café owner who had approached de Tonti earlier, pale beneath his ratty fez. He insinuated himself between the principals. "Not in my establishment, no trouble, no dueling, please, Monsieurs."

The adversaries ignored him.

The guard unsheathed his saber. The old man cringed back, making the sign of the cross on his stained linen shirt.

The Canadian stepped back and drew his own weapon. The sounds of six others joined the metallic chorus. La Salle was looking around for his defense alternatives when still another voice commanded attention.

"It's not gentlemanly to line up seven against one," de Tonti said as he leveled his lethal little cannon directly at the officer's face. The implication behind the authoritative click as the pistol mechanism rattled its tumbler to halfcock was not lost on its target. All de Tonti had to do was slightly draw back the hammer from safety to fullcock and the beautiful silver filigree piece would cease being an object of Italian artwork and fulfill its primary function. The hammer would slice down against the frizzen, igniting powder with a spark from the flint. This close, the .50-caliber lead ball could not miss.

De Tonti's hand was steady. There was a frozen moment when anything might happen. The guard officer snorted again and shrugged, but very carefully. "I don't need to teach you a lesson, schoolmaster," he said, disdainfully referring to La Salle's former profession among the Jesuits. As he spoke he lowered his saber back into its scabbard. "The king himself will put you in your place with your harebrained scheme."

"Well said," cracked Jourdain, obviously relieved that he could replace his own weapon. It was an antique rapier, which de Tonti suspected was worn for fashion rather than for fighting. Only then did de Tonti lower the pistol, but he held it at the ready as the smell of hostilities evaporated with the courtiers' rapid departure.

Then he put the gun away. He and La Salle were left standing there, eyeing each other. But La Salle still held his drawn sword as he regarded this stranger who'd spoken up for him. He had no doubt who this was, but his purpose was now to test him. Smiling without warmth, he raised the tip of his sword to the center point of the young man's chest. "Why would a stranger take my part in an argument that was not his?"

"Please, monsieur," stammered the café owner. La Salle took a step sideways to jostle him out of the way, keeping the saber point just brushing the dark green serge of de Tonti's doublet. His hand was as steady as de Tonti's had been out in the alley.

The younger man moved fast. He leaped backward into the typical crouch toward the pillar, his own sword drawn. It might have seemed La Salle had the advantage since de Tonti was using the cutlass, a shorter version of the saber developed for naval display. But where La Salle had been trained for sport, de Tonti's experience was hand-to-hand combat. La Salle hit with the slender blade but the captain was quicker.

The Canadian's saber struck plaster with a spark.

"Monsieurs, please," the café owner cried from behind an overturned table, a spot he abandoned with de Tonti's next move. The captain spun around the pillar, parrying each thrust La Salle made. His next pass overturned another table, which rolled against La Salle, causing him to misthrust a move that would have pierced his opponent's heart.

De Tonti leaped upon another table. La Salle was close on his heels, his blade moving like lightning in the firelight.

De Tonti was clearly the superior swordsman though it was obvious he protected his right. The Canadian did not use a left-hand weapon as custom permitted.

De Tonti detected this man was merely fencing with him. That was infuriating so he decided to teach this arrogant Canadian a lesson. His cutlass slashed La Salle's right sleeve without drawing blood, but it was obvious it might have been to the bone had the young man wished. La Salle decided it was time to end the fight. "I'm suspicious of friendly strangers," he called as de Tonti moved nimbly along the wall, which would have cornered a lesser swordsman. "Who are you?" La Salle demanded.

Another futile thrust missed de Tonti but slashed a rug on the wall. Out of sight the café owner wailed while La Salle worried de Tonti around the perimeter of the hall, sending furniture and metalware in all directions.

"Answer me, damn you!"

De Tonti's eyes glinted when he moved into an opening a botched riposte left in the Canadian's defense. The younger man uttered a growl that put genuine fear into La Salle's eyes. Now they fought in earnest, each man pushed to his extreme as their battle dance demolished the café. De Tonti relentlessly moved in for the kill. With a clean twist he disarmed the older man, who fell gasping to one knee.

Now it was de Tonti's turn to make his point on La Salle's chest.

The fire dampened in the winner's eyes. He moved the blade higher, brushing its tip along the other's lip where a mustache might have been had La Salle been more fashion-conscious. La Salle watched the metal with piercing intensity. Maybe he had erred and this was not the petitioner he expected. The implication forced him to gulp a dry swallow.

Finally, with inordinate softness, de Tonti remarked, "You are a mightily suspicious man, Monsieur de La Salle."

"I have mighty enemies." Now that he saw his life was not in real danger, some of his former arrogance was replacing the fear in his eyes.

De Tonti stood back and snapped the blade toward the scabbard. But he missed, the only awkward act La Salle had seen him make. Instead of helping it with his right hand as anyone would have done, he tried again to place the cutlass home by controlling it at the hilt with his left. The scabbard, in fact his entire right side, was hidden in the multiple folds of his cape. Finally he pressed the scabbard against a table and maneuvered the blade back into its slot.

La Salle watched every move. As he stood, the faintest smile touched his lips, not with mirth, but as though what he saw confirmed a suspicion. He'd been told that despite his qualifications the soldier who would approach him might not be acceptable.

"I fear you still suspect me," de Tonti said as he found La Salle's weapon and offered it pommel first to its owner. Still watching him, La Salle accepted the saber back.

"As I said, I have enemies."

"But, Monsieur, Henri de Tonti is not one of them." He thought as he said this, that perhaps he should tell La Salle about the man he'd killed this evening. Surely he had been La Salle's enemy.

La Salle made a crisp little salute that managed to say much, acknowledging the name. He offered his hand to shake. There was a brief awkward moment while de Tonti stared at the proferred hand. La Salle gauged his hesitation and immediately offered his left, which de Tonti shook with uncommon strength.

De Tonti's name was famous in France. It wasn't too large a conjecture to connect this accomplished swordsman with the man who had made the name so famous at a terrible price a generation ago. This would be his son, La Salle concluded.

"Well, Monsieur de Tonti, I believe I owe you a bottle of wine." He turned from the café owner as though he were a toad and drew on a pair of pigskin gloves. "I know a private place to drink to your good health."

His lighthearted mood was contagious. De Tonti felt accomplishment, and was glad of the lift it gave him. Despite the bold front for his servant, Sabat, and for others, ever since his capture de Tonti had been consumed by hopelessness. Even freedom hadn't dissipated the gray despair.

Walking beside this remarkable man, who lived up to his

reputation in every way, de Tonti felt that persistent *tristesse*
vanish. In its place he felt returning to him something he'd
grown up with but feared he'd lost with his hand, something
that told him he was destined by fate to help change the world.

12

De Tonti considered it ironic that La Salle was living on the
Rue de la Truanderie. So many people at Court considered the
arrogant Canadian a ne'er-do-well anyway that his address on
the Street of Vagrants seemed an apt joke.

But de Tonti kept these thoughts to himself as La Salle's
man, L'Esperance, served them a simple but adequate supper
in the L-shaped suite on the second floor of the ancient hotel.
The room was a delight, a crowded museum of New World
artifacts—primitive weapons of stone and bone, smoking pipes
of red stone emblazoned with wild feathers, skin-taut drums,
quill-beaded shirts, beautiful red clay bowls, and a gigantic
woolly hide of an animal La Salle said was like domestic cattle
but roamed wild in tremendous herds across the prairies on
the western side of the Mech-a-si-pi. The explorer also had a
bundle of what he called above-average beaver pelts.

"That business about the savages rubbing off the coarse
outer hair—that was surely a story to widen those gentlemen's
eyes," de Tonti said.

La Salle had paused during a soliloquy on his favorite
subject, the course of that great river. They had talked until
traces of dawn appeared. De Tonti was beyond fatigue and into
his second wind. "So tell me, did you make up that part about
the greasy savage bodies?"

"Not hardly," his host replied languidly. The hour and a pale
yellow wine he sipped as they talked had mellowed him. "I did
dramatize a mite. . . ."

"What part was drama?" de Tonti asked as he helped himself
to the last of a third bottle of the brilliant vintage.

La Salle tapped a small bell that signaled his manservant to
bring more wine. "Well, the so-called savages of America are
often cleaner than we Europeans who imagine ourselves to be
their betters. They are always bathing, either in the rivers and
streams or in steam huts. They do like to rub their bodies with

bear grease. Especially the women. They oil their hair and for some reason I never figured out, they smear red paint in the part of their hair. It's hideous—" he said with a little shudder of disgust, "—but all in all, they are human beings just as we are. Men who don't speak Latin, I dare say. But men nonetheless. All that is superior about us is our mechanical arts— metallurgy. Worked metal seems like magic to them. They call metal objects 'big medicine.'"

The servant entered from the adjoining room with an uncorked bottle on a tray. He set it down before his master, then handed over a small folded note with unbroken purple sealing wax on the flap. "This just arrived by courier, sir."

"They are highly civilized in many ways," La Salle continued as he took the note. "They do practice excessive barbarisms. . . ." A shadow crossed his face as if he were recalling unmentionable savage acts he'd witnessed half a world away.

De Tonti hoped he would elaborate on the details but La Salle directed his attention now to the note. Whatever it said, the note left him unmoved, and he nodded for the servant to leave.

"I personally don't call the Americans savages. In many respects they're more noble than European kings." In some quarters his statement would have been considered treason. La Salle distractedly stared at the note.

"What do you call them?" de Tonti asked.

"Indians."

"One thinks of the Hindus."

"Old Christopher Columbus thought he'd found India and the name stuck." La Salle peeled off the wax and popped it into his mouth. While he continued talking, he chewed on it as his hands idly folded the note again and again on itself until it was no bigger than the original blot of wax.

"The word *Indians* is a misnomer. So much is. Like we Europeans, the Americans are many nations: the Iroquois, the Sioux, the Illinois, the Arkansas. God knows how many different tribes—all fighting and hating one another just like properly civilized people should." He watched de Tonti to see the effect of his demonstrated worldliness on the younger man as he chuckled cynically. He saw but misjudged de Tonti's questioning look.

"Cleans the teeth," he explained.

But it was the folded note, not the wax, that interested de

Tonti. He knew that only the Crown used purple sealing wax.
Yet, La Salle was so casual. In fact de Tonti was brimful of
questions to ask his host. But La Salle's curiosity outranked his
own. La Salle had opened their long, rambling conversation
with inquiries about the young man's famous name. He
appeared now to wish to return to that subject, rather than
satisfy de Tonti's curiosity about the royal communication.

"Is your father still in the Bastille?"

"Unfortunately, yes. I suspect he'll die there." De Tonti was
uncomfortable discussing his father, Lorenzo de Tonti, the
Italian banker who had fled uprisings in Naples with his wife
and infant son, himself. They begged political asylum of
Cardinal Mazarin, also Italian, who was then prime minister
for the boy prince—now Louis XIV. De Tonti considered La
Salle's pointed questions rude in view of the delicate political
nature of his father's imprisonment, but in his job-seeking
circumstances, he decided to answer.

"As prisons go, the Bastille isn't so bad if one has the
means," La Salle observed. The fact that the Bastille imprisoned indebted noblemen and political prisoners rather than
common criminals meant that a prisoner with money could
buy almost any privilege except release. "I assume Monsieur
de Tonti's illustrious financial talents have given him the
means."

"Oh, yes," de Tonti agreed, giving in to the fact that La Salle
was going to pump him dry. "The insurance schemes that bear
our name set him up comfortably. Unfortunately one of his
tontines put him where he is today."

"Could it be that your honorable father made the mistake of
entering a tontine with some, uh, highly placed person?" La
Salle ventured as he removed the wax from his mouth and
tossed it with the meal's debris. De Tonti noted that the royal
wax had left a faint violet film on La Salle's incisors and he
couldn't help musing that it was often that way with a gift from
a king; once accepted, it left its mark on the recipient.

"Surely he didn't enter a tontine with the king himself?" La
Salle asked with disbelief, amazed that a man smart enough to
make a fortune would do such a dangerous thing.

With a nod, de Tonti explained, "All the other members
have either died or disappeared. The late Cardinal Mazarin
invested the king in this particular tontine when His Majesty
was a teenager. Since his maturity the king has decided that
was an unwise investment. Now only my father and His

Majesty remain to collect the fortune that will go to the lone survivor."

"Surely His Majesty doesn't fear that your father might arrange to be that lone survivor?" La Salle's hands ceased playing with the note.

"Perhaps by locking up my father His Majesty has merely taken out a supportive insurance policy. Perhaps he thinks that fortune might be worth the risk of regicide. Who knows what goes on in the mind of a king?"

"But the survivor would be the first suspect."

De Tonti shrugged. "It's a very big world to get lost in, especially if one has a fortune with which to accomplish a vanishing act."

La Salle shook his head sympathetically and tossed the royal note beside the wax. De Tonti yearned to snatch it up and read it. "My own parents joined tontines when your father's invention was the rage of the Court. It seems the depth of ingratitude for the Crown to imprison the man who helped bail the government out of debt."

De Tonti had pretty well resigned himself to his father's incarceration. He figured it was the just result in the high-stakes game the old man had chosen to play. Speaking of it now was unpleasant, however. "Well, as you say, the Bastille is a luxury prison," he said as if dismissing the subject, hoping to turn the conversation in another direction more to the point of his endeavor.

But La Salle would not let it go. "And how is the old gentleman?"

"I've been denied permission to visit him personally but I understand he's living in a modest but well-appointed apartment, has plenty of food which my mother is allowed to bring to him, and even has conjugal rights. They've let him have his papers and books. I'm told he's gotten religion."

La Salle was silent as de Tonti continued, "I've asked again to be allowed to see him but since I am first a servant of the king, I don't have much hope." His words reminded him of what La Salle had said in the coffeehouse, about one's allegiance belonging first to oneself. There was a wry look on the Canadian's face that let de Tonti know they were thinking along similar lines and he wondered if La Salle were judging him as having no courage in the matter. But La Salle's features were inscrutable.

"His treatment at the hands of what appears to be an ungrateful sovereign might leave one bitter."

Here was dangerous ground. De Tonti considered his words with great care lest La Salle be baiting him or the manservant be listening from the other room. "The Crown has treated me without prejudice. In fact, with generosity. I was one of the first to be admitted to the marine cadet program under War Marshall Vauban. I received an honorable commission and have been awarded stipends above salary twice for military service." Here he met the eyes of the explorer, who was intent on his every word. "Now I go before His Majesty with another petition, if I can get an appointment."

La Salle sighed and retrieved the note, with which he casually picked his teeth as he spoke. "Every Thursday the king grants personal audiences to worthy subjects. And he loves his soldiers, especially war heroes."

De Tonti blushed. It charmed La Salle to see such an honest emotion.

"Well," the young man said modestly, "I suppose."

"But why did you brave this evil night to look for me?"

De Tonti looked up again. Now his gaze was direct and his response unhesitating. "When I was a midshipman at Marseilles, I heard the old sailors talk about the New World but it seemed merely a dream. It wasn't until I was taken prisoner of war, when my life took a downward turn, that I began to think that dream might be my only hope. I have little inheritance, no holdings, and no commission now that His Majesty is making peace with the Spaniards. There's nothing left for me here. My one chance for a new life is in the New World."

"You don't need me for that," La Salle observed, laying the note aside.

De Tonti took a deep breath and launched into what turned out to be his final point. "The Prince de Conti has honored me with his patronage—I suppose the king may have something to do with it because of my father—you know, imprisoning him on such slim suspicion. Anyway, the prince arranged my ransom and helped me find you." He leaned closer. His golden eyes seemed to throw off shafts of light. "Perhaps, monsieur, you could use a fighting man at your side, one who proved his loyalty to you. For a chance at the New World I'd pledge my loyalty to the death."

La Salle had to look away, so intense was the young man who leaned imploringly toward him, his left hand flat on the tablecloth almost touching the note he was so curious to read. After what seemed an interminable time La Salle said, "Read it." He needed to know if this man could read. So few, even army officers, were literate.

"Monsieur?" De Tonti appeared surprised. He understood what La Salle was saying. It was just uncanny, as though La Salle had read his mind.

"The note there. Read it."

"Awfully early in the morning for the king to be sending messages," de Tonti said, picking up the note. He skillfully unfolded it with his left hand and scanned the brief message in purple ink. "Your appointment with His Majesty is for luncheon two weeks hence. It's signed, Colbert."

"The king's minister of marine is known to start his working day before five." La Salle tented his fingers beneath his pronounced chin. He stared out the east window, where he perceived a change in the light that preceded dawn. A single pink cloud marred the indigo sky, where one star, perhaps that of morning, winked. "France never sleeps," he said casually. He was privately pleased de Tonti could read. He had passed La Salle's final secret test.

De Tonti stared at the note. It was as close to royalty as he'd ever come though he knew his parents had been often in the royal presence in some mythical past he could never quite recapture. But here was a note on behalf of the monarch written in quite ordinary, though purple, words implying that His Majesty ate, made appointments, and generally went about the business of life like any mortal.

La Salle's voice snapped him out of his reverie. "I am looking for a special man . . ." he said, turning his gaze from the window. He had de Tonti's complete attention. ". . . to be my second in command on an expedition to find the mouth of the Mech-a-si-pi River and claim all the land it waters for our glorious king. I think, Monsieur de Tonti, that you might be that man."

"Sir, you honor me beyond my wildest dreams." De Tonti wished his voice didn't quaver. He could not have known La Salle was impressed by such a sign of passionate interest. He was used to men who masked their motives and desires. This young man's natural honesty was refreshing and his enthusiasm potentially useful. He was just plain likable. Instinctively, La Salle knew that other men, subordinates, would react to de Tonti in the same positive manner. He suspected that this man was a highly popular commander of men rather than a military genius. And he found favor in a petitioner who could be hardened by battle yet still express his feelings. It was something La Salle himself had lost in Jesuitical training and something he mourned like a dead child. He hated the Jesuits for draining that quality from him, for extinguishing his emotional spontaneity. But in truth his own nature had aided them.

"No, monsieur. It has nothing to do with honoring you. I merely see in you a practical solution to my own needs." What he didn't say was, I see in you a likable, earnest, intelligent young man who can handle the human dregs I must recruit to help me take this expedition to its successful conclusion. Neither did he let on that this young Franco-Italian came with excellent recommendations for honesty and loyalty. La Salle had been like a spider in the center of its web waiting for de Tonti to find him so that he could use him. There was much more of the Jesuit left in La Salle than he would admit to himself.

"You are a brave man. And tonight you proved you value my life. As I see it you have only one obstacle in your path."

De Tonti's face darkened with the obvious question. This, then, was the difficult part, La Salle thought. To confront the worst. He filled both glasses with more of the beautiful wine from his home province. After a hearty swig he leveled his gaze at this young man he'd grown, despite his own suspicious nature, to like in the short time he'd known him.

"With all due respect for your courage and skill with that deadly sailor's blade, you are still one-handed."

De Tonti had not expected to keep it a secret, of course, but only to forestall La Salle's knowledge until he was convinced the handicap would not be a liability.

"Though you compensate courageously, I became suspicious when we dueled."

De Tonti suddenly realized that La Salle had fought him only to confirm that suspicion. That's why he tried to fence with him, why he used only the right-hand blade to equalize the match.

But if he did suspect the Canadian's duplicity, he would never mention it.

His unblinking gaze caught La Salle's attention: God, what strange eyes this man has, like a cat's. He couldn't help but anticipate with appreciation what effect such eyes would have on the superstitious Indians along the Mech-a-si-pi. La Salle was a man who sought any advantage. This would definitely be one. "Please, Captain. I personally don't give a thread that you lost a hand—" He caught himself; one of his worst traits was blurting out something he did not mean to say. "That is, I believe in your ability to be my second in command as ably, even more so, as any two-handed man I've interviewed."

"Then what is the problem?"

"The king is the problem."

The question deepened on de Tonti's face as La Salle continued, "Oh, the king loves his soldiers, all right. He adores the veterans like yourself who've won him glory. But it's a well-known fact that His Majesty will not confront any unpleasantness he can avoid. He's been known to completely ignore members of his own family who've had the bad taste to get sick."

"I certainly don't plan to wave the stump of my arm in his face," he replied in honest exasperation.

"Of course not. But he'll know, don't you see?"

Plainly de Tonti did not.

La Salle leaned forward to explain. "May I be perfectly frank?"

De Tonti nodded in exasperation.

"That cape of yours may do for streetwear, my friend, but you cannot wear such an antique to an audience with His Majesty King Louis the Fourteenth of France. A regular greatcoat is mandatory, and it will at best display an empty sleeve. I tell you," he continued in response to the protest de Tonti was framing, "His Majesty will not confront an empty sleeve on one of his war heroes." He paused to let that sink in. "It would churn up the royal conscience. He would have to honestly admit that His Majesty's glory is won at a very high price which His Majesty does not personally have to pay."

The fresh pinkness of dawn invaded the room. For a while neither man spoke. While he wrestled with this information, de Tonti was unreadable to La Salle. It was obviously a situation he had not imagined. La Salle hated to hurt his pride but the truth must be said. Besides, he had other reasons for broaching this subject, reasons having to do with his own private feelings about meeting with the king. He was giving de Tonti all the time he needed to come to a conclusion La Salle had reached long before.

"Perhaps," de Tonti began tentatively, "I don't have to approach His Majesty in person."

La Salle wearily shook his head. "Then the chance of your

getting the commission is greatly reduced." He drained his
glass as if the problem were his own. De Tonti could not know
that it was because the explorer had set his mind on having this
greathearted gentleman as his lieutenant. The Prince de Conti
had given him the idea. Now that he had seen de Tonti and had
tested him, he was sure. This man had just the qualities of
leadership and empathy that La Salle did not have when
dealing with subordinates. La Salle knew his weakness, knew
he rubbed people the wrong way. He had to have someone to
act as go-between with the men who would make up the
expedition. Even de Tonti's handicap fit into La Salle's
maneuvers, if he could just persuade de Tonti to take the
measures La Salle envisioned. But he would not unfold his
plans yet. What he had in mind for the benefit of impressing
both the king of France and the natives of the Mech-a-si-pi
Valley must appear a natural course of events.

While de Tonti continued to stare at the note, La Salle idly
picked up the wad of wax as if he were unconscious of doing so.
He began playing with it, touching the tablecloth here and
there. Each touch left a lavender mark.

De Tonti's eyes were drawn to La Salle's doodling, but
distractedly, as though he were already far away on the shores
of the New World where he was certain destiny meant for him
to be. Soon, however, he saw there was a design in La Salle's
random marks.

13

La Salle was drawing a hand.

De Tonti watched a minute before his eyes narrowed with
inspiration. He pulled his chair around to see better. La Salle
added more lines, watching de Tonti furtively; it was obvious
that the soldier was fairly itching to grab the odd writing
instrument and work on the design himself.

Casually, La Salle laid aside the wax. De Tonti picked it up
as La Salle knew he would, pinched it for a finer line and
started adding detail. But the Canadian's mere doodle was too
small for improvements so de Tonti began another larger than
life on the tablecloth beside the first. La Salle knew his fish had
taken the bait. To conceal his delight he stood and stretched.

"Look here—" de Tonti said with excitement.

La Salle watched over the other man's shoulder as he sketched a precise engineer's drawing. "A brilliant idea," he mused over the other's design.

"It was your idea, really."

"But you've made it workable."

La Salle made a couple of suggestions, but mainly left it to de Tonti, to set the hook. "It just might work."

"Of course it'll work," de Tonti replied. Almost to himself he muttered, "It's got to have some weight to it."

"To serve our purposes it must be more than merely practical," La Salle said with that irritating superiority of his. He suggested a movable pinky to hold a snuff box.

"But I loathe snuff."

La Salle took the wax from de Tonti without asking, saying as he did so, "The king, man! We're designing this thing for a king's amusement, to take his mind off the fact that it's an artificial hand. A hook—or something just as crude, though merely practical—would revolt him as much as an empty sleeve." He completed his drawing of an elaborate mechanism that would allow the thumb to rotate, revealing another device inside.

"What's that?"

"A music box," La Salle replied with satisfaction. "The king loves mechanical devices as much as music. This serves both pleasures. I wonder if I can find out his favorite tune. . . . Anyway, it'll fascinate him," he said with a happy chuckle as he added a flourish here and there.

"Looks impractical to me," de Tonti said, but his heart was pounding. He hoped that La Salle couldn't hear such an obvious display of emotion. But privately he knew this thing would work—why hadn't he thought of something like this before? The king would not be the first person to be revolted by the amputation. He'd had that response from others, even from Sabat, who had suggested that he knot his shirtsleeve lest someone inadvertently glimpse the stump under his cape.

"Ah," La Salle said, hunched over their improvised drafting table like one of the schoolboys he had taught back at the seminary. "Here, see?"

"What's that in the palm?" de Tonti asked, scrutinizing the drawing even closer.

"What else but a watch."

"A watch?"

"His Majesty loves timepieces. He has the largest collection in Europe."

"A watch in the palm of my hand . . ." de Tonti said with high disbelief. But hope had snared him.

"And here, under the middle finger, a coinpurse!" La Salle made a happy noise in his throat. De Tonti looked at him in wonder. This was a side of the great man's personality he had not been ready for, this delight in pure engineering. De Tonti's own education had been as a military engineer so he understood the math La Salle scribbled in the margins of the tablecloth, but he was startled when La Salle, running out of room, elbowed the wine bottle and dishes to the floor. The clatter brought the sleepy-eyed manservant stumbling in to clean up, but La Salle waved him away with the same impatient disregard he'd thrown the dishes off his working space.

"A coinpurse," de Tonti repeated, laughing, his gold eyes sparkling like the spilled wine. But a thought clouded the gold. He made a disparaging sound.

"What's wrong? You know it'll work. *Mon Dieu*, you know it will work like a pontoon bridge or a siege scaffold."

"The coin, monsieur. The coin. Where will I ever get enough money to pay for such a fantastic device?"

La Salle's eyes lost their brilliance. He himself was deeply in debt. His family here in France had advanced him huge sums for his expeditions of discovery, and he'd mortgaged his Canadian estate to boot. But he did not wish to admit such unpleasantness to this man whom he wanted to enlist in his grand scheme. If de Tonti knew how little financial reward he'd be getting, he would most surely back off. La Salle knew he needed de Tonti as much as the other needed him. The Canadian scanned their ambitious design again. "Surely you can find a way to pay for it, since it means your fortune." After all, a gentleman was expected to find his own funding. It was a long-standing tradition among the French nobility. De Tonti might not realize it, but there would be no financial support for the Mech-a-si-pi expedition; La Salle had to pay for it himself. All he asked from the king was permission to descend the river and claim it for the Crown.

La Salle stood so quickly he knocked over his chair.

"L'Esperance!" he called, forgetting that his man stood just behind him. The servant made a compliant sound.

"The wine-colored greatcoat, the one I can't get into—" He grinned at de Tonti. "I always eat too much when I'm in Paris." He patted his ample stomach and turned to the servant. "Get it for Monsieur de Tonti."

De Tonti framed a protest, but La Salle was removing his baldric and cape and would hear none of it. However, de Tonti was unable to see La Salle's expression as he touched the cape like a dead rat and tossed it deprecatingly aside. It landed on a tall dressing mirror.

"We have an errand to perform and you can't do it in that."

L'Esperance appeared with a resplendent greatcoat over his arm. Wordlessly, with impeccable manners, he approached the embarrassed young captain, who complied as La Salle looked on with the air of the director of an elaborate court pageant.

L'Esperance was of that variety of man who makes the perfect servant; dignified but deferential, as his father had been for La Salle's father, and his grandfather for La Salle's grandsire. Without seeming to intrude on the intimate act of dressing, he helped de Tonti into the magnificent but tasteful daycoat.

De Tonti's right sleeve was knotted just below the elbow, but L'Esperance directed the truncated arm into the coat sleeve with the grace of the king's own dresser. De Tonti looked down at himself and groaned.

The coat was frogged with loops for at least fifty self-covered buttons of minute size.

"Monsieur?" L'Esperance inquired solicitously.

De Tonti stared at the impossible buttons.

L'Esperance was too polite even to smile at the captain's ignorance of fashion, but La Salle openly laughed. "You don't button them, man!"

He grabbed up his own dull orange brocade coat and slipped into it before the servant could assist him. "Like this." He turned toward the mirror, to see the old cape hanging there like a drab shroud. He motioned to it and quietly ordered L'Esperance, "Take care of that." The servant wadded up the cape and set it aside, wiping his fingers against his thigh as if they'd been polluted.

La Salle observed himself in the glass, flipping the lapels of the heavy coat. "See?"

De Tonti stepped closer to the mirror as La Salle stepped aside.

"Let's see now, 'Per . . . what does it need?" La Salle mused.

"A cravat, monsieur?"

"A cravat, of course." La Salle fretted like a tailor over the shoulders and general hang of his coat on the lean young man while the servant dug into a sea chest, then approached with a cream-colored lace neckpiece, which he proceeded to tie around de Tonti's neck. He fluffed the frills and positioned the lace just so on the collar, then stood back with his master to assay the effect.

De Tonti looked down, feeling miserable under all this attention. He was used to having Sabat assist him, but this broke his usual pattern. To be fussed over by strangers made him distinctly uncomfortable, but when he looked in the mirror, he had to admit, albeit to himself, that the effect was a good one. He no longer looked so downtrodden, so fresh from ordeal. L'Esperance reached across him to take the sleeve cuff, also elaborately frogged with nonbuttoning buttons, up and across de Tonti's chest. This was the military manner of displaying a sleeve left empty by war. He searched his own person and came up with a silkpin from a pocket. This he attached invisibly to the underside of the sleeve to secure it to the coat front. He flattened the cuff and stood back to see how it looked.

De Tonti reached for the leather baldric that held his cutlass and pistol. L'Esperance relieved him of it and slipped it over his head, then smoothed it out. De Tonti set the sword at the right angle for easy purchase and tested the draw of the gun from its pocket. He nodded to the servant, who smiled back at him without looking directly into his eyes.

La Salle watched all this with pleasure of a serious order on his long face.

De Tonti again looked into the glass. All in all it wasn't half bad. He felt odd about the sleeve; he had not wished to flaunt the hand's loss but this was much less awkward than the cape and it looked more handsome. And the burgundy velvet contrasted perfectly with his black hair and ruddy complexion. He flinched, however, when the servant made to untie his braid. L'Esperance looked toward his master for support.

"It has to go," the explorer said. "When we get to New France you may wear it any way you wish, but here in Paris we observe the conventions. Gentlemen do not wear sailors' braids."

L'Esperance's nimble fingers were already at it. He observed that his master's new acquaintance was free of vermin—in fact his hair was clean and shiny. He combed it out with his fingers, then drew a tortoiseshell comb from another pocket and began to groom the captain's hair.

Another glance in the mirror confirmed for de Tonti the improvement. His hair fell naturally into the shoulder-length fashion of the day, just as the king might wish his own hair fell, but for which effect the king was forced to wear a wig.

La Salle chuckled to himself as the servant went to brush flakes of dry mud from de Tonti's short boots. La Salle walked around him as if inspecting a battlement. "You have a natural nobility, sir, improved by a light edit." He clapped de Tonti's shoulder. "Well then, come on," he commanded with his usual imperiousness. He picked up the wine bottle to judge the amount as his servant began to collect the dishes from the floor.

"But—" de Tonti started to protest.

"Come on," La Salle said with a hand on de Tonti's right shoulder as if placing him under arrest.

"Where are we going?"

"To see Mansard, of course."

He propelled de Tonti toward the door. The manservant watched them, catching de Tonti's questioning eye. With a shrug, hands full of broken pottery, he seemed to communicate that this was his master, who must be obeyed without question.

"But it's barely dawn."

"Come, come," the explorer said, taking his own hat and de Tonti's from a brass hatstand by the door. He turned back briefly to grab the tablecloth, ripping it from the table as if performing a parlor trick. He gave de Tonti his hat, set his own in place, rolled the unfortunate cloth up under his arm, and herded de Tonti toward the door, which L'Esperance trotted to open.

"Who is Mansard?"

"The king's armorer. Only man for the job."

"But how will I pay for it?"

"A mere detail."

"But—"

La Salle pushed at de Tonti's back as they descended the narrow stair, tramping noisily in their heavy boots. Someone yelled through a wall, demanding to know what in the king's

name was going on. A woman screeched for silence. But this
was La Salle's stairway, just as it was his world to conquer, his
river to find, and his man to propel along without regard for
the sleep of others. De Tonti was glad he was on the side of this
great mover of men.

In his mind he was already wearing the magnificent hand he
was certain would be as real as La Salle's own between his
shoulder blades.

When the Sun King was still a boy and France was ruled for
him by his Prime Minister Cardinal Mazarin, there had been a
long civil war egged on by disgruntled nobles, called *La
Fronde*. The unsuccessful revolution was named after a mean
street game that urchins played against the windows of Paris in
which they threw stones with *frondes*, or slingshots. Since
only the well-off could afford glass, there was the flavor of
political action in the game, which Jacques Mansard was sure
was being played against his second-story bedroom window
one misty April morning. He clambered from his warm bed, in
which his plump wife still snored gently, to see which of the
neighborhood brats was at it this time. Bleary-eyed, he threw
open the window with his permanently blackened and heat-
scared hands, leaned out, and yelled a filthy word in his
smoke-coarsened voice before he noticed the two gentlemen
standing in the courtyard looking up at him.

"Who's that pelting my windowpanes?" he demanded with
some deflation of anger. His striped nightcap was askew and
the damp air threatening his arthritis put him in no mood for
antics.

"Mansard, have the fumes baked your brains?" the taller of
the two men called amiably. "Don't you know me?"

Mansard squinted and leaned farther over his sill. "Is
that—? No, it can't be—" His anger totally dissipated in recognition. "I thought the Jesuits got you."

"Black wasn't my color. Come on down. I've a wonderful
proposition for you. There is much to talk about."

Mansard chuckled and replied, "But the sun's not up yet,
Robbie, and I'm still in my nightshirt."

"We've been up drinking all night, planning your work for
you." La Salle held up the bottle. "Come take the hair of the
dog with us."

Mansard's wife sleepily asked what was wrong as he grabbed
his robe and shuffled from the bedroom. His career had been

launched by La Salle's father many years ago; they had fought while they were both boys in Flanders in what had come to be called the Thirty Years War. The elder La Salle had given him much work improving the defenses of his Norman estate, and the man who played *la fronde* against his window this morning had been baptized from a helmet that was Mansard's work because the local parish baptismal font had a crack in it. Mansard had always thought that the unconventional baptism was behind the boy's unconventional personality but he had always kept this opinion to himself. Few men could have raised such delight in the smiling blacksmith as he threw open the double doors of the shop. His apprentice was already growling at the intruders who were pounding at the courtyard entrance.

"Let them in," Mansard commanded, not unkindly, "and get the forge going before my joints freeze."

He hugged La Salle warmly and was deferent with the young man with him though Mansard was unnerved by the stranger's yellow eyes.

La Salle wasted no time in getting down to business. After introductions he whipped out the tablecloth and spread it out on a trestle.

Before long they were improving the design. Mansard found a gauntlet in a pile of scrap. De Tonti tested its weight. "It's the right size, but it needs more heft." Mansard nodded, but told him some other craftsman would have to build the music box.

"Perhaps you could bring me the apparatus, monsieur, and I'll build the hand around it. Also the watch."

De Tonti had anticipated this. "I know where I can get the timepiece, but maybe we'd best forget the music box."

"Absolutely not," La Salle said adamantly, not without anger at his new partner. "I told you the king loves music boxes. There must be something splendid to divert his attention from what this thing really is."

De Tonti doubted the practicality of a watch in what he anticipated would be a defensive weapon but he held his tongue. "At least I'd like to be able to remove the googaws in case I have to use this thing."

La Salle shrugged. Clearly he didn't want to argue.

Mansard understood La Salle's strategy. "Very clever of you if you mean to present Monsieur de Tonti to His Majesty." For many years he'd dealt with the king's eccentricities.

"Well," de Tonti conceded. "Perhaps my mother . . ."

"Yes, yes," La Salle said impatiently, "every noblewoman has a few music boxes tucked away. Gifts from admirers, and all." It was clear that he was growing impatient with this discussion, perhaps even bored with this project now that it had been launched, and wished to be elsewhere on other business.

"I must see her anyway," de Tonti said, and La Salle threw him a warning look because they had discussed how to finance this project as they walked to Mansard's forge. De Tonti had admitted that he had only one choice, and that was to approach Isabelle de Tonti to claim an inheritance, a mature tontine she was holding in trust for him.

But La Salle's look commanded him to say nothing about payment. "We do have a time element against us, old friend," La Salle remarked, lest de Tonti say more. Mansard, who was bent over the drawing in the craftsman's delight at a difficult challenge, looked up.

"We see His Majesty in two weeks."

"Two weeks!" the old man shouted. He had one of those aquiline faces in which all the features point to and culminate in the nose. Mansard's was fairly twitching at the impossibility of such a deadline.

La Salle shrugged away all responsibility. "Well, if it is beyond your skill . . ."

Mansard glared at the ruined tablecloth as if it were whispering unwanted advice to him, rather than directing a disrespectful glare at this man he'd known to have such an insulting attitude since boyhood. Finally he said, "If Monsieur can get the music box and watch by tomorrow, I may be able to complete the hand in a fortnight."

They looked at de Tonti.

He was by now bent with fatigue. His second wind had been leached away by strong wine and many hours without sleep. He had not fully recovered from his prison ordeal anyway. The past twenty-four hours showed on his face. But he nodded. "I think the music box will be no problem. But the watch . . ." He shrugged. "It all depends on whether I see my father."

Mansard looked questioningly at him, but La Salle said quickly, lest de Tonti reveal his father's whereabouts and cast doubt on his ability to pay, "I will speak to the Prince de Conti about that." His rapid reply gave away more than he might have liked of his secret machinations. De Tonti looked at him oddly, understanding the man further. Now he realized that La

Salle probably knew more of him than he had revealed. But, de Tonti thought, of course those two powerful men had already discussed the prince's suggestion that the young officer contact La Salle. He let it go.

Mansard had turned back to the design. He took the cloth from the trestle and tacked it to the wall with a couple of nails. He tapped it with swollen knuckles. "It's a pretty thing, I'll say." He glanced at de Tonti. "Has Monsieur given thought as to how it will attach?"

De Tonti was rubbing his right arm with his hand. The pinned sleeve was restricting the stump under the heavily lined cloth. "I figure it would simply slip over the end of my arm."

"May I see?" Mansard requested.

De Tonti hesitated only a moment, then took off the coat La Salle had given him. His benefactor became suddenly interested in a magnificent suit of armor on a wooden dummy. De Tonti wondered if La Salle shared the king's aversion to grim reminders of war. He would have thought the man's time among the aborigines would have hardened him. Instead it had made the explorer more sensitive.

Mansard helped de Tonti shed the coat and carefully hung it on a peg. There was no way de Tonti could untie the knot in his linen shirtsleeve so he offered it to the smithy, who went about the task with unperturbed efficiency. He had seen everything in his day—a thousand rotting French soldiers on a Flanders field and every wound men and metal could inflict. De Tonti's healed stump was nothing. He had about half the forearm left with a jagged but clean scar that presented no problem Mansard could see. "Does it bother you?"

"I always know when the weather's going to change."

Mansard nodded sagely. "Sensitive, yes. My wife's a seamstress. She'll know how to line the socket with something soft. Maybe lambswool. We'll bring the lining up like a sleeve above the elbow and strap it with a buckle."

"I don't want it falling off."

"Yes, that could prove embarrassing," Mansard said with a sympathetic chuckle. "Then we'll make a half sleeve of it and buckle it above the elbow, like so." He sketched what he had in mind in charcoal on the rest of the tablecloth. De Tonti glanced at La Salle, who had wandered far enough away so that he couldn't hear a whisper.

"Mansard, instead of a snuff box in the finger could you

install a dagger? It would be of far more use to me. Besides, I hate snuff."

"I presume the snuff box was his idea?"

De Tonti smiled, yes.

Mansard, this close to those golden eyes, was transfixed. "Whatever Monsieur wishes."

"There's room for a stiletto. I want it spring-driven. Will this blade be small enough?" He drew a fine slim knife from his boot.

Mansard studied the knife with appreciation. "Shame I'll have to shorten it but I know exactly what you want. A sudden efficient weapon for close work."

"Or," de Tonti said wryly, looking at the grimy fingers of his left hand, "to clean my fingernails."

Mansard's eyes twinkled. Despite the weird cat's eyes looking back at him, he liked this spirited man. He clapped him on the back as a comrade. "Where did it happen?"

"Sicily."

"Grenade?"

"So they tell me. I remember nothing. I woke up weeks later in a Spanish prison."

Mansard nodded understanding. "That's common, and a blessing."

He helped de Tonti back into the greatcoat.

La Salle approached them with the bottle, sloshing its contents. "I think there are three swigs left in here, just enough to seal the bargain."

"But, Robbie, it's not a bargain until we've discussed terms," Mansard said with a mercenary gleam in his eye.

De Tonti was not enough of a gambler to keep from shooting a glance at his new partner, but La Salle fielded Mansard's comment like a pro. "Don't you know who this man is?" He put an arm around de Tonti's shoulder. "He's the son of the Italian banker who saved France."

Mansard shrugged noncommitally. He glanced at the design hanging beside his forge. "Two thousand *livres* to build this device."

De Tonti's knees almost buckled under him. He steadied himself against the table.

"And cheap at half the price," La Salle said with confidence. "But we are keeping you from your work." He drank precisely one third of the bottle's contents and handed it to Mansard. The smithy didn't take his eyes from La Salle as he drank another third and handed the dregs to de Tonti whose face had bleached ashen. He swayed slightly. La Salle was quick to give him support. "My friend stayed up all night and he's only recently home from the wars," he said in explanation lest the crafty Mansard suspect he was really faint from the news of what the hand would cost. He tilted the bottle for de Tonti to drink. The young man drained the bottle and wiped his lips with the back of his hand.

"So you will bring the devices tomorrow? I must have their dimensions to cast."

De Tonti nodded, unable to speak. His stomach was churning.

"And you," Mansard directed at La Salle, "tread very carefully."

"I shall do my best."

"Your enemies can be unforgiving."

La Salle arched an eyebrow and gave de Tonti an I-told-you-so look. "They've already been at work."

"Poison?" the smith asked. La Salle nodded grimly.

"Hmmm, it's popular these days." Mansard appeared to be considering an alternative. He held up a hand to stop the two from leaving and momentarily left the room.

La Salle cast a worried look at de Tonti, who might be about to pass out. "Get some water," the explorer said to Mansard's apprentice.

Mansard returned with a small cedar casket, which he handed to La Salle.

"A present?" La Salle asked.

"An antidote."

"What is it?"

"I don't know, but my wife has sources for this sort of thing. She's Italian, you know." He looked at de Tonti, afraid he might have offended him. A spirit of nationalism made some Frenchmen bigoted, which Mansard hated. But the young man wordlessly gestured that no offense was taken.

"Thank you, old friend," La Salle said, pocketing the casket. He hugged Mansard.

"For your dead father's sake I take care of you," replied the smith. His apprentice brought de Tonti a bucket and dipper, which he gratefully took. The water was sweet; it might settle his stomach.

They said their goodbyes, leaving Mansard at his doorway as they stepped out into the courtyard and then the street already beginning to fill with early traffic. De Tonti saw La Salle glance

suspiciously over his shoulder, and thought now might be the
time to tell him of the duel outside the coffeehouse. But he was
distracted by his own body. A few steps and de Tonti paused to
wretch into the rain-scrubbed gutter. La Salle looked away
until de Tonti had finished throwing up, then they continued
along the street that paralleled the Seine. In Paris the streets
couldn't remain clean for long. Not a block farther the warning
cry of *"Gare l'eau!"* came from a second-story window. They
barely had time to avoid being pelted with a bucket of nightsoil
a woman threw, as was the custom, into the gutter.

"So good to be home," de Tonti cracked sarcastically with a
sickly grin, though his color was returning. After they walked a
few paces he said, "Where am I going to get two thousand
livres?" He was hunched by deflated hope and the cold chill
that follows nausea.

"Time to go see mama."

"Hmmm," the other growled doubtfully.

"You certainly are returning with your shield," La Salle said.
It was a reference to the advice ancient Spartan mothers were
supposed to have given their warrior sons: *Return with your
shield or on it*. That is, a hero or not at all.

"I don't feel like a hero."

"You have the right to claim your reward for bringing honor
to her name."

De Tonti didn't answer. La Salle did not know Isabelle de
Tonti.

14

Isabelle de Tonti was living in the same fine brick house
much closer to Versailles than the Bastille. De Tonti stood
across the tree-lined boulevard in a residential district a league
from the king's favorite palace. He was chewing on a fingernail
to clean it. It didn't do much good; it had been too late to go to
a barber, for the hour was near four in the afternoon of the
same day he and La Salle had seen Mansard. He had returned
to La Salle's suite, where he had slept far past noon, awakening
with late sunlight in his eyes. La Salle was absent and
L'Esperance offered no explanation though he did offer de
Tonti a meal of cheese and fine white bread. De Tonti had

momentarily thought of skipping the ordeal of confronting his mother and instead asking the servant for his recommendation of a good *tripot*, he felt so enlivened. But he decided there would be time for pleasures of the flesh after he had seen Isabelle. He felt good about his desire, though; it was a further sign of his recovery from the persistent depression. Before that moment, he hadn't wanted a woman since he had lost his hand.

It was a dazzling spring afternoon. Last night's rain had polished every leaf and bud. The sky was a blinding blue with the sails of cloud galleons riding a low breeze on the western horizon toward the Atlantic—toward the New World, he reminded himself. It was a heady thought that recalled the stakes that rode on the success of this interview with his mother.

Her house was almost as he remembered it, red brick with cut white stone outlining doors and windows. He knew Isabelle conducted his father's financial and real estate business from here. The old man had invested in Parisian houses when he'd first brought his young family to France in 1650. Now the rents on his investments supplemented other financial dealings so that if Lorenzo de Tonti had not been a permanent resident of the Bastille he would have been a prosperous banker and moneylender, with many retainers and, no doubt, a coach-and-four. Through the shrubbery he saw the carriage house and stables in back, large enough for a small two-horse shay.

Only one thing was missing from her home as he remembered it. Gone was the expanse of lawn he had loved in childhood. In its great green place was a splendid though cramped example of the gardener's art—flowers, trees, borders, and precise paths.

He stifled a nostalgic sigh and gave his fingers one more scrutiny. There was nothing to do but approach the door. He took a deep breath and crossed the street behind a one-horse shay driven by a smiling girl who giggled to her pretty companion when they saw him. He couldn't miss their admiring glances as they passed. That gave him even more confidence as he walked through the unlatched iron gate. Behind a low hedge surrounding the front of the house lay the immaculately formal garden, where roses were just budding. Here and there were geometric beds of purple lilies—the symbol of France, idealized in the symbol of the *fleur-de-lis*.

She was using every opportunity to announce her patriotism. But the flowers were exquisite, whatever the motive behind them. Their perfume faintly touched the air as he pulled the front door knocker.

Somewhere deep in the house the bell chimed faintly. He waited some time then tried again, watching the street. There was a chance he'd been followed.

He'd been put on guard when he left La Salle's hotel. For the first few blocks he walked before taking the commercial coach, he was sure he'd been followed by a fellow in workingman's breeches and a slouch cap of the type affected by stevedores. But since he had arrived in this pleasant suburb, the suspicious figure was gone.

His encounter with La Salle after the mysterious duel last night left de Tonti ready to fight, hungry for another chance to draw the cutlass. Now, standing on his mother's front step he scanned the residential street but saw no threat, only the green and brick-red civility of the good life.

He was of a mind just to leave and try to meet her another time. But something pulled his eye to the side lane, where a line of paving stones meandered in an inviting way toward the back of the house. There had been a great deal of landscaping since he had been here last, but the less polite carriage house still communicated with a hedge beyond the humble backyard. Gardener's tools were scattered about, but there was no sign of a workman. Through open stable shutters he could see that the vehicle was absent; the horses, too, judging from the two stalls and the lingering but not unpleasant odor of manure in the bright air.

He was somewhat relieved that his mother wasn't at home, though he found it odd she'd left nobody to see after the household in a city of thieves.

Her absence meant he could postpone the dreaded confrontation, leave these proper environs, and head back into the heart of the city, where he felt more comfortable and where he could spend his last *sou* in some friendly female company. That's what his body was telling him to do and he was about to follow the inclination when he heard something in the carriage house.

His hand flew to the pommel of the cutlass. It was quiet for a moment, so quiet he was startled when a bird burst into song from a nearby chestnut tree. With soundless steps over the packed ground he moved to the open stable doors, drawing his blade with a thrill of anticipation at hacking to death anyone who dared to spy on him. And it was the sword, his pet, not the pistol that could give satisfaction.

The renewed sound of something larger than a rat moving in the gloom seemed to follow him as he stepped from the late sunlight into the stable. It took a moment for his eyes to adjust to the dimness; he saw a quick flash of movement along a back wall. He sprang to slash at the spy he was sure had followed him from the Rue de La Truanderie to this law-abiding neighborhood.

He lunged at a dull flash of color but he felt the blade cut only air. There was the unmistakable rush of someone else's breathing and a scramble through hay piled by a stall. He brought the blade down and out in the path of the moving shadow, silhouetted as the enemy now was against the doorway glare.

The other screamed. He had less than a second to deflect the blow, a dangerous and difficult thing to do. But he had no other choice because now he could clearly see that what he'd thought was a skulking spy, an agent from La Salle's cursed Jesuits, or some other enemy attached to him now that he was attached to the controversial explorer, was not an adult paid to deter him.

He'd almost killed a small boy in a red velvet doublet.

The child lay on his back, eyes round with terror as the blade struck the post beside him instead of himself.

He was no more than eight. De Tonti was weakened with the thought of how close he'd come to slaughtering a baby. He expected the child to cry. Instead, the boy spat an obscene curse at him.

"You brat, where did you learn that word?" de Tonti asked, trying to silence his pounding heart with deep breathing. With more force than necessary he yanked his sword from the post and replaced it, an easier task now that he wasn't wearing the cape.

The boy scrambled to his feet. De Tonti grabbed his curly brown locks while the boy began to scream again, this time in fury as he aimed a kick at de Tonti's groin.

He held him at arm's length while the spitting little animal clawed and kicked until his force was spent. De Tonti hauled him a good way off the ground, full of his own muted fury that such an innocent had brought him close to foul murder. In all his fighting days he'd killed neither woman nor child, not even

Spanish. He would hate to have such a deed on his stern conscience.

"I'll tell my mother on you," the boy snarled as though this were the worst threat he could imagine. He stopped trying to kick.

De Tonti gingerly lowered him, letting his shiny black-shod feet touch the hay and dirt of the floor, but he kept a tight hold on the curly locks.

"Let me loose, you bastard—"

"Here, that's no way for a gentleman who wears dancing shoes to talk."

"Who are you to speak of gentlemen, you whoreson—"

"There must be saddlesoap around here somewhere so I can wash out your filthy mouth," de Tonti said, looking around, but he was mostly amused by the fiesty youngster.

"*Larron!*"

A line of spittle almost caught de Tonti, who gave him another stout rattle by the hair of his head so that the boy looked cross-eyed and dizzy.

"Most likely you're the thief, brat."

"I live here," the lad replied indignantly.

"Tell me who you are." Another brain-rattling shake did not loosen his tongue. "If you live here, then tell me when the mistress of this house will return."

"None of your business, *larron.*"

"I'm no thief, boy. Now tell me where your mistress is."

"I'm not a servant. My mother left me in charge and I order you to leave. You have no business here."

"How old are you?"

"Eight and a half, but I can pass for ten."

"You have a big mouth for such a baby."

The boy sneered, but his anger was obviously spent, and was rapidly being replaced by curiosity. He eyed de Tonti craftily.

"You dress like a gentleman, but you don't fool me. What happened to your arm? I heard the Turks cut off the arms of thieves."

De Tonti couldn't help but laugh. "Where did you hear that?" He let go of the child's hair and straightened his own new coat.

"My friend Andrew. He's already a king's page. I'm to be a page too, this summer. But I'd rather not because I have to help the king put on his bedroom slippers, and you know what? He doesn't smell so good."

"A king's page, is it?"

Mother says I have to, but I'd rather be a soldier and shoot Spaniards—is that a pistol there? Are you a soldier? Is that how you lost your hand? Did the Spaniards shoot it off or are you really a thief?"

"Too many questions," de Tonti replied, brushing dust from his velvet. "I asked you first, what's your name?"

"I'm the master of this house."

"Spunky brat, I'll say that for you."

"Mama says I'm the man of the house. She's gone to see father."

De Tonti knew now for certain that this was his baby brother, born out of the conjugal rights his rich, imprisoned father paid for. He felt a wave of fondness for the boy and realized now what had seemed so familiar about him: the brown curls, the pale skin, the eyes so unlike his and his mother's golden ones but ash-colored as were his father's. Thank Jesus he had stayed the cutlass.

Unencumbered by adult scruples, the boy stared at the pinned sleeve. "How did you lose your hand?"

"I asked you a question first. Answer who you are and then I'll answer a question of yours." But when the boy obeyed, de Tonti nearly fell over.

"I am Henri de Tonti," the child proudly replied.

Stunned by this disclosure, de Tonti couldn't form a reply. Why would Isabelle give another son his name? Dark suspicions flooded his mind; he felt sorry for this child being born into such a sultry family.

But he finally managed to say, "Well, Henri, I'm here to see your honored mother, Isabelle de Tonti. If I were a burglar, how would I know her name?"

"Do you know her?"

"From a long time ago. Now, when does she come home?"

"She stays a long time when she goes to visit Papa," he said, dropping his glance to his princely shoes.

"Where are the servants, then?"

"The housekeeper always goes with her because they take huge baskets of food for Papa." The boy bit his lip and looked shyly up. "He's in the Bastille," he whispered. "Mama says it's a terrible injustice, but I'm forbidden to speak of it."

"I won't tell on you, Henri."

The child thanked him with a rich smile.

"Where's your big brother?"

"With Mama—he's on leave from the seminary."

So, de Tonti thought, she finally has a son in the clergy.

"Are you an officer? You are, aren't you? May I see the pistol? Will you show me how you fire it?"

"Perhaps later. I've come to see your mama on important business."

"That's all she ever does—important business. She'll be home soon—do you want to come inside and wait for her?"

He nodded, warming to the child.

"What's your name, monsieur?" Henri asked as they walked to a door in the back wall of the house. The heavy wooden door squeaked on its hinges when they entered, just as he remembered from years ago.

"We have something in common, you see. My name is Henri, too."

"May I call you that, or do I have to call you Monsieur?"

"You may call me Henri if you wish."

"Tell me about the war," the boy said inside the brick kitchen, where gleaming copper kettles still hung from sooty beams and the fragrant aroma of a soup drifted from a pot on a hook over the banked fire in the huge fireplace. "Was it terribly exciting?"

"Terribly boring. Soldiers spend most of their time waiting for generals and kings to decide what to do."

"Mama says I must never criticize the king."

She's not taking any chances with this one, de Tonti thought.

"Did you kill many Spaniards? Did they scream horribly— my mother hates Spaniards. They made her and father leave Naples—that's a city in Italy."

De Tonti smiled, charmed by his little brother. "You've ruined your doublet I'm afraid."

The boy twisted to see the spot of manure on the fine cloth. "I'd better change before she gets home." He looked up at the stranger. "Do you promise not to steal the silver if I leave you here for a while?"

"I promise, Henri. And when you come back I'll show you the pistol. It's from Italy, too."

"You *will*?" The child scurried two steps at a time up a narrow flight of steps in a corner of the kitchen.

De Tonti wandered through a long hallway and into the formal dining room furnished with a dark wing table and chairs covered with striped silk, through an archway into a parlor where the late afternoon sunlight slanted, turning pale cream walls to pink. Isabelle had completely redecorated the house since he'd been here more than eight years ago. All the furniture was new; she was prospering. He was inspecting an ornately carved mantelpiece when he heard the back door squeak open and close amid a flurry of female voices.

Well, she was here.

La Salle's coat felt suddenly too large; he was aware of all his imperfections. The mirror above the mantel could tell him nothing to ease his mind.

He had to bite his tongue to keep from answering when a familiar woman's voice piped from the other end of the long hall.

De Tonti turned from the mirror, feeling so much like a boy again. He was dismayed to see a straw in his stocking.

Suddenly she was there.

Her hair was still raven black. She entered in a sweep of taffeta the color they called hennecin, henna and cinnamon. Behind her stood his brother Alphy, grown to peach-cheeked young manhood. He was handsome, right at twenty years, dressed in blue with wavy brown hair and gray eyes like their father's. But de Tonti gave Alphy only a fleeting glance; it was their mother who arrested his attention. He straightened slowly, dropping the straw.

She was still so beautiful his heart jumped beneath La Salle's velvet. She stopped short when she saw her visitor.

At her side Alphy misunderstood her surprise. His slim hand dropped to his dagger hilt, although de Tonti suspected that as with the other courtiers the gesture was ceremonial.

Madame de Tonti drew a breath, hand at her throat, then said to Alphy, "There is no danger, darling." She touched his arm. Alphonse stared at her a second then looked again at de Tonti. In that moment he recognized his older brother and would have said something but his mother asked him to leave. He hesitated. "Please, darling, leave us," she said sweetly and the young man departed.

She composed herself, steel beneath the perfume and lace. "So, it's you."

"Mother . . ." De Tonti's voice caught in his throat. He stepped closer to her, dismayed that time had defaced her. Mentally he calculated her years: He was almost twenty-eight. She had been twenty-four when she and her husband had fled across the Franco-Italian border. She had given birth somewhere *en route*. He'd actually been born in Italy but she shrewdly called him by a French Christian name and placed his nativity on French soil with an eye for where their future lay. He had not seen her for eight years.

Her eyes were the same. He'd forgotten what a shock gold-flecked eyes could be to the onlooker. They sparked at him now in a confounded mixture of well-bridled emotions he'd swear even she could not sort out. All the emotions between a mother and her firstborn who had disappointed her, plus the feelings of eight years of separation. There was something else, too, that looked like fear.

He ached to ask her why she'd given his name to another son. But he held this bitter question until its time.

She looked at him as if he were a stranger—tall, bearded, hardened, and with that sleeve pinned so emptily across the froggings of a coat that looked too large for him. No feelings showed on her face, but in her deepest heart she cursed, Goddamn you, Louis, for all that you've taken from us. "I thought you were dead."

"There have been times I wished I were."

She glanced at the sleeve. "How terrible for you."

He was about to shrug it off and give her the good news that it had opened a door for him to the king, but just then the little boy, Henri, burst into the room.

She didn't give him a chance to speak. "Leave us now."

"But—"

"Leave us," she said sharply in a tone that sent a chill of memory through her eldest son. She'd grown even harsher, he thought. At least she will have one son who obeys her.

"Go to the kitchen with Marie."

The boy left reluctantly.

Her hands were clenched. De Tonti realized she was afraid. Understanding burst upon him: She didn't want him to know she'd named another son Henri.

"My baby brother, *maman*?" he asked too severely.

"You know I'm allowed to visit your father," she spat defensively.

He was being too hard on her. This woman would do whatever she considered necessary, but she'd stop short at infidelity. He knew she adored Lorenzo. "Of course—I didn't mean to offend."

She dropped to a striped setee and rolled those eyes as if she might faint. He couldn't tell if she were really ill or if this was a diversion from discussing the child with his name. He sat beside her, feeling helpless, any anger he may have had dissipated by the sight of her discomfort. She looked up at him. For a long moment their matching eyes confronted each other in a battle of silent will. It was she who broke the silence: "You should have let me know you were coming home."

"There's been so little time. Only a few weeks ago I was in prison."

"Spanish pigs," she hissed.

"It's war, that's all."

Other bitterness, which she didn't mention, traced her features. He could guess that some was directed toward the king though it was impolitic even in her own home to express those feelings when her fortune was based on the Crown's ironic goodwill. They spoke for a few moments about the family business. "It makes me old worrying about such things," she said, lightly patting her elaborately styled hair. It was piled in front under a lacy doily with curls around the hairline.

"You're still so beautiful and you always were good at business. Even better than Papa."

"I do what I can," she said, not without pride. It was true. She looked up with new wetness in her eyes. She was holding back so much, it was bound to explode. "If you'd listened to me this would never have happened to you," she growled to keep from raising her voice.

"Mother—"

"If you'd gone into the priesthood you wouldn't be like this!" She gestured vaguely at the sleeve as though it were too obscene to mention. "Damn you, damn you—"

He knew from long experience there was nothing to stem the tide of her emotion. It could only run its course. He'd once seen her put out a servant's eye with a thrown bookend.

"Your father and I begged you not to go into the army."

He reached out but it gave her no consolation. Unexpectedly she grabbed his fingers and scanned them as though he were five and she was inspecting him for Mass. "Look at this!" The ungentlemanly calluses were all the indictment she needed. "I gave you the blood of Caesars and you give me back the hand of a common laborer." She threw his hand at him as though it were a disgusting object. Her sense of *dérogeance* was badly bruised. That ancient law that demanded no physical labor by the nobility was as stern as her Catholicism—even more so, because he knew she was about as religious as a rock.

When it looked as though she was calming down, he said softly, "Mother, I didn't have the call to be a priest."

"*Mon Dieu*, who's talking about the call? I mean a profession that befits your station."

"I just didn't believe enough for that life."

"I suppose you never even go to Confession."

"My conscience is my own—" he replied, starting to flare. Then he caught himself. In a calmer voice he said, "I'm to be honored by the king himself. I wanted to share the honor with you, so you'd be proud."

She refused to look at him but she gave him her attention. That remark about the king had snared her.

"I had the good fortune to be introduced to the Sieur de La Salle—"

She sneered; she'd heard of that Canadian, a madman, or worse, a charlatan.

"He proposes a great expedition to increase the king's lands in the New World."

"The New World, agh—" She paced around the setee, balling her fists against whatever was handy.

He stubbornly continued, "On an adventure that can't help but bring fame and fortune to us all."

"Pirates and brigands."

"And priests," he added. But it was a futile appeal. It was *sous* not souls this woman cared for.

"I stand to make a good deal of money, too."

She scowled, highly doubtful.

"I need your help. The tontine. The one you said was mine."

She was already shaking her head.

"I know it's mature. I've come to claim it."

She twisted away from him.

"You can't refuse a tontine in my name—" He stopped short, realization like a club striking his forehead. She stared at him.

"What you ask is not mine to give."

Nobody but Henri de Tonti could claim his tontine. It was suddenly so obvious. The caustic pain of knowing what she'd done pierced him. He would have done anything at that moment to hurt her as she had him. But the only weapons he had against her were words. "That boy, mother. Is he my father's?"

She struck him and would have hit him again but he grabbed her wrist. "Damn you again."

"I am my father's son and I claim my inheritance as firstborn."

"I cannot give you what you ask."

He was almost crying when he asked, "Why did you give that boy my name?"

She let her hand go limp and he let it go free. In an altered tone of conciliation she continued, "Henri, we thought you were dead." She saw disbelief unfurl in his eyes. "We really did."

"You knew I was alive eight years ago when that child was born."

Defiance etched her face.

"You knew exactly what you were doing," he continued. "This way there would be a Henri de Tonti around when all the other members of that tontine were dead." •

"So few boys ever come back," she moaned. "Henri collected that tontine. Nobody asked any questions."

His face was cold, so she continued, "I couldn't let it revert to the Crown."

From another part of the house the boy's laughter echoed, a foreign sound amid their argument over blood and money, a sound out of place and time. It could have been de Tonti's own boyish voice down the halls of years, laughing as he caught a ball this woman threw to him on a wide lawn in the sunshine of another spring. She heard it, too. When she looked at him again, he saw no anger for himself, but only love gone sour for what the years had brought her for her labor pains. He supposed a parent had some kind of claim, though dammit, he would not put such a claim on his child if he ever had one.

She saw condemnation in his eyes. "I didn't do this to you, Henri. I did it so that boy would have a chance. The tontine exactly pays for his commission as a page."

"I wonder if father's prison cell is big enough for two?"

"You wouldn't turn in your own mother?"

"You turned against your own son."

She was paralyzed by his logic.

"It's my money." He doubted he'd really turn her in, but she had to believe he would.

"Tied up in trust for Henri."

"I remind you, I am Henri de Tonti."

"To the Merchants' Bank, he is Henri de Tonti."

"Then you give it to me. I don't care if it's from the bank or your mattress."

She licked her lips in calculation. "I'd be foolish to keep that kind of money around this house."

"How much do you have on hand?" he asked, willing to negotiate. "Be honest, now," he warned. "I can smell it when you lie."

"About half the tontine's value."

"And," he added, "I want something else. A small thing." She watched him.

"That music box, the one you played when I was afraid of the dark."

"*La Pomme Rosace*," she whispered. Something broke in her. He hadn't expected this reaction. He knew she wasn't sentimental, but here she was, usually all nails and grit in the arena, suddenly spilling hot tears over a childhood fancy.

"If you still have it . . ."

She leaned limply against him. He couldn't help but love her all over again. He took her sobs as though he were the parent and she the child. "It's all right, *petite maman*."

"Life's been so hard, son, with your father locked in that horrible place like a common criminal. It's affected his mind." She sniffed and gazed up at him earnestly. "He even talks to Jesus."

He had a swift moment of empathy for his father.

"Life is so sad and having money is never enough."

He helped her to the setee again, where she sniffed into a handkerchief. "I've more than four thousand *livres* in gold and silver. You can have it all, including the music box, of course, with my love."

He waited for her terms, which surely would come next. She didn't disappoint him. "But I ask that you sign a paper abjuring further rights."

"Of course, darling Mama." He could never hate her for being strong, for imparting that life-sustaining strength to himself.

She stood, straightening her skirts, and crossed to a desk, which she opened with a key on a chain around her neck. She extracted a bag heavy with coins. He could almost smell the gold in it. Then she dropped it into his lap and scribbled her contract on a piece of monogrammed paper.

He tested the weight and couldn't resist a peek inside at the sparkle there. This would be more than enough to pay Mansard. He barely glanced at the simple contract before signing it with the pen she handed him. She clicked her tongue disapprovingly when she saw his left-hand scrawl. He'd been trained to fight ambidextrously but had been hopelessly right-handed when it came to script.

"I suppose I'll get no letters from you still," she said with a trace of bitter humor. Then she did an unexpected thing. Standing behind him still seated on the setee, she bent and kissed him on the top of his head. He started to respond but she was already moving toward the door.

"Thank you," he said, meaning it with all his heart. She hesitated as if she would have said more, then walked from his view with her head held high.

He sat there in the anticlimax of gathering shadows as the aroma of soup drifted into the parlor to replace her exotic perfume with the common smells of leeks and basil. He rubbed his eyes, wondering if he'd seen the last of her. Presently he heard light footfalls approach.

"Monsieur Henri," the boy said tentatively. He offered the familiar small jasper box. "She says to give this to you."

A few slow notes trickled out, but de Tonti snapped the lid shut before the melody brought tears to his eyes. He put it and the canvas bag into his wide coat pockets.

"Are you really going to the New World?" the child asked.

"How did you know that?"

"We listened behind the doorway," he replied secretively, reaching toward the place where he'd been standing. "Me and my big brother." He pulled Alphy's hand, drawing the young man into de Tonti's view. All the years he'd spent as the adored big brother and this one as the droopy-drawers who tagged along, getting in the way of games, tattling on him to Isabelle—all this flooded between them. Alphy was dying to speak with him alone, de Tonti could tell. He would have begged to accompany de Tonti away from here if his own little tattletale brother were not listening. But de Tonti wished only to get as far away from this house as possible.

"Are you going back to war?" the little boy asked.

"I hope I'm through with war forever."

"Is that the way you lost your hand?"

"Henri!" Alphy said. It made de Tonti start, hearing his familiar but changed voice call his name. For the second time that afternoon he was awash with *déjà vu*.

"It's all right, Alph," de Tonti replied then nodded to the child.

"Does it hurt? May I see?"

"I must go now, but someday maybe I can tell you the story."

"Are you a hero?" the child persisted though Alphy clamped his hand on the lad's shoulder.

"No, just an ordinary man."

"Mama says you are and she says it's rude to ask questions about your hand."

"Henri—"

"It's all right, Alphy. You know how it is with snot-nosed little brothers." He opened the door.

"Alphonse, his name's Henri just like mine."

"So you're going to the New World," the middle brother said.

"Looks very likely."

"That's my dream, too."

De Tonti understood that a plea was coming. "Alphy, stay here and learn from mother. Save some money, get some experience, first."

"But you—"

"I am another case entirely. I made mistakes you can avoid."

"But you told her you liked the way you live. Are you just giving a little brother hypocritical advice?"

"Just give yourself a few more years under her wing. You can learn much from her."

"May I ask just one more thing," the child said, tugging on de Tonti's coat. "Am I supposed to know you?"

The innocent question wrenched him as he wouldn't have guessed. He realized he'd probably never see his brothers again. His own future in the wilderness of the New World was a long way from Versailles, where their futures lay.

"Perhaps you can explain it to him, someday," he said to the older boy.

Alphy squeezed his hand and said, "And after I get experience, save money, and all that, I'm going to join you."

De Tonti walked away with great relief. He didn't blame Alphy at all for wanting to get away from Isabelle's velvet prison either, although he was not prepared to be his brother's immediate keeper on an enterprise as uncertain as La Salle's. But he did wave back at his two brothers standing on the handsome marble steps of the fine brick home so close to Versailles, so far from the Bastille.

He went immediately to Mansard's forge. The doors were locked but the smith was still working on the wax model. He took measurements of de Tonti's arm, then showed him an idea about how to fit in the music box. "Monsieur wants the hand to be solid, yes? A movable thumb, as Monsieur de La Salle suggested, would defeat the purpose. But look." He unrolled a drawing that showed a ring band on the third metal finger. In a cutaway drawing de Tonti could see a square compartment in the fist. "The box will fit there," Mansard said proudly, removing the false bottom in the jasper box to get at the works. "It will fit perfectly!" He set the mechanism on the drawing.

"Brilliant," said de Tonti. "Give the box to your wife." He was glad Mansard had defense in mind over decoration.

"Thank you, sir," he replied, taking out another drawing. "See how the watch will fit into the palm with a lid to protect it. You can also remove it if necessary."

"We'll have to wait on Monsieur de La Salle for the watch."

"I suspect this is what we're waiting for." He produced a parcel wrapped in baker's paper. "There's a note for you."

While Mansard unwrapped the package, de Tonti read the note. "I regret," it began after a salutation, "that I have been unsuccessful in securing an interview between yourself and your father. The king himself forbids it. At least I was able to secure the watch which Mansard has. Be assured your esteemed parent forwarded the watch of his own will and wishes you great good fortune in our venture. All that remains now is to prepare for our royal audience scheduled for the third of May upcoming. I am off to La Rochelle in the meantime to purchase the rigging for the two vessels which you will build for our passage down the Mech-a-si-pi River, which I have decided to rename the Colbert in honor of the great Minister of Marine who has favored our project before His Majesty. I am also recruiting men-at-arms and workers for the expedition. I send my highest regards with my assurances that our fortunes are made as I am convinced our interview will be a success when we go before His Majesty, our most beloved sovereign, King Louis XIV of France. Signed, Cavelier."

De Tonti had the impression the letter had been composed for eyes other than his own. It was another unexpected sting to realize he would not be allowed to see his father. He looked up to see Mansard holding the gold watch in its inner wrapping of red cloth.

"*Mon Dieu*, monsieur, the engraving says this was a gift from the late Cardinal Mazarin."

"He and my father were friends long ago."

"Look here, the crystal's a magnifying glass," Mansard exclaimed, setting it on the drawing, which the lens gracefully distorted. De Tonti listened politely as Mansard explained details, how the hand would be etched with fingernails, how the fingers would be slightly separate so he could wear a glove. But the captain's mind wandered. He was numb with the realization he'd never see his father again. His eyes were dry and there remained a bitter taste in his throat. He bit his lip and listened to the smith's enthusiastic plans, then took some coins from the bag and handed them to him. Money was in short supply so Mansard took the silver *écus* hungrily.

"Tomorrow I cast."

"You're a true artist," de Tonti said as Mansard covered the wax hand with a white cloth. As the smith walked with him toward the door, de Tonti crumpled the note then threw it into the forge with a silent curse. It was the only expression of anger he'd ever allowed himself toward the monarch who'd behaved in so unkingly a manner toward his innocent father.

That grief was just another coal heaped upon his head. He hadn't recovered from what Isabelle had done. Intellectually he understood, even forgave, her because of her circumstances. But there still remained the emotional residue of being betrayed by someone he adored. He supposed he'd never get over those conflicted feelings for her—love and betrayal.

He aimed himself toward Les Halles district, where he planned to get very, very drunk and make something approaching love to as many women as he found willing—blondes, brunettes, redheads, any woman as long as she didn't have raven hair.

He vowed never again to give any kind of love to a woman with raven hair.

15

The little slingshot revolution broke more than a few windows. During one episode of *La Fronde* a Parisian mob forced its way into the royal palace demanding proof that their thirteen-year-old prince, now Louis XIV, was still in residence. No harm came to anyone in the royal household but the prince never forgave Paris for the terror he went through that night. One way to get even was for him to build a fairytale castle called Versailles out in a swamp far southwest of the city limits. The king was still fond of his vacation palaces, but Versailles was the permanent royal address by that May morning when La Salle and de Tonti arrived.

They came in a rented coach too early for their noon appointment, and spent the extra time in the already-famous garden in resplendent blossom. La Salle nursed the coals of his pipe until the two men were within earshot of no one but the king's roses. Between puffs to keep it going this far from flame, La Salle told his lieutenant of problems at La Rochelle. Customs regarded the masts, anchors, and lines stowed aboard the *St. Honore* as two more vessels even though they were not yet assembled.

And the Jesuits continued to vex La Salle's venture. "Even today the king is speaking with one of the good fathers before seeing us," he said.

"Surely they're not just miffed because you left their service."

"It's much more than jealousy at losing another slave." He looked suspiciously over his shoulder. "They hate me because I'm their main competitor in the fur business which has been their sole monopoly. You will stand with me now, my friend, so take great care at every turn." His nervousness made de Tonti edgy; he thought again about disclosing that he'd killed a man outside the café because he warned him away from La Salle.

Again the Canadian looked this way and that. Clearly nobody was within hearing, much less striking range. La Salle reported that there had been no more poison attempts. "But I tell you I fear eating at the king's own table, so close to the royal person are my enemies."

De Tonti didn't want to insult La Salle but he found this last suspicion hard to credit. The king was heir to generations of suspicious survivors. The families of all his chefs and other servants were virtual prisoners of the Court. Besides, de Tonti knew that surplus food from His Majesty's table was sold daily by the stewards, who would not allow any adulteration to interrupt their business. He did not express any of this, however, but politely suggested, "But your enemies will surely stay away from a man who has the king's support."

La Salle stopped walking on the noisy gravel and threw the younger man a look that stuck to him. "You have much to learn about our business." He took a deep breath on the pipe. "We get no money from His Majesty, Henri."

De Tonti was disappointed. He had supposed himself to be asking for a monetary award as he had done in the past. Those stipends had been rewards for meritorious military service over and above his salary as a marine captain stationed on Mediterranean assault galleys. He said as much to La Salle.

"We only ask the king's permission to open new lands for him. Make no mistake about it, Hal," he said, tapping de Tonti's chest with the pipestem, which had the acrid smell of having gone out. "He'll not spend a *sou* for our expedition even though it stands to enrich him with country ten times the size of France."

"Then what is our profit?" De Tonti found it annoying that the Canadian would use so Anglicized a nickname on him. Hal, he mused privately. Because it was an English name, La Salle's usage lent a slightly scandalous ring to his words. The Canadian was already *avant garde* at Court. To sling about the language of the erstwhile enemy, Protestant England, was flaunting his already unconventional reputation in the face of a Catholic Court. Likewise his tobacco habit glorified England since its New World colony of Virginia was prospering because of "the weed." La Salle was skirting treason. Yet de Tonti could see nothing to gain from this except self-indulgence on La Salle's part. De Tonti hoped La Salle would not publicly demonstrate his radical arrogance in the presence of the king or any of his "ears."

La Salle took a couple of futile drags on the pipe and continued his lecture: "We must earn our way with fur. My creditors own me down to the hair on my balls," he laughed sourly. "I had to mortgage my Canadian estate back to the monks who granted it to me. I owe everyone in New France and half the Mother country, but," he was quick to add, "we will make a fortune on buffalo fur alone, and who knows what mines of gold or silver we will find? Better than old Cartier's diamonds, right?" La Salle chuckled, referring to another Canadian explorer, who years before convinced himself he'd found a diamond mine and, to the delight of a malicious Court, had sent back a crate of quartz crystals as proof.

But La Salle couldn't lighten the disappointment of de Tonti, who had planned on more of a sure thing and less of a gamble. Undaunted by de Tonti's look of skepticism, La Salle continued, "We shall be granted huge provinces out of the lands we claim for Louis." La Salle looked around again, this time to gesture at the lovely palace the king was building for himself. La Salle no doubt imagined himself ensconced in such a New World manse. Now, at peace with Spain in Europe, His Majesty was turning his attention to the New World.

"This is our edge on the Jesuits, Hal. Even though they have his ear, and he grows more religious each day, he still has a practical eye. He knows there must be civil authority in New France." He slammed the pipe into his fist, scattering ashes on his cuff. "And our reward will be to be made lords—kings of our own domain."

De Tonti allowed a mirthless chuckle to escape his lips. How proud Isabelle would be to hear that, if she believed it at all. Despite the *de* on both sides of his family's name, which she used to remind him meant "of the land," he'd never held any real estate of his own. "I had no thought of owning any land."

"Well, think about it."

A light wind came up, smelling of the sea. De Tonti, leaning now with La Salle against a banistered wall, imagined himself on a gently rolling deck facing the spray. "It'll be good to be on the open ocean again."

"There's another small problem," La Salle added, almost as an aside. "A mysterious passenger booked way on our ship. I was told this passenger booked months ago and cannot be denied."

"Who?"

La Salle shrugged, glancing around again as though the roses might be sharpening their thorns against him. "I was told only that it's a member of the clergy."

"A spy?"

"Perhaps only a Recollect or Sulpician. I have no general enmity toward men of God. Only for that sect of fanatics who would destroy the human personality in the name of God."

"Then we'll have a chaplain."

He eyed de Tonti sideways. "Our most Catholic Majesty may have been soft on Protestants when he was fighting Catholic princes. Now he wants all his kingdom pure. He made it clear there will be no Jews or Protestants in my company."

De Tonti absorbed this in silence, idly kicking the yellow gravel at his feet. Frowning absentmindedly, he bent to pick up a pebble.

As though trying to lighten the conversation, La Salle

added, "Thank the Virgin you're only Italian instead of something worse."

The humor was lost on de Tonti, whose attention had been diverted by the stone in his fingers. There was something familiar about it. He sniffed it with an offhand chuckle at La Salle's attempt to joke about his ancestry. They strolled along the path toward a hedge labyrinth, quiet for a time, each man given to his own thoughts.

De Tonti was thrown into reverie; when he smelled the sulfuric rock he knew with certainty which Sicilian quarry it came from. This knowledge gave him a useless but clear insight. The gravel and other barter payments were part of the reparation between the two kings. That's why there had suddenly been a new gravel quota back on the prison island. The King of France needed more for his pathways here at Versailles, and the King of Spain, having conceded the war, was quick to make his payments. The irony of the mundane coincidence silenced de Tonti. He was glad La Salle, too, had fallen quiet.

The Canadian was burdened with private doubts behind his expressed optimism. He was morbidly afraid to approach Louis. The several other times he had been in the king's presence he felt himself an utter fool, base of manner and mean in appearance. The past week he'd driven several tailors to near collapse with his inconsistent, extravagant demands. Though few of the shopkeepers were aware of the cause of this difficult customer's contrariness, his tantrums were part of the gossip of Paris, thus adding to his already shady reputation. Privately, La Salle had nightmares about his lowliness before the king and had to seek spiritual advice for the coming ordeal. He'd told only one man about his anxiety, the abbe with whom he planned to correspond from the New World, a trusted old friend in the Church who would copy and edit his reports to the king. In his latest note to this confidant, La Salle confessed, "The fear of making mistakes makes me more reserved than I would like to be. So I rarely expose myself to conversation with those in whose company I'm afraid of making blunders."

He hinted at none of this to de Tonti. Part of the secret reason he'd encouraged the man to design the metal hand was to draw royal attention from himself and his feelings of inadequacy. It was with great relief that he saw de Tonti was wearing it with ease and skill. He was gloved, however, the fashion for such an audience.

De Tonti teased him when he asked to see how it worked. "No previews," he told La Salle, refusing to remove the glove even to show off the metalwork. His jibe was to hide his fear of hurting the Canadian's feelings about modifications in the design. Mansard used almost none of La Salle's impractical ideas. The switchblade no longer erupted awkwardly like a bayonet from a fragile finger. It popped out in place along the base of the fingers, where one would more naturally hold a knife. De Tonti had practiced with it until he was comfortable with the added weight both in everyday actions and also in the fight. Sparring with Sabat he had come to appreciate the hand's advantage in combat. De Tonti loved the watch in the palm. In a way his father was with him always. And he had become so adept at winding the ring with his left hand, Sabat complained about the incessant melody back in their garrison quarters.

La Salle was so pleased with de Tonti he forgave him his stubbornness. He prided himself on his choice of a second in command. The Italian looked every inch the gentleman in a well-tailored greatcoat of crushed velvet in deep Parisian blue. The effect with his coloration was stunning. The old black beaver-felt hat had been reblocked, and his curly hair was groomed in a stylish but understated masculine way that fit with current fashion without pandering to it.

It had been necessary a few days earlier for La Salle to track him down. First he'd gone to the garrison, where Sabat told him the captain was taking rest and recuperation in the traditional manner. Sabat had some other things to say but didn't speak his mind to this La Salle, whom he regarded with a jaundiced eye. To Sabat's mind this was a shaky venture. La Salle's personal fastidiousness and arrogant intensity put Sabat off. He had no regard for this dilettante, whom he'd heard had commanded only schoolboys and savages. He also sensed in the Canadian some unchristian mystery, perhaps learned from the heathens of the New World wilderness. Sabat's neck hair stood up in the man's presence. He always crossed himself thereafter when La Salle departed.

Sabat was prejudiced beyond La Salle's offense, too. Though often at sea, Sabat had never been out of land's sight. Despite de Tonti's explanation with a cannon ball, the old servant had grave doubts concerning the curvature of the Earth. But there was no doubt in his mind concerning La Salle's demonic possibilities. However, he knew it was too late to change his master's mind. Besides, hadn't Sabat once vowed he'd go with his master into hell if need be? So, he thought as he watched La Salle leave, it wasn't odd that this demon would lead them.

La Salle, who considered the task of rounding up help beneath himself and would have let L'Esperance do it if he hadn't sent him ahead to La Rochelle, didn't give a tinker's damn what the servant thought. He was out the door and headed toward the brothel, feeling not a little preturbed at de Tonti for running off for low pleasures.

"But, Robbie, it may be years before I see another white woman," the Italian had answered, ensconced on silk pillows and sheets with two plump girls, a redhead and a stately blonde. He and the ladies seemed well-disposed to having a visitor. De Tonti was half clad in a loose shirt, but the women were pear bare. "Come on and join us," de Tonti teased, "I think the blonde likes you." He was munching on a halved pear as he patted the silk sheets beside the blonde's nearest thigh when he saw the Canadian trying unsuccessfully not to look at her rosy nipples. They all three laughed though La Salle was unable to see any humorous point and had clearly been abashed when de Tonti offered again, "Come on, hop in."

La Salle declined with a blushing scowl. He had been distressed to find his second in command in such a disreputable place. But now, strolling in the brassy sunlight almost at meridian, La Salle congratulated himself on having chosen a fine-looking partner, whatever his private proclivities. Despite what La Salle considered an unfortunately lusty nature, he was sure this fellow was going to bring him luck. "You look the part of the landed *sieur*," La Salle commented, squinting up at the light. "The Sun King awaits."

Falling quiet again, they retraced their steps, each in his own manner preparing for what lay ahead.

They approached the person of the king through a long narrow hallway where a servant pushed brusquely past them with a heaped food tray. De Tonti quickly imitated La Salle, who was sweeping off his hat, bowing, saying loudly, "Salutations to the king's *bon appétit!*" Then by way of explanation he told de Tonti that this was a palace convention, to salute the king's meal.

"I thought it would all be more formal."

"If the ladies were present it would be. But these are just

some of the boys he asked over for luncheon." He understood
the machinations of Court better than many of its participants,
noblemen and women the king kept as pampered prisoners on
his whim. Occupied here in gambling away their fortunes and
trying to top each other spending money, their minds were
kept from more serious entertainments and their purses from
more seditious investments. The lessons of La Fronde had not
been forgotten by Louis XIV.

He was sitting at table dressed rather severely in gray and
black with no jewelry save the gold buckles on his shoes,
which could be seen below the tablecloth. His Majesty was
drinking from a crystal wineglass that held clear liquid. His
elaborate wig curls kept getting into his drink. He appeared
serenely unaware of the twenty or so guests, all male, who
occupied the wide sunlit room on the west side of the royal
apartments. The guests were sitting or standing, some eating,
some drinking, their throng punctuated here and there by
splendidly liveried servants bearing huge trays of food and
beverage. The servants were far more decoratively dressed,
like gaudy birds, than the assembled gentlemen, almost to a
man dressed in somber blues, browns, and grays. The king set
the fashion stage.

Remains of the royal meal were scattered before the king,
who was involved in what apparently was a light conversation
with a black-garbed Jesuit of middle age and inconspicuous
demeanor. Bearing witness to their discussion were the shells
of several boiled eggs, huge crusts of bread with the "soft" torn
out, and two other half-full goblets in different shades of red.
The priest finally departed, backing deferentially from the
salon.

La Salle threw de Tonti an ironic gaze; de Tonti was sorry to
see him so stiff and uncomfortable. It was obvious he
considered the priest an ill omen.

A valet led the two newcomers to a table not far from the
king's right. On the chessboard of tables he and his partner
were a knight and a castle. The chessboard effect was further
heightened by black and white tiles in the floor. There was no
change in the genteel buzz of several conversations in the
room, but de Tonti could feel eyes observing him. What had
they heard about him, the new man in the crazy Canadian's
search for the back door to China?

La Salle seemed less at ease under the same scrutiny. The
king was already engaged in another animated dialogue and

did not seem concerned that other guests had joined his company. It was a cheerful relaxed scene but La Salle hurriedly whispered that it was all engineered to appear thus, when in fact each audience and the procession of events was strictly designed by Colbert, the king's most trusted advisor.

"That's Colbert he's talking with now," La Salle informed de Tonti. A servant appeared at their elbows with lettuce soup, truffles, and dainty conical rolls. A steward brought a choice of wines.

The windows directly behind the king's table threw a calculated glow on the royal position. The ceiling was twice as high as in an ordinary drawing room, and the room echoed slightly despite grand tapestries on three walls. A magnificent hunting scene was painted on the ceiling, most likely a mythological incident involving Apollo. De Tonti didn't recognize the tableau but knew the entire palace had the theme of that Greek god associated with the sun. Louis had taken the solar emblem as his own several years ago. He loved being called the Sun King.

The food delighted de Tonti. He hadn't eaten, saving his appetite so he could enjoy what was his first and most likely last royal meal.

But La Salle was only drinking, and that slowly.

The king and Colbert were head to head. It gave de Tonti a thrill that there were matters of state under discussion. Colbert himself was nondescript, dressed well but with no flare. He looked exactly like a worried clerk, which of course he was though he sat a very high stool.

De Tonti tried to engage La Salle in conversation about the meal, but all he got for his trouble was a sour word. De Tonti hoped it wasn't a breach of Court etiquette for La Salle to spurn the king's meal. Without being obvious, from time to time he sampled a morsel from the Canadian's plate to make it appear he was eating.

The lamb was excellent. De Tonti considered La Salle's suspicions about poison unfounded and saw himself as a nursemaid to this grown but socially inept man, despite his noble pretensions. He supposed privately that this was his reward for daydreaming of some adventure that might mitigate reality. Maybe Isabelle was right, de Tonti thought, and I have finally found a way, through this strange person, to destroy myself.

La Salle stared too pointedly at the king. De Tonti remarked on the excellent seasoning of the sauce on the squab. La Salle muttered some indistinct reply.

"Try it," de Tonti urged, greatly relieved when La Salle withdrew the spear of his gaze, which would have insulted the meanest fishwife. He studied de Tonti eating as though this ritual disclosed some secret about him. "You're missing something very fine," de Tonti said, wiping his lips with a gold embroidered napkin.

How could the man so heartily wolf down these victuals without concern that His Majesty holding their combined destinies sat near enough to ask, please pass the salt? And him with that already famous metal appendage the entire assembly was just dying to see demonstrated. Besides, de Tonti looked quite fit, quite unpoisoned. La Salle mustered as much casualness as he could find within him and took up a fork. Very daintily he picked at the food on de Tonti's plate.

He grinned at La Salle's suspicions. "You think they're less likely to poison me, yes?"

La Salle gave him a wry look and ordered, "Hand me an apple there."

De Tonti removed his right glove and, with a magician's dexterity, secretly popped the stiletto blade. Deftly, as though he'd been performing the act all his life, he reached right-handed over where a platter of fruit was stationed and speared a big ripe apple. He sat down and began methodically to peel it.

La Salle watched the perfect strip of peeling unravel in an alternately red and yellow ribbon as neatly cut as a barrel band. De Tonti was obviously attempting to take it off in one unbroken piece. The right hand did not grip the knife; it protruded from the side of the palm in a way odd enough to excite the attention of several men who had heard of this marvel. By the time he had the apple half peeled he had a considerable audience. Yet there were others unaware of the minor drama to the king's immediate right and so they kept up the conversational buzz so that the performer was unaware he'd drawn attention. Intent on making it perfect, de Tonti sliced off the final south pole of the apple and gracefully tossed it into the air. The blade tip caught the naked fruit exactly on its equator.

He offered it to La Salle, happy to see pleasure on his master's face. So he was distracted when a voice spoke behind him.

"Monsieur?" Colbert said, startling de Tonti, who rose when he saw it was the Minister of Marine. Too late he became aware of the absolute silence in the room as the true master performer took center stage.

"Monsieur de Tonti," Colbert repeated.

De Tonti's movement knocked over his chair but La Salle saved the moment by catching it.

"May I present His Majesty, the King of France." Behind Colbert stood that famous dour face, which was smiling directly, one would have to say warmly at Henri de Tonti.

Later de Tonti would remember how familiar Louis had seemed, though he did not make the connection. It's true as a child he'd probably seen His Majesty when Louis was in his teens because de Tonti's parents orbited the Court throughout Louis' boyhood. The familiarity, however, went deeper than mere appearance and into manner and, ultimately, style.

"Monsieur Henri de Tonti, Sire," Colbert said in his flat, bored voice.

And of course, much later, after they had reached the shores of the New World so that the reality replaced the fantasy, de Tonti would realize exactly why the king of France had seemed so familiar.

De Tonti saw La Salle on the king's left looking less comfortable now than a spider in a jar. De Tonti remembered his instructions: he swept off the hat and bowed. All this time his mind was racing with alacrity. How much easier this seemed, meeting the sovereign, than meeting Isabelle. If he could pass her tests, he could pass any. As he went through the motions of paying homage, de Tonti couldn't help but remember that a little boy had found the king smelly.

He could not have known why everyone around them was so silent—that the king simply did not approach others, but in a fittingly royal manner was approached by others. One old courtier muttered he'd never seen such a breach of habit in His Majesty, who usually insisted on the staunchest protocol.

But since it was the king and his primary minister doing the breaking, none could take offense. But men who had known Louis for years, in fact, had grown up with him, had never been approached in so casual a manner as His Majesty reached out to de Tonti. It was not exactly a handshake; it was more a fatherly pat on a favorite son's shoulder.

La Salle was fairly beaming. He had calculated this, known that the king would see the young man's worth. Besides, the

Canadian loved to throw a wrench into clanking Court machinery but would never be able to accomplish such a daring public act himself. He could smell the Mech-a-si-pi Valley country fair with honey locust blossoms even though it was only a draft through the western windows behind the king's empty and quite ordinary chair.

As if on command, the sun dropped to just the right angle to mellow the proceedings even further as the king leaned to say something only de Tonti could hear. Some courtiers would have given their fortunes to have received such a gesture from Louis. De Tonti answered as though the king were merely an ordinary man, albeit his superior. La Salle had not dared hope it would go this well. He knew Louis was a soldier only on the gameboard of international politics and rarely took to the field, but His Majesty loved the flattery de Tonti innocently gave him. De Tonti's natural conversation was that of a young officer with a respected field commander. Men who fight together must always be comrades, no matter what gulf of station separates them.

"Yes," de Tonti answered in full voice. Everyone in the room could hear him yet his answer was not so loud as to be pretentious. The whispers of gossip surrounding his reply made it stand out. "It was my privilege to serve under Monsieur General Ronsain at the Battle of Messina."

"He has spoken highly of you, monsieur," Louis replied in his own slightly high-pitched voice.

"We felt it a shame, Your Majesty, that the battle was indecisive."

"Yes, well . . ." Louis' bottom lip drooped as he recalled his strategy in the Mediterranean, where he'd put his pawns and knights against the stronghold of King Philip's Sicilian castle. Though Louis might dabble in every art form, including dance, music, and drama, his true art was military politics. Though he may have forgotten the color of his wife's eyes, the king remembered in etching-clear detail each maneuver he'd taken against the madman on Spain's throne. ". . . That one was a draw."

De Tonti nodded. He was fascinated by the king's habit of letting his mouth drop open when he was thinking or listening. It gave His Majesty the unpleasant aspect of an idiot child. It occurred to him that if Isabelle had been this man's mother, she would have broken Louis of the habit or killed him in the process.

"It's a heavy responsibility having the lives of brave men on one's conscience," the king replied candidly. "But one compensation is to reward the splendid quality of Frenchmen who act out the terrible game I must play for France."

One senior courtier reported later that this was the first time in public he'd heard the king use the first person singular. Louis turned slightly to include today's petitioner: "We congratulate you, Monsieur Cavelier de La Salle on your judgment of men."

The Canadian gave precisely the perfect bow.

"I trust you gentlemen have enjoyed my little meal?"

"The sauce on the squab was excellent," de Tonti replied.

"And the apples, sir, how did you find the apples?"

"Picked at the perfect moment of ripeness and gallied, I daresay, from the Neapolitan valley made famous by those apples."

"Beautiful country, Naples."

"Yes, sir."

"Would you be so kind as to peel one of them for us, monsieur?" the king requested, watching like a child enraptured by jugglers as de Tonti began his apple-peeling act again, creating another red and white strip. The whole room breathlessly observed, from the noblemen and the hushed servants to, it seemed, the very demigods on the walls.

Casually, as de Tonti carved, Louis said to La Salle, "So, my dear 'Chinese' person, tell us this plan of yours." De Tonti, confident at his task, caught the look of mingled anger and terror on La Salle's face as the king slapped him on the back like a crony.

"Come walking with us, you and your dexterous young friend here, and explain how you design to reach California on this Mex-aux-sip River of yours." Louis turned his back on Colbert to offer this invitation. To de Tonti or just about anyone else it was obvious the king was merely being friendly, elevating a former insult to a royal salute. The compliment was lost on La Salle, however, who was mortified that the king had referred to him as a Chinese. If it had been anyone less, the Canadian would have brought it to a duel.

"Begging His Majesty's pardon," he replied with a tight lip, "but this humble servant of the king believes that it's not into the Gulf of California that the great Mech-a-si-pi, now called the River Colbert, empties." He gave a small nod to the Minister of Marine, who coolly acknowledged it.

"It is my humble opinion," La Salle continued, "that the river empties into the Gulf of Mexico."

Probably only de Tonti, still at the apple, detected that La Salle's voice quavered. The Canadian's words got Louis' attention, although only briefly from the apple—could de Tonti peel a second one without breaking the strip?

Part of the pleasure the opposition took from La Salle was the implication that he could reach China from the New World. But Mexico, that was something else. China was little more than a myth but Mexico was the seat of New World Spain, treasure of silver mines and Aztec gold. Mexico was the prize old King Philip clung to, was so protective of. Even though France and Spain were at peace, the Gulf was off limits to any but Spanish vessels. Any others caught in those waters would be confiscated, and any seamen aboard would be hanged without benefit of confession or tribunal. Louis couldn't resist such a challenge. So as the young officer handed him the peeled apple, the king took up a stroll, moving toward the west, where servants hurried like a silk broom before him to whisk open the windowed doors.

"And perhaps when we return we can have some music?" Louis said, not without irritation, in Colbert's general direction. Colbert made the merest of gestures that acceded to the king's desire, and spoke quietly to the majordomo, who nodded his head defensively. Louis preferred to eat to the accompaniment of his musicians; some of the gossip among the nobles just prior to de Tonti's arrival had concerned where they were this afternoon. Their instruments stood beside the waiting empty chairs in the nook painted with appropriate Greek muses. But so far this luncheon, the instruments had remained untouched; the clatter of silver against china had not been softened by the strains of mandolin and flute.

De Tonti and La Salle were now on either side of Louis. Behind trailed Colbert, a little stooped, preoccupied with problems of his own, not the least of which was the royal musicians, who were all but out on strike. They'd been performing here at Versailles away from their families in Paris for months without a break.

Behind these four in spaced ranks trailed the nobles carrying last fragments of squab, cheese, or apple. Some continued quaffing wine. Servants orbited all with trays.

The somber-colored line punctuated by gaudy servants and glinting silver service slowly gained the private gardens that

warm afternoon. Someone standing on a palace roof would
have seen the thin dark ribbon thread out through the cool
willows that crowned the swan lake; then through the royal
forest, restored at great expense to look like natural growth
down to the two-hundred-year-old giant oak trees and verified
to be haunted by Druid ghosts. The snaillike ribbon found its
way through the royal aviary and zoo; but most of the beasts
were snoozing in their cool lairs away from the heat.

The procession lost momentum at the crest of a gentle rise,
where the king and therefore all assembled paused to marvel
at the work in progress on the palace down below. At present
the Hall of Mirrors was under construction. On the far side of
the compound was a staggered line of waiting teams and
wagons festooned with heavy burlap. Every now and then a
flash of mirror would echo blindingly up to the observers on
the hill and someone would exclaim that certainly there was
the world's largest or most perfect or most ornate looking glass
going into the palace.

Yet through all this, every moving ear strained to hear what
the king was saying to La Salle. Not a few small fortunes were
being wagered. The king could go either way on this Mech-a-
si-pi venture. Everyone knew he and Colbert wanted to
solidify the gains made in New France and develop the rest of
France's American holdings slowly without competing with
Canada. But everyone also knew that France was land-hungry.
Having achieved his military dreams His Majesty now wanted
to challenge the other European kingdoms on the commercial
and colonial front. The Spanish, Dutch, and English were
already ahead of France in this game of colonial expansion.
France could not, for glory's sake, lag behind.

His Majesty continued to direct questions between La Salle
and de Tonti as he once again took up his path among the
blossoming vegetation that led back to the dining salon. He
continued to question La Salle about specific points having to
do with the proximity of the Mech-a-si-pi, or Colbert River, to
the regions of New Spain in Mexico. For a time, he and La
Salle were several paces beyond the rest of the procession,
deep in conversation, full of much royal gesticulation.

When they returned, the dishes had been cleared but there
was only a single flutist to entertain. The king barely restrained
his fury. He and Colbert had a sharp private discussion in
which Colbert was seen to shake his head several times and
His Majesty to stamp his foot at least once.

"Well, by God, if the King of France cannot have his dinner

settled by a pleasant tune, what's the world coming to?" he was heard to say.

De Tonti caught La Salle's eye; the Canadian looked much better disposed than when they had first entered this room. De Tonti wound the ring of the music box so that presently the echoing chamber resounded with the fragile notes of *La Pomme Rosace*. The king turned toward the music, obviously in midsentence to his minister of marine. A smile cracked his face; he recognized the tune but not from where it was coming. He walked toward the source with the delight of a little boy hunting Easter eggs, grinning from ear to ear. De Tonti held out his hand. The tune ended, and before it began to replay, Louis motioned with a snap of his fingers to a valet to bring him one of the mandolins leaning against an absent musician's chair. The valet scurried to comply, receiving the instrument from two others who acted in relay.

Thereupon the king began to accompany Henri de Tonti's hand in the ancient little song. The king, who in his youth had been known to sing love songs while playing guitar in his bathtub, had a passable voice that carried the tune well. Before long they were joined by others who knew the many verses of *La Pomme Rosace*, some of which tended toward the bawdy.

It was a long time before Louis grew tired of the music box, of explanations of how it came to be embedded in the soldier's hand. He asked more questions and expected detailed answers. He did not, however, exhaust La Salle's store of information on the New World and its waiting riches. Finally, it was time for His Majesty to attend some state matter, of which Colbert reminded him twice before the king would be drawn away. He tossed a general farewell to the assembly, which mildly applauded him. Then he turned to La Salle and said, "Well, sir, we shall see."

La Salle bowed again.

"Give us some time to think about what you propose. And thank you, Monsieur de Tonti, for bringing a measure of joy to your monarch, who thought before today that he had seen everything."

De Tonti returned the king's smile, which faded suddenly as he leaned closer to the young man. "Be careful of one thing should your destiny take you to barbarous places," Louis warned in a dire voice.

"Sire?" de Tonti was almost thrown off guard by this aside;

he'd been ready to bow and was now standing there holding his hat, suddenly self-conscious for the first time since the king had caught him apple peeling. He watched the king's face close to his own and noticed it was drawn in downward lines.

"Beware the savage call," he admonished in an eerie voice, and with a sweep of his hand, indicated the wild mythological events surrounding them on the tapestries and painted on the ceiling.

"Yes, sir," de Tonti replied, wondering if he had heard correctly. What did the king say, the savage call?

"The holy fathers tell me it's an awful thing to witness, a good Frenchman going savage."

De Tonti nodded; at least he had heard right, but what did the king mean?

"They say it happens to certain men hitherto constrained by civilization to be drawn into the savage way of life rather than convert the savage to civilization. At the cost of their souls, of course."

"Yes, Your Majesty."

The king leaned even closer to de Tonti, who could smell the boiled eggs on the royal breath: "We've lost sleep worrying about that."

Not knowing quite how to answer, de Tonti placed a low bow before his sovereign that perfectly imitated La Salle's. When he stood again, the king was gone.

16

"Louis, by the grace of God King of France and Navarre, to our dearly beloved Robert Cavelier, Sieur de La Salle, greeting," opened the document La Salle unrolled less than a week later. "We have received favorably the humble petition made us in your name, to permit you to labor at the discovery of the western parts of New France."

Within three hours of its receipt the explorer had removed himself and all his belongings from Paris. The next day de Tonti and Sabat followed in a public coach over the highroad southward across the wide flatlands toward France's western coast. It was an unremarkable journey that brought them on the second evening to La Rochelle's docks. Their luggage was light since most of their belongings had been sent ahead and were already aboard the ship.

The coach rattled away. Stretching, Sabat strolled toward the quay, where a man was cleaning a mess of fish beside a launch that bumped leisurely against the wet stones. Sabat haggled with the ferryman to take them to the 200-ton *St. Honore*, which loomed with its skeleton of naked rigging out in the bemisted harbor. The brigantine was by far the largest ship anchored against the low blue silhouette of Ile de Rea off to the northwest. On the left was the Bay of Biscay topped by the point of St. Denis, where the crawling fog crept in from the Atlantic.

Suddenly the sound of two men's voices pitched in violent argument burst with a water echo from the direction of the silhouetted *St. Honore*. One of them was La Salle's, flatly adamant while the other was higher with emotion.

De Tonti and Sabat exchanged a glance. The servant pulled out some coins demanded by the ferryman and without a word began loading his and de Tonti's luggage into the boat.

"It's dinner time," replied the ferryman, about forty-five, leathered to the neck by the sun, his eyes slit in a permanent squint. During his quibble with Sabat he hadn't missed a stroke in cleaning the fish.

A new burst of dialogue erupted between La Salle and his adversary. Then, after the sounds of wood striking wood echoed by water, silence.

Sabat started to reply but was halted by the quick report of a gunshot from the ship. De Tonti began tossing luggage into the boat.

"Here, now—" said the ferryman as he stood, the scaling knife still in his hand. He was a burly fellow with thick overdeveloped shoulders and arms, a thin waist, and scrawny legs—a powerful physique that told of a lifetime of rowing. Some of the creases in his face were scars. "I'll have my dinner first, gentlemen," he snarled, getting a different grip on the scaler.

Sabat behind his master was climbing into the dinghy.

The ferryman advanced. De Tonti stood between him and his boat, legs planted, hands out. He had not made to draw his weapons but he had removed the pigskin glove from his right hand. "This can be a friendly business proposition or not. As you wish, boatman."

The ferryman was a bigger man than de Tonti. On his face

was the sign of glee in taking on these two just to break his
boredom. He slashed with the fish scaler, noticing that de
Tonti's right hand was slightly forward. The scaler pinged off
the brass, reverberating back up through the scaler, and into
the ferryman's hand. His features betrayed surprise. When he
took a closer look at de Tonti's hand, he saw the glinting blade
spring into view. He jumped back, giving himself barely
enough room to miss de Tonti's lazy sweep that could have
disemboweled him. The ferryman danced backward, throwing
his hands out, discarding the fish scaler, which clattered to the
flagstones.

De Tonti accepted the surrender with a nod. The ferryman
tossed his fish beside Sabat. He bent to pick up the scaler with
de Tonti watching, put the knife in his belt, and stepped into
the boat.

"Lean on it, man," de Tonti ordered, casting his glance
toward the ship. New sounds of argument floated across the
water, but there was no other gunshot.

The ferryman took up the oars. Presently they were moving
toward the ship at a reasonable clip, though the ferryman was
grumbling below his breath. He muttered something about
"crazy warts, causing trouble . . . going to New
World . . ." while Sabat watched him.

De Tonti's attention was on the ship. The mist dulled
fragments of angry phrases coming from her decks:

". . . demand immediate . . ."
". . . according to our agreement . . ."
". . . warn you, sir . . ."

God only knew what trouble La Salle had gotten himself
into, de Tonti reflected. His stomach rumbled; they had not
eaten since before noon. How pleasant it would have been to
stop in a tavern for the night before boarding in the morning.
They were close enough to the *St. Honore* for him to see two
men at the railing face to face screaming at each other. Several
men, some with belaying pins clutched in their fists, stood
behind each of the two debaters. La Salle held command only
because he held a flintlock on the other, a robust, rotund fellow
whose bearing indicated he was the unfortunate captain of the
vessel. La Salle motioned with the pistol toward the landing
skiff bobbing like a chick beside the fat mother ship.

"Under protest, sir," steamed the captain.

The Canadian gestured again with the gun.

"When I chartered this wreck it was specifically the ship and crew plus a pilot. I was guaranteed that I could act as captain, otherwise I would have used another company," La Salle replied, urging on the departing officer. He was followed by three of his staff officers, who tossed aside their hastily grabbed weapons. When the captain and his four men were aboard the skiff, La Salle whipped out his saber and cut the line.

"You will regret this act of piracy, monsieur," yelled the captain with a shake of his fist. His lowest-ranking officers had taken up the oars and were pulling them toward the dock. They approached and passed de Tonti's commandeered boat. The *St. Honore's* erstwhile commander called a warning to him now only a few oar pulls from the great ship. "Beware, sir," called the captain, "you are boarding with a madman!"

"Hal, is that you, my friend?" called La Salle, leaning over the rail.

"Permission to come aboard, sir," de Tonti replied sarcastically. But La Salle missed the tease.

"Permission granted," he called back, putting away the pistol. He said something to a man he called La Forest, who in turn dismissed the others. They drifted away but watched from the sidelines as La Salle greeted de Tonti stepping from the boarding ladder. "Nobody I'd rather see, I'll tell you," La Salle said warmly. He clapped de Tonti on the back. "I have brandy below—come and let me bring you up to date on our situation. . . ."

Which turned out not to be so bad after all. The good news was that they were within days of sailing. The bad news was that La Forest, whom La Salle had made recruiting officer, had been unable to fill their quota of thirty carpenters, wheelwrights, mechanics, etc., who would also be citizen-soldiers under de Tonti's military command through La Forest as second in command.

La Salle had signed on only seven men. So it fell to de Tonti and La Forest to return to shore in the morning to sign on some more members of their ragtag army. Although many had not yet reported, the ship's complement was complete, save for the pilot. La Salle was confident he would report that afternoon. Instead the owner of the ship paid him a call. It was later reported that there was another violent argument in the captain's quarters, which La Salle had appropriated.

He insisted on the terms as he understood them. The shipowner insisted that Monsieur was mistaken and that under no circumstances could a ship be taken out by one of the passengers even if he did own the king's ear.

La Salle was afraid he'd have to send word to Colbert to get him out of this mess. But the shipowner, a former captain himself, agreed at the eleventh hour to permit La Salle the dual captainship along with one of his pilots, who would have charge of the mariners and the actual disposition of the ship. This agreement was sealed with further monies and a note on La Salle's first year of revenue from buffalo hides. When the owner left, mellowed with fine brandy and the warm contract in the coat pocket closest to his heart, he was smiling. All this transpired in de Tonti's absence that first day. Over the next week he and La Forest found another twenty-two men to fill out the company. La Salle was worried about the caliber of persons they hired—tavern pillars and idlers for the most part. Some of the recruits had seen military service; most had seen the insides of too many jails. All were unschooled except for their tasks and had borne enough abuse to make them mean and desperate. The ferryman who reluctantly took them across that first night was among the band.

But whatever their evil reputations the men were all strong, with that hardiness born of desperation that could endure much if wisely directed. De Tonti interviewed each man, memorized his name and his hometown. There were several nationalities, French, German, and three Italians. One afternoon a couple of days before departure, a huge shadow fell over his company manifest spread out on a tavern table. De Tonti looked up to see a familiar smile.

"Once again, Señor, I ask to accompany you." It was De Arcos, the Corsican who had shared de Tonti's escape adventure. He rose and hugged De Arcos with genuine elation and offered him a tankard. The shy muscular young man grinned acceptance of the invitation and explained how he'd been freed along with all the other prisoners a week after de Tonti and Sabat had been ransomed. He had traced the captain through mutual acquaintances and was here to join the expedition. "Your talk of the New World saved my life," he said, clutching his hat. De Tonti looked around to see if La Salle was nearby. When he saw they were alone, he advised the Corsican to change his name.

He looked offended. De Tonti was quick to add the reason. "Our charter is strict on nationalities, my friend."

"But my war record for France is impeccable."

"Monsieur De Arcos," de Tonti whispered knowingly, "my family are Italian bankers—"

The Corsican's face paled by three shades. "Yes, Monsieur," de Tonti continued. "I know that you are not Spanish Corsican as you claimed to be."

De Arcos dropped his eyes. "Then you know."

"I only know that a Jew of the Venetian merchant clan, Arcan, has even less chance than a Spanish Corsican of signing aboard this expedition."

De Arcos shot him a pained proud glance.

"But," the captain was quick to add, "a French Corsican named D'Arcy, who served under my command, is already on our books." As he spoke, his handsome mouth curved in a wry smile and his eyes dropped to his left hand, which was writing in that name on the company roster. So Michelle D'Arcy completed the complement.

July 13, the day before the planned departure, a final wrinkle developed. De Tonti was standing at the rail, staring toward the far western horizon and feeling peaceful and ready for whatever lay ahead. Behind him the sailmaster's hands were working on a spread of canvas on the deck. A freshening breeze promised good weather. The mighty, deeply laden ship rocked serenely on the harbor waters; gulls punctuated the sky.

He heard one of the mariners behind him bark an exclamation but thought nothing of it until another remarked with a low whistle, "Look what we have here—"

The other sailors commented in tones of astonishment on what the first had seen. Their chuckles drew de Tonti's attention. He pushed away from the starboard rail and ambled over to the knot of men gathered at the other rail watching someone approach the ship. They were silent now, having spent their wonder. De Tonti looked past them, narrowed his eyes in disbelief, and joined their silence.

A skiff drew near, rowed by an apprentice ferryman who had trouble getting his craft alongside. His passengers were looking toward the St. Honore over their shoulders; the breeze slapped their faces, wide-eyed and female, and snapped the starched wings of their wimples. Five black-clad nuns bobbed under the boarding ladder, unsteady even while seated and threatening by their uncoordinated motions to upset the skiff. Nestled among the sisters were three little girls of eight or nine years, each in an identical navy blue traveling cloak that looked like a uniform. Finally one of the sisters took charge by ordering the others to be still as she engaged the ladder and pulled herself up with her great belled skirt flying.

The seamen instinctively stepped back. A couple whisked off their woven wool caps. One even crossed himself but another swore under his breath. Bad luck, having females aboard.

De Tonti recalled that La Salle had told him passage had been booked for a member of the clergy. No doubt he interpreted that to mean a missionary priest. What would he say to three orphans and five Capuchin sisters?

Not very much, it turned out. De Tonti entered the slightly open door of the captain's cabin after knocking. La Salle stood in the middle of a pile of cartons and barrels he'd been unpacking. Rolled maps and his sextant were already out on a large table. "Nuns?" he asked as though he hadn't heard from inside the barrel he was rummaging through. He straightened, holding a wad of excelsior.

"Five of them. And three children. Their superior, Madame Ormonde, wishes to speak with you."

La Salle shrugged approval and continued rummaging through the barrel. His search for a specific object was upper-most in his mind. De Tonti left him at it.

"Right through there," he directed the leader of the nuns. She was a stiff-faced woman in her early forties. She had married a widower to help him raise his small children. It was said they never lived together as man and wife because of the lady's piety. Upon his death she took up the cloth and was the foundress of a school for Iroquois girls in Quebec. She gave off very little personality on this first meeting, but de Tonti was put off by Madame Ormonde's manner. He'd always considered it a waste for women to thus employ themselves. It distressed him to have seen two beautiful young women among the clutch of nuns. And those little girls; they'd never have a chance to escape the Church's grasp on virgins. But he was polite, having removed his hat in this woman's presence. He held it now as he stepped aside to let her pass into La Salle's cabin. The hatch closed.

De Tonti didn't know what to expect. He waited in the officer's wardroom with La Forest to see what would happen.

"He'll be wise to put those ladies in the skiff and take the next tide out," said La Forest. De Tonti had grown to know the man in the past few days. La Forest was his first encounter with a *coureur de bois,* or "runner of the wood," that particular breed of men the French Canadian venture produced. They were generally lawless, high-spirited, highly competitive in

the gathering of furs, and often enamored of savage ways. La
Salle had known him in his own early days among the
Canadian Iroquois. De Tonti liked La Forest and instinctively
sensed that this man could teach him what he needed to
survive the New World wilderness.

"Legally he can't deny them passage."

La Forest chuckled cynically. He was wilderness-thin, a
sharp-featured fellow of about forty, as leathery as his strange
fringed clothing with a once handsome face that retained some
of civilization's restraint but was pitted with the round scars of
smallpox. This gave him a wild look; de Tonti couldn't help but
recall the king's admonition. Was La Forest the product of the
"savage call"?

The pilot, an amiable fellow in his midthirties named Gabin,
joined them. "The men are divided," he offered without being
asked. "Some like it, some don't."

"She's still in there with him," de Tonti observed.

"The other ladies are reading Scripture up on the poop,"
Gabin said as he unrolled a small chart of the harbor. "An' over
on the wharf is a pile of their luggage, boxes, barrels, and
crates. I'll wager Master La Salle will have us sleeping two to a
hammock." He shook his head. "The men won't like it."

As Gabin thus gossiped, he continued poring over his chart.
De Tonti and La Forest watched him trace a channel with his
stubby finger. He'd apprenticed in this bay and knew every
twist and turn getting out of it. He remarked that the strait by
St. Denis was tricky; but if the weather held out, there was no
reason why they couldn't take the tide out on the morrow.

17

De Tonti stood at the prow of the ship thinking of making
love with that marvelous whore. He couldn't remember her
name but he'd never forget the way she had moved beneath
him. Something like this magnificent ship trembling against
him now. The movement of the ship through the waves did
that to him out here on the forwardmost point of their
advance. Like twin needles thrusting them into the foam, the
extra mainmasts for their two unbuilt ships pointed their
course. They'd been lashed to the prow. He stood with one of

the great logs at his right, the rail just at his belt. A baluster curved into his groin to rub against his sex with each high-headed thrust of the ship through the waves. Nothing lascivious was on his mind; just good, healthy swiving.

The spray filmed his beard. His eye was caught by the sparkle of a fin too rounded to be a shark's. Probably a dolphin. Gabin must have taken them on a more southerly course than he had anticipated.

He leaned idly forward tasting the sea, feeling liberated as the mean smudge of Europe diminished on the horizon behind them. He felt so good his sex stirred. He pressed even closer to the balustrade, letting the ship caress him, when suddenly from behind a woman's soft voice startled him out of his fantasy.

"Monsieur de Tonti?"

He twisted his shoulders toward the voice, so unusual a sound aboard a ship. But he kept his hips against the railing, where the vibration of the sea up through keel and beam, deck and rail awakened his erection. It was diminished in a blink when he saw Madame Ormonde approaching him in a shadow of black serge, her gray eyes observing him below the crisp white beak of her wimple.

"Do I interrupt a prayer, perhaps?" There appeared to be no guile in her. Her voice was nobly softened, almost demure, but that couldn't hide this woman's strength. It was merely part of her self-discipline. Her slate-colored eyes fairly brimmed with piety as if she had obtained her forty-odd years of spiritual development by squeezing all sensual thoughts down to the hard silver spots of her asexual eyes.

"Madame," he replied noncommittally, not lying but not informing her of his privacy. But some small squealing part of him cringed at being caught in the act of sereptitiously having carnal knowledge of a 200-ton brigantine.

Almost without exception this man liked women, preferring their company generally to that of men. But he instinctively drew away from this one. He saw she was aware of his reaction. It shocked her but only for a flutter. In that fleeting moment he saw her burnt-to-ashes eyes flare with a coal of emotion, not sex, not attraction, but fury that he would dare spurn her and thus spurn her immaculate piety, nay, even the Church itself if he dared to spurn this beloved daughter.

All this flashed in a glance. De Tonti wasn't sure a second later that he'd seen so unbridled an emotion in the stern nun because her eyes changed again, veiled by piety and a reserve of forgiveness she maintained for just such moments with unremitting sinners. These two were the exact antithesis of each other. But they were also the twin products of a civility that insisted on a show of politeness.

De Tonti wondered what the hell she wanted. She wondered what hell was in him, what thoughts had so engrossed him that she had had to speak three times before he had taken notice, and then with a vacant look that turned quickly to the scowl he still wore. She pitied this man lost within a soldier's many sins, then chided herself for committing the sin of hubris, spiritual pride. She cranked her soul's wheel a notch or two while continuing to speak with him, of course, and silently set herself a penance of fifty Hail Marys for pride. She'd even say them in this wretched sinner's name. God knew, every little prayer helped. She could tell by the arrogant scowl on his face that he was hardened. The set of his hip told her too much. His golden eyes were unnerving, too much like an animal's.

"I see you love the ocean as much as I do," she said modestly, joining his angle at the rail. He saw her lean slightly into the bath of the spray, but without losing her rigid demeanor.

"We are blessed with a good sea," he replied, facing the water again, watching her from the corner of his eye. She tilted her head up, smelling the spray, straining the stiff white material of her wimple. He observed that she had a well-arched neck. Her hands on the rail were frail, thin-skinned, freckled, and laced with blue lines that marked a woman's passage into age. But her hands bore no trace of callouses. These hands had been used only at the labor of prayer. Years ago Madame Ormonde had taught herself to recite prayers in her head while engaged in other activities, even conversations. Rather than diminish her clarity, this practice seemed to make her sharper. "Mother of God . . . Mother of God . . . Mother of God . . ." she silently chanted now, a metronome inside her skull. But she said, "This is your first visit to New France, I believe?"

"Yes, ma'am."

They chatted like this for a time until she complained of the damp spray and excused herself without bringing up any request. He puzzled very briefly about what might have brought her to interrupt his thoughts. But the rocking of the ship called him back again.

Madame Ormonde departed with satisfaction. There was a concern on her mind about the proximity of her party's quarters to Captain de Tonti's own. Her intention was to find out if she should worry. She was confirmed in her suspicion that passion ran deep in the man and he was not to be trusted within an *arpent* of a young female. For the nonce the cabin arrangements would have to suffice but she must remain on guard every moment lest Satan employ this young man in some evil design upon her charges. He did, however, seem to be a gentleman. She reminded herself that hell would be paved with the charred souls of many gentlemen.

There was very little for de Tonti to do aboard the *St. Honore*. Once a day he inspected his "troops," as La Salle referred to the company of ne'er-do-wells, pickpockets, tax dodgers, and pig thieves La Forest was shaping into a military company. But La Salle, having rigid ideas about military discipline, had strictly forbidden him to have anything to do with the day-to-day training of these men, whom La Forest practiced at drill twice a day on deck.

The women had their hymns and vestment embroidery, the crew their stations, La Salle his plans, La Forest his recruit tormenting, and the recruits their musketry and march. Even his own servant served as La Forest's sergeant since Sabat was the most experienced of the recruits. In this way La Salle paid the servant's passage, which otherwise would have fallen on de Tonti. So while everyone aboard had occupations, de Tonti alone was idle. He'd be busy enough when they landed. His first task would be to supervise construction of the *Griffin*, the ship they planned to use on their descent of the Mech-a-si-pi. But he couldn't start that task until they reached Fort Niagara, where La Salle planned to build the little ship. To take up the slack and to keep from going mad with boredom, de Tonti designed a model of the three-masted barque. When he mentioned the idea of building the model, the explorer was delighted and ordered his lieutenant to begin without delay. De Tonti scavenged scraps of wood from the carpenters' bench, resin and pitch from the sailmaster, unraveled a mateless stocking for string, and confiscated several of La Salle's silk handkerchiefs for sail material.

By the tenth day out under a benign sky and before a snapping breeze that promised an uneventful crossing, he had the skeleton of the model ship assembled. His cabin was so small there was barely enough room to turn around. Like all the sailors aboard, he used a hammock, an ingenious device of knotted ropes borrowed from the Cuban Indians. He'd always wanted to use one of the things and had made it a point to have one on this trip. With his bed hung to one side he had just enough room for a makeshift table under one tiny port, half of which was obscured by the beams of a partition hastily thrown up to provide a cabin for Madame Ormonde's use. There, using a discarded barrel as a chair he toiled for hours happily oblivious of all other events aboard the *St. Honore*. In the close quarters of this closet with no perspective except a scrap of sky through the halved porthole, the miniature ship under his hands became a full-fledged *Griffin*, forty-five-ton berthen, proud and finely plowing the imaginary waters of the lake La Salle reported was as large as a sea.

Making the model improved his use of the knife embedded in the hand. He grew adept at extremely fine work, slicing minute strips of wood for the ribs and planking. He was so proud of his work he'd sit back for long minutes at a time just looking at it. Late the morning of the twelfth day, he was intensely at work. He had completed the ribbing of the barque and was working on the prow La Salle wanted built high to protect against arrow attack. He had not yet affixed the two masts to the keel but had cut and paid the ship's carpenter to turn them. A third would point out at an angle aft somewhat like the long lateen sails of the Mediterranean galleys he'd served on as marine captain during the recent wars. Now he was working on the scalloped straking that would armor the prow.

Up on the main deck he could hear Madame Ormonde's nuns sculpting a hymn from the wind. Sister Beatrix was at the wheezing little portable organ, which kept the ladies fairly in tune. The wind threw the holy melody about, too far away from him to hear the words they sang. Beatrix was the sloe-eyed youngest of Ormonde's ladies. She had the most beautiful cheekbones he'd seen in many a day, but she did not have eyes for him. She, like a newer edition of her superior, was sincerely pious. On her it was a sweet sad veil where it had hardened on Ormonde into a mortared wall. The tune the young sister played was an old familiar one, pleasant accompaniment to de Tonti's labors. He decided to work on the sculpture of the griffin, the fierce mythological animal with the wings and head of an eagle and a lion's body on the coat of arms of Count Frontenac, governor of New France. La Salle had chosen the creature as the insignia for his expedition vessel. He had bragged before their departure from Paris that he'd make the *Griffin* fly above the crows, referring to the black-robed Jesuits whom he planned to best at the fur-trading business. De Tonti grinned. His little wooden beastie that would ride the stern of the model grinned back maliciously from his hands. He leaned against the near bulkhead to appraise his work.

The sea was rising. The familiar creak and groan of the larger vessel around him, the nodding line of the horizon through the open port, and the tasty smell of salt spray all added to the illusion that his little model was in fact the real vessel he'd soon build on the Niagara River.

"You will fly proudly, little bird," he said to the carving. He observed the model for a few moments before he reached for the figure to refine its evil features when he heard a less familiar noise from somewhere nearby.

It sounded like a human cry. De Tonti paused, the carving in his hand, listening. He opened his mouth slightly to hear better but the strange cry was not repeated. Up on deck the ladies had changed songs. Now they sang a fierce old hymn accompanied by the organ and a sailor's accordion. But de Tonti paid it no attention as he listened for the arresting noise that had seemed nearby but muffled. He looked around blinking as his attention was drawn from the fantasy of the model to the reality of the suffocatingly small cabin. Probably just the wind in the spars, he thought, or a sour note from the windy musical instrument. He turned again to the beastie, popping the blade in his palm, and meticulously went about the task of coaxing an even more maleficent grin from the griffin's wooden lips.

The moaning sounded again. This time it was louder, apparently coming from the direction of the adjoining cabin, the one sectioned off from his own. He'd been led to believe there was nothing in that compartment but teaching supplies. In fact he had seen that it had no entrance, no true door. It was closed off behind crates of books, French primers for the savage maidens, and was entered from the main hold only by sliding a panel to one side.

There was another moan accompanied by a scraping sound and a muffled little cry that went on and on then trailed off, lost in the surge of the waves.

In the last few minutes the sea had grown, the waves spaced closer together so that a small file rolled off his workbench onto the rough floorboards. He bent to pick it up and heard a small crash of something metal, a tin pan perhaps then the eerie cry again.

De Tonti stood, listening with keenly attuned ears for the exact source of the distressing sound.

Again, a moan, a cry like a human baby, and the scraping of something metal. Now it sounded heavier than a plate but though he strained he couldn't place the sound. He set down the carving and leaned his ear against the paneling between his cabin and the next.

Someone, most likely a female from the sound of it, was sobbing on the other side. The chorus up on deck swelled with the addition of a couple of male voices. The sailors didn't usually like having women aboard. It was an old seagoing prejudice. But they liked the nuns, felt they were good luck against inclement weather or the icebergs that frequently drifted from more northern waters into this increasingly used sea lane to the New World. The wind changed abruptly, shifting the singing in the opposite direction. De Tonti took an empty cup from a cupboard, placed its mouth against the wall, then leaned against it with his ear pressed to the metal. The moaning sound was amplified through the sides of the cup directly into his hearing.

A human girl was definitely in distress the other side of the wall. He glanced around to see if there was a crack or ill-fitting plank in the jury-rigged bulkhead but it was tight. He put his ear to the cup again but the sound had stopped. He stood that way listening while shallowly breathing but there was only silence now from the compartment next door.

The wind was rising, causing more creaking from the ship around him, but still he listened attentively for a few minutes. After a time he returned to his carving but with less concentration now as every squeak of wind, waves, or wood around him drew his attention from the work in his hands.

But there were no more mysterious moans and after a while he was able to finish the griffin's grin and cement the malicious figure into place on the model stern. When the ship's bell clanged the late meal above the music out on deck, he realized he had whiled away several hours. His stomach growled. He secured the model against the ship's increasingly agitated motion and departed the cabin after one long last look at the creation of his hands.

By now de Tonti figured he'd been mistaken about hearing a human cry next door. It had to be a trick of the wind and the rising sea. He closed the door on his work and on further thoughts concerning the distressing sound. In fact in the ensuing events he completely forgot the moans he may have heard, and because of those events he didn't spend any time in the cabin for the next few hours anyway.

As he mounted the companionway stair, the ship reached at a steep angle for the crest of a large wave then lunged down the trough. He instinctively grabbed the rail but was off balance because the right hand couldn't grip. The motion slammed him against the bulkhead. He thought for a moment his nose was broken. He staggered onto the deck, a scene of Pandemonium. It was, as a sailor would say, a very grown sea, heightened into a white-flecked gray wall behind them, a long sloping green-glass valley ahead.

He'd never seen a sea come up so fast. The crew hastened to get the cloth down. The company scurried after cooking pots, bedrolls, weapons, then dragged them all belowdecks. The ship groaned at every joint. Loose rigging whipped about, lashing the unwary. He saw blood on more than one face, but everything was moving too fast to focus.

One of the nuns screamed as she huddled with two of the children near the mainmast. De Tonti instinctively glanced about for the third little girl but didn't see her. If the third child had been on deck, she was now lost. The other nuns scampered for the companionway, clinging to mechanical devices and lines.

He didn't see La Salle but Gabin at the wheel was working his men with a swift calm command de Tonti had not thought he possessed. Sometimes a mild-mannered man could fool one. De Tonti silently thanked heaven that dealing with the ship this afternoon had not fallen to La Salle.

The nuns floundered toward him. He guided them down the stair he'd just taken, screaming into the wind to Ormonde, "Anyone else out here?"

She shook her head. Either the answer was negative or she didn't know for sure. Or maybe she just couldn't hear.

"The other child—where is she?"

Madame Ormonde shook her head as she grabbed the stair rail. "—seasick—" was all he could hear of what she said, pointing downward.

Then from belowdecks one of the other nuns screamed, "Sister Beatrix!"

Madame Ormonde cast a furtive look around the streaming deck. People hurried about but none wore a black habit. Then she pointed. The young nun had somehow missed the companionway and was huddled at the stern, clinging to the giant anchor capstan.

There flashed in de Tonti's mind what would happen if in her desperate terror she freed the anchor. Their only hope was to get the sheets lowered, batten down, and with Gabin's masterly hold on the great wheel, keep the ship with the wind until the storm blew out.

The weight of an escaped anchor would spin them down without a chance. He never remembered crossing the deck that was now a capricious river with water washing first in one direction, then another as the ship bottomed out, yawing badly in the trough, and began a groaning climb to the next crest. One moment he was at the hatchway, the next he was trying to pry the beserk girl's hands off the kingpin that held all their fates in its socket. He saw that the little pump organ was wedged there. She must have gone to retrieve her musical instrument. She clung like a clawed demon, her strength redoubled by hysteria.

Her hands were clamped to the pin; he didn't dare yank them loose for fear of unleashing the anchor. Himself, the nun, the instrument were all but swimming in salt water. His fingers found no purchase on her slick paralyzed grip. With a quick snap he used the metal hand, for the first time lest he hurt her, to strike her wrist, hoping to God he didn't break the bone.

It hurt her enough to startle her out of her paralyzed trance and she let go. He threw her over his shoulder, clamped his right arm across her thrashing legs, yanked the organ free of the capstan apparatus so it wouldn't devil the anchor, then dragged himself and his double burden back across the liquid deck where Madame Ormonde had been swept off her feet but still clung to the stair rail. Her face was a muddy mixture of terror and anger. She grabbed for the nun, and unable to separate Beatrix from him fast enough, she hit impotently at him, raging for him to get his filthy hands off the innocent.

He barely felt the blows but her response bewildered him. He had saved Sister Beatrix's life, and perhaps the entire ship. Why, he'd even saved this stupid pump organ. Finally she managed to rescue the sister from him. He stood there with a puzzled look on his dripping face, holding the soggy wood and leather musical instrument. It made a strangled cry when he threw it with disgust down the companionway.

Amid the wind's shriek the last of La Salle's company continued to crawl past them down into the hold. The blacksmith was dragging a box of tools across the deck. As de Tonti helped him guide it down the stair, a stout crowbar rolled out and tumbled down into the hold, followed by someone's cry almost drowned out by the storm.

Madame Ormonde gained her feet, and in the face of the screaming wind, tilting with the great beast-ship up another wave, she said something to him. He couldn't believe that this bitch was calling him a demon, a lustful—what? How dare he do *what* to the nun? The wind slammed her words so that all he got from them was the emotion. Her face contorted in fury. She even tried to strike him again but he stopped her with the metal hand; she drew back as if it had the devil's face on it, making the sign of the cross. No use trying to explain about the anchor. If there was going to be trouble over his striking the nun, every man aboard would side with him. He reached out deliberately with his left hand to urge Madame Ormonde to go below but she twisted away from his touch, hissing, "—show you what the power of righteousness can do—"

"Go on down—" he commanded. A fan of spray as high as the mainmast lapped over them, momentarily blinding de Tonti. He blinked the salt from his eyes in time to see one of the sailors who was working the last bit of rigging disappear into the angry water. He saw a knot of faces just below on the stair and a sweep of black soggy cloth slap past him. He tried to stop her but Madame Ormonde was not going below. She staggered up the sloped deck toward the prow of the *St. Honore*. Gabin, who had lashed himself to the wheel, bellowed for her to get below. He tried to catch her skirt but she yanked it free of his grasp, trudging updeck, pulling herself along with whatever was handy. Her cries were inaudible.

Then the wind changed. She was praying! De Tonti could now make out the cadences as he held on to the stair rail by crooking his right arm under it. He couldn't look away from the nun, who had now gained access to one of the huge extra mainmasts. By using the thick line around it for handholds she pressed on until she was nearly standing up against the tilted deck. She wedged herself against a huge hempen knot on the lateral mast, threw her arms up in a posture of supplication, and screamed at the Creator to stop the storm.

The wind threw back her words. At least fifteen of the sailors and recruits and two drenched nuns peered up out of the stairwell. The women mouthed prayers, their beads in their trembling hands.

"In the name of the Mother of God, we command the sea to calm—"

Oh my God, de Tonti thought; she's using the imperial, or was it the papal, "we." It was obvious by her posture of holy defiance that she was speaking for none but her exalted self. He truly hated the woman's arrogance at that moment, found himself hoping that if there were a Creator, He would send another lateral wave to wash her overboard. But he instantly retracted that foolish request; there was every chance one more of those huge side waves would capsize the *St. Honore* and carry them all to the deep.

She didn't hold on. She just stood there with her back against the lashed extra mainmast, arms up commanding the elements to abate. She addressed the weather directly, no longer calling on the deity but telling the seas on her own power to die down. She slid into Latin, reciting prayers and Scripture intermittently, her voice growing more strident.

"'Hear my cry, O Lord, hear my cry for mercy when I call for help from thee,'" she raged out of the Psalms. "'When I lift up mine arms, do not drag me down with the ungodly— reward them for what evil their hands have done!'"

This stung de Tonti. He'd never been prayed against before. Despite his disregard for religion, her vehemence over his rescue of Beatrix gave him a chill that went deeper than the cold water that drenched him.

Another wave washed over her but she wasn't moved. It sent her off into another harangue at the waters. She commanded the sea to hear her voice as a representative of the Church, of the Creator Himself. He didn't know how long they were all frozen in the tableau: the mad woman at the prow admonishing the Atlantic Ocean, the watchers from below drawn up into the elements by the drama on deck, himself clinging to the stair rail in complete disbelief at what he was witnessing. But some time later—maybe an hour, maybe minutes—the sea reached a plateau of violence, screaming and spitting, where it seemed to sigh. Then it just dropped off.

It died. Captain Gabin released himself from the wheel,

swearing mightily, but under his breath and with respect. It was difficult not to use the word "miraculous" to describe the way the sun broke through a crack in the black storm clouds that held over the sea like a kettle lid. Below this lid lay the summer sky in a band of dazzling azure with sharply defined golden rays illuminating patches of the calm sea below.

As quickly as it had come up, the squall was over. He went out to assist the exhausted mother superior. Despite his dislike of her, he couldn't help feeling respect for her bravery.

She wouldn't let him touch her. She pushed at him, stumbling away on flotsam that littered the sparkling deck already steaming in the calm golden air.

The ship's company was coming to life, taking to the deck at assigned stations or just to look around. Everyone watched Madame Ormonde. Someone tried to thank her but she only shook her head, whispering, "The Lord, not I."

A couple of the sailors dropped to their knees, hats in hand, as she passed. At that moment the lady wasn't sure what had happened. She'd swooned at the prow, having entered into the automatic trance of ecstasy that was for her a normal attitude of prayer. She'd practiced the asceticisms of Loyola and the self-denial of St. Theresa too conscientiously not to assume the state of bliss that was the central meaning of her life. But the flesh-and-blood woman was exhausted, a little bewildered that the body had worked so handsomely under the most severe test she'd ever encountered. She fought the demon Pride in that stroll to the campanionway; not even her confessor could have found fault in the battle she fought in those few short steps. She routed that demon and nearly put him down, but in the end, by the time the fourth person had genuflected at her dripping skirts, Madame Ormonde was fairly beaming with satisfaction. A thousand Hail Mary's wouldn't dull the gleam on her pride. This was something she'd been striving for all her life, to be able to enter into that bliss and by the sheer force of her spiritual will affect some physical change in the evil, incarnate world.

Sainthood was what this woman had in mind and nothing less. To her credit she was already framing the confession she'd make as soon as she set foot in the cathedral at Quebec. In her saltwater wake several men crossed themselves out of sincere piety and not a little fear. Even the more worldly of the entourage displayed a distant respect. She hoped her act might help to save their immortal souls, though if it didn't, just

seeing the looks of doubt crack their cynical faces was quite
rewarding. It would not be the first time, she reflected, that
someone had hell scared out of them.

De Tonti heard La Forest grumble that now it would be
church services every hour for the rest of the voyage. But a
sailor growled at him. Wisely, de Tonti thought, the Canadian
shut up.

The sea had abated. That was an undeniable fact. But were
Madame Ormonde's prayers the cause of it? Ask any sailor
aboard and he'd say yes and throw you to the sharks if you
denied it. He'd seen those hardened scalawags fall to their
knees because that brave foolish woman had stood at the prow
and ordered the storm to die.

And it worked. It had been quite a thing to see the
mountainous waves lower like obedient puppies at her feet.
He thought of all the stories this afternoon would generate
among the men in a hundred taverns a thousand leagues and
many years removed from this time and place.

All just coincidence, he argued with himself. Perhaps he
had inherited it from his mother, but de Tonti put no stock in
religion. He paid diplomatic heed to the priests simply
because one could do no less in his position. He served a
religious king who had grown even more religious during de
Tonti's eight years in the military. But long ago he had privately
decided there was little likelihood of a God looking down on
His suffering little human beings. That was a fantasy for
children, old women, and gullible sailors who were so likely to
perish at any moment that religion dulled the mean pain of
their lives. De Tonti remembered how once in the middle of
High Mass when he was nine, he'd assessed religion as nothing
more than a cup of flat wine. He learned to do whatever would
keep Isabelle or the nuns off his back.

But in his heart he did not believe. Yet he'd seen the waves
recede when Madame Ormonde commanded them in the
name of the mother of her God to do so. It was at the very least
a striking coincidence, a gooseflesh sort of thing, he had to
admit, lying in his hammock swinging with the motion of a
tame sea under the ship. If he hadn't experienced it himself,
he wouldn't have believed they'd ever been in danger of
swamping.

But was it a miracle? No, he thought, then said softly, "It

was just a coincidence." The sea would have gone down in any case, without the nun's assistance. Still it was a most amazing display of precise timing. He'd never forget it as long as he lived. Though not religious, he'd been a sailor long enough to be more than a little superstitious. It was something he hated in himself because he considered himself a man of reason. The logic of the philosopher Descartes had taken the place of faith in his logical engineering mind. Since his cadet days when he'd been introduced to the writings of the great French mathematician, he'd been convinced that this way of thinking was superior to the assumption that spiritual forces were at work. He prided himself that he'd worked through nearly all his earlier superstitions. He would not refute any of them to sailors aboard a ship, however. That would have been courting dangerous argument. His naturally diplomatic turn of mind allowed him to keep Cartesian philosophy to himself, where it stood him in good stead through the trials of a rigorous life. But unlike La Salle, he had no need for public debate.

He held out one event from this critical examination, however. Once right after he lost his hand, he'd seen Jesus Christ. It was the only event he remembered from that night. He wouldn't tamper with that memory. He couldn't explain it, but he would not believe that it was only a fever vision. The number 13 also bothered him. Several negative events in his life had occurred on that day of the month. But he rationalized that this could be the result of mere association. Coincidence could explain misfortune rather than outright bad luck or spiritual forces.

These were his thoughts as he lay there trying to get some sleep. It was at that moment he heard something in the next cabin. Whereas before he'd heard a mere sob, now there was a scraping sound, as if heavy wood were being dragged against a wooden floor. Then there was the soft clatter of footfalls. There was another moan followed by a quiet but harsh-toned voice. He couldn't make out the words.

The response was another moan. The ocean was so flat and serene the ship did not creak as usual for a brief time. So he plainly heard the human cry coming from the compartment next to his. This time there could be no mistaking it on the calm sea and the quiet ship where all but the watch were supposed to be asleep after an exhausting experience. He had been causing the hammock to sway slightly as he grasped for slumber. He let the motion slow then stop as he listened with tensed stillness.

There it was again. A soft cry, a muffled sobbing. There was definitely a distraught, even despairing, human being on the other side of the bulkhead. And now there was someone else in there speaking sternly to the one who cried.

Soundlessly de Tonti escaped the hammock. He found the brass mug he'd used earlier to listen through the partition. All was quiet for several seconds. Then he distinctly heard the speaking voice say, "Look what you've done, you filthy witch." More muffled sobs and the sound of scraping, again as if a metal utensil were rolling around on the deck. What was that sound? He knew he'd heard it somewhere else, but he couldn't place it.

"Filthy!" the voice, thoroughly female, repeated. "Don't touch me—" Something unintelligible amid more sobbing and a sharp crack, like a blow with the flat of the hand. More sobbing. "Oh, Lord, help me in my hour of trial, help me to deliver this pitiful sinner into thy hands," the speaker intoned in the unmistakable attitude of ardent prayer. Madame Ormonde's voice was indelible in his mind after this afternoon's events. He had no doubt that's who it was saying, "Be quiet, I say. Here. Eat."

There was a series of sounds he couldn't identify because they were too muffled through the thick bulkhead. The cries ceased, however, and what may have been the light tread of a woman's boots sounded in his direction. Then more scraping on wood, a couple more steps, more sliding of wood that ended with a thump.

Then silence. De Tonti stood leaning against the wall, ear to the cup for some minutes until his muscles cramped. He moved to take the kinks out of his left shoulder. He stood listening a while more. But all sounds had ceased in the next cabin. He returned to his workbench. The little *Griffin* was taking shape fast. The tall scalloped prow was complete; the gunwale was in place, plank by miniature plank. The side straking fitted perfectly, and tonight he would fix the masts in their sockets. Next would come the task he anticipated as the most difficult—sewing the sails and attaching them to the yardarms. He hadn't worked out how he would accomplish that. He could do a great deal but such delicate work was not in the hand's repertoire. He spent a while fussing with details, wishing he had not already glued the mascot in place. During this busywork he listened for sounds next door. The lantern above him on a bracket swung slowly with the ship's otherwise imperceptible roll.

He heated glue over a brazier and dipped the smooth shafts into the hot liquid. With steady concentration he set the masts. He loved this work, even the smell of heated horses' hooves, but his mind was elsewhere. He sat watching the glue congeal, his attention keen for any sound. But except for the soft murmur of the waves and the occasional creakings of the ship, it was quiet. He smothered the charcoal fire, then listened to the creakings, the sizzling of the coals, the faint metallic clickings of his hammock hitches in their clips.

His own breathing sounded loud. The sobbing started again. It was a regular muffled cry that tore something apart inside himself. He was sure there was a little girl suffering over there. That would explain why, since Madame Ormonde's party boarded, he'd seen only two of the children who'd originally accompanied her. He listened once more with the cup. The liquid sounds of bottomless anguish were clear. He swore under his breath, his empathetic heart churning for that sorrowing child next door, so close but so far from his assistance.

The lamplight was golden, reflecting off the glass of the port beyond which the dark sea sighed. With imperceptible tread he walked to the port. This small opening was two man-heights above the waves. The spray refreshed him as he leaned his face as far as possible into the night. He was unable to get his head completely outside the portal because of the partition that halved it. He couldn't see around and into the other cabin.

The sea hissed gently just beyond his vision. He could still hear the sobbing, clearly audible under the ocean's own moan. The other compartment was to his left so it was impractical for him to reach his left arm around and into the dark other opening. But by facing the partition and reaching through the port and around the partition he could put his right hand into the cabin. He would have crawled through the port and into the other side if it had been possible. As it was, he could only reach into the unknown space.

The sobbing continued. In the darkness the one who cried there couldn't see his hand. The night was moonless and even though there must've been some small glow from the sea the cabin was probably velvet black. Only a faint greenish phosphorescence touched the water at the foamy tips of the waves. He silently cursed the dumb hard wall that kept him on this side unable to rescue the girl who cried there, imprisoned for God only knew what reason. He'd thought about that while working on the model ship. Whatever Madame Ormonde was, she was no tormentor, he argued fairly on her behalf. She probably was doing what she considered necessary for one of her recalcitrant novices. Maybe a penance that was as distasteful to her as to her charge.

No, his harder side rebutted. He remembered her voice next door, railing against her prisoner. No, Madame Ormonde was not innocent, but most likely about what she honestly considered the Lord's work. He shuddered to think of what that could involve, having seen what the Inquisition in the name of the Prince of Peace could inflict on a human body. There was no doubt that Madame Ormonde in that same spirit of righteousness could act as inquisitor for a transgressor if the sinner was a child. He withdrew the brass hand and looked at it in the umbrance from the lantern.

It was such a beautiful object he still liked just observing it. Thoughtfully he twisted the ring. The faint lilting notes of *La Pomme Rosace* tinseled the deeper music of the sea. For a moment the sobbing continued as if the pain and sorrow on the other side of the bulkhead were too deep to be touched.

Then, slowly, like rain seeping into the parched earth the music seemed to pierce the anguish. Silences lengthened between sobs.

She had heard the music box. By the time the melody repeated, the crying had ceased entirely. The music slowed as the spring inside the instrument wound down. He wound the ring again and this time thrust the hand out into the darkness and around to the other side behind the partition. As the melody quickened, let in where his larger body would not fit, he heard another sound. The metallic tapping drew closer to the port, closer to the music.

He had a sudden recognition of it. From his own imprisonment he knew with certainty that what he'd been hearing was the sound of a chain dragged across the floor. His shoulder was cramping as the song died a second time. He hurriedly brought his salt-sprayed hand back inside and wound the instrument again, quickly, lest that awful sobbing begin again and tear out his heart. He heard a small voice above the waves, above the creaking of the ship's body around him, above the springing whisper of the music box innards.

"Oh," the voice cried, "please come back." It truly was a
female child, he thought, giving the music back to her and
silently thanking Isabelle for this gift.

The tinkling notes sang again. He felt something bump
against the brass fist, something tentative and not at all hostile,
as if someone reached out and deliberately touched what must
appear to be an apparition floating in the pale sea glow.

The music stopped. He couldn't bear to withdraw his
unfeeling hand from that touch.

"Who is it?" the small voice asked tearfully but no longer
crying.

His memories of ghastly imprisonment flooded back in on
his mind from the dark recesses where he'd pushed them. He
tried to imagine what it would be like for an eight-year-old
child. No adult human being, however sinful, should have to
endure such treatment, his inner voice insisted, much less an
infant. Times like this de Tonti experienced an overwhelming
sense of getting justice done. In his cadet days he'd dabbled in
alchemy, a fashionable hobby for young engineers though
pragmatists considered it arcane. He'd even gone so far as to
attend a secret meeting of outlawed Freemasons, some
members of which played a personality-reading game with
Tarot cards. He'd given up all that undergraduate superstition
after encountering Descartes. But he still recalled with a
comfortable feeling of recognition the Knight of Swords as a
personal symbol of his own knighthood. The bold character of
the card expressed a generous, brotherly desire to right all
wrongs. It was the only idea of nobility he'd allow himself. He
felt like the Knight of Swords at this moment, ready to take up
a weapon and expunge evil from the face of the world.

"I'm in the next cabin, reaching through the portal," he said,
surprised at the tremble in his own voice. He sensed again that
the hand was in contact with something, feeling a gentle tug
against the metal fingers.

"Who are you?"

He imagined her leaning as far as the shackles permitted
against the bulkhead and open portal, her tangled hair perhaps
misted like his own by spray. He told her his name. "And
you?"

There was a long silence as if she'd drifted off. He recalled a
time in the Sicilian dust when he lost the thread of who he had
been. Imprisonment did that. It took away any other life the
prisoner had and replaced it with walls of confinement in an

eternal present. The cell became all existence, without past or future so that the self retreated namelessly into the shadows of the mind.

"Jeanette," she finally answered.

"Sister Jeanette?"

"That is all I can tell you." He felt another tug. "What is this?" she asked, less frightened than curious. He convinced himself it was the saving grace of childish curiosity, painting a mental picture of a little girl slumped painfully on the other side of the wall touching his hand in the darkness. What a wonder it must seem in her dim incarceration.

". . . a music box shaped like a hand?"

"A music box inside a metal hand," he replied. Now he was grateful La Salle had insisted on what he'd disdained as a frivolous addition. A king's amusement, he had said. Would La Salle be able to appreciate its use tonight?

"Are you a spirit, a demon come to taunt me?"

"No, a man with a metal hand."

"Please make it play again." The chains rattled minutely; she let go. He pulled back and wound the ring. His flesh hand was shaking, his mind rushing with plans to free this innocent child no matter what Madame Ormonde had to say. The Knight of Swords would take on the Hierophant, the card that represented the strange figure of the legendary Female Pope. But for now all the help he could give was the pleasure of music, which he handed back through the darkness.

La Pomme Rosace played again and he talked with her for a long time of innocent things, trying to detect from her answers who she was and why she was here. After a while his shoulder went to sleep. When he withdrew his hand again, fatigue needled his muscles but he continued to play the music in the uncomfortable position.

Finally there was no response from her. He was sure she'd gone to sleep, lullabyed by the music box as he had once been.

"Little girl?" He took back his handful of music and let it wind down as he lay back in the hammock after snuffing the lantern. She didn't answer. There in the darkness he listened alone to the final slow notes, asleep before the song was finished. But it was a sleep troubled by dark dreams, by a moving shadow. He pursued it through lonely wastelands but couldn't catch up though he knew he must try. Deep in the dreaming self he decided it was time to climb upon his war horse and right a wrong.

18

The next morning, a Sunday, dawned with resurrectional brightness. De Tonti woke with the ship's bell tolling the watch. Because it was Sunday there would be a service on deck. Not a mass, of course. They had no priest on board. But a service nonetheless with La Salle as nominal captain giving a memorial address for the dead sailor and the company would be led in singing. There would be no accompaniment; besides the one sailor de Tonti had seen wash overboard the only other casualty of the storm was the pump organ though Sister Beatrix had refused to give it a burial at sea until she had exhausted her skill at repairing it. So, a short time after the bell, the sounds of *a capella* hymns crystallized on the fine morning.

De Tonti roused himself with a cup of wine to clean out his mouth. In his mind was a fuzzy plan that clarified as he dressed then took his time finding below-deck passageways around and under the singers up in the sunshine. He had a fairly good idea of the ship's layout and felt he could locate the cabin next to his without having to go on deck.

It turned out to be more difficult than he'd imagined because the temporary bulkhead that halved his compartment ran the width of the ship about two-thirds of the way to the stern. He had to make a roundabout detour down through the dank dark bilge, which stank of rat droppings, fetid seawater, and piss—sailor superstition hinted that human vinegar killed wood worms. But he finally found the place where the cabin should be. He recalled that it closed with a sliding panel. He figured that accounted for the wood-on-wood sound he'd been hearing next door. He pushed aside huddled crates and barrels, long wooden boxes of muskets and tools, crates of lead bricks for ball. He saw evidence of rats back here but when he reached the panel he found it bolted with heavy hardware and a fancy warded Dutch lock that required a notched key.

"Monsieur de Tonti?"

He froze. It was Ormonde. Yet up on deck they were singing the *Vexilla Regis:* ". . . mystery of the Cross shines forth . . ." the sweet feminine voices sang.

186

"Ah," he said to give himself a moment, "I thought you were leading that beautiful chorus."

"Sister Beatrix is our musician."

"I'm glad you're here," he said casually, bending to see something on the floor. "I want to show you something. I'm afraid rats have gotten to your books."

She frowned. With a whisper of yards and yards of cloth around her, she moved to stand just behind him. The light was subdued down here but there was enough coming from a lattice hatch above their heads to see a pile of shredded printed pages behind a gnawed crate. She growled in her throat. He was sure she was not one of those women who'd faint at the sight of a little mouse. She was angry at the rodents, not cringing. "Looks as though only one book's lost. Thank you for noticing. How did you notice, by the way."

"I'm second officer on the Mech-a-si-pi expedition," he said, not without pride as he stood. "It's my duty to find trouble before it starts," he remarked noncommitally, without indicating he'd heard anything suspicious next door. He wanted to find out what was going on before she corrected the abuse.

She watched him closely.

"I'll have our carpenter repair this crate and the cook put out poison and traps," he offered.

"Thank you."

He touched his hat respectfully and made to leave but she stopped him. "I want to tell you that I'm sorry I struck you yesterday."

"Madame, I'm sure the excitement of events—"

"No. I wish to apologize. Honor me by accepting."

He acknowledged with a nod but he gestured toward the stair. "We are missing the service," he said softly. "May I escort you?"

She took the stair. He followed, but as he ascended, he spied the blacksmith's tools they had dragged below during the storm. He found the crowbar easily enough, hiding it in his right coat sleeve. Then with in inward groan he stood at the foredeck for the duration of the service, clear through La Salle's rhetorical comments that ended with his invitation to Madame Ormonde to speak to the assembly. They had to beg her, but in the end she let herself be convinced. She spoke for thirty minutes on the importance of right thinking, urging each man to make his confession at the earliest possible moment after their arrival. But finally even her sermon was over and with a closing hymn the company on deck and sailors in the rigging went about Sunday morning in a leisurely fashion.

De Tonti whisked himself and the commandeered crowbar to his compartment, where he worked in shirtsleeves on the *Griffin* all day and into the early evening while the nuns sang vespers above his head. He didn't take supper. His stomach was uneasy in anticipation at the coming revelation. He waited until after the wood-on-wood scraping noise, until after the second voice, which chose this night to recite scriptures to the prisoner, until after the forlorn ship's bell tolled midnight. When all fell into stillness, he adjusted his lantern to give maximum light and removed the crowbar from his coat sleeve where he'd left it. He set the crowbar between the partition and the outer bulkhead, and leaned on it until the rough planks groaned apart. It was amazingly easy.

Within seconds he stood in the debris of his victory. Holding the lamp he stepped into the cabin. He was prepared for anything, but still what he saw there shocked him. The room was half the size of his own closet and had been in total darkness. There were no amenities, no bed, nothing except a shadowed form down on her knees and two small points of light—her eyes reflecting his lantern light back to him.

The room was bare except for thick metal rings fastened to the floorboards, which were in turn connected to the chains he had heard drag across the floor. A chamber pot sat off to one side near a tin plate on the floor with a few scraps of bread on it next to a jug of water.

It was the girl herself who shocked him. She was dressed as near as he could tell in the dimness in a roughspun shift that covered most of her. He could barely make out the small bumps of her toes at the hem as she hunched under the rag.

He took a step nearer. He could see food on her face, the face of a child who could be no more than seven or eight at the most. He couldn't see her bare arms because the sleeves were too long. He took one more step, towering over her uncomfortably. She shrank back as if expecting a blow. She looked so small she hunkered down; he saw her eyes were blue, her hair the finest spun-gold ringlets. Her legs were tucked under her so he could get no real idea about her height. Her hands were in her lap as though she were in church. Her face was round, her forehead high with the mark of intellect.

His throat constricted with deeply insulted dignity that any

human being could do this to a child. What he mainly wanted
to do was strangle Madame Ormonde. But instead of considering the prospect further, he pulled out a linen handkerchief, dipped it in the water jug, and began washing the child's
face. She watched his eyes as he want about this task.
Underneath was revealed the pearly skin of a beautiful girl.
She didn't even pull back when he tilted her chin up with the
brass hand. Everyone else had displayed at least awe toward it;
few would let it touch them and none could do so without an
involuntary flinch. But this child showed none of the reactions
he'd come to accept as a matter of course.

He couldn't speak because of the emotions he found sticking
in his throat. But he forced a smile back at her serious
unreadable expression. Since she was a child who'd been
abused, he figured he was watching passive acceptance
mingled with fear that made her silent. She seemed unable to
take her gaze from him. The child had probably not seen
another human being except for the starched nun since they
had left France. No telling how long she'd been kept in such a
state before embarkation. Something of these thoughts must
have shown on his face because she mirrored it gravely in a
pouting expression that further bent his heart.

"There now, that's better," he said, dipping the cloth again to
wash her hands but she took it from him and continued
scrubbing her little fingers as she asked, "Are you Henri?" Her
hands were pink under the dirt, her wrists bruised from the
metal bands around them. They must have had to make special
shackles for such slim wrists. They were fastened with pins
that could be removed if one could see the trick. Her hands
were tiny, even more dainty in proportion than the rest of her
appeared in the shapeless shift. He carefully unfastened the
handcuffs. She watched intently, as if in a dream, glancing from
his face to his hand.

"Is that the music box?"

He tossed the hateful shackles aside and sat cross-legged on
the floorboards in front of her in the attitude of telling a
friendly story.

"Want to hear it?"

She brightened, smiled, and nodded. There was a lassitude
about her. She hadn't moved from the position in which he
found her even though she was free to do so now. The air was
chill tonight with a breath of the north. He removed his coat
and put it around her shoulders. It swallowed her. Briefly she

stroked the velvet; it wasn't the wine-colored coat La Salle had given him but another of russet he'd bought the day before they sailed. She touched the cloth as if petting a dog. He wound the music box and let the song begin. She closed her eyes and continued to stroke the soft material. Rapt, she listened without moving as it played through twice then halfway through a third run. He saw her fingers reach tentatively for the ring so he offered it to her. It delighted him that she didn't act as if the hand were anything unusual, neither revolted nor respectful. Her movements were jerky. Her muscle tone was bad from this confinement. She had the gray look of malnutrition. If she didn't get some fresh fruit, she'd be scurvied in no time.

The song played again, but she had not wound the ring enough. He did it for her. *La Pomme Rosace* played again and again as he began to talk with her.

But she grew reticent, reluctant to speak of her crimes. He tried another tack. "Where are your parents, dear?"

She regarded him with widened eyes that showed far more maturity than her apparent years and not a small measure of madness. "My parents?"

"Your mother and father. Why have they let this happen to you?"

"Oh, they approve." She gestured that he needed to wind the music box again, but he pressed her for information.

"But why?"

"Why, to save my soul, of course."

"A radical approach, I must say. Who are they that they would so abandon you?"

"They didn't abandon me. They gave me to Madame Ormonde."

He looked stunned.

"My father is . . ." Her eyes glazed. She looked away, picking at the tattered hem of her garment. "Well . . ." The words would not leave her lips. Her color heightened. "He's a rich and powerful man. Very pious. He loves God and he wants me to love God, too." She gave him a look that gave him the shudders. "But I've been very, very bad."

"I don't understand," he said, afraid he was beginning to understand all too well.

"I disobeyed him, my father. He did what he thought was in my best interest. If I get better, if I mind Madame Ormonde and do as she says and give up my . . ." She looked away again, either embarrassed or secretive. De Tonti couldn't tell. "Well, my sins, I suppose. Then she says I can become a sister in the order and serve the Lord." She fell silent. De Tonti didn't want to push her so he waited silently with steady patience. Finally she said, without looking at him, "But I will not give up my sins. I will never obey Madame Ormonde." She turned fiercely on him. "I hate that old bitch. I hate the Church and all those stupid priests. I don't want to serve God. I hate God. I hate the Virgin Mary, but most especially I hate Jesus Christ that he would let this happen to me." The outburst appeared to tire her.

Such vehemence shocked him. He didn't care much for the Church himself. A personal God he doubted. Nuns he loathed. But Jesus Christ was another matter. "Hate them all, child, except Jesus. He suffered unfairly too. He weeps for all prisoners, especially innocent ones like you, and would free you as he freed the lambs and doves outside the temple if he could." He'd never said anything like that to anyone. He stopped himself because such a speech made him suddenly self-conscious.

"You're not like the rest of them," she said, touching his face with one fingertip.

He smoothed hair back out of her eyes.

"Play the music again," she said.

He obeyed. The song filled the dank room. When it was finished he stood. Tears glistened in her eyes. She reached to pluck at his shirttail. "Please don't go."

"Does she more often come to you at night?"

"She doesn't like to come here at all—she says the night air makes her less nauseous."

He knew he was taking a chance by making her life more bearable with a blanket and a pillow. But if he left the boards down, he could retrieve the bedding in the morning. He'd only once heard Madame Ormonde visit the girl at some time other than early evening. He'd gamble she would not break her pattern. If she did find out he'd been in here, all the better; he was ready to do battle with the nun if that's what destiny prescribed.

"Don't go—"

"I'll be back," he said, taking the lantern to his own compartment, where he dug in a sea chest for a blanket. As he grabbed his pillow from the hammock, he saw a tin of dried apples and took several slices back to her.

She was standing now, a porcelain doll, a little bent by poor food and the cramped posture. His coat still on her shoulders dragged the floor. She stood no taller than his waist. He felt like a giant looking down on her. While she gobbled the apples, he knelt and spread out the comforter, folding it over on itself to make up a bedroll, hoping privately that she didn't get sick from the fruit. He placed the pillow at one end of the pallet and sat back to offer it to her.

"Tomorrow I'll bring you some real food and water to bath in. We have to be careful, but I don't think she'll know if I remove everything before dark. I've heard her come here only once during the day. Does she mostly arrive in the evening?"

She thought a minute. "A couple of days she didn't bring me anything to eat at all."

He grimaced.

"Oh, she doesn't consider me human, you know. That's why she treats me this way. She thinks I'm possessed by the demon Lust. It's the demon who makes me do bad things. She says she treats the demon badly so it will depart. She's going to have me exorcised by this special priest in Quebec." She was suddenly embarrassed before him. She dropped her eyes and looked back at him through the veils of her lashes. She was so beautiful in his eyes. She looked like a miniature goddess from ancient Greece, a statue of cream-colored marble tossed aside by barbarians who could not know her worth, but unbroken and shining through dirt that could not despoil her.

He shook those thoughts from himself. This was a child; he was her protector. That was all.

"I am going to help you, Jeanette."

She shyly took his flesh hand in her own. He led her to the pallet and tucked her in. He smoothed the curls that refused to stay off her forehead. She regarded him with an enigmatic look, a blend of wry amusement and innocent devilment. "Will you kiss me goodnight, Henri?"

He leaned over gently and placed his lips on her brow as he imagined a father would do.

She flung her arms around his neck with amazing strength. "I shall never forget you," she whispered in his ear. "Not in a million, million years. Even if I roast in Hell as they say I will, I will say your name while I burn, my Henri." Her breath was hot on his neck; his response to the child's innocent gesture disturbed him and so he left her quickly. She had roused him

in a way he did not want to be aroused by a baby. It shamed
him that his own body added to her degradation. She was
innocent and couldn't know that her femaleness was as ripe as
Isis' even if she weren't yet a woman.

Once again on his side of the bulkhead he heard her say,
"Will you play the music again so I can go to sleep with it?"

"Yes," he croaked. He wound the ring. His own clothing
smelled sour but he felt the chill so he wrapped in a light
blanket after disrobing. He would not acknowledge his own
arousal, but quickly slipped into the hammock. The music
slowed so he wound it again. He blew out the lantern, liking
the way the cool blanket took the warmth of his body, tired
beyond mere events and desiring sleep.

But sleep did not desire him and he tossed about, swinging
the hammock in the inky blackness.

"Goodnight, Henri."

"Goodnight, Jeanette. Sweet dreams." He felt foolish with
such a command to a child in her situation. How could she
possibly have anything but nightmares? Maybe the music
would sweeten her sleep. He wound the music box three
times more and when the last note was finished he wound it no
more. The darkness was red around him as he stared into it,
full of hateful thoughts, angry and indignant at the length
righteousness could extend itself to inflict such punishment. At
that moment he hated the Church for giving a woman like
Ormonde power over children. Truly, he thought, Jesus weeps
tonight.

For a long time he lay on his back relishing various plans for
putting Madame Ormonde in her place. She could drown in a
cider vat down in the hold. Everyone would think she'd been
washed overboard. With these thoughts he slept. His dreams
were of straightforward, thoroughly satisfying sex with that
whore in Paris.

Later when he tortured himself with guilty thoughts about
that night, de Tonti would blame what happened on the fact
that he was in a fitful sleep when the warm little body crept
into the hammock with him. She might have just been a lonely
child responding to the only adult who'd been kind to her.

At first he didn't know that he was not dreaming. The
hammock rocked minutely. In slumber he detected a shift in
movement he ascribed to the helmsman's wearing ship, a
tacking maneuver to keep them reaching into the wind.

Then warmth like liquid along his naked left side roused him to semiwakefulness. He slid his left arm under her head. Her doll-like body pressed against him. It was a peaceful position to be in. He could have returned to sleep like that, holding on to the dream and nothing more. He woke finally with a start. There was no mistaking her intention as her small hand groped for him.

"No!" he said, twisting in the confinement of the hammock, throwing them both onto the deck. There was a shocked silence between them in the nightglow, then she began to cry. Only one other time had he heard as sad a sound of rejection, when years before, a dying soldier had cried out for his mother.

He felt helpless against her sobs. He wanted to reach out and touch her, yet he did not dare.

"Please, please don't hate me because I'm small," she begged.

"I don't hate you," he tried to explain. There was just enough light to see the glimmer of her wet eyes regarding him. "It's just that, well, you're innocent, and—"

It was she who reached out; her hand found his face in the darkness. She drew toward him, warm and womanly against him. When he lifted her it was as if he held a child but her hand found what she'd been looking for. She caressed him as he found the hammock and lay down with her. It was the first time he'd been in a hammock with someone else. Though she was small the added presence skewed the hanging bed. Their friction, as they found their balance together, kindled desire.

She was very tiny in every part, warm and sweet-smelling despite her neglect. Passion removed the lassitude that had imprisoned her movements, which were now strong and graceful. Presently she began a small crooning sound that was both soothing and arousing. It could never be mistaken for her solitary cries. She blew the humming song into his left ear while her hand found responses in his body. Now he knew the level of abomination, as Madame Ormonde would have called it. For this child to be so sexually sophisticated would indeed drive a nun to lock her up. From whom had this babe learned her lessons? He'd heard of infant prostitutes, but had never had any desire to see a child degraded. But with all her skill, she didn't seem to be a professional. She was in no hurry.

She replaced her song with her honeyed tongue in his ear. Her breath was fiery. When he could stand the sublimely soft probings no longer, he inclined his face to hers and met her mouth with his own. He surrounded her with his arms and legs. She seemed as small as a pillow but she did not protest. Behind his desire he feared that he might hurt her in some way, and was ready merely to touch her here and there and leave his own pleasure for another time, for the years it would take her to grow up, his conscience whispered.

But she would have no mere petting. How could a child so young be so advanced? He dared not enter her. It might break her, and though he wanted to sink himself into the cave of her more than he'd ever wanted anything, he feared to do so. She grew impatient with his hesitation. She insisted without words. When he tried verbally to protest, she silenced him with her lips, shaking her head as she kissed him, informing him that no words should delay their union.

The hammock described increasingly wide arcs in the steamy glow from the portal.

The girl was strong in her limbs, entirely adept at several signals of passionate intensity. She had either learned from a master lover or instinctively knew the art in her very bones. She'd thrown off the rough shift. He felt the hard buds of her breasts the size of demitasse cups between his own nipples. At least she's pubescent, he thought, refuting his screaming Christian soul. She was no virgin. That's why she was under Madame Ormonde's guard. This ardent skill was her sin, the devil propensity the nun was trying to beat, starve, and abuse from her. For a moment he pitied Madame Ormonde and her futile self-appointed task of training this one from the path of passion. This one would have to die to be turned from her direction, child or no.

She jibed her pelvis expertly to receive him. They shuddered together long and sweetly. He imagined that his seed would fill her body and spill over like a wine bottle overflowing under the drunk vintner's hand. She took him, all of him, and covered his face with a hundred kisses when they were done. He could only lie there in wonder. No woman in his life, whether master whore or inspired lover, had ever brought his passion so high or fulfilled it so perfectly. He felt no trace of the *tristesse* that too often followed sex. "I promise you, I will free you from your prison," he whispered.

She made more small purrs in his ear like words but without language. Before long she was admonishing him in courtly French to think about it, *"Mon cher beau Henri*, think about not rescuing me from my prison."

"How can I leave you like that?"

"While I am Madame Ormonde's prisoner, if we are very careful, we can be together every night of our journey with nobody the wiser."

That was undeniably true. He felt a stab of conscience upon agreeing with her. To take his pleasure at such expense flew in the face of his pride and morality even if it pleasured her, too.

"No," he answered, but with no heart. "I cannot bear not to try and ease your predicament. Surely you've done your penance."

"I can never do my penance," she flared. "Don't you see it is what I am that Sister hates and I will never be sorry for what I am."

Her words made more sense in this harsher light. "She might even kill me," Jeanette said in the tone of thinking out loud. "She vowed to cleanse me of sin and save my soul from possession by the demon Lust which she believes makes me wanton."

De Tonti listened, thinking not so much about her words as the girl speaking them. He almost asked how old she was, but hesitated, afraid she'd say nine or ten and he'd be pierced anew by conscience for raping a baby. But he knew this had been no rape—seduction, perhaps, and there was no doubt who had seduced whom. But who would believe it? What would La Salle do? This could destroy everything between himself and the Canadian and endanger de Tonti's hope for a new life. These thoughts muddied his clear-seeing conscience and quelled any curiosity about Jeanette's exact age.

"I heard her tell father that if the body had to die to save the soul then it was a bargain and she'd take even murder on her own soul for the larger good of saving mine."

It gave de Tonti a steady set of chills. He knew Madame Ormonde was capable of such a thing. La Salle was afraid of her because he suspected she was an agent of the Jesuits. The more he saw of the Canadian's fear of the order, the more it looked like imagination. In any case, it paralyzed him where Jesuits might be concerned: he would not make a move against Ormonde.

"So my beloved—and I shall truly love you all my life—you must not rescue me. You must not tell anyone you've found me. And each night after she brings me supper and scripture, you will break down the wall, remove the bindings, and I shall

join you in this funny bed and we'll make love until dawn.
How long does the journey last?"

"Two or three weeks depending on the winds."

"Then let us pray for contrary winds."

19

Each night after Jeanette was fed, de Tonti removed the
bulkhead boards to bring her more dried apples, the music
box, and his passion. She blossomed under this attention.
When she had been beaten down, she played the victim,
willing to do nothing to better her condition. Now she
emerged as a new personality able to change what was within
her power. She kept herself and her quarters clean without
anyone's suggestion. Fully within the length of the chain she
was able to get to the portal to throw out her own night soil.
She put the daily pitcher of water to use before she saw her
lover each night. All the time he spent with her she would
watch him with wide adoring eyes that made him uncomfortable. It delighted him to see these changes in her but he had
no wish to be adored, so he engaged her in the work he was
doing on the model.

"I have a problem with the sails," he told her. He was not
able to stitch them, and wondered how else to attach the lines,
hoping she'd volunteer to sew them.

"You could glue them," she said with the first intellectual
excitement he'd seen in her. "You could even make them look
blown by the wind. . . ."

He'd already cut with difficulty the miniature sails out of
handkerchiefs. She used a splinter to dip glue from the brazier,
applied it along the raveling edge of one of the sails, then
folded it over one of the strings that would be a rope on the
model.

It thrilled him that she'd shown so much initiative. He
praised her and let her begin work on the rigging immediately.
He was careful each midnight to make sure there was no glue
on her fingers or chemise before he left her.

Still he had done nothing to free her. He felt the overwhelming might of the Church behind Madame Ormonde and
continued to have no doubt that La Salle would side with her.

Until they reached land he saw no way to approach the problem. If he confronted her on it now, there would be the strong suspicion he had taken the child as his lover. The woman could turn the men against him if she so much as hinted that he might have swived the child.

The joy he saw growing in her dispelled any doubt that he'd done the right thing. He felt no guilt that he was her lover, but another kind of guilt had begun to nibble at him. As long as she was a prisoner, he felt he should somehow free her.

So his conscience ate at him even though he was able to give the girl precious human comforts within the limitation of their magic time together.

It could not go on forever. On the eighth morning after he'd broken through the bulkhead he had a chilling moment on deck when he saw Madame Ormonde exit La Salle's cabin, a staunch, self-satisfied turn to her lips. He inwardly groaned as he watched her cross the deck to go below; maybe he'd been found out.

The truth was, though he'd never know it, that Ormonde had become suspicious of the girl's altered behavior. The very changes of attitude de Tonti was so happy to inspire gave the liaison away. Jeanette no longer hissed and spat at the nun. Her quarters showed a marked improvement. The girl herself seemed to be concerned with her own appearance, in contrast to what could be interpreted as demonic lack of regard in the past. Far worse, and one which the nun could not bring herself to relate to this male person, was that the girl fairly reeked of sex. So Ormonde loosened upon La Salle only her strong suspicions. She was certain the security of Jeanette's cabin had been broken. But because de Tonti had so carefully disassembled the bulkhead so it showed no trace of tampering, she couldn't figure out how it was happening. She suspected him, of course, but he never gave her anything substantial to complain about before La Salle. So she swore him to secrecy and told him about her demonic charge. La Salle was horrified at a girlchild on the lusty rampage and quickly offered to help any way he could.

"One of the sisters must be with the poor child at all times," Ormonde said with a sigh. "You can help by giving me the use of the cabin next to the girl's so we may keep better care of her."

La Salle's own desire that Madame Ormonde send back a good report, for he correctly deduced her connections, made him happy to comply.

The same evening, Sabat brought word to de Tonti that Monsieur wanted to see him in the morning. This was the traditional way for a commander of a ship to get such a request to one of his officers, down the line. La Salle was playing the part to the hilt.

So it was to La Salle's well-windowed cabin after the eighth night of hammock assignations that de Tonti reported the next morning. The huge barkentine was sailing as close to the wind as the pilot of a square rig dared, making the finest time crossing the north Atlantic anyone aboard could remember. On crossing the deck, de Tonti was sorry he couldn't stay and enjoy the air that was enthusiastically slapping them westward.

La Salle stood at the spray-hazed many-paned captain's window watching the swells drive them on to New France when de Tonti entered after a knock. Tobacco smoke thickened the air. The explorer had just laid aside his long clay pipe. Messily unfurled on a table was his principal map, copied from those of Marguette and Joliet, who a few years earlier had been the first Europeans to explore the middle Mech-a-si-pi as far as the tribes of the Arkansas. A sheathed sword held one side of the map, while an inkwell sat on another corner. The fourth curled freely.

"I have something for you," the Canadian said, turning to the desk, where he took a small cheaply bound book from a drawer. He handed it to de Tonti, who took it, saw it was blank, and put it in his pocket without further inspection.

"Time to start a journal."

De Tonti groaned. He hated writing reports, the most onorous part of command.

"I know you don't like it but it's necessary. Our enemies will fill the Court with rumors which we must counterbalance with a flood of letters and journals. Now's the time to begin. My own editor will work over your raw notes for Court presentation, so don't worry about style and spelling."

"Or handwriting?" de Tonti asked wryly.

"Print if you must. Make it legible, that's all."

De Tonti shrugged grudging compliance, tasted the claret his host poured for him, and waited for La Salle to continue. He was obviously nervous.

"So," La Salle finally said, pacing behind the desk. This was not his usual manner and it put de Tonti on edge. He watched the explorer roam his confines like a caged wolf. "How is the model of the *Griffin* coming?" He slapped his hands together behind his back apparently enjoying his usurped role of sea captain.

"She's a fine little ship more than half done," de Tonti replied, sipping. "Come down to my cabin and see for yourself."

"Perhaps you could bring her up here."

De Tonti didn't know how to react. Surely he jested—bring the whole spread-out mess of a half-constructed ship's model? What was La Salle thinking?

"The hull, have you completed it by now?"

De Tonti nodded. "The masts are in place and I'm working on the sails."

"The sails?" La Salle said incredulously. "Really, Henri, you amaze me. What you've done, well, it's truly amazing. You can even sew sails?"

It was the first time he felt himself patronized by La Salle. What did he want that would make him step so out of character? "Well, Sabat has assisted me with the detail work," de Tonti said, hoping that white lie would cover his true assistant's contribution. "I couldn't have gotten this far without his help."

"You miss having him at your beck and call after all the years you've been together, yes?"

De Tonti changed position in the leather sling chair, feeling more discomfited by the impression that there was something La Salle was trying to say but was taking a long time around the deck to get out.

"He's close enough, I suppose," he replied cautiously. "Is something troubling you?"

The Canadian regarded him. "Nothing at all. What could be troubling me?"

"I don't mean to be personal, but something seems to be troubling you."

La Salle poured himself a glass of purplish wine. "I have no objections to your personal concern, in fact, I'm touched by your solicitation. What is occupying my mind is a small logistical problem, nothing more. I'm hoping you'll see your way clear to helping me solve it."

"If I'm able." What was coming? The hair on the back of his neck told him he wouldn't like it.

"I need you closer to me for private consultation, for example with this map—" he shuffled the heavy parchment.

"See how Marquette and Joliet showed the conjunction of the Illinois and the Colbert Rivers?"

De Tonti looked at the map of their proposed route traced in red: Into the St. Lawrence River southwest to Lake Ontario; a short portage around Niagara Falls to the Niagara River south to Lake Erie, west and north to Lake Huron through Detroit; west by the Isle of St. Ignace of Michillimackinac, south into Lake Michigan to *Chicagou* on the west shore, portage to the Illinois River, and finally on southwest to the Mech-a-si-pi. On the map the journey was less than two hands wide; in reality it was across a vast unknown wilderness. La Salle told him it could take months, even years if luck was against them. Still, de Tonti didn't see what his presence could do for it at this point, but he didn't make a comment.

La Salle jumped into his silence. "We need to speak of portages, of how we'll team the men. I know a bit about canoeing, and I think I have a guide in mind for us. A fine man, an Illinois named Nikanape. I know him from the time I spent in the forest." La Salle had referred very seldom to that almost mystical experience of his young manhood, when, having grown bored with squirehood and business in Montreal, he had ventured alone into the Great West, where he saw for the first time the Mech-a-si-pi River. It was where he received his vision of a vast kingdom of plantations owned and operated by ennobled Frenchmen for the king and for their own profit, and where he had first seen himself as one of those New World noblemen overseeing his own kingdom of gentle *habitants* and menial slaves. "And," he concluded, "I have tricks to teach you. How to recognize a genuine letter from me, for example. There's a way to make a secret signature—oh, there are many things we need to speak of."

"So," de Tonti said, having drained his glass and faced the inevitable, "you wish me to transfer my belongings nearer to you." It was not a question. He knew. He simply did not want to drag it out as La Salle seemed bent on doing. His heart was sinking. Had Ormonde found out about his relationship with Jeanette and told La Salle? Or was he sincerely, innocently bringing his second in command closer to his beck and call, as he had suggested de Tonti might wish to do with Sabat?

"Actually in here with me, if you have no objections. Spacious quarters, yes?" De Tonti looked around merely to prevent disappointment from showing on his face. "You could sling your hammock there, and see that small nook with the pull-down surface? A good place to continue building the *Griffin*." He studied de Tonti's silence. "I'm invading your privacy, but I think we need to start making plans." De Tonti had never heard La Salle so inoffensive before. In this he smelled more than a rat, but could not let on that there was any reason he would prefer the cramped privacy of his closet amidships rather than this luxury apartment where the motion of the ship was almost imperceptible, where there was light and fresh air away from the grinding confinement of the lower deck.

"Well?" Some of the imperiousness crept back into La Salle's voice.

De Tonti shrugged as though it did not matter. Inside he was wrenched, thinking what would happen to Jeanette if he completely abandoned her.

"You thought something was bothering me; I say the same about you."

"Monsieur?"

"My friends call me Rob and now we are surely friends as well as business partners. Please." He sat heavily in the captain's chair behind the huge table that served as a desk.

"I am yours to command, Rob."

"But you do not wish to leave your quiet privacy, yes?"

"At sea privacy is a treasure."

La Salle nodded, unblinkingly observant of de Tonti for some sign that would give him information. But the young man was well cloaked.

"Well, then, it's settled. Have Sabat move your things up here on the morrow."

"There is one small problem. A mere inconvenience, really . . ."

"Yes?" La Salle suspiciously drew out the word.

Ah, thought de Tonti, he may know about Jeanette after all. "The sails," he said innocently. "I had a fancy idea I've incorporated into my design. I devised a way of draping glue-wet sails over a candle butt to give them a fair appearance of billowing in the wind. It's a pleasing effect, and I've adopted this plan into the sails already spread out in my cabin. This damn fog has prevented their drying. I'm afraid if I move them now, the whole lot will be ruined."

La Salle tented his fingers beneath his chin and appeared to be studying the problem. Finally he said, "Perhaps Sabat can rig up a little oven."

De Tonti adopted La Salle's studious mien and chewed on this suggestion with an attentive incline of his head. He coursed his flesh fingers through his beard, nodding slowly. "Perhaps he can put together something with a lantern. I'll have him get on it straightaway."

"Excellent. L'Esperance will hack out a spot for you. Any overflow of your personal gear can be stowed in the hold along with my own trunks."

"In any case, the sails should be dry by day after tomorrow," de Tonti said, maneuvering for any small time at all he could manage with Jeanette to explain to her that they were going to be separated. "Actually it's a pretty conceit putting wind into their cheeks," he said to draw away attention from his reluctance to leave his cabin. "One I can certainly forgo. I can flatten them out if you wish." He might never see her again after Madame Ormonde inflicted her holy proximity on the child. But he dared not excite La Salle's imagination, for how could he admit that he had broken into the girl's cabin and spent every morning in her arms? If La Salle was scandalized by de Tonti's whores, how would he react to a baby lover?

The very fact that de Tonti had made no objection to the girl's situation would cast suspicion on his own motives. The dilemma caused him to ache inside, but he was proud that none of it showed. No telling what the prudish La Salle would do if he even suspected. How would he go about decommissioning de Tonti on the open sea? Would he have him clapped in irons to be tried by an ecclesiastical court at Quebec, or shipped back to Paris to stand trial in a civil court? Or perhaps he'd leave de Tonti to the swift justice of the sharks.

"No," the explorer drawled, soundlessly clapping his fingertips together with a kind of contained pleasure. "I rather relish the idea of seeing our little *Griffin* fly into the startled beaks of the crows!" He chuckled wickedly, leaving no doubt which black-feathered birds he was referring to.

"As you wish, monsieur—Rob," de Tonti caught himself.

La Salle grinned at him, not unlike a crow in his own appearance, dressed as he was today in a slate gray coat, black doublet and stockings and with dark circles under his eyes.

"That may take some getting used to," de Tonti said, "calling you by your Christian name."

"You're no longer in the military, my friend. You are now in the fur business. Get used to the idea of *La Sieur* as the title of your own name, as befits your station." The Canadian saw a cloud cross de Tonti's features when he had meant to enliven him. "What's wrong?"

"Oh, that phrase. 'As befits my station.' It reminds me of my mother."

"You never told me about your meeting with the honorable lady."

"Nothing to say. She honorably gave me four thousand *livres* in gold and silver." He held up the beautiful hand.

"Ah, yes. The brass fist. I tell you, Henri, you will someday thank the Lord you lost that mere and common flesh-and-blood appendage."

De Tonti's wry look said he hardly thought so. La Salle had no idea what he was saying; surely he was just being insensitively glib. De Tonti fought down the offense, hiding it all behind a cynical chuckle.

"No, no, I tell you our red friends will strongly revere you."

"Big medicine, I suppose."

La Salle nodded.

"You never told me what that means, big medicine. Will they fancy I can cure the gout by touching them?"

"Oh, no. They say 'medicine' in our best translation of their word, similar in all their various languages, which means much more." He searched for a better translation. "When the American savage says something is *wa kon*, he means a wonderful, in the sense of wonder, a wonderful mystery to be accorded the highest honor."

De Tonti zeroed in on him. "Is that why you insisted I spend my birthright on this 'thing'?"

"This is the second time you've made reference to my motives concerning your hand. How could I have any design except to help you?" Actually he was pleased to see cynicism sprout in de Tonti. He had wanted to toughen him up, mold him more on the lines of, say, Rob La Salle. "Are you sorry you spent the money on this wonderful device?"

"Not at all. But I've suspected since we met His Majesty that you had in mind more than a king's amusement."

La Salle appraised him with keen pleasure. "You are learning, my friend, you are learning your lessons well."

"Are you trying to create another Robert Cavelier de La Salle?"

"Ah, but there can never be another one of him," the Canadian replied, as close to glee as his serious personality would ever come. He tossed off the last of his claret.

De Tonti, smiling, but aggrieved inside, stood to take his leave.

"Before you go, tell me: Have you heard any . . . any, well, strange noises from your part of the ship?"

Like a nail sunk in wood, de Tonti felt surety sink into him that somehow La Salle suspected what was going on below-decks. But how? "Noises?" de Tonti repeated with artful insouciance.

"You know, through the bulkhead or such?"

"As a matter of fact, yes." The truth always served better than any lie.

La Salle's gaiety evaporated like water on a hot griddle. "Yes?" He leaned forward over his empty glass.

"I believe one of the pious sisters shares a wall with me."

"One of the nuns?" Disbelief riddled La Salle's voice.

"She cants most beautifully from the Bible every evening."

"The Bible," La Salle repeated woodenly, trying to piece this together with what Madame Ormonde had told him.

De Tonti stood with his hand on the hatch lock as he turned to offer a quote that left La Salle staring after him. "Psalms Twenty-one, Twenty-two, around in there, I believe it was last night," he said, staring off into space as if trying to recall the words. In fact he knew them perfectly from a scriptural passage learned what seemed like eons ago under the whipping stick of some nun who shared the philosophy of Madame Ormonde. He had been about eleven and for punishment of some forgotten infraction was forced to read the entire Bible aloud. Many fragments of scripture stuck to him. He quoted this, which seemed so apropos: "Be not thou from me, O Lord, deliver my soul from the sword and my darling from the power of the dog."

Despite his coup at leaving La Salle speechless for once, de Tonti returned to his cabin with a heavy heart. He desperately wanted to visit Jeanette, but dared not break the pattern imposed on him by the nun's schedule. He puttered at the *Griffin* and was dismayed to find the sails drying nicely. He listened next door for a while but hearing nothing, abandoned the eavesdropping for the fresh air on deck. Later he reviewed his men, chatted again with Sabat, and ate a light supper in the officers' mess. But throughout the day he could not pull his thoughts from the fact that very likely this would be his last night with Jeanette. How could he break it to her? How could

he confess that his own security forbade his trying to improve
her plight, that he could not so much as lift a hand or speak out
on her behalf lest the full fury of his prudish superior and of
Mother Church fall on his head for debauching a child?

Maybe he would keep their last night sweet and simply not
tell her. But, his conscience argued, that is the easy way out.
That would leave the girl to pine for him, and thinking for the
rest of her life that the one who should have rescued her had
deserted her. But, his other more practical side argued, what
did he truly owe this unfortunate, precocious infant? He had
done nothing to hurt her and had only given her what he
could, human companionship and hope.

These thoughts chased him all afternoon. When the sun set
behind the unseen New World toward which they were so
damnably hastening, de Tonti retired to his cabin. He waited
impatiently for Madame Ormonde's nightly readings to be
finished so that he could give the child all he could offer her, a
last night of pleasure.

But the reading seemed incessant this evening. He listened
with the cup through the bulkhead; the good sister was
reading from the New Testament. After an interminable two
hours or more, the buzzing chant ceased. He waited for a long
time, listening for the telltale sliding of the panel before going
to Jeanette.

He must have dozed because he came awake fully aroused
and listening for the scrape that would signify the dog's
departure from his darling. Still in a semidream state, he went
to the removable part of the bulkhead and listened.

"*Mon amie?*" he whispered.

There was no answer. He cursed himself. The poor child
must have fallen asleep waiting for him, the bright spot in her
dreary day. Quickly he removed the plank and stepped into
her mean quarters.

What he saw first drew the breath from him. It was the
nearly bald head of young Sister Beatrix like a man's three-day
beard in prickly spines all over her cranium where a woman's
locks should be. The sight was grotesque. He stopped so short
he almost tripped. For a drawn moment the sight of beauty
insulted for piety's sake so startled him he couldn't speak even
to offer apologies.

Sister Beatrix was preparing to retire having removed her
small black boots and wimple but thank God nothing more of
her habit. She was sitting on a stiff-backed land chair silently

reading from a missal by lantern light. She had turned to look over her left shoulder at the sudden sound of his entry so that the glow illuminated only her poor shaved head. In this light it was like a huge overripe peach, utterly ugly. She jumped to her stockinged feet, which had been propped upon a small but neatly made cot.

His eye traveled the room. It had been immaculately combed of any trace of the unfortunate habitation it had been such a short time before, turned by swift cunning from a prison cell into a nun's cell complete with the single glint of a crucifix on the wall above the sister's waiting pillow.

"Monsieur!" Beatrix exclaimed. Yet somehow when he considered the tableau in retrospect, she did not seem startled enough. Madame Ormonde must have told her something untoward could happen so she wouldn't scream. Had she been instructed to report any such occurrence? Back in Paris, La Salle had planted these suspicions in his mind, warning him that outright physical attacks would be replaced by secret maneuvering. Now, he argued, since the king had given La Salle the stamp of approval, the Jesuits would be much more likely to discredit him. Or, de Tonti reflected sourly, discredit his trusted officers. De Tonti was already backing out. He averted his eyes from the shorn girl, not out of respect but out of revulsion. Again behind the bulkhead, but before securing it, he said, "Most humble apologies, Sister. I thought I heard a cry and had no idea I would be violating your privacy." Awkwardly he set the boards back into place.

She said nothing in response so he shoved home the plank that held the ingenious wall together and called hoarsely through it, "Please, I beg you forgive me, Sister."

At first she didn't answer. He had a fleeting cold fear that she may have gone to sound the alarm. So he said by way of explanation, "There has been an infestation of rats down here. I spoke of it to Madame Ormonde."

The young nun must have been standing very close to the panel, for he could plainly hear, "I shall pray that the rats will go away." There was a long moment filled with the creakings of the ship. Then she added, "Thank you, monsieur, for saving my life in the storm."

He muttered something self-deprecating. After a few quiet moments he relaxed. The worst had not happened, she was not immediately reporting his intrusion, but she continued, "And, monsieur, I will pray for your immortal soul."

What, he wondered as he leaned against the bulkhead, did she mean by that last remark? Her calmness after what should have been so unexpected an event as a man bursting through her wall left him with little doubt that the whole scene had been engineered.

He found himself trembling as he moved away from the bulkhead. That foul deceitful Ormonde had planned this to trap him. How had she found out? Had he been stupid enough to leave some trace of his presence? No, he had been most careful, making a list of every item he took to Jeanette's cabin, which he checked each time he left. Had the unfortunate girl somehow let slip a hint of their liaison? He doubted that. Their time together meant too much to her, and besides, all her intellect was sharpened against her tormentors. She simply would not give them any clue. God only knew what might become of her now, moved to some more wretched area if such were possible.

There flashed in his excited imagination a mental image of the poor chained creature in the sloshing bilge in the nethermost regions of the ship's body, green with seasickness from continual motion, her skin wrinkled in the fetid seawater. These gloomy thoughts persisted while he undressed silently in the dark. No light fell through the cracks from the other side of the wall. The sister apparently had no fear of further intrusion because presently when he pressed the cup to the partition he heard her gentle snore.

He paced barefooted, letting cold sweat evaporate from his prickling flesh. He chewed his thumbnail, seething with trapped energy, ready to run yelling up the companionway for all hands to help him locate the pitiful prisoner. He would search every splinter of the vessel for her, uncover the inhuman power that could mistreat a child of God in the name of that same God. Any sane and just mariner would rally to such a cause against whatever authority, he argued later, tossing in his hammock deep in the night. Later he dreamed about a knight made of metal save for his flesh right hand, and of his daring rescue of a tiny fair maiden from the talons of a hideous Psalm-quoting dragon.

But when consciousness assailed him, eyes full of grit, he knew suspicion would go against him from every goatish seaman aboard the *St. Honore*. None of the crew would take up his cause if it were known he'd swived the child. None would believe she had seduced him. As time ripened his memories of Jeanette, she would become the fairest, purest of women, unsullied by dirt, pious abuse, or the abuse of other men.

Even so, he hated himself that morning. The ugly truth was he dared not endanger his own enterprise in a cause that had so little chance of success.

His guilt from then on about Jeanette was that he had not lived up to his dream of being her hero. Despite the label "hero," and that given by a king, de Tonti never did feel particularly heroic. Wounds and imprisonment had soured his war experience for him. No accolade could ever make up for what it had cost. But he had no regret. He hadn't been lying when he told La Salle he never looked back. When he thought about it at all, he considered his loss a result of life's force on himself, similar to the fate that had thrown his father into lifetime imprisonment. In the son's case life had taken something from him but it also opened a door to fame and fortune in the New World that might have remained closed without the sacrifice. So much to gamble on the slim hope that he could somehow wrest the child from Ormonde's power, take on the entire Holy Mother Church, for Christ's sake. . . .

No, he countered. He'd never been afraid of the Church before. He was taking this line of inaction because it benefited himself and to hell with Jeanette. La Salle was right; men do what they must for their own motives. He could choose to help her and endanger them both, or he could remain silent and leave her to her fate while he pursued his own unencumbered by a runaway girlchild whose parents would surely come after him with the combined might of the law and the Church.

This was where guilt bit him. And because guilt was salt on so many recent wounds he found a place to hide it where he wouldn't have to feel it so keenly. He managed to misplace it in his idealized memory of Jeanette herself, the perfect infant woman, what a meditating priest would call his *anima* or spiritual female side. He grew more and more to remember her shining and golden in the first lantern light he brought into her darkness rather than sweaty and heaving with him in the hammock. All this was unconsciously born in de Tonti that first morning after he had burst into Jeanette's compartment to find her gone, completely eradicated from his current reality, thrust suddenly into the past where her perfection ripened in him as the embodiment of Woman, innocent and waiting for Hero.

But what he was consciously feeling that morning was self-reproach because he knew he wouldn't attempt a rescue. He had little power on this ship under La Salle's command. All he could succeed in accomplishing in the matter would be his own dismissal and more injury to Jeanette. If the hands were stirred up—and Madame Ormonde was not above using her influence to stir them up—they might toss him overboard as a bad luck Noah whose sins could sink them all. Sailors were a superstitious lot. La Salle wouldn't be able to stop them or might not even wish to. Jeanette was under lawful authority; he had no right to remove her from it. On land he might accomplish it and disappear, but even if he located her on board, where in the middle of the ocean could they find refuge?

So, with these thoughts souring him, the only person he located that morning was Sabat, whom he gruffly ordered to move his belongings to La Salle's cabin.

Only his old aide noticed an uncharacteristic reticence in the man, but their former familiarity was tarnished. De Tonti wasn't as approachable now as captain of the company as he had been when they shared their prison experience. Sabat hesitated to draw him out. But the old man did not like what was happening to his commander. He was sure La Salle was harassing him. But, he resigned himself, the die was cast. There was no turning back to France now, not with the faint blue smear on the northwestern horizon, which, the old hands assured him, was not the cliff of Hades but Newfoundland—truly the New World.

III

ARKANSAS

20

It was Mad Moon. Weeononka felt so warm and snug in the fireside of Cornsilk Weaver she almost forgot the old stories about how this month got its name. Some tribes called it Cannibal Moon. But because of all the beautiful dried corn, not to mention many horses, hides of beaver, and other trade goods, the people of the Iroquois village were enjoying a comfortable winter. Game was unusually plentiful that season; she heard the hunters speak of the abundance of eating animals as well as beaver they had trapped for the whites.

Weeononka didn't understand what the whites did with all those beaver skins. The Iroquois were vague on that point when she asked. The best she could determine, the whites came from a region where all the game animals had fled. To get fur they had to hunt in other lands. But what did they do with all that fur?

The few white trappers she saw in the village seldom wore fur. In a snowstorm they might wear a robe with the fur unshaved but unlike all well-dressed braves they didn't keep a rolled buffalo skin on their backs.

Nor did they use the hides in their ceremonials, at least from what Weeononka had been able to tell by watching the white sachem. Many things about the whites thus remained a mystery. It wasn't until the last quarter of Mad Moon that she got her chance to see a white man up close under circumstances where some of those mysteries might be explained. It was very close, as a matter of fact, because once again he walked into her on the path to Weaver's fireside. From time to time she had caught glimpses of the blackrobe white man that Walking Many Mountains had named for her the first night here. Brother Martin was a frequent sight at major village pathways or at the communal spring, where he spoke at passersby in his lovely language and in another language that gave Weeononka flight of heart when she heard him. The white sachem was muttering to himself in Sioux and his own tongue, gesturing wildly with his fingers this way and that, pointing, fisting, fanning like pale old birds.

213

It had been many moons since Weeononka had heard anything close to her native dialects, Osage and Quapaw. Very few similar words appeared in both Iroquois and the Siouan language Fleet Woman had grown up speaking. In many ways captivity among the Iroquois was a good life: She had been accepted and was not ill-treated, but she still hadn't warmed to their speech. She missed her own language. Here was the sound of home being spoken with a funny French accent by this crazy white sachem.

She was on her way back from a visit with one of the Weaver's relatives, who specialized in gathering herbal mixtures for pregnant women. She'd traded a pair of moccasins for three pouches of herbs, including ground maidenhair fern for cramps, in her parfleche this moment. She had decorated the trade moccasins richly with glass beads that Weaver had given her. She loved to work with the European material and had not touched a porcupine shaft since her introduction to the other alien kind.

It was getting dark. The snow that had softened in the afternoon sun had crusted. The path was slick. She had taken a shortcut hoping to beat the quickening dark when she heard the familiar cadences of her native tongue. She stopped, fascinated and delighted with the sound.

The old man almost walked into her. He stopped short in his conversation with nobody. He was so used to preaching to the air he was surprised to find one of these savage sinners actually listening to him. What's more, he saw with unconcealed joy that this one was with child. His only converts among this obdurate race had been dying infants, the only Iroquois he'd been allowed to baptize. This woman wasn't so far along that he wouldn't have time to talk her into letting him baptize her baby as soon as it was born. His many months of proselytizing among these heathens would not be in vain if he could snatch at least "one soul from the infernal wolf," as one Jesuit put it.

These thoughts were in his mind as he recovered from their mild collision and asked her who she was.

"Weeononka of the Quapaw," she replied, standing back from him. Walking Many Mountains said he was crazy; he might be dangerous, too. His eyes were an unbelievable color for human eyes, but there seemed to be kindness in their watery blue depths.

"Ah," he replied in French, "Then you would be *La Vite*." She asked him to say it again.

He patiently explained that in the French language, "Fleet Woman" would be translated as *La Vite*.

"How do you come to speak Sioux?" She had to repeat her question more slowly for him before he could answer, "I was stationed among them for a time," in halting Sioux and handsign.

"I would like to speak this French."

Brother Martin was in such feverish anticipation of saving her soul his hands were shaking. "I would be happy to teach you," he said, bidding her sit with him awhile. She looked negatively at the darkening sky.

In stumbling Sioux he invited her to come to his lodge the next day. She discovered that he knew little of her language— some memorized phrases of greeting and some of his scripture. He said he would serve her some white man's tea if she could find time. So she sat on a bench beneath a rough-hewn cross outside his lodge learning French. The Jesuit ran out of Sioux words immediately and neither of them spoke much Iroquois. He was surprised how fast this young woman learned his native language, which he'd been trained to teach in a proper seminary. At every opportunity Brother Martin guided their lessons toward his major goal, telling her parables and speaking of the Virgin and the Holy Child.

Walking Many Mountains would be furious if he knew Weeononka was learning French from the blackrobe. His own father, a Huron, had been converted by these same priests. Later when the Iroquois massacred the Christianized Huron, his father was among the martyrs to the new religion. The son never forgave the father for being taken in by what he considered a silly, womanish religion.

But Walking Many Mountains wasn't at the fireside these days. He spent most of his time translating for the war chief, who was talking to the whites. The last time he warmed his fireside bedroll, he told Weeononka to prepare to travel come spring. They were planning a big raid on a Kickapoo settlement west of here. And since it might be a long campaign, the warriors could bring one woman each to keep them fed and happy. He assured her the chiefs wouldn't move until spring, however, so she needn't be afraid of having to travel in the last moons of pregnancy. Now, she reasoned, if they were going among the white men, she wanted to be able to talk to them. Maybe some white women would appear to finally prove these whites were mortals after all. Also, in the back of her mind was the idea that this white sachem could interpret why the cloud in her dream had obscured her unborn child. A sachem was a sachem, no matter what his nation.

Several days' journey eastward overland and across Lake Erie from where Weeononka had grasped her first French words, De Tonti was about to experience his first view of Niagara Falls. He'd spent only a hurried afternoon in Quebec running errands for La Salle. When he returned to the *St. Honore* for the journey to Montreal, the nuns and their charges were gone.

He had missed even a parting glimpse of Jeanette. It depressed him to think he'd never see her again. He vowed that someday he'd come back and find her though he knew there was little chance he'd keep that promise. Meanwhile he had more than enough to occupy his time.

After a short time in Montreal they continued on to Lake Ontario via a rented barque. Nothing had worked out as planned; half the men deserted, they lost provisions through carelessness and theft, and the weather turned nasty in early November. Despite all obstacles La Salle pushed them on.

Primarily because of the brutal weather de Tonti took to the frontier style of dress immediately—leather suit, heavy Indian moccasins, a rolled-up buffalo hide that served a multitude of purposes. But he kept the old felt hat although the plume drooped under the barrage of snow and wind that accompanied their trip from Montreal to Ft. Frontenac, the first outpost on the frontier of the great unexplored West.

By the time they left that place the plume was gone. The beaver hat itself proved to be a marvelous umbrella, keeping rain off his face and neck most of a wet day before becoming saturated. De Tonti was pleased to hang on to the hat and vowed he'd never part with it. But it iced up several times while he was on shore hunting and the fire they crowded around wasn't enough to melt and dry it so he found himself looking out between miniature icicles on the eaves of a frozen hat. He wrapped his head in leather bands and wore the hat anyway. He knew the men laughed about it behind his back but it didn't bother him. He was glad they had enough spirit left to laugh at anything.

Christmas Eve in a bitter silver sleet they crossed Lake Ontario. For three days there was no change in the dreary weather.

They sang hymns on deck with little enthusiasm because the sleet turned to snow the next day. Beyond the slate-colored water, the forest rose immediately up into the low cloud that changed from snow to cold shrouding mist after noon. La Salle distributed a holiday drink. The winds were so contrary the following morning they were unable to buck them to get to the Falls. The pilot wouldn't move the ship but La Salle wasn't about to postpone his plans. He decided to haul half the supplies overland to the Falls.

"Why not just stay with the ship and wait it out?" de Tonti asked La Salle in a moment of privacy.

"You don't know this weather like I do," the Canadian said, perturbed that his second in command would argue with him. "It could freeze up overnight and stop us for weeks."

De Tonti morosely regarded the men struggling to offload the provisions. This arduous labor at least accomplished one thing—it kept them warm.

"Believe me, this is the only way," La Salle insisted shrilly, then dropped his voice in dark sarcasm. "All I need is for you to turn against me." He stamped off to supervise, leaving de Tonti to simmer in his doubts. It seemed insane to leave the relative comfort of the little ship and hike off into a blistering cold wilderness. Despite the grumblings of everyone else, La Salle had his way.

They left the pilot and his small crew on the barque with orders to proceed over the lake to the Falls as soon as the weather permitted. With him was the extra ship rigging and the rest of the expedition's supplies. The pilot and La Salle had been at each other's throat since the trip began. The commander ordered him to tie the barque up beneath the Falls but they found after struggling overland with the cargo for two days, that he had disobeyed orders. Afraid of Iroquois on shore, he had anchored in the great pool below the Falls.

An unfortunate combination of wind and undertow swamped the craft. They were able to save the anchors and masts for the *Griffin* but they were unable to catch months of provision from the current. La Salle's hope could not be dashed though it seemed to de Tonti that fate was inventing further obstacles to throw into their path.

All this left him in no mood to appreciate the beauties of nature. He'd heard about the Falls, however. Few white men had seen it and the reports he'd heard sounded almost mythical. The real thing proved to be more than the stories

and he never tired of watching all that water falling in an
awesome white wall and a cloud of mist that rose like a tower
into the winter sky. La Salle had appraised his situation
quickly; he knew he must press on or lose all his hands in the
face of these disasters. He sped up his plan to haul provisions
and rigging above the Falls and on to the *Griffin*'s construction
site. After only a day of rest he had his men groaning at the
task.

De Tonti stood now above the Falls, lightly burdened with
two coils of hemp rope. He'd gone ahead alone as a scout. The
scene below him brought back a sharp memory. From the
gorge ridge he watched the line of burdened men snaking up
toward him. He recalled a line of courtiers behind His Majesty
that had seemed like a dark ribbon unrolled through the
greenery. Now another human ribbon laced another land-
scape. The only reason this line of men reminded him of the
other was because of La Salle. Now he knew why Louis had
seemed so familiar: There was La Salle carrying nothing
himself but setting the pace for all. La Salle from this distance
in his billowing dark cape might be the king in stature and
posture. He walked at the head of the caravan with a long staff,
shepherd to the flock. Yes, de Tonti thought, that's the secret of
La Salle's personality. Because he saw himself as a king, he
imitated Louis' personal style. Maybe that's why he was so shy
about meeting Louis—he wished to be His Majesty, and was
afraid his arrogant envy would show.

It would be more than an hour before the rest of the party
reached de Tonti's position where he was enjoying a few
moments of reflection alone. His last bit of solitude had been
aboard the *St. Honore*. He repressed those memories because
it hurt to think of Jeanette, where she might be now and under
what circumstances. That time seemed a hundred years ago.
He fondly recalled the model of the *Griffin* he had given to La
Salle's fiancée in Montreal. Now the real thing lay ahead.

21

Building the real *Griffin* proved to be less difficult than
building the model. De Tonti had only to supervise construction of the larger vessel. Whatever visionary enthusiasm or

military prowess La Salle's recruits lacked at least they were
fairly skilled at their several occupations.

The master himself went back to Montreal to replace lost
supplies. In his absence the men were restless and quarrel-
some. When La Salle returned to the camp where they had
built the *Griffin*, he brought more bad news than good.

"My creditors have seized all my property in Montreal," he
confided to de Tonti as they stood on the raw new deck. De
Tonti couldn't believe that this might be the end of their
enterprise even before it began.

"What do we do now?" he asked, almost hoping it was over.
He had been thinking about going home. He'd never spent a
more miserable time in his life, even as a prisoner of war.

La Salle grinned at him. "We're going to take this bird to
Michillimackinac."

Which is exactly what they did. The *Griffin* wasn't the first
sail on Lake Erie; Indians often stood in their canoes with bear
robes stretched on their arms to catch a wind. But the *Griffin*
brought the first large sail to the lake. The piercing cold
remained but a freshening breeze favored her passage southwest then north through the narrows at Detroit on up Lake
Huron to the island named after the Great Turtle situated in
Lake Michigan's northern bottleneck. There they found that
La Salle's advance party had collected a good store of peltries.
The commander was nearly hysterical with delight as he
supervised the loading of his beaver fur fortune.

"This'll bail us out," he said gleefully, looking across the
rippled water at the Jesuits' log headquarters on the island.
"They thought they could stop me by hiring that pilot to lose
my provisions at the Falls." He laughed unpleasantly. "I'll
show the crows what competition can do."

De Tonti was astounded at this surmise. "You don't think the
pilot risked his own life to thwart you."

"The crows will stop at nothing, Hal. Nothing. Thievery,
destruction, even murder."

De Tonti bit his tongue at that hated nickname and at this
revelation of his master's instability. There was no evidence
that the pilot's loyalties were divided. Losing the ship was a
natural event made worse by human error. But he knew it
would do no good at this point to oppose the wild-eyed
Canadian.

La Salle dispatched two men aboard the *Griffin* to carry its
precious cargo back south over Lake Huron while he made

preparations to continue with the remaining force via canoe to the country of the Illinois.

De Tonti stood on the gravel beach watching the sails of his beautiful ship disappear around the headland. He shivered with a disquieting chill that came from more than winter when his mind flashed an intuition: He felt this might be the last he'd ever see of her. He tried to ignore the gloomy hunch. They faced more grim weather but La Salle was determined to press on. The two score Frenchmen and native guides took to their canoes southward on Lake Michigan the next morning. La Salle was a madman; he couldn't sleep and groaned with an upset stomach. He disdained any food offered for fear of poison, certain that his enemies would not relent until they had stopped him one way or the other. Publicly, however, he praised the Jesuits and even took on two of them as chaplains of the expedition. They also took on several civilized Shawnee guides. De Tonti had yet to encounter Indians in the wild and was looking forward to the experience. Those with the expedition seemed to him little different from the white men whom they tended to imitate. They all dressed in the leather uniform of the frontiersman, used firearms, ate the same wretched dried venison, and shared the same luck. So far, he had not seen an Indian woman closer than several paces.

The winter grew even worse with snowstorm after snowstorm that distressed the French and put religious terror into the Indians. They feared that *Michillimackinac*, the Great Turtle who held the world on his shell, was angry. Seeing the Indians in terror sent fear through French hearts. More men deserted, stealing trade goods and provisions. De Tonti went after some of these men. La Salle chased down others and brought them back to the grumbling ranks. Only sure death in the icy forest kept the rest with the party. Everyone was sick, cold, and discouraged. All except one.

La Salle drove them on. At the river called *Chicagou* they portaged across a barren frozen wasteland to the Illinois River. It was the most miserable time in a journey beyond misery. Provisions were short and game nonexistent. They fought each other over wild onions grubbed from beneath the snow. The third night of the ordeal La Salle hunkered down by the fire with de Tonti. The commander was silent for a while, blowing into his gloves because his spit was crystallizing on his lips. De Tonti knew the commander's unexpressed worries: The men who were supposed to report back from the *Griffin* were long overdue.

"I must go back and find out what happened to her," La Salle said softly so the others couldn't hear.

De Tonti remained silent, snuggled into his buffalo robe, thinking as La Salle continued, This man said "her." He didn't care about the men at all, only the ship.

"But we're going to meet some friends before I go," La Salle continued, insensitive to de Tonti's judgment of him. "I want to prepare you for your first meeting with the Illinois."

De Tonti couldn't feel his feet; he was cold down to his bowels, colder than he'd ever imagined a man could get and still be breathing. He was nursing a bad freeze burn on three fingers from touching the metal hand ungloved. He hurt in every part, his bowels were torn up from the bad food, and he was plagued by nightmares when he was lucky enough to fall asleep.

La Salle appeared impervious to everything around him. "No matter what they do, don't become distressed."

"What are you telling me? Stand still while they chew on me?" he replied, in no mood to be told that he must endure more discomfort of any kind and savoring the blemish of warmth cast by the fire on his otherwise perfectly cold body. His anticipation of meeting wild Indians was dampened anyway by his misery. He didn't feel he was welcome here, but La Salle assured him that the Illinois would be glad to see them. "These Indians are going to shock you with benevolence."

De Tonti turned his face from the flames to study La Salle. His cheeks were pink with the wind and the glow of ambition.

"They will touch you."

De Tonti prayed La Salle would commission him to open the brandy barrel. He imagined the chemical warmth of the liquor seeping down his throat and into his numb innards.

"So, don't insult them by turning away when they put their hands on you. Especially the women, but the men, too. It doesn't mean any danger."

De Tonti nodded. He wished La Salle would get to the point. Giving up on the brandy, he wished to do nothing less than lie down and go to sleep.

"And I suspect Nika will give me a . . ." he hesitated, watching de Tonti, "a special dinner, a feast of honor. They might put some, well, unappetizing things into your mouth."

"Into my mouth?"

"It's how they honor guests. And it will offend them if you don't eat."

"What sort of things?" Jesus, he was thinking, not human flesh.

"Well, meat. Like frogs."

De Tonti considered frog legs a delicacy.

"And raw oysters."

"I love *escargot* from the shell." He was feeling relief that his worse fears were unfounded.

La Salle smiled. "And dog." He watched the color drain from de Tonti's wind-burned face.

"You must not offend my friend. It will be the greatest honor. His favorite hunting dog."

"Christ—"

"But don't you see—it's the highest gift to give one's animal friend to one's human friend."

De Tonti looked sickened.

"Besides, the meat's rather good."

Weeononka went into labor right on the moon four days later. Cornsilk Weaver officiated in the birthing hut, certain this would be an easy one. But it was not. It was taking too long and by the second day of Weeononka's labor the old woman was worried. It looked as though the blackrobe would get this one. Just when she saw the little head and thought, Well here we are, it disappeared back up into the exhausted girl's body. Weeononka was sleeping in the hunkering birth posture; it would only be a nap between contractions. Two assistants supported her. They both knew Grandmother was fatigued. With a look the eldest assistant said, Why don't you get some air. The mother will be all right for a little while.

So Cornsilk stepped stretching out into the frigid blue evening. Behind her, Weeononka trilled again the vibrating song of birth. The weaver glanced over her shoulder until the girl slumped back into a brief nap. Going on three days now, she was thinking as she walked down to the lake's crusted fringe. She watched the last light seep from the sky, then took up a handful of snow. It tasted good after the stuffy hut full of its elemental smells and heated activity.

She heard the dry bushes crackle behind her. She looked sideways and saw the muted flash of feathers and a shaved scalp. "Surely it is not some warrior this close to the birthing hut."

"No warrior would dare to come this close," said her unseen grandson.

"Then a bush is speaking to me. Surely the prolonged birth of the Quapaw woman's baby has addled my poor old brains."

"But if a warrior did come this close to the birthing hut, it would be advisable to quickly give him the information he wants so he can hurry away."

"If some warrior did such a thing I would tell that warrior he's a fool. Glad such a foolish man is not among my kin." She rubbed snow onto her face, relishing its refreshing bite.

"Some warrior wants to know if the Quapaw woman is going to die."

"Some warrior better leave this place immediately."

"Some warrior might count this as coup, coming so close to the birthing hut."

"Some warriors are ignorant. I have to get back and save that baby."

The bush rattled. She clearly saw Walking Many Mountains in silhouette against the evening sky. "Save the woman instead."

"No warrior has the right to make such a suggestion. One who has already offended the Mother by approaching the birthing hut wouldn't dare risk doing it a second time in the same night."

"It's not an Iroquois baby."

"Some warrior must lose his infatuation with this woman."

"She'll accept an Iroquois warrior only after she has a baby of this fireside."

But Cornsilk Weaver had already turned and was headed back to her work when she heard a woman scream inside the hut. She thought it must be a further complication of birth and ran in small old-woman steps to the deerhide flap. A figure came running out of the lodge, not one of the birth assistants and certainly not the laboring mother. It was the blackrobe in a lacy surplice, cowering before the stronger assistant's blows as she screamed, "—offending the Mother—" and pushed him out.

He sat down heavily in dirty snow. "Oh no—not the holy water!" he cried as he crawled to retrieve the little metal bottle.

Weeononka, deep in the throes of labor, screamed words in her own language Cornsilk Weaver couldn't understand: "Southern barbarian, southern barbarian—"

Meanwhile some warrior who had been passing by came running up to the blackrobe. "Women—?" Walking Many Mountains queried, not daring to actually inquire inside.

Honored Grandmother stuck her head out of the hut. "Get him away from here," she ordered curtly, gesturing at Brother Martin. Behind the Grandmother, Walking Many Mountains could hear Weeononka scream with terror and pain, "Southern barbarian!"

"What did this worm belly do to her?" the warrior demanded, dragging the blackrobe up on his toes, shaking him so that his knobby head rattled and he dropped his holy water. He began screaming in his own language to add to the noise the Grandmother was sure would hex this birth beyond the damage that male presence had already accomplished.

The apprentice midwife fumed. "Came in here with his filthy medicine sprinkling it all around—"

"—must baptize the child—" Brother Martin sputtered, grabbing handsful of snow where the holy water had spilled. He haphazardly threw these holy snowballs at the open flap, all the while intoning his chants. Weeononka in the birth squat cried out again when she saw him through the opening.

Snow sizzled loudly in the firepit, threatening to extinguish the flames. The other assistant hurried to save it.

Cornsilk Weaver dropped the hide, stopping another salvo. The flap closed in the brave's face. He had nowhere to turn to vent his frustration, anxiety, and anger except on the old man who was trying to retrieve the vial. Walking Many Mountains dragged him screaming away from the birth premises, "Lord if this be my time I greet thee gladly." His voice faded out in the cadences of Latin echoing through the fog and off the trees. "Forgive me, Father, for I have sinned . . ."

That was the last the Honored Grandmother saw or thought of the blackrobe until after the birth early the next morning. The infant was frail, exhausted from its long passage. He was already a squaller, colicky and fussy. But the mother was strong and pink as she slept off her grueling work.

The next day, when the blackrobe was found tied upside down to the cross outside his hut, his blood had seeped out of him through the slash in his throat. He, his blissful smile, and his scarlet stream were frozen hard as pipestone. The war chief was furious because he had "smoked a peace" with the Jesuits. Now he would have to explain its egregious breach. He arrested seventeen braves of firesides surrounding the priest's hut. He instructed them to inform on the murderer; otherwise they could begin their death songs.

People said their terrible music of preparation brought the

long snow that night. None of the men relented because they were in a brother warrior pact with Walking Many Mountains. He stepped forward when he heard about the chief's ultimatum.

Weeononka watched him paint himself for the ordeal. His personal bodypaint signature was dramatic: expensive French vermilion on his entire head, neck, chest, and arms with a single line of long circles in stark white running like footprints from the center of his forehead down the right side of his neck diagonally across his heart and down his left arm to the back of the hand.

She considered that it was the most stunning body-name she'd ever seen. The sight of him coming upon an enemy must be terrible. He spent that afternoon applying this distinctive coat, then went to Weeononka resting on a buffalo robe beside the whining baby. Without words he offered her a rope of red braided leather, then extended his crossed hands. She took the rope, not sure what was expected.

"Tie my hands," he said softly. Behind him she could see everyone watching them. She sat upright and did as he asked. He pulled against the bond to test it, then said, "That baby is a brat and a weakling."

The infant was asleep but had a cloudy look on his pinched little face as he made miserable-puppy noises.

"I'll make him strong."

"Can you shut him up?" He offered his wrists again so she could add another knot.

She tied it elaborately, saying, "He'll settle in."

The man sprang to his feet in one swift graceful movement and turned away from her without further comment. He walked purposefully out of his grandmother's lodge with his fireside following and headed directly to the lodge of the war chief.

Along the way curious villagers attached themselves to the entourage following him through the new high snowdrifts.

The seventeen death songs echoed nearby. He walked into the chief's lodge without announcement, where the headman was getting a massage from one of his women.

"My father," he said to the startled warlord, using the honorific title, "let the ten and seven brothers cease their death songs and return to their firesides. I tell you I found great satisfaction in killing that blackrobe dog." He proceeded to explain why with dramatic punctuation.

There was nothing the chief could do. A warrior had a fundamental duty to protect the women of his fireside. The Honorable Grandmother confirmed his report about the blackrobe. What the chief would tell the other blackrobes when he must was that their man went *windigo* and had to be put out of his misery before he hurt somebody.

His great aunt sewed the corpse and its glassy blood stream into the finest buffalo hide and raised it to the highest branches of a sacred juniper. The chief sent a runner to the nearest Jesuit mission requesting it be claimed at their earliest convenience, preferably before the thaw. The great aunt reported to the women that the corpse had been smiling.

Meanwhile, Walking Many Mountains informed the Quapaw woman that he had been her champion. "I have done my duty," he said, "now you must do yours." He said this in public, before the Honored Grandmother, but Weeononka made no reply and he left her without pressing his point. There would be enough time later, after she recovered sufficiently to reason.

Cornsilk Weaver appraised the new child as inferior. "It's your decision but I tell you this baby won't live out the Hungry Moon." She urged the mother to expose it, fully her choice without sanction until the naming.

But Weeononka of the Quapaw gave the baby her breast. She sang to him, naming him Moon Runner because of the dream she'd had about him even though she still didn't understand it.

This baby was going to live.

22

Twenty-one Frenchmen, two priests, and their Shawnee guides brought their several canoes down the Illinois River directly into the startled midst of the temporary Illinois hunting camp. Six hundred or so Illinois looked up to see the foreigners with metal weapons gliding down their river. Women shrieked, braves grabbed their headknockers and the headmen came to the riverbank in person to receive the white men when it was realized that they were friendly Frenchmen.

Here were de Tonti's wild Indians, finally, clustered around them as they left the canoes and walked with the chiefs to the council lodge.

De Tonti found everything La Salle had said to be true. The women reached out to touch his clothes as he passed by. He had the distinct impression that they were all one many-armed creature. Their skin was as red as he'd been told, as red as clay, but with another hue, a pleasant but strange tone of rubbed copper or polished wood. Their dark eyes stared in uninhibited curiosity. All of them, men, women, and children were in absolute awe of the metal hand. He had never felt himself such an object of interest, not even at Court, and it made him distinctly uncomfortable.

But at least inside the huge skin-covered, loaf-shaped lodge it was warm. De Tonti had been cold for so many weeks on end, he'd forgotten what warm air felt like as he sat on the pile of buffalo skins beside La Salle. Behind him the rest of the men nervously took their places, their knives and guns handy.

But the Illinois were glad to see them, as La Salle predicted. They put out the best of their winter stores and fresh game. Two young women moved among the guests with food that they insisted on placing in their guests' mouths. De Tonti thought the women very beautiful, but couldn't catch their eye; they kept their glances demurely downcast. He didn't know what he was eating but it tasted good, better by far than the jerked meat they'd subsisted on since leaving Fort Frontenac. It was mostly concoctions of corn and dried meat, but he couldn't tell what animal it had come from and hoped nobody told him.

The elaborate meal was attended by the entire full-feathered council. Afterward, the chief, a middle-aged man of great dignity, undraped and lit the sacred calumet, and passed it around. He then gave each of the white men a personal replica of his own red stone pipe, decorated with feathers and colored strands of beads on leather.

La Salle opened his parfleche to give his hosts generous packets of tobacco while de Tonti and De Arcos passed out small hatchet heads. These gifts were received with great ohhing and ahhing among the Illinois braves.

La Salle had explained that an exchange of gifts over the calumet opened the way to negotiations with these people. De Tonti could see the Canadian was delighted with the pipes. In a way the calumet ceremony was a kind of native notary public that made any meeting official. Later the pipes could be used as passports among other nations, since each group had its traditional, distinctive way of decorating the pipes. La Salle finally made a grand speech in their hosts' tongue, French, and handsign, in which he said he had come to protect them from the Iroquois, to bring them knowledge of the true God, and to bring them trade merchandise to make their lives easier.

His speech caused great ripples of verbal response from the gathered chiefs, who obviously were not in agreement about the benefits just promised. One of the old men politely asked why the French would do all this for the Illinois, and why they were traveling here in the first place.

"We plan to descend the Mech-a-si-pi in a big wooden canoe."

This provoked even more astonishment from the Indians. Nikanape, who had greeted La Salle like a long-lost brother when they had first entered the village, stood up to respond to his white friend's remarks. "We welcome you, brothers, but would not consider ourselves dutiful if we failed to warn you about the dangers that await any traveler down the Great River."

The chiefs all agreed with a show of head nodding and enthusiastic comments among themselves.

Nikanape continued, "If you make it past the whirlpools and rapids, there are cannibals who will attack you a little way down the river." The Illinois headmen further agreed with the spokesman, and continued adding comments after he'd finished saying, "Man-eating alligators as big as a war canoe live in the lower reaches, and beyond that the river falls into a deep pit."

La Salle waited for the concert of agreement to die down, then replied with a steady gaze that swept each of the chiefs, "If the Illinois don't have the heart, we'll go to the Osage—"

It was as though he tossed pitch onto a fire. The red faces around him blazed in a flurry of indignant protests. De Tonti, who was still learning to speak their language, was near enough to La Forest to hear a translation of what La Salle had just said in Sioux, the language of the Illinois, Osage, and several other Mech-a-si-pi nations. The other white men were distressed to hear about the monstrous alligators, whirlpools, and cannibals. More than half the expedition had been lost to desertions; these disclosures might thin their numbers further, which La Salle could ill afford.

"We thank our friends for the warning," the explorer was

saying above the din, which ebbed as his forceful voice filled the smoky lodge. "But we are men of honor who welcome challenge, even as Illinois braves." He let that manipulating compliment settle in as he picked up a small iron cooking pot that held *sagamite*. "This is not French made," he said in a stern voice. Nikanape sprang to his feet as if to make a defense, but La Salle continued, "You have taken gifts from the English, like this. Their friends the Iroquois have polluted your mind against us."

"No, brother—" Nikanape started to say, but La Salle turned on him in genuine anger.

"Are you playing both sides, Nika?"

Nikanape protested, greatly affronted, and the first meeting ended shortly afterward. The whites had been given lodges in the village but La Salle set out a watch. Late that night when the watch was to change, his men woke him with the news that the first watch had deserted. Now there were only ten Frenchmen in the expedition, plus the civilized Shawnee guides, who stayed loyal. At dawn La Salle addressed them. "I can do without any one of you," he told them.

De Tonti shouted, "I am with you all the way!" D'Arcy, La Forest, and the fur trader Couture cheered their agreement, and La Forest gestured that the others should join them in affirming their loyalty.

"No, let them go," La Salle petulantly insisted, turning from them in disgust.

De Tonti saw the men expected more from their leader, who appeared to be sulking. "Listen," he said in a friendly voice. "You are free men. You may leave us, of course, but think of the glory and the money that will come to the first white men to explore the mouth of the Great River."

They muttered among themselves, for the most part unconvinced.

"Then leave us," he said with a gesture at the forbidding frozen woods around them. Beyond their circle several Illinois watched their every move. What chance would a lone white man or two have in that wilderness with these same strange eyes following? And north and east beyond this forest where one would have to go to get back to civilization waited the Iroquois. "But we offer this to you," de Tonti concluded, "Stay with us until the weather breaks. We welcome you and would not have your mysterious deaths in that forest on our conscience."

There were no more desertions. In fact, after that there seemed to be some small renewal of hope among them. The Illinois gave them stores of corn and meat and sent along two of their own men as guides. One was Nikanape, who begged La Salle to forgive any unintentional offense. From then on, he never left La Salle's side. The chief told La Salle the next day that his people were forever allies of the French. La Salle said they would build a fort on the river near this tribe's permanent village to protect them against the Iroquois.

Against de Tonti's advice he named the place *Crevecoeur*, Fort "Brokenheart." While three men felled trees for the stockade, he put his carpenters to work on the *Griffin's* little sister. Meanwhile, there was still no word concerning the fate of the *Griffin* or the fortune in furs aboard her. As soon as the second barque's keel was laid, La Salle left for Fort Frontenac to find out about her and to replace the supplies lost below the Falls. With him went Couture and La Forest and a handful of men and guides.

Not a week after his departure two of those men returned to Fort Brokenheart with new orders for de Tonti. Since this position was secure among the Illinois allies, and three carpenters could finish the little ship without him, de Tonti was to go to another river location where La Salle wanted him to build Fort St. Louis of the Illinois. This was all part of his master plan: A string of military and trading posts along the water highway of the Great Lakes–Illinois–Mech-a-si-pi system.

The two men La Salle sent back came with trade goods and brandy, which enlivened de Tonti's men. But they also brought bad news. Rumors had it that La Salle was broke and maybe dead. There were reports the *Griffin* had been wrecked on purpose so La Salle's peltries could be stolen.

The couriers brought a message from La Salle, which de Tonti read to the assembled men in the front room of their new stockade. The message was a joke that dispirited him because La Salle seemed to have no understanding of normal human doubts. He believed so completely in his vision he could not see that other men just wanted to be warm, to be fed, and especially to be fairly paid. Basically his note said everything was all right and they must be patient a little longer.

"We'll never get our money," said an older Canadian, speaking for the others, who growled their agreement behind him. "I vote to break up this party now."

"No," 'Per insisted. "My master has never left his servants without their reward. Besides, you are all under contract."

Sabat gave de Tonti a significant glance. He knew his own servant would keep quiet.

"No offense, monsieur," the Canadian replied, "but your loyalty as the Sieur's servant has been bought over many years. He hardly knows any of us.

"He don't care if we live or die, much less if we're paid," said the ferryman who had signed on at La Rochelle.

De Tonti let them argue awhile. Along with Sabat he sat silently to one side. He had ordered the two couriers to keep their mouths shut but it wasn't healthy to squelch honest speculation. They had not been invited to this meeting; neither had the two priests, who had other loyalties and did not depend on La Salle for their livelihoods. He only wished La Salle had had the foresight to send a small advance on the men's pay. It would have been a gesture they'd respect. Privately he had his own doubts that La Salle cared for any of them, including himself. In the dark of many nights he'd reflected that perhaps he and all of them were just pawns to someone who wanted to be a king. His experience showed him that kings had a way of ignoring the consequences of their kingly actions on ordinary men.

"Contract be damned," spat the fur trapper who went by the name of Jollyheart but who belied it with a perpetually sour disposition. "I'm about ready to take my chances among the Iroquois. At least they honestly call themselves snakes and don't pretend to be anything else."

"I for one will wait for Monsieur de La Salle before I make my decision," said D'Arcy. De Tonti silently thanked his own foresight in hiring this quiet loyal fellow whom he trusted more than any of the others. "I can't see throwing away a chance of a lifetime just because this enterprise is difficult."

The men rolled this around among them as D'Arcy concluded, "And we knew it wouldn't be easy. We're doing something that's never been done before."

"Besides," 'Per interjected, not sounding offended that they suspected him, "where would you spend your salaries in this godforsaken place?"

At least that provoked agreement. De Tonti motioned for Sabat to pour another round. They tossed out more objections in a halfhearted way and finally when everyone had had their say, de Tonti took the floor. "He owes me more than any of you, in salary and advances on the furs I've gathered for him. I'm willing to wait and I think, considering our position in this hostile country, you should wait too." Privately he was wondering if there was any truth to his own words but was determined not to show loss of heart. "He's never proved false to me and he certainly can't be blamed for the weather and natural disasters."

The men listened. It was Jollyheart who replied, "Sir, I wish to the Lord it was you who was my master." The others agreed heartily, though de Tonti suspected the brandy might have had something to do with it. "I don't blame La Salle so much for our circumstances. It's his disregard for us that worries me."

"Here, here," Sabat said from his corner, speaking for the first and only time in the meeting.

To a man they nodded their heads as the fur trader continued, "I'd follow you anywhere, though, and because of you I'll stay my plan to strike out on my own for a little while. I'll give the Sieur one more chance."

A mild agreement rippled through them and after finishing their brandy they dispersed to the other room of the poor fort.

Sabat lingered. De Tonti looked up at him, warmed by the look in his eye that asked if there was more he could do for de Tonti. "That's all for tonight, old friend." Without comment the old man departed, loosening the bearskin that served as a door between this and the common room, leaving the commander to his thoughts.

A private addendum on La Salle's message reminded de Tonti to work on his diary. "We cannot relax for a moment," it concluded, "because our enemies surround us with lies and innuendo. Only our own true reports can balance their falsehoods."

So it was with aching feet and dire forebodings that de Tonti traveled a few days later with his best men to Starved Rock, where most of the Illinois lived. Because of their mission, the two priests asked to go with him. He left 'Per in charge of Fort Brokenheart.

De Tonti reflected that he'd begged La Salle not to condemn the place to such a name. Why tempt fate? But Rob, who thought to sidestep fate by coming at it directly, wouldn't listen. He never listened to any advice, and here again de Tonti was left to pick up the pieces.

He had set the men to work under Sabat's supervision up on the bluff and headed for the Illinois encampment. The priests welcomed this chance to preach among the Illinois with the hope they'd be more amenable to the Faith than the Iroquois. It was very quiet, one could almost say boring, in the Illinois village beside the river named for these Indians, the day L'Esperance brought the news from Fort *Crevecoeur*.

De Tonti sat cross-legged outside their bark house in the middle of the Illinois enclave, working on the damnable memoirs Rob had ordered him to keep.

He'd put off the onerous task because of the press of events. But during this lull he finally set himself up with sharpened turkey quill, local sumac ink, and the cheap blank book La Salle had presented to him for the purpose. The damnable thing had columns marked on each page; back in France the Canadian had picked up a deal on a case of ledgerbooks. De Tonti hated looking at the banal notebook.

Its coarse Dutch paper was an offense, bound to display scribbled words forever inadequate, even though he knew an editor would transcribe them before they were read by any courtly eye. Still, de Tonti felt woefully inept. The experience of having a writing task reminded him of all his miserable years in the classroom under some nun's switch.

The impression of a classroom was vaguely supported by a couple of Indian boys who squatted in a position that de Tonti found uncomfortable but that seemed easy for these people. At any hour of the day or evening a silent audience of villagers encircled the white men's lodge. They seemed to come and go in shifts, ever polite, ever unobtrusive, but ever observant of these interlopers in their midst.

De Tonti didn't mind; while they were studying him, he was studying these strange humans. He was convinced they were men just like himself despite French prejudices. He liked them. His interest made him facile at learning their various dialects. He knew instinctively that an understanding of their ways could enrich him and maybe even save his life in this wild country.

He winked at one of the native boys, breaking the child's stoic concentration. The children weren't used to being regarded by white men, who ignored them for the most part. But they liked his attention.

"What are you doing?" the boy asked shyly in sign, edging a little closer like a frog in his unnatural crouch.

"Drawing words—see these marks?" He was fairly proficient in Iroquois, thanks to Father Ribourde's tutoring, but he felt

barely able to talk to children in Sioux, the language of the
Illinois.

The boy giggled, joined by his friend, who wouldn't dare to
come closer. They knew words were spoken into the air; it was
utter nonsense to think they could be drawn into the crazy
white man's little box, which they called a "book."

"Funny spirit," said the boy gleefully, then commented to
his friend, "Sometimes he just sits and stares at the little box.
My mother says it's an exercise for sore eyes." Mirth convulsed
both the boys.

De Tonti understood just enough to catch a glimpse of how
odd the act of reading must look to these people who had a rich
diverse verbal language but had no concept of the written
word.

He was glad for the diversion, but returned to his work.
Each word constipated him. How could he distill the past two
years' events into a few scratchy pages of his crabbed left-hand
scrawl?

He reread his opening lines. Those at least seemed to the
point: "After having been eight years in the French service, by
land and by sea, and having had a hand shot off in Sicily by a
grenade, I resolved to return to France to solicit employment.
At that time Monsieur Cavelier de La Salle, who honored me
with his favor, came to Court seeking to obtain leave to
discover the Gulf of Mexico by crossing the southern countries
of North America. . . ." On second thought even this seemed
somehow wrong.

He was about to cross it out and start all over again when
'Per entered the village with a three-man Illinois guard on his
flank. De Tonti helped him get his pack off then offered him
Indian tea, which Father Ribourde was kind enough to get.
The several Frenchmen with de Tonti were all eager to hear
any news. As always, a few adult Illinois joined the two boys,
aroused to curiosity by the arrival of this other spirit.

Poor old 'Per looked about to drop, and even before he said
hello, de Tonti knew the worst had happened.

"All the men deserted," 'Per said miserably. "Burned our
stockade to the ground." He took a gentlemanly sip of
steaming tea. "Took everything they didn't burn—powder, ball
lead, stores, pelts—everything."

"Did they burn the little ship?" de Tonti asked, and was
surprised at the answer.

"I guess they figured there wasn't enough of it finished to
trouble with," replied the servant, taking a fresh cup from the

friar. "They scribbled a message in charcoal on a plank
. . . 'Nous sommes tous sauvages.'" We are ourselves all
savages. "I guess they figured my master wouldn't be able to
pay them," he offered as explanation.

De Tonti nodded. Those two Frenchmen who had brought
La Salle's new orders had done far more harm than good.

He was still mourning the loss of his beautiful *Griffin*. This
venture was not turning out at all as he had envisioned it back
in that café in Paris. How grand and noble it had seemed then,
how anxious he'd been for La Salle to accept him. Now he
wished he'd never gone after the man. What he wouldn't give
to be back home in Paris. Maybe he could have gotten on as a
guardsman of the royal household. . . . If he'd just been
patient, the peace with Spain would surely have been broken.
A few more months and he might even have gotten a
European commission.

His own optimistic words on the breeze-ruffled diary page
mocked his regret. . . . *La Salle, who honored me with his
favor* . . .

"At least you saved the forge and most of the carpentry
tools," said 'Per, glancing inside the cabin, where the crates
were arranged as pieces of furniture.

Everyone's attention was on de Tonti, who appeared to be
woolgathering, staring into space. He became aware of the
silence around him and shook himself out of his reverie.
"We've got to get this news to Rob."

"I volunteer to meet him at Fort Frontenac," said 'Per
without hesitation.

De Tonti started to argue but La Salle's servant persisted.
"This wilderness is killing me, Monsieur de Tonti. Please let
me return to civilization where I might have a chance of
serving my master a few more years."

De Tonti saw the old man was pleading for his life.

He assigned a couple of trusted men to accompany 'Per.
Maybe La Salle could find a way to save the enterprise if he
was informed immediately of Fort *Crevecoeur*'s loss before his
enemies found out. He remembered La Salle's comment about
his fiancée's desire to assist the expedition. He knew La Salle
would take on any debt, even risk marriage, to get his chance
at the Mech-a-si-pi.

By the time 'Per and his escort pushed off in their pitifully
understocked canoes, de Tonti's spirits were again high. He
had been able to buck up the others but privately he'd begun
to doubt. Now, hope crept in again.

He was working on the diary on another afternoon of the week 'Per left. He had gotten over his initial reluctance to write; now he was scribbling furiously, knowing that he'd copy this later, probably editing most of it out.

It was another quiet afternoon. The great village around them hummed with activity. Most of its population was off hunting. Those left behind were not fighting the heat to do any heavy labor. Everyone, including numerous yellow dogs, found their spots of shade and settled down for a nap.

De Tonti's spot was just outside the bark house, where he spread a buffalo robe under an evergreen that smelled particularly nice on the warm air.

The two Jesuit fathers were off in retreat. Their original joy at preaching to these Indians had dimmed. Both were dispirited because they hadn't won a single convert here. These Illinois were just as obdurate against the Faith as the Iroquois.

Sabat, D'Arcy, and two other Frenchmen were occupied up on the rock where La Salle wanted Fort St. Louis of the Illinois to be built. He alone of the whites was in the village that afternoon, scribbling in his journal details of the sea journey that had brought him here. He liked the atmosphere and hum that hung above the Indian camp. It was made up of cooking smells, dog barks, children's cries and laughter, and the buzz of human activity behind leather tent skins. All together this produced a soft aromatic murmur he found peaceful.

If Father Ribourde had been there, de Tonti would have been studying Iroquois. With his teacher gone de Tonti found no excuse to avoid the dreaded diary. But once tackled, the task wasn't so bad. He was completely absorbed in recollections, some of which he reported but many he did not.

As he worked, D'Arcy returned to the bark cabin to fetch up more spades—the shafts were breaking against the rocky escarpment into which they were sinking foundations.

He didn't bother the captain at his labors, but went immediately to the crated tools, where his scrapings barely penetrated de Tonti's concentration. After a while D'Arcy found the last of the spare handles and began the walk back up to the rock, giving the commander a friendly wave when he saw him glance up from his writing. De Tonti acknowledged the greeting and was about to stand and stretch when a commotion arose on the path where the man was headed.

A warrior came running between the lodges, gathering an excited crowd around him. He didn't stop to speak but in the tradition of runners continued his inexorable trot toward the chief's counsel lodge. But by his demeanor and by the painted symbols on his face and chest, the Illinois villagers knew that this man had spotted an Iroquois war band not far away and heading in this direction.

De Tonti threw the journal into the cabin and grabbed up his weapons, knowing by the chatter around him what was happening. His mind raced with questions and probable answers. What had happened to the Iroquois peace with the French?

Women moaned and children screamed. The few warriors in the encampment swabbed themselves with paint and clacked lances against headknockers in the opening chorus of the war song. If any Iroquois were about, the din would guide them directly here, he reflected.

But it didn't matter anyway. If Iroquois were on the warpath, they'd been reconnoitering this place for days.

Remembering La Salle's lessons about the superior person being approached, de Tonti stood outside the cabin, forcing himself to be still and to patiently await what would surely be a delegation of his Illinois hosts.

He was not disappointed.

It was difficult not to feel threatened at the sight of the two headmen approaching with their armed entourage trailing behind, followed by a horde of angry villagers, crying women, and barking dogs. The dust they stirred up was stinking with animosity.

"Why have you lied to us, Iron Hand?" the headman demanded, not waiting for the interpreter. De Tonti was fairly proficient at understanding the meaning of what was being said, though the speed at which the man harangued caused him to miss a word here and there.

But not the emotional message. De Tonti wished now that Nikanape were here to mollify them but he'd gone with La Salle.

"You French spirits have caused the Snake-persons to make war on us. It is your fault the Iroquois attack. What are you going to do about it?"

"Is this why that rascal chief of yours left, to join his allies against us?" demanded one of the senior warriors, who had already put on war paint.

"There was a blackrobe among the Iroquois—I saw him up close taking a piss from under his black skirt," said the scout. He used the word for a woman's garment, which made a couple of the warriors snicker. He was sweating profusely from his run and from the excitement he'd stirred up.

The mob around de Tonti growled like a single wolf. He felt himself their prey, but he forced down panic and said in an even voice, "There must be some mistake—it's well known that some Iroquois mask societies dress in long black robes."

Someone in the angry crowd around him agreed but the majority remained unconvinced.

"Because of your lies we've lost time getting the women and children to the island where they'll be safe."

"Why have you French lied to us?"

"Tell the truth!"

One of the warriors in a growing rage pushed over a crate of tools, which clattered to the dusty floor of the cabin. Many hands reached out to grab the spilled axes, shovels, and crowbars; de Tonti was sure they were stealing them but then he saw several burly braves hoisting the various pieces of the forge between themselves.

Others were hauling out the bellows and other forge instruments. De Tonti protested but was forcibly stopped by the growling mob. As he watched, they dragged everything metal to the river and from a ledge over a deep channel tossed it all into the swift current.

"You bring evil *wa kon* among us with bad metal, Frenchman—"

"Prepare to eat your own fat."

But the headman called to them to be silent, having let them vent some steam by destroying the metal objects.

He ordered everyone to leave him so he could speak alone with Iron Hand. With several demonstrations of anger and many muttered asides, the people complied, retiring a few paces from the lodge while the two men conferred.

De Tonti was able to convince the old man that he personally would lead an attack on their mutual enemy. He volunteered to go with his men, who were returning even now from the construction site after hearing the commotion down here.

Later, scouts brought further bad news.

Iroquois indeed were massing not a league away, armed to their ear slits and dancing to the song of war. They further disturbed the people with a rumor that La Salle had been seen

among the Iroquois. It was only the headman's word to de
Tonti that kept him off the torture pole. When the headman
explained that Iron Hand would lead the attack on the enemy,
the people were somewhat mollified.

Still, the women packed their belongings and rounded up
their children to leave camp. Through the restless night,
family after family canoed to an island refuge downriver.

The night air was full of smoke from the fires lit by warriors
who were dancing for battle. They danced through the night,
the eerie sounds of their drums throwing a mounting tension
into every living thing in the vicinity. De Tonti felt it as an
almost unbearable tightness in all the joints of his body, a
knotting of the stomach.

Animals fled. Birds shrieked off into the forests.

As if the Illinois war preparations weren't enough, the
Iroquois over the rise could be heard at their own hostile
music, screeching for blood.

Only the dead knew any rest that night.

23

De Tonti dozed fitfully in the bark cabin with his men,
everyone sleeping lightly with weapons under their hands.

In the false dawn all the dancing and war songs ceased. A
stealthy quiet settled over the birdless forest. The river level
seemed to drop, sucking air out from between the trees.

This silence was in its own way more terrible than the chants
because nightmares crept into the holes left by the absence of
sound. The uneasy stillness woke de Tonti like a shot. He
slipped outside without waking the men to think things over.
His body was aching from a tossed night of no deep sleep. His
eyes stung and he felt in the cold morning there was no
comfort possible to body or soul. Unable to sleep further, he
walked under the pale sky by the river trying to see if the forge
and its accoutrements might be salvaged, but the current by
the rock was rapid. He found no trace of the apparatus.

Leaning against a tree, he watched the sky lighten. Far
away, on the fringes of the uplands a hoot owl called. By dawn
he had devised his argument for both the tribes he stood
between.

When he saw the number of Iroquois assembled against them, he knew the less-warlike Illinois didn't have a prayer. Their only chance was negotiation and he knew without a doubt who'd get the job of mediator.

Here alone would La Salle have been welcome, for even if he didn't know how to handle his own people, nobody knew better than he how to deal with the tribes.

De Tonti hoped he could remember all the Canadian had taught him. The most important thing was to appear courageous, unperturbed by the odds or possible outcome. They placed a high store on style. In those early morning hours de Tonti planned the style with which he'd meet the enemy.

In the morning he left his hat behind so as not to have it shadowing his eyes. Also, he didn't take a weapon. Instead he borrowed a thick strand of wampum from the pitiful remaining stores and walked toward the knot of Iroquois headmen with the beads swinging on the fingers of his raised right hand, hoping Rob was correct about it possessing *wa kon*.

He ordered D'Arcy and another Frenchman plus one of the Illinois braves to follow him only so far. Every few paces one of them had been told to stop walking and wait at parade rest.

He planned for them to accompany him back out of the Iroquois midst when his mission was accomplished. In this way, with his obedient, disciplined retainers, de Tonti would look more the chief to the status-conscious Iroquois.

Finally in the increasing sunlight he was walking alone, his moccasins crunching on the dry grass and gravel of the sloping meadow just outside the Illinois village, where all its inhabitants stood with the remainder of his men in a silent rank watching him proceed.

He was sweating. His heart pounded as he observed from the corners of his eyes the wild soldiers flanking him as he approached their war chiefs in full battle array.

Flashes of red, white, and black paint seemed to shoot out at him from the chiseled faces. They were silent, not seeming to breath as he passed their squadrons.

But he had heard them last night screaming for blood. They would cut him up and eat him this moment but for their curiosity.

He was thinking that war had never been like this for him in the past. Among civilized men, war was an art, a game. One went at an enemy who fought by the same gentlemanly rules, whether upon playing fields or behind fortress ramparts. He noticed that many of the Iroquois women were standing behind the warriors. He hadn't known it was traditional to bring families on long sorties.

These thoughts played across his mind as he advanced among the fiercely painted savages. The sun sparkled off the white-and-purple necklace of strung beads on his hand. The beads slapped against the metal with a shushing sound, a whisper of brass brushed by glass. His steps were measured. He could see what must be a head chief ensconced on a bear robe litter and surrounded by his naked, bald, and feathered lieutenants. What felt like a thousand glinting eyes needled him.

Step, step, step, now silent in the beaten dust he made his moccasin prints. About ten paces away from the headman he stopped with military precision, leaving the only movement around him the beads swinging on his hand.

He imagined he could hear the warriors' hearts beating around him. Suddenly in a flash of copper-colored flesh and vermilion something moved toward him from the left. Metal hit metal. He was face to face with a young Iroquois decorated with many scalp tassels. The Iroquois had a look of perplexity as he regarded his deflected French knife blade, which should have been dripping gore. He knew where he'd placed it. Instead the sunburned man regarded him with puzzlement, looking at the cut string of wampum between them. The beads dripped off the gut wire, raining into the dust.

The brave saw something different about the stranger's hand. It seemed to infuriate him because he swung the knife again, aiming for the heart. But the white man was quick; the metal hand shot out like a snake's tongue, as the brave would later describe it, deflecting the blow with its own to his jaw. Both men heard the crack of bone. The warrior staggered back, feeling his chin with his free hand.

At first de Tonti felt nothing but as he stepped closer to the headman, who was now standing in surprise and anger at his uncontrolled soldier's actions, he felt the warm trickle of blood under his leather clothing. He didn't dare look down for fear the sight of his own blood would weaken him. Instead he stared with as much steel as he could forge into the eyes of the headman.

The Frenchman still held the battered rope of wampum. It was so obviously a gesture of peace after the unwarranted attack, no reasonable person could resist him. His gaze didn't waver; that impressed the war chief, who remarked with harnessed fury to the young brave, "Once again you behave rashly, Walking Many Mountains. See this spirit does not have pierced ears, therefore he cannot be an Illinois or an Iroquois or any red man with whom you are familiar. This is why the decision to make war resides in older more experienced men, and not in young braves."

It was crushing for Walking Many Mountains to be thus admonished by his war chief. He hung his head, shamed beyond endurance.

The war chief immediately ignored his unruly man and gave his attention to the wounded Frenchman, whom he personally touched to assist in sitting down. He ordered with succinct gestures that his aides bring something to soothe the visitor, some bandages and ointments to take away his pain. Already his personal sachem was helping the white man to expose the wound—thank the Mother it was superficial. The young fool could have killed this foolish spirit, the old man thought to himself as he watched the sachem's quick hands apply a sponge of cattail fluff to the profusely bleeding scratch above the white man's left nipple. What a filthy hairy people these whites were, he observed.

The headman was interested to see buckles and straps under the spirit's clothing; it satisfied him to know that the metal hand was held on in a quite explainable manner and was not growing with the flesh as some of his more gullible spies had reported.

He glanced at Walking Many Mountains, ignored by all now, slinking over in the shadows. The warrior had been eager to catch his chief's eye, to glean some gesture from him that would help him recover some face. In succinct handsign the headman gestured that the brave was forgiven. He must make amends with a suitable gift to the Frenchman whom he had insulted.

The warrior's face brightened and he dashed off, left to determine what the gift should be.

The chief turned back to the Frenchman, who looked less likely to faint now. He nearly laughed at the white man's look of astonishment as one of the elder braves lifted his long braid with a knife.

What sort of Frenchman was this who braided his hair like a civilized person? Most of them wore it long and tangled like a girl's. The chief realized that this man's clothing, so unlike other Europeans' in its leathery practicality, as well as his plaited hair and dark skin had misled the hot-tempered youth to attack what he thought was an Illinois. So, this was a different sort of Frenchman.

De Tonti was sure the warrior holding his hair meant to scalp him. He wasn't hypocrite enough to mouth a formal prayer, but he silently asked Jesus to forgive him all his many sins in preparation for what surely was coming. He fervently hoped they'd simply knock out his brains instead of torturing him over a slow fire. One of the other chieftains advanced the opinion that that's what they should do with him.

The headman disagreed. They debated with great civility like this for a while as de Tonti listened. He was dizzy from loss of blood but he didn't miss what was being said. Where his Iroquois was ragged, he took the meaning from their handsign and the emotional import from their heightened tone of voice. He had already noticed that these people didn't hide their emotions like Europeans. They wore them blatantly on their faces.

"I tell you sincerely," he said when the agreeable chieftain posed a question to him, "the Illinois are ready to bring twelve times one hundred to battle." A rude round of disagreement pulsed through the chieftains. "You heard them dancing last night—their song was even louder than the song of the renowned Snake-persons." De Tonti supplemented his Iroquois with handsign. They were surprised the white man spoke fair Iroquois. And they would discuss for some time to come his intelligent modifications of sign used tolerably well even with an inflexible right hand.

"Besides, we have sixty Frenchmen with muskets to defend their Illinois brothers, who are under the protection of the Great Ontonio, the King of France."

These numbers impressed the assembled generals, who murmured among themselves. Their scouts had told them only about five hundred Illinois and less than ten Frenchmen occupied the village on the river.

Finally after a long debate between the Frenchman and the two Iroquois factions, the headman spoke. "My brothers. If we can get our designs without killing then we will do so. This Frenchman has a brave heart—you saw the way he approached us. Despite attack he did not fight his attacker. I believe his suit for peace is sincere. We have been friends with this La Salle. Let us not break our word, but send this worthy opponent back to his camp with a token of our goodwill and a pledge to meet with the Illinois elders two noons hence on the meadow between our encampments. This man will be there that day to *parley* with us." They had already borrowed a French word, one the French used a lot; Frenchmen loved to talk. He gave de Tonti a beautiful beaded belt for La Salle and asked him to take word of the proposed parley to the Illinois chiefs.

Sticky with blood under his clothing and sick with the taste of it in his mouth, de Tonti retraced his steps, picking up his men along the path where he had stationed them and to their credit where they waited per his instructions even though they were the targets of Iroquois stares and hostile imprecations.

D'Arcy whispered at his elbow as he helped him to walk, "Why would they be building such big canoes?"

Without pausing, de Tonti eyed several Iroquois braves working on the largest canoe he'd ever seen. "Not for a fishing expedition, I'll wager."

They didn't waste any time leaving the Iroquois encampment. D'Arcy and the other Frenchmen supported de Tonti right and left as they returned to the Illinois village, where the two friars had returned from their camping retreat when they heard there was trouble. Father Ribourde gave him something to stop the flow of blood, which was great considering the shallowness of the cut. He cleaned the wound and bandaged it, using a poultice offered by an Illinois sachem and known by the priest to cut infection. As he worked, the old priest said, "I will hear your confession, my son."

"Am I that far gone?"

"I think you'll be all right. But it wouldn't hurt. . . ."

"You're wasting your prayers on me, Father," de Tonti said playfully. "The Lord has given up in my case." Of all the priests he'd met on this venture so far, Ribourde was the most sincere and most humane. He was a slender, continuously high-spirited man in his middle sixties whom de Tonti understood to be the scion of a wealthy French family. To give up the life he inherited to come to this place was evidence of his genuine love of his work. He was an excellent teacher with a gift for language. Between the friar and de Tonti had sprung a friendship despite their unbreachable differences.

"The Lord never gives up, my son," the priest replied seriously. But there was a twinkle in his glance as he bandaged

the captain's wound, which was closer to his heart than
Ribourde wanted to admit.

Even with news of the parley, the Illinois were nervous.
More and more of their tribe found reasons to cross the river
and join the women on the safe island rather than be there
when the Iroquois attacked, as most believed would happen
despite the friendly words. De Tonti agreed. He told them
about the war canoes the Iroquois were building. The Illinois
war chiefs could only conclude their enemy meant to take the
river deeper into Illinois territory.

The Iroquois deliberately added to the tension even further.
They loitered on the fringes of the Illinois village in twos and
threes, making guttural comments that no one could hear
distinctly but that held menace in their very utterance.

Finally because of mounting anxieties the Illinois chiefs
decided to abandon the village entirely to the Iroquois rather
than face so many of the enemy with only a handful of braves.
They dragged off everything portable to the island to await the
day of the parley. The Iroquois took up residence in the
village, where de Tonti and his men nervously remained. The
Snake-persons danced noisily that night, making sleep impossible for the surrounded Frenchmen and turning the horizon
red with their fires.

The parley was tense; some concessions were made but de
Tonti and the Illinois entourage returned with discouraging
reports that they didn't trust the Iroquois promises.

This uneasy situation prevailed for several days when an
Iroquois messenger again invited de Tonti to parley. He had
healed fairly well and was ready for action. This meeting was
conducted with a great deal more ceremony than the first
session. The Illinois delegates and de Tonti were honored with
a feast and elaborate calumet ceremony and dance. The old
chief who had spoken up for him before appeared wearing an
awesome feathered headdress and many cords of wampum,
which he stroked during the proceedings. One of the Illinois
told de Tonti that the old man was remembering some
agreement or contract, probably refreshing his memory of the
treaty with France. De Tonti was fascinated; he was struck
with the similarity between the Iroquois and the Catholic use
of beads as mnemonic devices. This raised his respect for the
Indian intellect.

After they smoked tobacco with the great ceremonial
calumet pipe of red stone, the braves played a wild elaborate
ball game de Tonti found a splendid entertainment. Then the

chief offered him generous presents. Besides several strands of
wampum the Iroquois chieftain gave de Tonti six bundles of
excellent beaver pelts valued on the Montreal exchange at a
fourth of his accumulated debts. But along with the skins came
an admonition, which was dutifully translated by the warrior
who, de Tonti noted, had struck him that first day.

"These six packages of beaver skins are profound in their
meaning," said the translator after the chief began his speech.
"The first two bundles represent the good promise of the
Iroquois not to eat the Illinois, whom you say are the children
of the Great Ontonio, the French chief with whom the
Iroquois are at peace."

Many smiles and head noddings followed this announcement. But the demonstration had a forced quality to it; the
Seneca who had suggested de Tonti be burned at the stake sat
off to one side in stony silence. Had Old Feather Headdress
forced this show of passivity? La Salle had made it clear that
the chiefs were not the same as French kings; they did not
have absolute power. Each decision could and most often was
dissented with. These people, in almost all the tribes, held on
to a kind of personal individuality a French king might
withhold from the nobility.

The chief continued in measured, formal tones and the
young warrior translated into French that was not half bad:
"The third bundle holds sweet herbs and ointments to help
heal the wound which was inflicted on the honored guest by a
too-ardent warrior. . . ."

De Tonti nodded with formal politeness to the chief and to
the translator who had inflicted the wound.

"The next bundle contains body oils and paints to do further
honor to the esteemed guest and to aid him in his further
travels."

De Tonti nodded again, knowing that to an Indian this was a
valuable gift. But the reference to traveling was a veiled hint,
he was sure, and more so when the chief continued, "The next
bundle of fur celebrates the generosity of the Sun, which has
benefited us by shining down upon all, Iroquois and Frenchman alike.

"The sixth bundle symbolizes our desire that you take
advantage of the favorable traveling weather to leave these
regions.

"We understand your party is headed for the Great River
where you wish to travel southward. Perhaps we can offer you
aid in accomplishing this desire."

The hint was unmistakable. But de Tonti was polite. He thanked the chief for the gifts. "But when do the Iroquois plan to take equal advantage of the same good weather and leave the Illinois in the land that is theirs?"

The chief, who had remained silent, spat a curse; others muttered menacingly behind de Tonti's back. He was sure he heard someone say something about eating many Illinois before that happened. He saw he must do something to show strength because the old chief might not be able to hold off the more aggressive of his men. Old Feather Headdress glared at the other chieftain, who disdainfully looked aside.

De Tonti shot out a hard-soled moccasined foot to kick aside the pelt bundles. "Why would I take presents from liars?"

The old war chief stood up in rage, for to be called a liar was the highest insult. He demanded that the honored guest depart or he would depart, unable as he was to remain within the same shelter as such a perfidious barbarian.

De Tonti felt this was the time to leave and did so without further conversation, abandoning the chiefs to yell at each other.

He was walking to the lodge where he and his several men had been put up by the Iroquois, glad to be out of the dark smoky council chamber and into the autumn sunlight, when he felt someone at his elbow. He looked up to see the rash young translator pacing him in a conciliatory manner. "Sir," he said in French, "my chief instructs me to tell you that you and your party may stay tonight, but should leave in the morning."

De Tonti nodded curtly, not about to give this one any leverage.

"I humbly ask your forgiveness for my rash act. You looked like an Illinois—I hate the Illinois dogs because they are weak women."

De Tonti nodded again. He'd never heard such a long speech from a common Iroquois brave before. They were normally a taciturn people. "Wherever did you learn to speak French?"

"I lived many years of childhood among the blackrobes," said the brave with a frown at this digression. "Permit me," he continued, "to show my apologies for attacking you."

De Tonti regarded him. "Why should I?"

"I would give you a gift that would greatly aid your journey."

"Well?"

"A servant to ease your travels."

"I already have a servant," the Frenchman replied, starting
to walk away.

The Iroquois reached out to touch his sleeve. "Permit me to
give this servant to you. She will make your travels less
weary."

"I don't want an Indian woman. We have different customs,
which you offend with your offer."

The brave looked stricken. He'd been ordered to give a
suitable gift and must comply. Besides, he was glad to be rid of
the woman. Despite his generosity and patience she continued
to turn a cold heart to him. Her baby was a constant nuisance;
all the fireside was complaining. He told her to leave it with
the Honored Grandmother lest it start to bawl before the
white man agreed to take her.

"You will want this one," he said quickly.

"No, thank you," de Tonti replied, moving quickly to
forestall further argument but was arrested when the brave
called out, "But you must accept the gift!"

"Will you leave me alone," he said flatly, turning to deliver
this remark eye to eye. The warrior was caught short, almost
bumping into de Tonti.

Over the brave's shoulder de Tonti saw a moving figure in
the shadows beneath the trees. It was a woman.

"But you must take her." He was unused to having a gift
rejected.

The woman stopped walking, matching their pace. She
stood quietly watching the proceedings without a ghost of
emotion on her extraordinary face.

"My chief has ordered me to make fitting restitution for my
error. This woman was the best I could think of," he said,
turning slightly to include her with a gesture of his hand. The
woman stepped out into the sunshine but stayed several paces
away. De Tonti was greatly attracted to these women though
this was as close as he'd been to one so far. Some were too fat
for his taste, and most seemed beaten down in a way that
saddened him. But this woman was another matter entirely.

He was shocked by her beauty. She stood proudly, gracefully, without a trace of nervousness, her eyes daring to peruse
him unlike any Indian woman he'd seen so far.

"Uh, no, really," he said, his voice changed.

The brave smiled. "She is desirable, yes?"

Ah, but she has raven hair, de Tonti thought with an ache.
And she has that beauty that gave a woman so much power
over a man. The warrior sensed his hesitancy.

"You are a man traveling without his woman. You plan to head for the Mech-a-si-pi, which is strange country. You need someone to take care of your daily needs. This one's name is Weeononka—in your language that means Fleet Woman."

De Tonti firmed up his resolution by turning away from the sight of her exquisite face. "I am not interested in any woman."

"This one is special."

De Tonti continued walking, shaking his head, avoiding any glimpse of her. He felt his body already responding. Damnation! How long had it been now? His last woman was on his latest trip to Montreal, a coarse whore in a shed on the riverfront. Distasteful. After the last one in Montreal, he'd made do with his own hand rather than face another discouraging encounter without passion. He repressed any thoughts about Jeanette: The last time he'd made real love it had been with her aboard the *St. Honore*. Now he fairly ached at the sight of this altogether desirable woman, so he must not look at her.

What trouble she'd be on the expedition. La Salle would kill him, or worse, dismiss him, leaving him at large in the wilderness with no credentials. Women. They always brought trouble but this time he would avoid it, nip it in the bud before it had a chance to grow.

"No women."

"She can help you."

He flared at the Iroquois with a swearword. "I don't want her. Now leave me alone."

"Very well, then," said Walking Many Mountains, dropping back, but he stopped de Tonti short when he said, "But Weeononka is from the Arkansas. . . ."

24

Actually, the word Walking Many Mountains used for Weeononka's people was not *Arkansas* but that's the way it sounded to French ears. What the Iroquois brave called her people that day sounded more like *Ugaxpa*. But de Tonti knew that meant the branch of the Illinois nation who drifted down the Mech-a-si-pi with the Iroquois hot on their heels. The other members of the migrating nation went west across the river to become the Sioux, and some went southwest to become the Osage. Others canoed down to the confluence of the Nigestai and the Mech-a-si-pi Rivers to later give the French-corrupted name of Arkansas to the region. This woman was a Quapaw, familiar as only a native could be with the unknown country into which they were about to descend.

De Tonti would have taken her with him if the choice had been his. But he wanted to discuss her with La Salle before he committed himself to taking along a woman who might not be welcome.

"I will pass this way in the spring," de Tonti said, and gave the warrior a coin to seal the bargain. "I'll take the woman then." Walking Many Mountains was thrilled to have the metal piece though he would have preferred that the white man immediately relieve him of Weeononka. He did not want to look at a woman who rejected him. But the bargain was sealed when he accepted the coin.

De Tonti was sure La Salle would want to replace his Arkansas guide though he wasn't sure if he'd want a woman along.

The next day, he and his party of six Frenchmen, three Shawnees, and two priests traveled via canoe up Lake Michigan, staying near the western shore because of bad winds. They stopped to dry out their leaking canoes at *Chicagou*. This was the territory of the Kickapoos, who hated the Iroquois but who had been friendly to the French.

The sun came out the next morning, raising spirits and a hunting party to supplement their meager supplies. De Tonti saw Father Ribourde strolling in the dry grass of a nearby meadow, his long nose buried in his breviary.

"Stay close!" he called to his friend. The priest waved, his warm smile evident from across the field.

He did not come back by sundown. De Tonti and D'Arcy beat the bushes for him, finding his tracks intersected by those of several moccasins. It didn't look hopeful.

That night they knew they were being watched from the forest but there was no incident. The other priest begged them to continue looking for Ribourde, and they stayed there at the useless task as long as de Tonti dared. But no trace of Ribourde ever turned up. De Tonti silently mourned him, for he had no doubt the old man was dead. They found out later the Kickapoos had thought the good father was an Iroquois priest, who wore similar long gowns for their ceremonies. They bashed his head in and paraded his scalp as that of a Snake-person.

That wasn't the only disaster between de Tonti and a reconnection with the main expedition. Lost provisions, more Indian threats, and crawling cold followed his group. They finally found refuge with an Illinois hunting band.

La Salle meanwhile suffered his own hard winter trying to get back to de Tonti. He and his men found the great Illinois village below Starved Rock deserted and scattered with moldering human bones. The Illinois had put their deceased up on scaffolds and the Snake-persons tore them down to vent their rage on the dead, since the living Illinois had all quit this place back when de Tonti had confronted the Snake-persons. It was onto this grim scene that La Salle stepped after the Iroquois had left the place. They had followed the Illinois to their island refuge, and had taken many more than seven hundred men, women, and children, whom they tortured to death or led as slaves to Iroquois villages.

The sky for several weeks was marked by a brilliant comet, which threw the superstitious of all nations into panic. Some blamed it for an increase in sickness and a scarcity of game. La Salle ate some greens that made him sick to death. He survived by using Mansard's antidote and made public statements that he was sure there was no truth to the rumor that the Jesuits' men had tried to poison him.

Never in one place for long, he eventually returned still another time to New France for provisions. There he caught up on his correspondence, threw promises to his creditors, found more recruits, all while recovering from snow blindness. He gave up ever finding the *Griffin*. He planned a new assault on the Mech-a-si-pi with canoes. He delighted in flaunting his renewed expedition, knowing the heavy odds being wagered against him.

Before he set out again for the Illinois village where he and de Tonti planned to rendezvous in March, he sent a snowstorm of letters to his family back in France, to whom he was deeply in debt. "This is all I can tell you this year," one of his letters concluded. "I have a hundred things to write, but you cannot believe how hard it is among the Indians. I must speak to them continually and bear all their importunity, or else they will do nothing I want. I hope to write more at leisure next year, and will tell you the end of this business, which I hope will turn out well, for I have thirty good Frenchmen and a few loyal Indians who all know how to use guns, as well as M. de Tonti, who is full of zeal."

He didn't mention he feared de Tonti was dead. That was the rumor through the Iroquois, who had passed along and changed the story of Walking Many Mountains' knife attack. However, March found the two men together again, as planned, and with great celebration the expedition started out finally for the Mech-a-si-pi. Because the rivers were still frozen, they pulled their provisions along the frozen ground on sledges through the farthest reaches of Iroquois territory.

Ten of La Salle's Shawnees brought their wives and three children so he was unconcerned about another female. He was delighted to have an Arkansas Indian on the journey, regardless of her sex.

They picked up Weeononka on their return to that country. Her baby was still a whiner, whom Cornsilk Weaver's fireside had threatened to drown more than once. She had given up on the white man but the incident gave her the impetus to leave whether he showed up or not. She didn't like being an outsider among the Snake-persons. Every time Walking Many Mountains came near her, she refused to look at him. It was becoming a point of pride that this woman was spurning him before his own fireside, which generally considered her a stubborn barbarian and a fool to pass up such a fine catch.

She was just biding her time until warmer months when she would have a chance to run away with Moon Runner. That's what her dreams seemed to be telling her. Throughout that winter she dreamed about her dead husband as though he were urging her to return to the Osotony.

So when one of La Salle's Shawnees entered the Iroquois village that spring day, she was ready to go. Cornsilk Weaver paid her the unexpected honor of saying farewell the night before her leavetaking. "I hope your path is clear," the old woman said in handsign.

Weeononka nodded.

"I liked you, girl. I think you might have been one of us, if you had tried."

"My way lies in another direction," Weeononka handsigned. She disliked the Iroquois so much she had refused to learn their language.

This time it was the old woman who nodded. The baby made a fussy squeak. "He's still collicky."

"Yes, but you have to admit I made the right decision."

"I don't know. He's sickly."

"But see how fat he's growing."

"Still not fat enough."

"You just don't want to admit you were wrong," Weeononka said, refusing to lower her eyes respectfully after criticizing an Honored Grandmother. The Weaver didn't react to what she considered the girl's impertinence. She had never shown the proper respect, always held out for her own ideas. Always wanting to win. It was good that her grandson had found an honorable way to get rid of her. After glancing around to make sure nobody was around to hear her concede, Honorable Grandmother drew closer to the girl. "It was a good thing that you fought me for this child's life," she admitted. "But let me tell you something."

Weeononka regarded her with the same unflinching gaze as that first night.

"You're too proud."

Now Weeononka looked down, not in respect but as if rejecting what the old woman said.

"But I forgive you," Grandmother relented. After all, the girl was leaving. Besides, her strength reminded Cornsilk Weaver of her own youthful personality so even though she was glad not to have to deal with this one anymore she grudgingly liked her anyway. She gave Weeononka a basket of ground corn, a clay boiling pot, jerked meat for the trip, and a strand of purple and white wampum beads she said counted Weeononka's days among the Iroquois. Weeononka was thrilled with the glass beads but was too proud to ask for what she really wanted—red earth to paint in her hair.

She and the baby were on the trail behind the taciturn Shawnee the next day. Moon Runner, who had been fairly serene, was having stomach pains again. He didn't want to take solid food and it was time to wean him. The old grandmother was right; he wasn't fat enough and by the second day on the trail to La Salle's camp he started crying in that annoying way that had so upset Cornsilk Weaver's fireside. He later settled into sleep riding her back as they approached the encampment. The first thing she saw was La Salle's white canvas tent with *fleur-de-lis* on the side flapping in a breeze off the Illinois River. With relief the next thing she saw were the women and children traveling with La Salle's Shawnees. At least I won't be the only female, she was thinking as the women gazed suspiciously back at her with Shawnee eyes at what they supposed was an Iroquois woman.

The Shawnee guide took her immediately to de Tonti's tent next to the commander's and left her there without a word. She looked around. Besides an unmade bedroll, a light backpack, and a map coming unpinned from the north side, the lodge was empty. There were no weapons about; she assumed he was out hunting.

It was early afternoon. What better way to greet her new master than by having something ready to eat with his game? She had no intention of staying with him, of course, any more than she had with the Snake-persons. But while she did, she might as well take as good care of him as possible. He would get her back to the Osotony; that was all that mattered.

She laid the sleeping baby on the man's bedroll and went out to gather firewood. By the time he arrived, she had a good pot of *sagamite* plopping in sticky bubbles near a strong, clear fire.

Weeononka stood to greet him. The sorry sight of him was discouraging. Much had happened to this white man since she had first seen him in the Iroquois camp. He was bent and walked in a crabbed way she had not remembered. True, she had seen very few white men, not enough to tell them apart since all of them were bearded, and had not seen this one close enough to remember his face, but the Frenchman seemed in her memory to have been more vital. Also he'd aged. His beard she remembered as being black as charcoal was streaked with white. The hair that fell from his tight little cap was stringy and grizzled. He had probably been sick during the last winter.

She watched him as he lay three folded homespun shirts on the bedroll—such finely woven cloth, like La Salle's tent, was something as alien to her as bearded men. She was fascinated and wanted to touch this material, but the white man made her nervous. She knew he'd seen her. He seemed to be pointedly ignoring her.

She almost said something to take the initiative but hesitated, thinking, This is the master who must be endured. After watching him a moment longer, she took a deep breath and greeted him in French she hoped was correct.

He stopped, drawing back from her with a look of surprise and then disdain on his face. "You speak French?" All these Frenchmen looked alike with their hairy faces.

"Yes, monsieur. Tell me if I speak the words wrong."

He frowned at her. "Now look, you. I wasn't asked if I liked this new arrangement so don't come bothering me, understand?"

She didn't; he was speaking too fast but she nodded anyway. His tone was nasty.

He sniffed her cooking with a scowl, grumbled, spat, and trudged off toward the big fire the company cook kept going on the other side of La Salle's tent.

She decided not to get angry with him. What could one do with such barbarians anyway? When Moon Runner woke, she fed him and ate a bowl of *sagamite*. Darkness was setting in. She wished her white man would hurry up and return so she could get a better look at him. But when the afternoon drew on, she wanted water so she put the child on her back and strolled over to the other women. Their expressions changed when she spoke to them; her Quapaw was close to their Illinois. She was welcomed like a cousin and after they talked for a while she accompanied them down to the river. She was delighted one of the women had enough vermilion to share. Weeononka wanted to look pretty for her new master, so she painted her part line as soon as she returned to her man's tent.

Later, after dark, she poured water into the cooking pot and put a handful of sandy river-beach soil and a sliver of soaproot into the water so that in the morning the pot would be clean; all she'd have to do was swish the dirty water around, pour it out, and rinse the vessel. She curled up under her buffalo robe with the baby. Near dawn she woke to a Frenchman's voice exclaiming, "Damnation! That's the worst tasting stuff I've ever eaten—"

Weeononka crawled from the warm robe, leaving Moon Runner to his whimpering sleep. Just outside the tent she stopped when she saw a man bending over her firepit with her cooking pot in his hands. He was just setting it down as he wiped his mouth with a sour look on his face.

"Get out of here," she ordered in French. "My master is due to return and will box your ears."

The white man stood looking at her strangely. *"La Vite?"*

It sounded strange to hear her name in French, which she had not heard since she last saw Brother Martin. She was distressed to see how tall this interloper stood. Her scrawny old master wouldn't be much good in a fight with him. The early light gave this one a dark sinister look. He was fully bearded, wearing an outlandish headpiece that drooped over one of his eyes—his eyes! She saw as he stepped close they

were the color of a cat's. He looked ferociously hairy despite a
smile hidden in his whiskers. She backed away from him; she
didn't like the few white men she'd met. This one looked
dangerous.

"My master is away hunting bear. He's very important and
will shoot you with his musket if you so much as touch me."

Behind her the baby started whining.

"What's this? More to the bargain?" the man said, trying to
see around her into the tent.

"The mother panther has a cub?" He laughed in a way she
interpreted as good-humored. This close she saw his eyes were
the color of the edge of the sun as it sets, shimmering yellow.
She thought him attractive in a strange unnerving way. He was
both like and unlike all the men she'd known. Despite his
masculinity, he didn't swagger like Osage or Iroquois men.
There was a gentleness about him that immediately confused
and fascinated her. He could have pushed past her but he
didn't. Neither did he touch her. "I can't understand why you
put that red paint in your hair," he said, "but you are very
beautiful, *La Vite*."

"My name is Weeononka." She shook her head when he
tried to say it. He wasn't putting guttural emphasis in the right
place so that what he said was her name before Dancing Buck
had changed it.

"Weeononka," she corrected.

He looked exasperated. "Sounds like you're coughing. I
shall call you Arkansas."

"That's not how you say my people's name," she started to
correct him but he hopelessly shook his head. She could not
help but observe that he too was beautiful. She almost said it
but bit her tongue. It would shame her old master for her to
have eyes for another, younger man.

"Please leave before my master returns and beats me," she
lied, knowing that old man she saw earlier would not be able to
catch her much less apply blows.

"Your master will never beat you."

"He's very fierce, my master—" Just then she saw her
master behind the stranger, walking like a spider with the
same scowl on his wrinkled face as when he'd left her.

Sabat said something to his captain, ignoring the Indian
woman, then walked off with a casual salute. When Weeononka saw by this exchange which man was servant and which was
master, she apologized profusely. Privately she rejoiced. She

had been troubled that the old man would try to mount her, but this one was entirely another matter. It had been a long time since her thighs warmed in anticipation of a man's touch. Suddenly she imagined what this man would be like. He looked strong and passionate, though he was more covered than any Osage warrior would have been and so she couldn't "read the loincloth," as an Osage woman would say. But despite the fact that she couldn't tell if he was responding to her directly, she sensed he was pleased to have her there. The more glances she stole at him the more she realized that this was the first white man who aroused her. To cover her embarrassment and excitement she revived the coals in her firepit and rinsed the cooking pot.

"You mean I was drinking your dish wash?" He spat several times but didn't seem to be angry. In fact he appeared to think it was funny. Walking Many Mountains or even Game Dancer would have reacted very differently.

"Why are you putting those rocks in the fire?" he asked, enjoying every moment of this. He had forgotten how lovely this woman was. He would have taken her to bed right then but he wasn't a barbarian after all.

"To boil water for tea, of course," she answered thinking he was kidding her, wishing that he would suggest they go to blanket before Moon Runner woke. Suddenly she felt deprived of pleasure, though during her stay with the Iroquois she never once felt desire. It was as though her body had been saving it up; she had a spontaneous flash of his manhood rising to greet her. The thought was so sweet she had to look away. "You would like some hot sassafras, wouldn't you?" She dared to glance up at him to see if he read her soft innuendo. It didn't translate, of course, but among her people the herb was known as a sexual stimulant because of its tingling flavor; the Sioux word was a double entendre. As she expected, he appeared oblivious.

"It smells wonderful," he said, looking forward to sampling some real Indian cooking. He was enjoying the sound of a woman's French. It was certainly not as lightly spoken as his mother's or even a Norman peasant's. The effect was somewhat spoiled by the line of red paint that reminded him of blood in her hair. But it was a young woman's voice speaking French nonetheless. Hearing the soft familiar cadences reminded him of hot baths, spiced milk, and green expanses of lawn. Hearing French from this savage woman stunned him in a pleasant way.

He'd never given it a thought of how one would boil water without a fireproof cooking vessel. But of course one would simply drop red hot stones into water. He stood there watching her as she continued to discuss casually without grammatical error but in her oddly pronounced Indian version of French the varieties of objects with which one can cook *sagamite*.

"I prefer a rock. But my aunt taught me this style." She set out three oddly twisted lumps of bright orange clay.

"Who taught you to speak French?"

Weeononka wasn't sure if the rules for not naming the dead applied to white blackrobes. But what was true for one kind of human must be true for all, so she discreetly referred to Brother Martin by his professional status and not his name. She threw the clay lumps into the coals.

"You speak very well, Mademoiselle *La Vite*."

"I am a married woman, monsieur." She had no word for the concept of "widow." Among her people a female was either a girl or a woman who had been married.

"Then you're Christian?"

She flashed obsidian eyes at him, the very picture of disciplined anger, then spat furiously into her cooking fire. Her saliva sizzled; her eyes were a little scary. "Blackrobes, ayi! Baby-eaters." Then in calm French she continued, "You see, in the lowland country we have few stones to boil water with, so we must make our own boiling stones of clay." She felt the memory of her first days with The Blossum.

Over the next few days de Tonti and Weeononka maintained a polite distance. By the time the expedition took them to the Illinois River, their relationship had warmed somewhat but they still were not sharing a bedroll. De Tonti, though he ached to take her in his arms, didn't want to lose her by breaking some taboo.

This was a new emotion in de Tonti, who had never hesitated to approach a woman before. But this one was different. It suddenly mattered what she wanted, whether she cared. He was dreaming about being inside her exquisite body, of kissing her sensuous lips. The more he thought about her, the more untouchable she seemed. Reflection was unpleasant but he knew his experience with Jeanette had sensitized him. Many times he felt he should have chosen differently, even though rejection would have wounded her. During this time he had several dreams about his baby lover in which she begged him not to take another. Their experience was still unsettling and was bound to have its effect now that he found himself responding to another woman.

She was always polite and kind, and tried to discern his needs. His seeming aloofness confused her. She thought it best to just wait and see what it was he expected from her. Once she offered to massage his shoulders when he complained they were hurting, but when she began, he thought he could not bear her touch without responding and broke it off abruptly.

He left her where they had been sitting. She stared after him, wondering what was wrong but as shy as he about asking. For her part, she wished he would take her in his arms and wondered why he hesitated. One of the Shawnee women told her he must already have a wife waiting for him where he came from, but she knew that wasn't so.

"Maybe he's a contrary," said the Shawnee, whose name was Little Bird. She shyly pronounced the word that meant a man who likes other men. The Shawnee looked down on the practice but everyone knew the Illinois and some other nations accepted such intercourse. There were rumors about Nika-nape because of the way he attended La Salle. Nobody knew for sure, but they gossiped quietly. "These whites are strange in so many ways. Maybe they're strange that way, too."

"Maybe some white men . . ." Weeononka said circumspectly.

Little Bird caught the subtle reference to the Canadian and shrugged without further comment on such an impolitic subject. Like most of the Indians, she did not like La Salle but she respected and feared him.

". . . but not this white man," Weeononka continued. "I just don't understand."

"Then, my dear, you must wait and see. That is all I can advise you."

De Tonti also sought counsel. "You're the first Frenchman I've seen stand on scruple over an Indian squaw," La Salle told him one night. It was incongruous to him that this lusty fellow was hesitating.

It irritated de Tonti that the Canadian disparaged her so. While he maintained polite intercourse with the Indians, he was possessed of that superiority toward them he held against just about everyone. Even Nika, his only true friend in the company, was subservient to him. On this matter he even felt superior to de Tonti. Nika was hunting with one of the

Shawnees. They were alone in La Salle's tent while the master re-tallied the worth of furs he'd bartered and left with the Illinois. De Tonti had approached him about Weeononka because he expected advice based on La Salle's greater understanding of these people. He saw he'd miscalculated; La Salle had never been with an Indian woman.

"There's something so reserved about her," was all de Tonti could say, "as though she holds some terrible mystery."

La Salle lay down his pen and regarded de Tonti. "If you want her, take her." Privately he was sorry to see such a display of lower-class emotionalism in his second in command and he blamed it on de Tonti's inflammable Roman heritage. He would have preferred that he plan a proper marriage based on property and respect rather than passion, thereby setting a good example, like himself, for the men. But he'd long ago accepted what he considered his man's lusty nature.

"She's so beautiful but so grave. You don't see it, do you?"

La Salle shrugged and played with the pen. "You're making too much of something insignificant."

De Tonti was put off by La Salle's insensitivity and found an excuse to leave. He further guarded his feelings after the disappointing counsel and stewed in his confusion. He watched the woman for some sign that she wanted him as badly as he wanted her. Then, he decided, he would love her as she deserved to be loved and La Salle's prejudices be damned.

The men gossiped. It was fairly obvious from the shy manner between de Tonti and the Quapaw woman that they were not yet lovers. The company was betting on when the captain would make his move.

Meanwhile, the larger effort continued. With the River Illinois as their highway, their canoes glided southward through the leafless forest. A day later they left the Illinois and entered the Mech-a-si-pi. Floating chunks of ice rattled their canoes; the sky was leaden but no storm hindered their progress into more southern latitudes. The air warmed. Birds sang from the riverbanks, which were as twisting as an unrolled skein of yarn.

By the time they camped near the mouth of the Missouri, de Tonti and Weeononka still were not sharing a bedroll. Moon Runner cried incessantly, apparently sick on this new water he was forced to drink. Everyone grumbled about the whining baby. During the day Weeononka and he rode with the other women and children; but even they were tired of the baby's cries. Past the juncture with the Missouri the river turned thick with mud. The stream grew from there on, enlarged by the Ohio and frequent swamp creeks.

They found signs of being tracked. Sometimes at night they heard calls echoing in the forest that terrified the Illinois. One of the Frenchmen failed to return from hunting. They looked for him and had just about given up when he came out of the marsh in an hysterical frenzy. "They were painted for war, I tell you," he babbled. De Tonti gave him brandy to calm him down, and while the company looked on with wide eyes, he told them of how they had captured him, taken his flintlock, and tied him to a torture pole.

"I thought they were going to burn me alive," he cried. "But their headman signed to me that I was to tell you, Monsieur La Salle, that if we don't get out of their territory they'll roast us all for dinner!"

La Salle listened to all this then ordered a round of brandy for all while he gave a speech. "We don't have to fear these savages and their puny arrows. With our guns they wouldn't dare attack us." He exhorted them not to be discouraged by a bunch of feathered idiots. The Shawnee looked dubious; Chickasaw were famous for butchery. The Frenchmen and Canadians couldn't miss their guides' concern. But La Salle passed out coins for everyone and another round of brandy, and the next morning they were on their way again. The western bank in this region was a swamp so that night once again they camped on the eastern beach.

Dawn brought a scream from Little Bird. She had gone for water and found one of their Shawnee lookouts on the sandbar with his throat slashed and his hair missing. The man was a Christian so the priest gave him a burial Mass. They decided not to attract any more attention by singing over the hasty grave but once again boarded the canoes, weapons at the ready, for further travel deeper into enemy territory.

25

Spring highwater pushed the river over its right-hand western bank in a floor of swamp. Using handsign across the water between their canoes, Weeononka suggested to de Tonti that they delay camping and instead canoe on down past hostile territory.

"Those bluffs are sacred to the Chickasaw," she signed.

But La Salle declined the advice. The sun was just setting. He wanted to dry his boots and eat something because he was suffering his constant stomach complaints.

Along that stretch the Mech-a-si-pi was particularly snakelike with switchbacks every half-league, oxbow lakes, and many islands. On the expedition's right was the swamp. To the left the relentless river had carved teeth, columns, and plateaus of sandy stone dotted with caves and smooth-sided recesses. From the lead canoe the commander signaled the convoy to beach left; for a hot meal he'd take his chances on the Chickasaw Bluffs to the east. The Shawnee quickly scouted a dry sandstone plateau that formed a second shelf above the water. They carried their bark canoes up with them so as not to attract attention.

Just as they unrolled La Salle's tent, a lookout ran from the bluff edge gesturing wildly and whispering that a large Chickasaw war party had just stepped out of canoes down on the graveled beach. As if mowed down by the brisk wind, everyone stopped what he or she was doing and fell to the ground. There were three times more Chickasaw down there than members of the expedition. This was a safe place only if everyone in the party remained absolutely quiet until the Chickasaw departed.

More lookouts crawled from the edge with grim intelligence; the Chickasaw were setting up camp. La Salle was furious with his scouts when he saw their mistake; the path from the river was well worn. The expedition had camped directly across from an old Chickasaw trace.

"Let us hope they mean to stay only for the night," he whispered, ordering in sign and soft words that his people not move around except on their bellies and not speak or light a fire. It wasn't easy for such a large group of people to be absolutely quiet, especially at sundown when food should be cooking and people should be preparing for sleep.

Dissatisfied with any but his own observation, La Salle bade de Tonti to crawl with him to the precipice, where they were dismayed to discover the Chickasaw had firearms. The Canadian spat a curse at the Dutch and English he was sure were selling arms to the Chickasaw. Some of the band were setting a bonfire. Smoke, ashes, and heat flumed up the sides of the bluff while down there the Indians began roasting some white man, an Englishman to judge by his voice. Their hollering and the victim's screams covered any noises those on the plateau made as they crawled behind a large outcrop and into their bedrolls with no warm supper.

After a while the victim below stopped screaming; the dancing and chanting went on into the night. Still none of the Chickasaw came up to the second level above the river, where the expedition crouched. De Tonti figured they were complacent because this location was deep in their home territory, where they assumed none would dare trespass.

He munched on one of the Indian journeycakes. "It's like eating a boiling rock," he whispered to Weeononka. She didn't answer; her attention was on Moon Runner as he fussily took her breast. But she felt Iron Hand's warmth against her shoulder. It was a comfort she appreciated. She leaned slightly against him and felt the sturdiness of him pushing gently back. Some of the expedition slept. After a time even the noise from the beach subsided as the torturers slept off their revels.

The wind polished the night sky so that the stars danced. Weeononka watched the sleeping Frenchman beside her with growing sadness. She wanted to put her lips on his but she hesitated. Perhaps it was a good thing that he had not taken her. Her choice would not be as clear if they were mated. In the starglow she could see his eyes moving back and forth beneath his closed lids. His lips formed a silent word and he smiled from the midst of his dream, endearing himself to her even as she sat there contemplating departure. What was he dreaming, she wondered. He turned in sleep toward her, his flesh hand reaching, then relaxing on her stomach. His graceful, strong fingers twitched. No sound came from the Chickasaw camp but the wind had picked up the fragrance of their smoldering woodsmoke. The smell jolted a memory in her. It had been such a moonless night when her husband went to the Chickasaw torture pole. She recalled the stars over his shoulder as he had held her in his arms. The sky tonight was the same; there was the Path of Ghosts dusty with starry grains like the river beach with pebbles.

Her dead husband was somewhere out there walking without sacred moccasins toward the country of the sun. She'd been scrupulous not to think his name yet she had dreams about him every night. In them he was standing on a high treeless bluff pointing toward a far blue ridge above a winding

ribbon of river. She knew he was urging her to take the baby
back to the Osotony.

Had The Blossum found the sacred bundle where Weeononka had hidden it in the corn cache? Had the elders rebuilt
the village on the river or did they move to another spot where
they could start anew from the ashes of their dead children?

She knew she must find out.

She'd advised La Salle about the exact location of the Kappa
Quapaw. It was the next stop on the river and the expedition's
first on the western bank. If the Chickasaw missed them,
they'd be honored guests of the Kappa tomorrow afternoon.
There would be a calumet dance and a feast. She knew the
Kappa Quapaw would welcome these white people because
they liked the two Frenchmen who'd come a few winters back,
the explorers La Salle called Marquette and Joliet. Some of the
Kappa had even taken their blackrobe religion, though the
Osotony and other locals looked down on them for it.

Tomorrow would mark the end of her assistance to this party.

She looked again at the sleeping man beside her. I would
have been your woman, she thought. All you had to do was
reach out and take me. I would have fed you and loved you; I
don't even mind that you have one cold metal hand. The rest of
you is warm and kind. I would have been happy to be your
wife all our days.

But he had not taken her. Perhaps Little Bird was right and
he was some kind of mysterious "contrary" who didn't need a
woman.

Warmth from his hand reached her flesh through her leather
skirt. She closed her eyes and saw with her stomach skin the
hot shape of it. How long would it take for his warm touch to
brand her and tie her to him forever? The time was fast
approaching when she must make a decision about him. If he'd
been a Quapaw or any other kind of red man, she would have
had no problem. They would simply go find the remnant of the
Osotony, set up a lodge as man and wife, and that would be
that. But this man was an outlander from who knew what kind
of strange nation. She recognized the mark of the warrior on
him but it had taken a different track across his white soul than
it would a red man's. She suspected that he'd never be content
without his fellows and their noisy metal articles of war and
everyday life.

With equally sad certainty she knew from this short time
with them that her soul would never be content to remain

among these white men, not even for the value of this one special white man whom she knew, despite the fact they'd never shared a blanket, that she loved. If she tarried long enough for him to consummate those feelings, the narcotic of his love and protection would numb her to her true direction, which was red and not white. Once again, she thought, I find myself with a man who isn't going in my direction.

She reflected again that it was right that they had not taken each other. It made the decision as clear as the passionless stars. She must have slept because muted dawn light startled her when she woke to the baby's mewings. Oh no, she moaned inwardly when she saw him arch his back in the way that signaled a screaming attack of colic. She forced him to take a nipple; it hushed him for a while. She looked at the bluff behind them where a narrow path led up to the plateau. Perhaps she could take him up there where his cries would not endanger the others.

A sentry returned from the precipice, waking everyone with frantic handsign that the Chickasaw were climbing the bluff even at this moment where the expedition had hoped to remain unnoticed. It would take less than ten times thirty heartbeats for the first Chickasaw to come upon them. La Salle and de Tonti made quick military plans. Their only hope was to let the Chickasaw enter an ambush, then take a surprise offensive since there was no quick way for all the party to quit the bluff at this location. But that meant clearing away every sign of their habitation. Their bluff could be attained only by one path up from the riverbed. Its back side was an unclimbable wall onto the final level of the eastern bank. Into its face was the single steep path Weeononka had considered climbing. She saw it was too late for that now; she would have had to expose her flight to all below in any case.

If they could remain out of sight until a large Chickasaw contingent walked into the trap, they could kill enough to scare away the others with the noise of firearms. The escarpment would hide the women, children, and provisions. The Frenchmen with muskets and pistols and Shawnees with arrows stationed themselves behind the scrub brush and sandstone palisades that littered the plateau.

A lookout handsigned that the enemy was moving up in larger numbers, evidently planning to reach this level and cross it via the steep path to an eastern inland village. The Shawnees were spitting on their headknockers, relishing the

chance to kill some Chickasaw, but the white men were
worried; they had only limited ammunition. They knew this
play would either work right away with the Chickasaw scared
by a sudden unexpected ambush or not at all. These Chickasaw would not be expecting trouble and so would not have
their few guns ready to fire. If they suspected how few whites
were here, it would be all over very quickly.

The morning lengthened. From the east came the first rays
of sunlight through a bank of cloud. Ten Chickasaw appeared
on the path and stepped out onto the relatively flat crown of
the bluff. Weapons loose in their hands, they glanced cautiously around, hunters always on the ready. But they appeared casual about it—this was too close to home for them to
be worried. The Chickasaw had a terrible reputation among
their neighbors and few dared to step over their line. The first
arrivals were followed by a flood of tattooed and shell-
decorated warriors who spilled up onto the bluff, crowding
into each other then moving on toward the back wall. De Tonti
was pleased to note that only one in about ten of the enemy
carried firearms; evidently only the war chiefs had the rare
weapons, which were newly introduced into the Chickasaw
mentality and probably still held in awe by the ordinary
braves. Still his men must wait until the main body of the
Chickasaw were within range.

At that moment de Tonti heard Weeononka's baby squall
from behind the escarpment. One cry might have been
mistaken for a hawk or a wind shriek in the palisades, but if
that child wailed more, the Chickasaw would know they
weren't the only people on the bluff.

De Tonti, primed to attack, mouthed what was possibly a
genuine prayer despite himself, that Weeononka could keep
the baby quiet. He listened, catching La Salle's round,
twitching eye. All that could be heard was frustrated wind
through the bluffs. La Salle had his piece out ready to fire, his
right hand up and about to drop when this next group of
Chickasaw gained the plateau. There were nearly a hundred of
the enemy assembled.

De Tonti groaned when he heard the baby scream again
against the wind, clearly not a bird or a wind whistle.

In the cover of the escarpment, behind the canoes the
women flattened themselves as close to the ledge as possible.
Weeononka behind the others saw Moon Runner was not
going to stop crying. The women frantically motioned for her

to keep him quiet. Little Bird pulled a heavy buffalo robe over the girl and her baby. Beneath it Weeononka tried to cover his mouth with her hand but he squirmed out of her grasp arching his back against her arm, full of fury that his insides were hurting him. He was stiffened and red and his next cry would be even louder, an infantile explosion of thwarted fury. She'd tried everything—patting his back, jiggling him up and down, but nothing would silence him. He adamantly refused the nipple, turning his pinched little face away when she tried to stifle his scream with it. He was nearly blue as he sucked in a breath so he could cry again.

There was no decision, no actual moment for her when she said to herself, This I must do. There simply wasn't time for reasoned thought. Her body thought for her, knowing only one way to silence its own offspring. Yet there was knowledge in her, too, cold and clear, so that later she would claim complete responsibility. No decision was necessary. She had tried all possibilities. This one recourse was left.

She pressed him close; his skin burned against her milk-full breast. She filled his mouth with the dripping nipple just as the cry erupted, then deliberately, relentlessly gentle, she lay down on the baby. It was as if her body was trying to reabsorb him, bring him back into its safe muffling interior.

She felt the struggling feet kick her ribs. It amazed her that this frail tiny bud of a human being was so strong, so full of the will to live. She placed her hands around his darkly swirled hair, cradling his head with her fingers so the rough ground would not further wound him.

Out beyond the escarpment the river breeze slackened. De Tonti with frozen heart saw a Chickasaw, who was casually holding a Dutch musket, look in the direction of the baby's last hidden cry. But when there was no repetition of the vague squall, the brave looked away. Like a swift silent red cloud his comrades moved past him into the wide funnel of the ambush.

The silence under the buffalo robe loomed over Weeononka like a great egg that would destroy her if broken. Gravel scored the back of her hand. She drew Moon Runner closer to herself. Her nose brushed his head; he smelled so good, like a corn cake just off a hot rock. His baby hair was as fine as cattail fluff.

"Goodbye, little one," she whispered, her eyes burning. "Forgive me." She felt her heart spasm with overwhelming grief then felt physical pain as he fought against the nipple. His

newly cut milk teeth were sharp. The pain brought her tears
faster; they splattered on her hand tightly holding the baby's
head. He was fighting for his life and she loved him even more
for it. She concentrated on the pain, willing herself to feel
every red arrow of it. Before very long the baby stopped
kicking but she wasn't aware of it. His strong jaws were
clamped onto her; finally she slipped a finger past his sweet
lips to try and force his mouth open. Her movement disturbed
the buffalo robe, letting light into the dim little cave she and
her baby shared.

She was oblivious of anything beyond herself, of the burning
sun now angling intensely down from the sky, of the grown
silence beyond the escarpment. Her world had narrowed
down to herself, those baby teeth, and blazing realization:
Now she understood why the cloud obstructed the baby in her
dream. She herself was the cloud that passed between her
child and his life.

This knowledge was almost more than she could bear, but
tradition was like a reflex in her. She spoke the ritual words
softly into his little shell ear, "Walk toward the sun, Moon
Runner, and don't look back. . . ."

Beyond the grieving woman and the rock wall that hid her,
the sequestered ranks of musket-armed Frenchmen held their
collective breath; surely the Chickasaw war party would soon
smell strangers even as the strangers now caught whiffs of oiled
and dusty red men. But for the freshening breeze from the
west over the river, they would have already known that their
bluff sheltered an invasion of aliens.

Suddenly La Salle's hand dropped as he gave an ancient
Norman battle yell, firing his pistol at the same time. The
explosion rattled against the bluff walls, followed by many
others, which threw the Chickasaw into disarray. De Tonti's
blood raced at the sound, at the sight of men falling where he
pointed his weapon. La Salle's Indians answered with their
own blood-freezing war cry and a volley of arrows and lances
while the whites reloaded.

All this Weeononka heard like a memory.

De Tonti out on the bluff reloaded the pistol, his face
streaked with sweaty tears. The old love of battle was giving
way to the old loathing of the kill. He walked among many
Chickasaw who lay bleeding, screaming, or very quiet. The
sounds of the dying tore at him. He put two out of their misery
with quick unflinching temple shots. Other expedition mem-

bers grabbed up enemy weapons and the Shawnees took scalp locks while the Chickasaw remnant scattered either back down to the river or up the narrow path that led to the highland. They could be seen jumping into their log bateaus and taking the current to safer places. The battle was over quickly, apparently without a single expedition death. They were all congratulating themselves, moving to capture those new Dutch guns and toss the enemy dead over the cliff. Others, including de Tonti, made for the sanctuary where the women waited.

When he first saw Weeononka standing, he thought she'd caught a musket ball in the bull's-eye of her left nipple, so neat was the ring of blood there. Incredulous that a shot could have found her behind the wall of rock, he stumbled toward her with her name on his lips.

Closer, he saw the sweet hemisphere of her breast was splotched scarlet and he gasped, weak-kneed as no battle could have left him, at the thought of her beauty cruelly disfigured. When she turned to stare at him, he saw that she hadn't been shot at all. It looked to him as if she'd been bitten. Even from here he could see the beginnings of tiny slashes, blue and swollen, the unmistakable pattern of small human teeth. The frail infant lay unnaturally still in her arms, his little mouth stained with his mother's blood, the tiny muscle of his lips twitching in a final spasm. De Tonti knew immediately what must have happened. Unable to stop the wailing baby any other way, she had suffocated him with her breast. He remembered the moment back there when the hostile braves were treading so closely to them when he had been suddenly aware that the baby's cries stopped. What relief that stillness had given him, making the ambush perfect. During the ensuing fight he had had no time to wonder what had silenced the baby so suddenly.

Weeononka's face was an unholy blank.

It was he who finally moved while behind him what had transpired to save them all dawned on less sympathetic men. He approached her, touching her sleeve to wake her up. The men gasped at the Quapaw woman's exposed breast. The other women stared in disbelief at Weeononka. Then one of the Shawnee women deduced what she had done and gasped. Everyone except de Tonti seemed paralyzed.

"You bitch—" he heard Rob mutter in a coarse whisper. "You filthy bloody God-cursed murdering savage bitch." He took a

few tentative steps toward her as if he might attack, but
something, perhaps de Tonti enfolding her in his arms,
stopped La Salle with his arms akimbo.

"May you rot in hell," La Salle finally spat, stamping away in
quiet fury as if he had no more stomach for the scene.

The priests crossed themselves, the men stumbled about as
if drunk. Several of them echoed their leader's contempt. But
they did it in whispers and with round-eyed stares, staying far
away from the woman who had killed her baby. The Shawnees
were awestruck at her sacrifice and stayed away out of respect.

Only de Tonti was close enough to see the wet track course
down her cheek. It wasn't a single drop but a continuous
current. Otherwise she hadn't moved since standing. He
gathered her in his arms, hugging her as she hugged the baby.

Sweet Jesus, he was thinking. She saved us all. She growled
like a mother cat at one of the priests who tried to sprinkle the
child. When she started wailing the death song, the Shawnee
women joined her. Little Bird helped prepare the body.
Weeononka went through the ceremonial she performed for
her husband, but was reluctant to bury the baby. In her mind,
though she couldn't explain it, it was clear she must take him
back to the Osotony. She found a knife and was about to hack
off a finger when de Tonti stopped her.

He turned to put the knife away. When he looked back she
was running with the sad little bundle to the edge of the bluff.
Without a sound she stepped directly off, disappearing like a
miracle. De Tonti cried her name as he followed, thinking with
horror that he'd see her mangled body on the rocks below. But
the river had caught her—a few steps farther south and she
would have hit the beach. Where she went in the water was
eating directly at the bluff in a deep pool. He saw her hit with a
splash and he was over the side, diving after her without
thought.

The current here wasn't as strong as out in the main channel
so he was able to grab her quickly, but she was deadweight,
eyes closed, head back, still clutching the baby. He called her
name but she didn't respond. The muddy water made her
slippery. The current was stronger than he had first thought.
He looped his arm around her from behind, determined not to
let go but too encumbered to pull her in and fight the river too.

There was no bottom. The river eddied fiercely, swollen
with six hundred leagues of floodwater, at the base of the cliff.
The lashing tongue of water licked them farther from the

shore. The current swallowed Weeononka. He could feel her tearing away then the world narrowed down to thick brown water no matter where he looked. He fought, screaming her name when he surfaced, and saw the dark coils of her hair coming undone in the tearing water. He grabbed her hair and went under again. But he would not let go this time and found the surface with the ropes of her braids in his clenched fist. He pulled her up. The cold water had stunned her into fighting where she would have let it kill her a moment before. Her arms flailed. The roar of the water drowned her scream. The frantic current was interrupted about a league away by a round island, remnant of an ancient loop on the western bank. De Tonti saw it looming ahead as a crown of budding trees. The river slowed, parting around the obstruction, so that he was able to drag himself to the shore. Weeononka found the bottom and struggled out, but she lingered in the shallows hugging herself, searching aimlessly among the skeletons of trees and other debris.

He urged her to abandon the search but she pushed him away. He pulled her arm and she wrenched from him, staggering in water up to her ankles toward a mudflat. So he searched with her, keeping an eye out for the familiar bark canoes that could appear out on the water. His eye took in the low tangled growth beyond the lee side of the island and this arm of the river toward the west. Here there was no sign of Chickasaw, who would cleave to their eastern bluffs, but there might be other hostiles coming from the western bayou.

"We are safe here," he was surprised to hear her say as if reading his thoughts. Her voice sounded flat. She was standing on the sandbar, trickles of mud and slime running off her every surface. About her was the attitude of acceptance: She wasn't going to find the bundle here.

He matched her stillness, waiting to see what she would do. She might still try to kill herself. He saw, however, that that desire seemed spent and she appeared only tired now, not suicidal. She regarded him.

He slung water from his beard and returned her glance.

The sun was warm though past its zenith. The gusty wind that laced the bluffs was more subdued out on this wide flat isle. Evergreens whispered a few paces from the water. Beyond that wash of green the bare wood at the center of the island was hazy with first growth.

It wasn't so much that he started walking toward her, or she toward him, as it was a single step toward each other. They

met in the shallow water. She began sobbing against him,
mourning the baby. He lifted her, saying soft things to
her while he found a dry spot of sand in the benevolent sunlight.
She cried for a long time until exhaustion finally overtook her.
When he was sure she was asleep, he started a fire with the
sun through the watch crystal. The beach was littered with
driftwood.

They might not have anything to eat, he thought, but at
least they would be warm that night.

26

After a while Weeononka stood and stretched. The nap
seemed to have enlivened her. "I'm hungry," she said as he
dropped another armload of firewood. He was amazed to see
her so refreshed. This was not the first time he'd seen
emotions ebb and flow in her. She put no bridle on emotion,
but didn't indulge it by lingering. Where she'd been bluish
pale the sun had now fired her cheeks and put a sweet pungent
aroma around her.

He popped the knife blade in his hand. "This is all the
weapon I have." The mechanism delighted her; he savored the
anticipation of how she'd react to the music box but decided to
save that surprise for another time after he'd repaired water
damage.

She tossed several beach pebbles into the flames, not
wondering how he had started a fire; a warrior always traveled
with his flints. He was thinking that the crystal would be
another delight for her. There were so many things he wanted
to share. She was so smart she'd learn civilized ways easily, he
was thinking. He noticed as she stood that the river had
washed the red paint from her partline.

"Why do you paint your scalp?" he asked, too bluntly by her
standards, he was surprised to see by the flash in her eye: Who
are you to be pointing personal questions at Weeononka? But
her verbal reply was gentle: "I don't know why it is done, but
it's a very ancient tradition." She saw distaste darken his
glance, and wanted to give him something to understand about
herself so she indicated one of her long thick braids that had
come undone in the water. She began combing it out with her
fingers. "But I know why we braid the hair." His beautiful eyes

the color of the sun glistened with interest so she continued to explain, "The spirit undisciplined is the hair unbraided. A child's hair flows free just as the child runs free from duties to the clan, but when a man or woman reaches a certain age, the hair and the wild spirit must be disciplined into the larger pattern." Her fingers worked quickly to restore the weave.

Without using her hands she stood, a sensuous unwinding motion like a slow spring or a beautiful snake. "We don't need weapons," she replied, looking toward the wood. Their long afternoon shadows followed them past the cedars to a dogwood glade. The trees had no leaves yet, just creamy flowers on bare silver branches.

By the time they crossed the forest to the western beach, she'd collected several kinds of tender young leaves from groundling plants as well as pokeweed shoots, the corms of small white flowers unearthed from the loamy forest floor, garlic and leek buds, chive sprouts, mint, and delicate uncurled fern fronds. He was dubious about the alarming red mushrooms but the oyster-white ones in choir ranks on a fallen oak looked quite edible. She found the grainy tongues of morrels he thought looked murderous. "These are treasures," she assured him. "The Osage call them land fish." She made a sound with her lips that said how tasty they were, her tongue a wedge of juicy rose-colored fruit between her lips.

A spring rattled from a rocky crack where they surprised a turtle napping in the last sun. She dropped her provender to catch it but it scuttled out of her grasp toward Iron Hand, who snatched it up by one stubby leg, dispatching it swiftly with his blade. While he dressed the carcass she found a bed of black mussels in the cove where the branchlet joined the river. With a stick she brought up handfuls of cattail shoots she cleaned and peeled at the water's edge.

During this time they seldom spoke but more than once their eyes met in shy unspoken dialogue. The sun stained the western sky a dazzling, dying orange as they carried their supper back to the fire, where her boiling rocks glowed redly. While he stoked the fire, she started a soup flavored with garlic and leeks in the turtle shell. She broiled the mushroom strips on a hot rock then wrapped each sliver in a pokeweed leaf. When the mussels sizzled open among the coals, they tonged them out and ate them from the shells, which they used as spoons for the soup. He thought the food the finest he'd ever tasted, made more succulent by the purple sky and the

woman's smile. After sand-scouring the turtle shell she
scooped up water from a pool trapped on the sandbar. When it
was hot she steeped mint leaves for tea, which they sipped
quietly watching fine crimson explosions settle their bonfire
into a sky-full of sparks.

Now they talked. In French, handsign, and a little Sioux,
they poured out their stories, told their deepest feelings, pain,
and triumphs. Treefrogs sang around them. The sand was
warm, the stories long. When the tea was gone and they'd
been quiet for a spell she said, "I just realized . . ."

"What?"

"Your hat. You lost that crazy hat."

He knew then he'd won her back from death. Joyous relief
pulsed through him. He could only smile, too full of feeling,
nodding that indeed the hat was gone.

"Because of me you lost your favorite hat," she remarked in
terse sign.

In uncertain Sioux he replied, "Everything would I lose for
Weeononka."

She scooted closer to him sitting with his back on the bank's
gentle slope, and stretched out facing the fire, sighing like a cat
in contentment. He could feel her warmth next to him,
relaxed and peaceful. Having begun, he said her great courage
had touched him deeply. His words seemed to stir the fire.
Lithe blue flames sprang to sudden life then settled down in
red and yellow flickers. "I have so wanted you," he continued
in handsign, words somehow being too blatant. "But you were
too fine and far away like that star."

Her eyes reflected the glow as she watched, fascinated by
what he was saying and by his mastery of the ancient hand
language. Few white men attained such subtlety. The sign for
"I love you" was simple: He pointed to himself, his heart, and
then to her. He saw her appreciation and put a flourish on it
when he said, "I want us to be . . ." He didn't know the sign
for "married" so he made it up on the spot by bringing his
hands together, joining the chief finger of each, watching her
eyes as he continued to pull with greater strength flesh against
metal; when he'd achieved maximum expression of insepara-
bility his mated fingers punctuated the idea with a final tension
that gave his hands the look in this ruby firelight of powerful
chain links. She sat up in surprised appreciation of his
invention, but didn't speak, so he continued in more conventional sign, "I'm ignorant of your customs and fear I might
offend you."

He knew the French female style was to make much of this moment, and accorded her the same privilege. She, however, was thinking about white and red, how his eloquent handsign went beyond his own personal meaning; red people could be symbolized by flesh, the whites by metal. Could a couple made up of such disparities travel for long in the same direction? Could they become a bonded pair? But here, the living answer to that question, was an honorable white man who'd found a way to live with metal, asking her to live as his woman. This was a potent sign that seemed to insist on a possibility she might otherwise have denied.

He was thinking she was still in shock. Later he would say all this again. What mattered tonight was that she understood he cared, that he'd help her start a new life and wanted to give her more babies. Whatever she wished. "I just want to comfort you."

"Sometimes," she replied enigmatically, "the only comfort is being warm on a cold night." But she snuggled closer to him. Near sleep and drifting nearer, he rambled on about what their life together could be. He wanted to settle down at Arkansas Post, make a living in the fur trade, experiment with crops and other domestic enterprises. Half the words he said she didn't understand but his voice was musical. When he realized she was asleep in his arms, he lay aside a strand of blue-black hair that had fallen over her eye. The last thing he remembered was the hissing fire and a nightbird's call across the river.

He woke in sapphire darkness to her crying. It was different from before when grief made her sob like a baby. Now she moaned in pain. She was sitting up, bent toward the embers, rocking forward and back.

"What—?" he started to ask then saw she was holding her breast. She'd unlaced the neck of her beaded dress as if to feed the baby. At first he thought the bite must be hurting her then he saw it was the unbitten, swollen right globe that had her attention. Eyes brimming, she looked around at him. He saw she was trying to milk the dry nipple with her fingers. The breast was distended, the skin drawn tight because no baby had emptied it. It looked about to burst but the nipple was puckered, sunken. The weight of the milk had squeezed off its release. She stared at it in anguish, holding the globe of her flesh with both hands to ease the weight as if it were some kind of fragile offering. Firelight licked her skin and turned it the color of molten gold. Her shadows were blue, her eyes dark coals with hearts of fire. He leaned toward her, but hesitated, his eyes darkening to amber. The air seemed to ripple, and understanding passed wordlessly between them.

He put his tongue tip to the nipple to awaken it. With severe gentleness he began to bring it into his mouth, wetting and caressing the hard stubborn bud of it. Her skin was feverish. Against it his own was cool. She felt for the first time the delight of a man's insinuating beard on her areola; milk sprang from her. They watched in mutual delight as it squirted a silken pinkish, salt-sweet stream he caught in his open lips and followed to its source. His kiss swollen with her milk pulled a gasp from her. She tensed with momentary pain, as sharp as that caused by those terrible little teeth. Instantly he paused, searching her face. New trails of tears pulsed down her cheeks. She, smiling down quickly, urged him, continue, continue (and he'd never know her smile hid a private, poignant chuckle at him with the childish dribble of her juices making a similar wet trail on his half-open lips as it might on an infant's). He thought only that her small nervous smile meant to resume. He sucked tenderly at first, then hungrily as her cries changed from pain to pleasure until soon she made purring sounds and stroked his hair, almost idly combing through his braid to untangle it.

The soft doeskin chemise opened to her navel, which he explored minutely with his tongue. Their dance intensified, moving her further out of the garment. He made the discovery of her unforested mound of Venus, something he'd never even imagined in a grown woman.

She found the lacings of his shirt and leggings. They grew chilled together as a northerly breeze found them. They reluctantly paused while he threw more wood on the fire. When it was blazing, she pulled him to the sandbar pool, still sun-warm and deep enough for them to stetch out together. They threw off their moccasins and stood finally in their sand-jeweled skins.

She stepped into the water, shattering the reflected stars, scooped up the fine sand, and began scrubbing her body. She was so beautiful he couldn't help watching her kneel there. When she saw him deep in observation, she playfully threw water at him.

He looked down at the hand at the end of the leather sleeve. The music box and watch might already be ruined by the river, but he didn't want to douse them further. It was time for her to see anyway. He quickly unbuckled the hand and stood before her as he was.

This was a new experience for Weeononka. She'd seen the stumps of fingers and toes. But in this wild land where hardiness meant survival, people just didn't live without arms or legs except for rare birth defects, which most midwives considered cause for birth cord strangulation.

"Were you born without a hand?"

Her unaffected curiosity pleased him. He explained his war experience as he joined her in the water, where she casually began scrubbing his back with the gritty sand. It felt marvelous, relieving tensions he had not been aware of. He felt her breasts and smooth stomach against his spine.

"I've never seen this battle wound before," she remarked, rubbing hard along his shoulders.

"Surely it must happen sometimes to braves."

She put sand in his hand and offered her own back to be rubbed. "But they die." She shyly made the handsign for self-murder, not wanting to offend him.

"Does my arm offend you?" he asked.

To answer she caressed both his arms with her hands, expertly massaging key muscles and stress points. Her fingers were strong, her touch exhilarating. She didn't stop there but descended to the amazing forest of his chest, to his thighs and calves. She tasted his milk as he had tasted hers, found it pungent, salty, knowing exactly when to hesitate, saving and savoring their building pleasure. She massaged his feet with her own, then awakened erotic sensations he'd never suspected hiding in places like the back of the knee, the palm of the hand, the scarline terminating his arm, the center of his forehead. They sampled each other like a feast. He seemed ignorant of "twin rowers," so she delighted in educating him.

Finally they were suspended and entwined so that they were one breathless creature on the sand, screaming in pleasure. They slept only to wake and love again then crawled beneath their clothes and fell asleep entwined. The fire smoldered. Dew covered them. She woke to the sound of crows somewhere in the island forest. A fog had moved in with the sun lost somewhere behind it.

"I think they're waiting for us at Kappa," he whispered in her ear.

"I don't know," she answered, close to him and relishing the warmth along that side. Cold damp air hit her along the right when she stirred.

"Where is it from here?"

"North across the swamp. Many days."

They had in fact passed the village on their swift downriver journey to this island. "I'm afraid of the swamp."

"We couldn't make it?"

She was quiet, thinking. "I don't want to try. There are alligators. . . ." What she then described sounded to him like a mythological dragon, surely an exaggeration.

"Will being alone with me for a few sunrises be so terrible?" she asked. He answered without words, exploring her in the soft morning light. He felt as though he could never know enough of her topography, the perfect hills and enticing valleys of her strong body.

After they had pleasured each other again, they went digging for sassafras roots for breakfast tea and crisp white tubers they ate raw. They explored their island the rest of the day, stopping to revel in each other's bodies as the mood struck, then taking their time to walk the sandy beaches. He knew she was looking for the little bundle she'd lost. She didn't make a show of it, but he could tell as she poked among the eddies and broken logs that she had not given up quite yet.

But her spirit was high. He felt enriched by her, burnished to a high shine that sparked between their eyes and fingertips.

Unspoken but lingering was his concern for the rest of the expedition. It surprised him when she remarked, almost as though she had read his mind, that they would be along in a while. "We have only this short time, I think," she said wistfully.

But he caught her up, pledging the rest of his life to her.

That night they spoke of possibilities. He repainted his word picture of their house at the Post, of a huge farm (this he had trouble explaining), of their children growing up neither white nor red but a new people.

"But you could live with the Quapaw," she suggested shyly. He agreed effusively, yes, he wanted to learn all the ways of her people, take the best of both their nations. This was not what she meant but she didn't argue. It was possible for her to take this moment suspended between what was and what would be, and enjoy it for itself alone. But the future had a stronger pull on the man than on her. He was full of plans he described in detail for their wonderful life that would be funded by the fur trade.

They returned to the smoldering fire and built it to a

conflagration—he wanted La Salle to see it from afar when he
took to the river again. She said the party was surely being
entertained by the Kappa, who would want them to stay for
many days, but he knew La Salle would be anxious to move
on.

"How far to the mouth of the river?"

She had never been that far south but she knew its
confluence with the Nigestai was only a short way below the
Kappa village. They had no mutual system of measurement
except time; she was sure the two rivers joined less than half a
day south of here.

"It's said by the ravens that the Great River spills into a big
hole less than two days' journey after it joins the Nigestai."

The third day he stayed near the fire, throwing on rotten
wood to make it burn in a column of thick black smoke. Surely
La Salle would see it, unless of course he and the others had
been detained by the Chickasaw. He thought that unlikely; La
Salle would have left that awful bluff at the first opportunity.

That afternoon the long Illinois canoes rounded the headland and beached amid cheers and celebration. The men paid
off their wagers when they saw de Tonti and the Indian
woman. Once glance and it was obvious they had found each
other. Even the losers of the wager were brightened by the
couple's good fortune. La Salle was frenzied with excitement at
finding the man he considered the most valuable in his party.
He saw the bond that was established between de Tonti and
the woman—that worried him—but she looked subdued and
happy to be at his side. She would keep him tame for the rest
of the trip.

He brought de Tonti up to date on the expedition at the
bluffs. They had seen no more Chickasaw after de Tonti had
followed Weeononka into the water. They had hastily buried
the white man the Chickasaw had tortured—he was a red-
headed Irishman. "The name *McQueeg* was tattooed on his
wrist," La Salle reported, disturbed that an Englishman of any
stripe was in this region. It made it all the more urgent that he
claim the river for France. As Weeononka had predicted, the
Kappa Quapaw joyously received the Frenchmen and their
Shawnee guides, who were cousins to the Quapaw. One of the
priests stayed with that village to baptize new Christians. In
exchange a Kappa warrior joined them along with a visiting
Taencas runner, who agreed to return to his southern delta
country with the expedition.

The two white leaders stayed up late that night setting their plans, so when her lover rejoined Weeononka, she was already asleep on his bedroll. He didn't wake her but lay there with her in his arms, full of visions about their wonderful future together. Later she woke him pleasantly; they shared each other's bodies again, apart from the main group. It was sweet but a little sad because the island was no longer their exclusive domain.

At dawn they left it, he in La Salle's lead canoe, she riding with the women.

Not a half league down the river she cried out at something she spied in the water. Oh no, de Tonti thought in the next canoe, she's found her dead baby in the eddies. She insisted that the paddlers aim for the spot where she pointed, excited by what she'd found.

"*Le chapeau fou!*" she exclaimed. Everyone was greatly relieved when she pulled de Tonti's waterlogged hat from a snag at the river's edge. She handed it to him across the space between their two canoes. He leaned over and kissed her, much to the delight of the company. Even La Salle was grudgingly buoyed by their affection.

They found the main channel again and headed for the juncture of the two rivers, as de Tonti wrung out the dilapidated hat, spreading it to dry in the sun. He saw her watching him from the women's canoe and waved.

The Shawnee wives were solicitous of her and very kind, happy that she'd found the strong white man they all respected. Little Bird told her of the unfortunate white man they had buried back on the bluff, remarking on his bright red hair, which she had never seen before. Weeononka became animated at this report and wanted to know more but the Shawnees woman could tell her nothing else. Weeononka hoped it had been the white man who had defiled her husband's death. It would be a just fate. Maybe her husband's ghost would walk easier now that he had been avenged.

Little Bird reported that the Kappa said the Osotony had not rebuilt on the former site but moved to the Lake in the Mountain. She glanced longingly at the western horizon. It was too far to see from here, but in her mind she knew the spot exactly. It was near the Osotonys' annual hunting campsite.

Even though there were no people here to greet them where the Nigestai met the Great River, La Salle still wanted to camp at the junction to scout a site for a fort in his grand scheme.

They were on the river by noon the next day, floating through pleasant country in the early bloom of spring.

De Tonti was in La Salle's canoe. The Canadian had not mentioned the woman since his explosion at her up on the bluff. But now he indirectly referred to her when he said, "Some of my advisors feared you were a treacherous Italian but I swear you are more French than I."

"What do you mean?"

"That woman, helping her—loving her—it's very romantic."

De Tonti snorted. "It's nothing of the sort."

La Salle shook his head. "Now I truly know you," he said, teasing.

"It's just nature taking its course." De Tonti glanced back to see that Weeononka was all right in the third canoe. From here he could see no emotion on her face. Her thoughts seemed to be lost in the water's movement as it carried them along.

That night she responded to his touch with some of the fire she had shown on the island. They made love until they fell into exhausted slumber and in the morning when he woke he found her and her meager belongings gone.

He ran out waking the camp with a cry, grabbing the Kappa guide. "Tell me where she went!"

La Salle had to pull him off the guide, who answered, "Don't you know, white man? That woman is going back to her people to die."

De Tonti would have grabbed him again but the Kappa Quapaw stepped back, his hands a flurry of explanatory sign. "It's a custom for a Quapaw chief woman to take her life out of grief," he explained gently to the white man. "Especially now that she grieves for her baby, it's likely she's going back home to join her husband, a famous chief who died at the hands of the Chickasaw. Everyone knows the story."

27

La Salle found him in the tent throwing articles of clothing into a pack, grabbing this and that, *pemmican*, jerky, bisquits, shot—items for wilderness survival. He dumped it all together without regard for use with the obvious intent of leaving as soon as possible. The Canadian stood at the door flap a

moment absorbing the import of de Tonti's actions. He went
about his haphazard packing, thin-lipped and silent though he
knew La Salle was standing there.

He buckled the whole mess together in his backpack. His
movements were harsh, overdone, but methodical. Nothing
would stop him, La Salle observed as he remarked, "I
understand perfectly what you're doing and why."

"I doubt that," de Tonti replied, thinking of Jeanette and
how he'd left her without a backward look. He couldn't undo
the past and take a stand back there on the dock at Quebec but
he could avoid making a similar mistake with Weeononka.
How long could a man bow to duty and lose all that mattered?

"There comes a time when every man must do what he
must," La Salle replied softly. Once again he had managed to
mirror de Tonti's thoughts.

He took a camp stool and watched his best man complete
preparations to desert his enterprise. "I suppose you'll take
Sabat with you."

"I wouldn't put it on him. He's too old."

"You're not thinking of following her alone in that bayou?"

De Tonti was grimly silent, his back to La Salle as he stuffed
two extra blades into the pack. He saw he'd forgotten to
include the damnable diary. He snatched it up and proceeded
to make a place for it.

La Salle couldn't miss the gesture. If he was taking a journal,
he must not be thinking of staying a savage forever. "What will
you do when you find her?"

"Whatever she wants."

"I fail to see what the savage bi—"

De Tonti glared at him. Only one other time had he allowed
his patron see that he might be able to kill him.

La Salle nodded, conciliatory, hands spread to indicate his
apology. "You're a free man. But I mourn to lose you, Hal."

"That's not my name."

La Salle was surprised but didn't respond since de Tonti's
reaction was actually a wedge in his stubbornness. Maybe La
Salle could still bring him around, save him from this grievous
mistake.

"I never liked that nickname. It sounds too English, if you'd
listen to the truth." La Salle settled back, arms folded across
his chest, so de Tonti continued, "You have no idea how it
sounds for you to be spouting Anglicisms in your position. But
I don't know why I keep trying to correct your errors since you
won't listen to advice."

La Salle was pink with delight at this outburst. If de Tonti had been undivided about leaving he would have done so without preparations and certainly without this discussion.

"You know, monsieur," the younger man continued, "that is a fault in you. You never listen to anyone. You don't even know who your best friends are, you're so damned suspicious."

"Henri, I've taken you for granted but I swear to you that I couldn't have come this far without you. You're the only man with me I can trust."

De Tonti snorted cynically. He was just about ready to go. He looked around to make sure he wasn't leaving anything he might need; he really had no idea what he was headed into.

"Please take one of our guides. He can carry provisions so you won't have to risk living off the land."

De Tonti stared at him without comment and grabbed his hat, his remaining civilized article of clothing, then hefted the pack. He took it outside, where he dropped it in the dust to inspect the bindings and mount it on his back.

The entourage was watching. The men made business appear normal, going about several occupations, all pretense. De Tonti felt the center of their attention. He knew that at least with a couple of the men La Salle would be at a loss without a mediator. Too bad. Let La Salle pick up his own pieces from now on.

"May I walk with you along the river path?" La Salle said politely as de Tonti hefted the pack, but the older man didn't hesitate even though de Tonti made no gesture that said he wished company. His mind wasn't even on La Salle. He looked for Sabat but the old man was nowhere about. He said a quick goodbye to La Forest, who appeared incredulous at what de Tonti was doing. All the men were now looking at him as though he'd turned green before their eyes. "Tell Sabat . . ." he started to say, but for want of words didn't finish the thought. La Forest nodded, understanding completely.

He casually saluted the men, forgoing any individual farewells, though something like a plea shot from D'Arcy's glance. De Tonti frowned, turned away before there were words, and began trudging off upriver toward the west, where he knew he could follow the *café au lait* course to Weeononka's village.

La Salle walked beside him away from the camp. De Tonti knew the Canadian had not given up but would probably make a dramatic play on his sympathies to get him to remain with the party.

The river was high and thick with mud beside them as they threaded their way along the footpath on its bank. In places, new rushing water had eaten away fresh morsels of the bank. La Salle bade him pause for a moment at one of these spots, where a huge crescent of rich creamy backflow nibbled at the jungle. To go farther one would have to either hack his way through the almost solid green wall or jump from one bank of the bight to another across a narrow tongue of snarling water.

"I ask only that you hear my proposal."

De Tonti's back was already aching; he had to balance the pack anyway. With La Salle's help he shucked it.

La Salle took in the view of the wide swollen stream flowing west to east, right to left as they stood on its raw northern bank. "No longer is this the Nigestai River. From now on it will be *Rivière des Arkansas ou Tonti . . .*"

"Hmmm," de Tonti replied. If this was a joke, he didn't find it funny.

La Salle was serious. His eyes glinted at the prospects he envisioned there, prosperous villages along this river, ships plying its waters with rich cargoes, the happy sound of French being spoken on wharves that might occupy this very spot if his dreams could be made reality. But he needed this man to pull it off. He knew de Tonti shared those dreams if he could only make him remember what was at stake.

Of all the men with him, this was the last one he would have expected to go savage. If it weren't for that bitch . . .

"I'll wait for you here," La Salle said evenly, betraying none of his anxiety about de Tonti's loss.

"Please, continue to prove your thesis that the Mech-a-si-pi River empties into the Gulf."

"It's the *Colbert* River—" La Salle flared, then cooled. "I won't proceed without you."

"La Forest is equal to me in command."

"But he's not the man you are, Henri de Tonti. No, I shall wait for you. Bring your bride back, if you wish. I will do anything to keep you with me."

"Flattery isn't going to work."

"How about an outright bribe?"

"What?"

"I wasn't joking. This is now the River de Tonti." La Salle turned a complete circle with both arms outspread. It was an unexpectedly expansive gesture from him. "All this, wherever my finger points, I grant to Monsieur Henri de Tonti this day the whatever it is—I've forgotten—"

"March fourteen."

"—on this day the fourteenth of March, 1682, a province of land between the confluence of the De Tonti and the Mech-a-si-pi Rivers."

"You are wicked, Rob La Salle."

"This grant will be part of my official report to His Majesty. It's already accomplished. I received his permission to reward you before we left France."

"You never said it would be so much."

La Salle shrugged as if he needed to say no more.

"But I can't accept this." De Tonti offered back the scroll with its official-looking wax seal imprinted by La Salle's ring. "I'm resigning your command."

La Salle shook his head adamantly. "This land is yours already. The very dirt we are standing on belongs to you at this moment. Consider it a bonus for your faithful service."

"But—"

"For past service, Henri, not to bind you in the future."

"This is most generous." He'd expected some trick from La Salle but nothing like this.

La Salle put his hand on de Tonti's shoulder. "Go with God, my friend. I hope you find what you seek." De Tonti saw La Salle's eyes were genuinely swimming. "Love is not the worst goal for a gentleman to have. . . ." Unexpectedly La Salle hugged him.

De Tonti blinked back astonishment at this unprecedented gesture of affection.

But he knew La Salle had something else to say: "Take your place beside me in history, Henri. Come with me to the mouth of the Mech-a-si-pi. When we return to this place I will personally help you find her. The whole company will help. But let's reach our primary goal first, since all our futures hang on it."

De Tonti seemed paralyzed by the choice, La Salle hoped.

"The land is yours. As titleholder here you literally own the woman and her whole godforsaken country. It's yours even if you break our contract. I was working on the paper this very morning. "But if you stay the course there will be a bonus of a thousand *livres* in beaver for you when we return to Montreal. I have it drawn up to that effect back in my tent, a thousand for you and the same for La Forest."

He could feel de Tonti straining at the decision. Around them the impenetrable jungle sighed with a thousand small voices. It was like a wall this close to the river, a green bastion festooned with ropes and creepers as thick as a man's thigh. A step off the path and one would be lost. Not even the Indians liked traveling there in this wet season. La Salle knew de Tonti was thinking about the futility of finding one person within its depths, especially a person who did not want to be found.

But he dared not press his point further. He let his hand slip from de Tonti's shoulder, turned, and walked back along the path in the direction they had come. Five steps and he was gone, swallowed up in the sultry foliage.

La Salle returned to camp alone but in high spirits. He was convinced de Tonti would see reason. But he asked one of the guides, the swamp-wise Taencas, to watch out after de Tonti but to say nothing of where the woman may have gone.

Iron Hand's fame had preceeded the expedition. The laconic old runner was beaming at the honor of accompanying him as he trotted out of camp and into the throbbing jungle.

De Tonti was glad to see the guide, who caught up with him only a few paces west of the spot where La Salle had said goodbye. The white man's first handsigned request was for help in finding the Quapaw village where Weeononka might be headed.

The Taencas, whose name was Handsome Frog because he was such a good swimmer, shook his head. "The Osotony are gone. The lodges are broken. Chickasaw . . ."

De Tonti nodded. "But she said some of the people survived that attack. I know she went to them. Do you know of another Quapaw village?"

Handsome Frog took him about three leagues that day into the woodlands beyond the swamp. There on a fair prairie where they encountered a herd of buffalo they found another abandoned Quapaw site. They camped there that night, dining on a buffalo calf that had gotten stuck in quicksand. De Tonti learned much from watching the Taencas prepare the meat. He unearthed white tubers, which reminded de Tonti of Weeononka and their island. He ate but the Taencas could see he was despondent over the woman. After they ate they smoked two bowls of de Tonti's precious tobacco, then some of Handsome Frog's private mix of powerful herbs.

"Do you really think she's killed herself out of duty to a dead man?" de Tonti asked after the smoke's effect loosened him.

"Who knows what a Quapaw woman will do."

"They're unusual?" De Tonti asked, using a sign that meant "wrong way." He recalled that the Quapaw had invaded this country that had belonged to the Taencas and other indigenous peoples.

"They're different. Quapaw and Osage allow it. Especially a chief woman. I think she may have done it. My own people have this custom, too, among the nobles," the Taencas added, using the sign for "mound of earth."

These lowland people revered high places, de Tonti thought, recalling Mt. Sinai, where Moses of another lowland tribe received the Ten Commandments. "But does she have to? I mean," he tried to explain in Sioux, thinking in Latin that duty must be a universal human concept, "is she duty-bound?" He used the gesture for "bound by the heart."

The Taencas shrugged.

Odd, de Tonti thought, how that gesture also seemed common human property, like the smile and the frown.

"She left. That's all that needs to be said. Why do you mourn one woman, white man? There are so many. . . ."

De Tonti had wild dreams that night. At dawn they returned to the burnt-out village of Osotony on the river. All that stood was a single lodge, which de Tonti couldn't know was the cabin Weeononka had crawled from to escape the Chickasaw. It was a dismal scene. He had dared to assume Handsome Frog could find some evidence of where the tribe had fled, but even for the experienced scout it was hopeless. All they found were human bones, some pitifully small, and charcoal.

Despite the melancholia that seemed to permeate the ruin, de Tonti couldn't help noticing that this was an excellent river location. The Quapaw had chosen it after years of observing the meandering water. It was a high spot on a wide bend not too far from the confluence of this river with the Mech-a-si-pi. It would be the perfect place to build a fort. The king had created Versailles out of such a swamp. Maybe a lesser mortal could drain these for some croplands. . . . He said nothing of this to the guide but made sure that he could find this place again.

The day had started out bright but by early afternoon the sky looked slate-green and sullen from the southwest. Handsome Frog looked anxiously back over his shoulder at the mounting thunderheads while aiming de Tonti in a more direct path toward the swamp.

"Let's go around it," said the Frenchman. He didn't like the bayous.

"Iron Hand, see that storm coming?" the runner said in Sioux, as if explaining something simple to a child.

"Looks like some squall."

"That's the thunderbird."

De Tonti scanned the clouds moving in rapidly, whipping the crowns of the willows near a small creek that bisected this prairie.

The air changed around them as they hurried to the shelter of the bayou. "For some reason the thunderbird avoids the swampland in favor of the prairie," Handsome Frog explained, pausing to gauge the storm.

It was an eerie sky. Half was still a dazzling blue in front of the stormhead. De Tonti saw lightning lace the front. Thunder sounded surprisingly close. He'd heard about a mounted field commander struck by lightning when every soldier on foot around him was spared. He felt suddenly naked out here in the open. A wave of wind almost took his hat.

The Indian silently watched the storm. He glanced at the fringe of lowland fully a quarter league down the sloping meadow dotted only here and there with low bushes. Handsome Frog suddenly shucked the large pack from his back like a chick coming out of a shell.

A burned smell filled the air. The sky was olive green at the violent heart of the storm bearing down as if it had spied them, playing hawk to their mice.

Handsome Frog was a dozen paces ahead of de Tonti before he realized it was every man for himself. He was out of his own pack and flying toward the forest before he realized he'd moved.

Wind now battered him from behind as he ran looking over his shoulder. He heard Handsome Frog's gagged cry as he plowed into him standing on a rock still facing the west. De Tonti recovered and looked to see what claimed Handsome Frog's stunned attention.

Dipping almost tentatively out of the storm's darkest cheek was the shrieking nodding snout of a swirling funnel. It spun leisurely from the cloud then swooped spinelessly through the tops of those willows. Like some kind of cloud-living animal of great size, the funnel snuffed up the entire coat of foilage, taking randomly a tree by the roots here and there but leaving the rest shuddering naked branches. The creek snaked impossibly upward from its bed and into the funnel tip, water suddenly running straight into the air as the monster took a sip.

Clearly snared in this great slurp were a deer, birds, reeds, rocks, and dirt. In a lazy dance the funnel whisked a clean narrow path up from the oasis and onto the rise de Tonti and Handsome Frog had just vacated.

"Come on—run—" de Tonti screamed, thinking the Indian was paralyzed by fear.

But he was not. He had begun keening in a deep even voice the opening stanza of his death song. De Tonti could bearly hear it under the funnel's scream.

The thing paused on the knoll. It lifted its dark skirts, grabbed their backpacks, and headed straight for the two men.

The Indian's eyes were wide open. De Tonti thought in those last few seconds the man had died of fright. He'd heard of such things.

But because he liked this rare individual, Handsome Frog turned once, looked at him with clear unfluttering eyes, and laid out some friendly advice. "Prepare to die, white man." In his next breath he found his song again, facing the oncoming funnel with his arms up and open.

De Tonti too was transfixed by that roaring inevitable cannon bore.

The cloud emitted a tortured sound. De Tonti had never heard anything like it. This must be what the gun hears when the bullet comes tearing out. It seemed to sear a grove inside his skull. He was looking directly at it, far beyond acceptance of the inevitable, when the tip lifted back up into the sky so fast the eye missed the movement.

The funnel was there one second, gone the next.

But that metallic gouging sound continued over their heads. Their faces turned upward as the funnel roared by, slamming into high ground a little above them to the right. As if the contact had nauseated the storm, it spat out their packs and staggered on, jumping in a crazy zigzag pattern northeastward along the border of the swampland until it and its shriek faded away.

It was suddenly very silent.

The terrible roar still echoed in de Tonti's ears. A wall of rain and wind battered at them from all directions but Handsome Frog was laughing and de Tonti was laughing with him, rain streaming their faces. They whooped in two languages, hugging each other, jumping with life renewed by close contact with death.

"That was my *fifth* thunderbird," Handsome Frog bragged, pounding his chest and singing out in the direction of the storm, "Come back, you thunderbird! You can never get me!"

They dragged their packs to the shelter of a great oak. The tree was so big the ground beneath it was still dry after the quick storm. By the time they had a fire going, Handsome Frog was calm enough to explain that the thunderbird was his manitou. A tornado had hit his village the day he was born. Since then he'd encountered many on the horizon but now had stood face to face with five. This experience was great *wa kon* for the runner. That night he tattooed further insignia on his thighmark and sang late near the fire.

De Tonti marveled at his own renewed spirit; yesterday he was ready to die because Weeononka had left him.

The next day dawned storm-scraped and shining. They traversed the swamp again, conversing about the inhabitants, animal and human. Handsome Frog taught him much about alligators.

"If you can get one on its back," the Taencas explained, "it will go to sleep. The problem is getting one on its back."

He said some of the people bordering the swamp worshiped the chief alligator. Siouan tribes considered it a degenerate practice since the alligator god demanded human babies as sacrifice.

"But when a big one turns maneater, as they do if a careless hunter leaves it merely wounded, many river people start secretly sacrificing to the chief."

De Tonti listened deep into the night to swamp lore. Survival in the bayous was a specialized art. Nobody with any sense went into the lowlands during the wet months, but even little children were taught what to do if they should find themselves in the great blue temple, as the neighborhood called the extensive swamplands.

"Main thing is to remember to watch the current," said Handsome Frog. Fire shadows played on his craggy face. His front teeth had precise holes bored in them. His nose was slit to the cheek and was decorated with feathers and beads. Despite the chill he was dressed only in a breechcloth and tattoos while de Tonti huddled near the fire in his heavy leather suit.

"Lose the current for long, you're dead."

The fire crackled. Around them the swamp whistled and sighed. De Tonti could not repress a shiver. What a dismal place to be lost in.

During those dark hours until dawn he slept lightly, waking with a start several times when he thought the fire had gone out. Even with Handsome Frog he had no desire to remain without the fire's warmth.

The Taencas watched the white man settle nervously into his bedroll. Funny people, these Frenchmen. Full of contradictions. Like this one courageous enough to face the Iroquois with a string of beads as he was reported to have done, and live to be frightened of crickets. Handsome Frog reflected on La Salle's orders. But he also liked Iron Hand. He debated briefly, before hearing the light snore across the flames, about telling him he knew exactly where the Quapaw woman had gone.

But he decided against telling him she would go to the Lake in the Mountain. The Quapaw were crazy enough to live up in that spooky place. Iron Hand was crazy enough to follow her there. Handsome Frog didn't want to lose the company and good *wa kon* of traveling with the man with the metal hand.

For two days La Salle camped at the confluence of the now De Tonti and Mech-a-si-pi Rivers. The men were busy refurbishing gear, repairing boots and holsters, which mildew was taking at an alarming rate. The plan had been to leave the seventeenth, tomorrow, a plan de Tonti was familiar with, having helped design it.

They heard shots from time to time but not the one-two-one signal they'd devised to call for help. La Salle told the men de Tonti had taken off to hunt because he was tired of dried meat. None argued, though there was stern disagreement behind La Salle's back. Secret odds were laid against the captain's return. The men, without coin, bet marked playing cards in lieu of money, and several lost a considerable sum when de Tonti and his guide returned the afternoon of the sixteenth with three large turkeys of flamboyant feather immediately confiscated by the delighted Indians.

They roasted the fowl that last night. La Salle broke out stores of brandy, considering de Tonti's return cause enough for a celebration to launch the final leg of the journey.

Packing the next dawn for the renewed journey de Tonti let slip with his half-inflexible grasp a pouch of lead ball into an iron kettle. The sound stopped him and he shook the pot as though swishing water to clean its sides. The lead balls rolled around and around building up speed and amplifying the sound.

Every Indian in camp dropped what he was doing and looked in the direction of the ominous sound this produced. Handsome Frog saw de Tonti was recreating the thunderbird's scream almost perfectly in pitch if not in volume. Once heard, that sound could never be forgotten. He and de Tonti started laughing, capturing the other Indians in the joke. Someone explained it to the white men, who thought they were exaggerating. Only de Tonti among the Frenchmen could claim firsthand proof that the Indians were telling the truth about the thunderbird. The storms, Handsome Frog explained, were entirely local. The one that nearly killed himself and Iron Hand was not even seen from afar by the main expedition six leagues away.

Everyone's spirits revived. De Tonti never mentioned Fleet Woman again. Nor did he speak of his journey to her village. He sometimes thought she might be dead, as the Indians said she was. If she chose to leave him, then she might well choose to die. But he harbored the hope that as long as he didn't know for sure, he could consider her alive. He consoled himself that it was her decision; he had not abandoned her to indifferent fate as he had Jeanette. He'd thought much of Jeanette while in the whispering wilderness. The guilt of what he'd done to her, he supposed, would be with him as long as he lived. His futile effort to rescue Weeononka from her self-appointed fate did not lighten the burden of Jeanette by so much as a pebble's weight.

Maybe fate was always self-appointed, and one could do nothing to help another forestall it. No, he thought bitterly, an early death from mourning did not have to be Weeononka's fate. I could have loved her enough to make her forget. If only she had let me try.

These were private thoughts, of course. All he communicated to La Salle and the rest was quiet enthusiasm. But he was detached. To the accompanying savage warriors it was obvious Iron Hand had left his heart back on the Arkansas. The civilized whites were impervious to such intuitions, all except de Tonti himself, who felt a gaping hole had been blown in his side. Instead of blood this wound spilled feeling. Although it did not impair his intellect, it produced a cool numbness.

The effect looked very handsome on him, according to La
Salle, who commented on de Tonti's maturation to L'Esperance. 'Per had the good sense to agree but he also heard the
hen cluckings of Sabat, who was sure the Quapaw witch had
put a spell on his master.

De Tonti felt nothing. He rode the swollen river and his own
writhing soul from far away. On a high updraft above the
growling Mech-a-si-pi's main channel, he saw an eagle soaring.
It was easy in imagination to take the same point of view. He
saw themselves as specks on the map he'd been studying for
two years while yearning for this river.

Now that he had it, he couldn't share the buoyant ambitions
of the other men.

They were on their way again.

28

It was a dream that helped her decide. She was with Iron
Hand that last night when she was awakened by the shriek of a
crane. She sat up and watched her dead husband walk from
the forest, where the persistent hum of treefrogs strummed
the night. He crouched beside her and the sleeping white
man. She was so happy to see that he was riding a little boy on
his shoulders. "Don't worry about us," said her husband,
patting the boy's leg. The child smiled shyly at her but said
nothing. He was holding on by clasping his hands under his
uncle's chin, looking safe and happy. Weeononka was about to
reply when her husband touched her lips with his ghost
fingers; the sensation was cool and tingling. "You're the one in
danger." He looked deeply into her eyes. There was no light
from the fire here where she and Iron Hand had pulled their
blankets for privacy. Yet she clearly saw her reflection in Man-
Who-'s eyes. That's when she knew it was dream time. She
looked back at her own sleeping body slumbering entwined
with Iron Hand.

Her husband stood. Her little boy squealed his delight. "Go
home to our people, Weeononka. You need them and they
need you."

He walked back into the shadows, turned with a wave, then
was gone. She liked this *wa kon* of being awake inside her

dream so she sat still for a long time, savoring the magic. A
sliver of a moon sailed overhead. For a long time she thought
she could hear her little boy laughing from the shoulders of his
protector.

It was a very good dream. She'd been worried for her baby
unburied and all alone on the Path of Ghosts. Now she knew
he was safe. When the ghost child had looked at her, he didn't
seem to bear her any blame. That gave her heart joy, even if it
meant he did not recognize her. She could almost not bear to
think about what she had done to him. When she did think
about it, she wished again that Iron Hand had not prevented
her from following the child into death. But seeing him as so
beautiful and healthy a spirit helped the pain of remembering.
He had grown under his uncle's guidance, and was no longer
just a dead baby. She was sure after this dream that he didn't
remember what had happened on the Chickasaw Bluffs. That
gave her hope.

She had meant to take her husband's advice and head for the
Osotony on the Lake in the Mountain. But when she came to
the fork in the trails—one leading west up the Nigestai and
one leading north back to the Osage mountains—something
made her take the northern route. Even as she slipped away
from this white man, she grieved for him. There was too much
mourning in her already. To replace this one whom she must
leave, she found herself thinking of Game Dancer.

So, despite the omens, she turned in his direction.

When Weeononka walked into the village of her girlhood,
there was something going on. Some travelers from the south
were clustered over near the council lodge where a knot of
villagers was idly watching a barter. Weeononka couldn't hear
exactly what was being said behind the wall of persons, but as
she drifted in that direction, she caught the gist of it. These
southerners from a tribe called Yaqui had come from far away
on a quest for the renowned Ozark bow wood. Several
villagers smiled in recognition but didn't interrupt the trade
with questions when she appeared among them.

She listened just outside the ring of people. She could hear a
familiar voice doing the bargaining for the Osage. It was Game
Dancer. She listened for a while, pleased at the manly wisdom
evident in his voice. He sounded older than the few seasons
she'd been away.

Presently the woman in front of her drifted off and
Weeononka took her place. In this way after a time she worked

her way through the crowd and could now see Game Dancer sitting on a buffalo robe discussing the trade with the southerners.

These strangers were short slender bronze-skinned people who wore woven shirts of cactus fiber through which their lean muscles could be seen. They sported turbans of wrapped material in bright colors and wore much silver embedded with turquoise.

She watched with great interest as Game Dancer negotiated a certain number of rough-finish bows in return for three silver-turquoise medallions and the metal heels one of the Yaqui was wearing buckled over his moccasins. The three Yaqui had traveled here on three *cabay* and a pack animal that was a stockier longer-eared version of a *cabay*, what the whites called a mule, though none of her people had heard the word yet. Weeononka saw these animals tethered over on a line between two trees bordering a meadow here Game Dancer's own white was staked, the same horse given him by the Quapaw chief.

Things were certainly changing in the sleepy Osage camp to have five horses at one time in the headman's corral. For surely Game Dancer had come up in the world.

But his trade displeased an old Osage man, who turned to a companion, another venerable warrior who now served on the council. They exchanged looks of disgust.

The first councillor made a disparaging hand gesture, turned, and walked importantly away from the proceedings. Game Dancer saw this action but kept an aloof face as though it were of no importance. The other old Osage folded his arms across his chest and watched the bargain continue with a look of grave displeasure on his wrinkled features.

The lead southerner, a man of middle years and a tough, toothless grin, did not want to part with his metal heels. When he moved, they sparkled in the sun, heavy silver with jangling spiked wheels inlaid with rock crystal and pale green stones.

They were carrying on the trade with handsigns and a few Osage words, which had been incorporated into the speech of many bordering tribes trading with Osage traders. But the southerners also spoke to each other, commenting on the trade in their own unknown singsong language. To Weeononka's ears the Yaqui tongue sounded beautifully exotic.

Obviously the other two were trying to get the old man to throw in the silver spurs. Neither of the other two Yaqui had

spurs anywhere near as fine as the old man's. They had a brief
argument, which ended in the old man's pulling rank. This
everyone watching knew even though none had ever heard
this tongue before. It was evident in their gestures.

She hoped Game Dancer would see her.

He sat patiently, hands on his knees, listening with his eyes
on the strangers. His gaze wandered down toward the old
man's spurs. Weeononka watched with great interest her old
friend and the undefinable look those objects put on his
beautifully chiseled face.

Just then she saw Crow Sister on the other side of the
trading circle. In a while Weeononka caught her eye. Her
joking relative smiled and moved out of sight as she circled
around to Weeononka. She too relinquished her ringside spot
on the bargaining since this negotiating session was coming to
a close for refreshments and a pipe. She left the throng to hug
Crow Sister. They walked a little way off, talking on top of each
other's words, touching hands.

"So many times I've wondered what was happening to you."

"Every morning I think your name," said Weeononka,
hugging Crow Sister again.

"The baby?"

Weeononka shook her head.

"You've been through much, I can tell."

They spoke for a few minutes of many things, catching up.
Weeononka was going to ask what had been going on back
there—why the old man had been mad at Game Dancer's
bargain—when his voice arrested her.

"Weeononka—" Game Dancer politely interrupted.

She turned to see him walking toward her with a slight limp.
He appeared to be on the long side of healing from a battle
where he took many wounds. There were random dry scabs all
over him. Crow Sister demurely dropped back. She wanted to
ply Weeononka with questions about her traveling life, but
Crow Sister was only a woman. A man, especially a chieftain,
could interrupt her discourse.

Weeononka's eyes were on the warrior, anyway. Crow Sister
couldn't help but notice that the girl's attention was already
stolen. They stood a hand apart but anyone watching would
have known each wanted the other.

It was a pleasant thing the village enjoyed gossiping about
that afternoon: How the Quapaw girl who grew up adopted
here had come home to take an old suitor as husband. Every
woman in the town greeted her that day. Even warriors who

had known her in former times nodded politely in her direction, showing her great respect.

She was flattered by this attention. She could not take her eyes from Game Dancer. For so long she had wanted him: That he was offering her meat at a dance that night surprised her and made her blush. The day had been cool but the night was warm now with a breeze up from the south that often tinged the mountain nights in the fall season. The fire added to the effect of extreme comfort and security.

Game Dancer didn't take part in the dance, a funny one the warriors liked to perform called the beggar's dance. Instead he sat to one side with Weeononka, leaving no doubt in anyone's mind that he was courting.

Two old powerful women passed them by, smiling cordially. "I think they like seeing us together," he offered, licking meat juice from his fingers. In this flattering light she could see none of his wounds. He looked polished and fine. When he looked up from his sticky fingers, his eyes were sparkling.

She had to look away, his gaze was so direct. She felt a warm glow on the inside of her thighs and a fleeting sadness for Iron Hand.

"How goes your barter with the southerners?" she asked when two of the Yaqui passed by with smiles of good humor.

He didn't answer. She thought he might not have heard her but when she looked he was glaring at the men's backs. She could not draw him out on the matter so she surmised that they were making a hard bargain.

But Game Dancer mellowed. Later, leaning back on his elbow he spoke to her of how he was going to change everything here according to his vision, that the Osage would be a powerful people even among the whites.

"The whites," he said, "are coming. There's nothing we can do about that. But we'll be ready for them like many people won't be. We'll have horses.

"As soon as I get my plan into effect, every Osage household will have horses which we will trade with southerners like those Yaqui. Bow wood is part of the past. Today, it's horses."

He searched her face for a response.

"Well, do you think I'm crazy, too?"

"Oh no—" She was horrified he misunderstood her silence. "Nobody thinks you're crazy, honored warrior."

She couldn't believe that he'd joke about it. "You have honor here. But your ideas are large, as a chief's ideas should be.

Maybe some of the people just don't have a large enough
vision to understand you."

That night she stayed in his lodge. Lovemaking with Game
Dancer was not what it had been with Iron Hand. Nobody
could be like the white man. But she must let go of Iron Hand.
She was sure her direction lay among her own people. Being
with this man tonight was safe-feeling, which she needed to
feel but doubted she'd ever feel again when she voluntarily left
the Frenchman.

After all, this was a reunion. Weeononka had lived in this
Osage village a dozen winters, seeing this young man grow up
even as she grew up. But they had not spent much time
together, since he was a far-ranging hunter and she a camp-
bound girl. Before, when he had approached the old chief as
her guardian, asking for her, their relationship had been formal
and guarded. Then almost as soon as their mating was agreed
upon, the message had come from her uncle in the south. She
had a feeling now that he had always been sorry he gave in to
her uncle's request and payment for her.

Lying in his arms that night sharing the same buffalo skin,
they entwined their bodies in unhurried peaceful sex. They
brought each other to climax several times, each time pulling
back to let the urge subside, only to bring it back again later
with a lick, a thrust, or a long, lazy stroke.

He was asleep as soon as they had finally pleasured each
other. Weeononka couldn't get to sleep so she lay there
watching his sleeping face, thinking how happy the last few
hours had been. This all seemed so right, as if this man and his
groundlodge had been waiting for her return.

He was up long before dawn the next morning. She felt his
movements even though he was trying to be silent. When she
offered to get up and make a morning tea for him, he wouldn't
let her. Very tenderly he forced her to lie back on the bed they
had shared, kissing her many times.

"Today I will give you a wonderful gift," he said with an air of
mystery. She teased him, she begged, but he wouldn't tell her
what the gift was. "But I promise you it will be wonderful, and
will bring us both honor."

His mood was so buoyant, spirited, and childlike, it was
contagious. She wished to have his body again but he said he
must not for he was to meet a challenge today and must
preserve his vital manitou, which sex ebbed from him.

"I should not have brought you to blanket last night, but

how could I resist?" How could she resist this wonderful man, she was asking herself, as he crept out of the lodge to fulfill the rituals he'd set for himself.

She nestled deeply into the warm covers, satisfied with herself. She could not believe she had only been here since yesterday. She felt already mated with this man as though her time with the Frenchman had been a dream and this was waking life; she supposed that she had been mated to him all along.

She lay there feeling slightly queasy. She had morning sickness early with the first baby, too. Soon she would tell him she was pregnant. Thinking about Iron Hand's baby brought sudden burning tears, and she let them flow into the fur for a while, let herself cry it out. Every morning since that first on the island she'd felt the telltale nausea. Would Game Dancer accept the baby? Would the baby have his father's wonderful eyes, which would instantly tell his ancestry? Maybe it wouldn't look white; customarily, the tribe accepted any healthy newborn with gladness.

Someday, she reflected, she'd tell him about their own son. She'd tell him almost all about him. Maybe she wouldn't tell him how the baby died. Game Dancer might not understand what she did to save white men and Shawnees.

She pushed these heavier thoughts to one side in her mind and allowed herself the luxury of thinking about Game Dancer's body, how she liked the smell of it, the soft strength of his muscles, his slow hand. Iron Hand seemed farther away with each moment she stayed here. This was what was right, she was sure. In time she would ask Game Dancer to travel with her to visit The Blossum and the Osotony up on their sacred mountain. For now it was good for her to be home healing wounds that didn't show. Later she spent midday down at the swift creek washing her hair and bathing, thinking of how they'd be together again that night.

29

At the creek the women pressed her about life among the whites. She said enough to be polite but told them nothing that hurt to speak of. When she returned from the creek she saw a crowd gathered behind Game Dancer's lodge.

The air above and around the corral was pale with dust. There were many shouts and screams from that direction. The village seemed deserted except for that area where all the women, children, and braves were gathered around the fence, sitting or standing, watching Game Dancer try to ride the *cabay*.

Even before she got a close look, she knew that's what was happening.

She saw him through the dust hanging on to the flying mane of the maddened horse, the same one her husband had given to him on that morning long ago. She had seen it tethered out in the meadow behind Game Dancer's lodge. Nobody had seemed to be paying much attention to it so she had figured when she'd seen it yesterday that it had lost its novelty. During all this time nobody, not even Game Dancer, mentioned the animal and until this moment she hadn't given it a thought. It was the same cream white creature but there the resemblance ended. She had only seen it docile.

Now the creature's every muscle was knotted in fury and pain. A tight rawhide bridled his foam-streaked cheek. He was sopping wet, matted with dust and sweat and blood. His flank lay open with ribbons of wounds. Game Dancer was wearing the metal heels buckled over his moccasins the way the Yaqui wore them.

The barter must have been concluded. She didn't see the Yaqui or their mounts anywhere. They had left with their Osage bows. She wasn't aware that Game Dancer had waited to try out the spurs without their expert eyes watching because he didn't want to lose face in front of men who knew horses and might scorn his unmanly lack of skill with this one. Still, he was determined.

He jabbed the animal with the wicked metal. Blood streaked with dark red fingers. She couldn't know but this was why the old men had watched Game Dancer's Yaqui trade with looks of disgust—they were mad at him for bargaining away their bows for these articles made to subdue the horse he swore he'd never try to ride again.

The horse screamed, trying to bite the legs of the man just out of reach on his back.

Game Dancer no less than the horse was maddened. He shrieked with each bucking lift. The animal was still tethered; all four hooves were bound by thickly braided rawhide tightly drawn on four stakes. So, it could barely move. But it seemed determined to break its own back by arching upward, squealing with each attempt to dismount the man.

Foam made pink by blood flecked its nostrils and thick lips. The horse ceased the heaving motion for a while and hung its head until its puffing nostrils touched the stirred dust. Its whole body began to tremble.

It went down on its front knees.

As horrible as the scene appeared to Weeononka, it was all the more so because of the deadly cold look on Game Dancer's face. She had never seen anyone like this. He had always been the most perfect model of meticulous discipline. He was the very ideal of self-possession in a human body. Now something else possessed him. She could tell by the way he yanked on the horse's mane, the way he hacked with the silver spurs, that he was out of control. He screamed at the horse to get up. It made a terrible liquid sound and tried again to shake off the man like water.

The horse drew several loud breaths, then sprang to its hooves, arching its back so fast that Game Dancer wasn't prepared. He fell off into the blinding dust. The horse, maddened anew by his victory in removing the hated weight, used what little slack there was in the rawhide to paw at the tumbled human body trying desperately to get out of the way of those slashing hooves.

The man rolled a little, but the action of the hooves pulled him back. Weeononka cried out with the others as Game Dancer's back was suddenly bright with blood. Several braves jumped into the corral and tried to get close enough to free Game Dancer from the attack.

One of them managed to take up the flying reins and draw the horse back so that his comrades could get Game Dancer out of the way.

She went immediately to his lodge, where they put him under a buffalo hide painted with his many war deeds. The medicine man came in without a word and began to make noises with his rattles, shaking feathers about. Weeononka was angry with the old wizard; why didn't he get on with the business of tending that leg? To Weeononka it looked broken.

After a long line of chants and powder burnings, the shaman began the more practical part of his visit. Almost perfunctorily he probed Game Dancer's body. It was as Weeononka suspected; the leg was broken midcalf. With quick, sure hands the old man lassoed Game Dancer's ankle with a rope he dogged around one of the lodge's exposed timbers.

He motioned for Weeononka to pull under Game Dancer's shoulders. He eased the leg straight. With one quick snap he jerked the rope that tensed the ankle and reset the bone.

The medicine man gave her precise instructions, which she knew anyway but to which she politely listened. Bind the leg—not too tightly—with wet inner doe hide strips. He whipped the end of the rope around the pole and knotted it. She was to splint the leg in this position to keep the bone ends in place until the strips dried.

"My boy will bring sleeping herbs. And vermilion to paint in bracelets around the leg at the top and around the ankle, to keep away the black bone."

While he puttered further, Weeononka watched the shaman and finally said shyly, "You don't remember a maiden who left this village two winters ago?"

The medicine man looked up at her, recognition glinting in his eye. "Everyone remembers the Woman Who Smoked. We heard some sad things about that Quapaw uncle of yours."

She shrugged. There was too much to say at this time, so she merely smiled.

"Welcome home," the shaman said as he stood to leave. "This man needs someone to take care of him."

She regarded Game Dancer with his head thrown back, his breathing hoarse, his entire body speaking of his failure to ride the *cabay*. He needed to be washed up, her task after the sachem departed with a final staccato chant.

She stayed with Game Dancer for two days while he was unconscious, then for another day of delirium. In his visions he rode the horse many times, and sang many victory songs. Then, exhausted, he descended into what appeared to be normal sleep.

She watched him often, thinking about how he had seemed in memory and how he was now in reality and how those two things did not meet. She thought about the child she was carrying. How could she provide a place of safety for it with this man as he was? Life with him would have been perfect if it weren't for the horse. If he'd only give up trying to ride it. Maybe he had learned his lesson this time, she thought hopefully. But her more realistic turn of mind said he'd never give it up, that he'd ride it or die trying.

Maybe he had gone *windigo*, she mused darkly the third rainy afternoon. The village was very still except for rain hitting the round lodge roof over her head. She had a good little smokeless fire going and plenty of firewood inside.

She'd started some tea, and as she sat there with it steeping in its crock, she regarded the man as she had done so many times in the past few days.

Yes, maybe he had gone *windigo*, a state of insanity reputed to hit great hunters who were unable to find game. It was said they would go *windigo* from famine and shame at not being able to provide meat for their families. And in the cold north, where Weeononka's people had been driven out by the Iroquois four generations before, it was said a *windigo* man could become so crazy he'd turn cannibal and eat the very people he was supposed to feed.

How can I bring a child into such a lodge? she wondered. She felt so dashed. Four days ago it had seemed exactly right that she had come here. It was a rounding of the circle she and Game Dancer had started but had been unable to complete.

For so long, she thought as she watched him sleep, you have been everything I could want. When I found you here, unmated, almost waiting for me, my heart was glad. I was willing to forget even Iron Hand for you.

And it seemed right for Game Dancer, too. He was so pleased to have her with him. He'd been so kind, honoring her because she had been the wife of a great chief. Because she had gone among the whites and came back full of knowledge. She had seen all this in his response to her. Such a short time ago, he was all she ever desired.

Now, a crazy *windigo*. She recalled that he had asked if she thought he was crazy, too. That had been a warning that something was wrong. I should have asked him what he meant, she thought. But who would think this fine man would go *windigo*?

But, her other side argued, nobody she knew had ever seen a hunter gone *windigo*. It was probably just a story the ancestors brought on their long flight from Iroquois terror. Stories get told under such circumstances and get passed along. Besides it wasn't even winter.

Ah, but perhaps a hunter could go *windigo* from other things, from the whites' liquor, from disease, from inordinate desire, such as Game Dancer's desire to best that horse. Another curse brought by the whites, she reflected, but not including Iron Hand among those other whites. She did not want to think of him now that she was certain she'd never see him again.

She felt it had been right to leave him. But it was not right to come here. It was her duty to go back to the Osotony as her husband had instructed her in the dream.

I have brought this sorrow upon myself, she thought, *by ignoring my husband's warning. Where would she ever find her path?* It should have been clear to her from before that Game Dancer was moving in the opposite direction.

When will I find a partner who's on the same path as me?

She knew with burdening certainty that unless this man gave up the horse her path and his were destined to fork. She couldn't change him but she could not watch him destroy himself. These dark thoughts occupied her mind when she heard a polite scratch on the rawhide flap.

Crow Sister entered at Weeononka's grateful invitation.

"How is he?" Crow Sister asked quietly, settling down on the buffalo robe. Weeononka set a horn of tea in front of her and poured one for herself. She settled back on another robe and took up her beading, the occupation she'd missed on the trail. "I think he'll be all right," she said guardedly. But she could hear the emptiness of her own words as she looked up at her old friend, her beadwork forgotten. "How can such a worthy and beautiful person do such a terrible thing to himself, Crow Sister?"

She shook her head. Over on his sleeping robe, Game Dancer moaned softly in unconsciousness, but he didn't stir. Presently he settled back without a sound except for deep, mindless breathing just below a snore. "It's that terrible *cabay*. At first it brought him honor, when he brought it into the village. The elders were so impressed they made him civil chief when the old man died." She did not mention the name of the old chief who had given Weeononka her name not so long ago. Still, she venerated his spirit by remembering him as he was the night he delighted in breaking tradition to help her gain back her lost face. Weeononka knew he had been old and had deserved his rest but she was sorry to hear he was gone.

Likewise, Weeononka was constrained from speaking further of the chief's death without breaking taboo.

"Right away Game Dancer took a bride, the tiny one, daughter of Winning Deer." Significantly, she did not mention the wife by name.

Weeononka nodded. She remembered the girl as a childhood friend. "Well, the Great Spirit blessed them immediately but the girl and the baby both died in childbirth. Game Dancer took it hard. Soon he began neglecting his duties,

speaking rudely to the elders, and arrogantly boasting his
superiority. He started trying to ride the horse, not as crazy as
he was the other day, but determined in a wild way that made
people dislike him. The elders requested him to stop, saying
that such behavior was not in keeping with a chief's duties. He
refused, saying it was a point of honor because some warrior
had bet him he couldn't ride the animal.

"Once the council gave him a leave for a while from the
chieftainship. He was furious and stalked screaming out of the
council lodge, holding a flaming torch and waking the entire
village. He set bushes afire and announced that at dawn he
would ride the devil *cabay* to prove that the council was wrong
and he had the *wa kon* on his side."

Crow Sister took a breath and a sip of tea then continued,
"And he did it. He painted himself as if for war and went out
and climbed onto that devil. Well, I tell you, he didn't stay
there long. That animal threw him off in one great leap. "It
took three of his friends to help him recapture it, and as soon
as they had it roped, Game Dancer climbed back on. He kept
doing that all day and into the night." She trailed off in her
story as if the sadness of it was an obstacle to its relation.

Weeononka during this time had been slowly beading the
cradleboard toy she'd been working on, but she was listening
to Crow Sister. From time to time she glanced over at the
unconscious man under the buffalo robe. But he was out.

Politeness forbade her interrupting Crow Sister to ask
questions once a story was begun. As soon as the older woman
felt like it, she picked up her tale's thread:

"He broke an arm that time and a couple of ribs. He had
bruises and cuts on every part of him. Both eyes were black,
one swollen shut for days where the creature's hoof caught
him. That was, let's see, not two moons ago."

Outside a wind came up, rippling the door flap with a new
chill. Weeononka threw a few sticks on the fire that was
burning low in the center of the lodge. A little smoke rose to
the draft hole.

"So," said Weeononka when it was clear that Crow Sister
was finished, "I came during a lull."

"Yes. He's been really good for more than a moon." Crow
Sister shifted position. "You see he promised them after the
last time that he would never ride the *cabay* again.

"He publicly declared that he was cured of his need to prove
himself against the horse, said he'd been out of his mind and

had now come to his senses. He was very convincing. The
elders were even talking about reinstating him on a trial basis,
he was doing so well. Until he traded for those spurs." She
looked at him again.

"Why didn't you tell me about this?" Weeononka pleaded.

"Well, I would have, of course. But you only just arrived,
and I couldn't insult him yesterday to his face."

Weeononka saw that she had allowed Game Dancer to take
her over since her arrival. It wasn't Crow Sister's fault.

"Besides, I hoped—we all hoped—that you would be good
for him. It would prejudice you to know what he'd done
before, and it wouldn't seem fair since he had been improving
before he got those spurs."

"And anyway you knew how I felt about him before. . . ."

Crow Sister showed her brown-stained smile. "It was a
second chance for both of you."

They were quiet for a few beats while the rain tapped the
roof.

"I think it's really going to storm tonight," the old woman
said.

"Yes." Weeononka had let her beading slip from her fingers.
She stared at the fire, Crow Sister's words still in her mind.
"Why don't you stay here tonight?"

The older woman looked as if she might, but she shrugged
negatively when Game Dancer in repose caught her eye. His
mouth gaped open hideously. He was drooling a little. His
spittle choked him and he coughed, still in troubled slumber.
Weeononka hurried to him with a soft skin, just in time to
catch the blood he brought up. But it was over quickly. His
eyes blinked open. They stared right through her before they
rolled back and he went out again. She tenderly wiped his lips
and the bloody spot on the buffalo robe, and backed away from
him.

"I would really like your company."

"No, dear. He's bad *wa kon*." She patted Weeononka's cold
hand. "You're still young enough to sleep with a devil but I'm
too old to gamble." She took up the hand of this young woman
she'd raised since girlhood. "You're cold."

"Your words have chilled me."

"I regret that I'm the one to have to say them to you, whom I
love."

Weeononka embraced her stepmother.

"Here, what's this?" She touched Weeononka's forehead. "A fever?"

"No, I'm very healthy."

Crow Sister looked at her a long time, glancing at the beaded toy she had been working on before she said, "Does he know you're pregnant?"

Weeononka was surprised but only for a moment. She shook her head. She was wearing her hair in braids rolled up around her ears in the Quapaw manner of a married woman. So her hair didn't tremble as the old woman remembered.

The girl was now a woman, Crow Sister reflected with a bittersweet twinge. What had happened to her along the way? the older woman wondered. But she didn't ask. She knew Weeononka would tell her when she was ready.

"I was going to wait awhile to be sure." She looked at Game Dancer again, then at the bloodstained rag in her hand. She set it aside and poured water from a jug onto her fingers.

"Do you think he's gone *windigo*?" Weeononka asked with trembling voice. To even utter the awful word was bad *wa kon*.

The soft drizzle turned to a driving rain pelting above their heads.

Crow Sister paused with her hand on the tent flap. "Some say it."

Weeononka could tell Crow Sister was distinctly uncomfortable staying here any longer. Game Dancer made another sound.

"I'd better hurry or it'll wash me away," said Crow Sister dashing out.

Weeononka was again alone with Game Dancer. The fire crackled. It rained all night.

30

For three days Weeononka nursed Game Dancer back to a portion of his former health. The medicine man came to look at his bound leg and said chants over him several times. His assistant brought infusions for him to drink, herbs to be boiled for him to breathe in the steam, and poultices to apply directly to any wound. Game Dancer spoke very little, but she could tell he was getting his strength back. She allowed herself to wait and hope. Maybe things would improve.

Maybe he had the devil horse out of his system.

She figured his unusual silence was from the injuries he'd suffered. He'd surely be his former self after a time of recuperation.

By the fourth day he was sitting up when she returned to the lodge from getting water at the stream. It was midmorning. The sun was welcome after a few cloudy days. It turned the inside of the lodge into bright orange light.

In it Game Dancer looked quite fit as he sat with his bound leg propped upon a powder keg. He was sitting on his sleeping robe, studying his face in the mirror he was so proud of trading the French for sometime back, grooming himself.

At first she was glad to see him performing repairs on his scalplock feathers, repainting with green earth the ends of his bound locks.

She had been gone for a while, getting water. He'd obviously been at this task for some time.

But her initial joy at seeing him occupied was dulled when she saw his eyes reflected in the mirror. He was battered still, with healing bruises and welts on his torso. He had a caved-in look around his fourth rib. He was even swaying a little and as she watched him she saw his eyelids droop, as if he were dozing off, but he caught himself and continued applying the paint to his hair with a small stick in a shaking hand.

"Well," she said, "it's good to see you up."

She was dismayed by his reply, a sidelong glance oiled with contempt.

He didn't speak.

She set down the water jug and took her place with her legs folded under her skirt, the skirt she'd made with the white man's cloth Iron Hand had given her. She hoped Game Dancer would see it and approve so she had been wearing it since he'd woken up.

He continued painting the hair strand, concentrating on it above all else.

His eyes drooped almost shut, and he swayed, but caught himself. He bit his lip in renewed concentration and tried to put some more paint on that coil of hair.

But his fingers would not grip the stick. He dropped it but apparently wasn't aware of it as he continued trying to paint his hair with a brush that wasn't there. He did finally see it missing and groped around for it, finding it stuck to his knee.

He reached to pluck it up with two fingers but again the fingers seemed to be refusing to do as commanded or perhaps he couldn't focus. Finally by shutting one eye and trying very slowly he managed to take hold of the paint stick.

It was painful to watch him debilitated like an old, old man whose hand shook with the palsy. He returned to his painting. He saw she'd been watching though she tried to turn away her glance lest it hurt his pride.

"What are you looking at, woman?" His tone of voice was a physical assault on her. She shied back.

"Get me a drink of water."

She poured the fresh water she'd just fetched into a horn cup and set it beside him. At that moment he lowered his hand to tip the stick with more paint, but his hand, none too steady, hit the side of the cup instead. She moved to help him clean up the mess.

"Get out of my way—" he snarled.

She moved back quickly, watching him like a hawk.

"That's not my cup," he said, smashing his hand against the container of water. Water sloshed into the mussel shell that was his palate. "See what you've done. It's too watery now and won't stay on the hair."

She started to get him more green earth from the cask where he kept it.

"Never mind," he snapped. "I'm through anyway." He flipped that coil of hair back and admired himself in the glass.

His face was a battlefield of healing wounds. His nose was still blue, turning to green. One eye had not opened; a watery mucous oozed from under the lid. He turned that side of his face from the mirror and looked at the slashes of red paint he had streaked with his fingers on his cheek. When she saw his reflection she knew instantly what he meant to do.

That was his own personal war signature, those five bars of red across his right cheek.

She tensed visibly.

It was as if all her thoughts of the past few days suddenly came to a single point before her eyes as she stared at his comical, pitiful appearance. His mouth drooped open; she'd seen an idiot child once, born to a woman of this village and allowed to live until it mercifully died from weakness that one famine winter. Its lips drooped like that, its puffy eyes lidded almost shut from eternal drowsiness.

Here was illness deep inside the body.

She was sure the horse's hooves had done more than the obvious physical damage. Sometimes warriors returned from battle with no blood on them, but so badly broken inside that they died shortly afterward, often maddened and having to be restrained.

Game Dancer had that vacant, personless look about him. But he appeared to snap out of it again.

He focused on her standing now, her head almost touching the sloping side of the lodge because she had moved as far away from him as she could get without actually departing.

"Why are you doing this to yourself?"

A mad mean spark flew through the mirror from his eye to hers.

How she hated those mirrors, another white curse.

She was near the tent flap; she could get out in one bound. But he could see none of this in her eyes. Once known for his keen eyesight he appeared to have trouble keeping her in focus. He rubbed his eyes with his scabbed hands, and as she watched he slipped his little finger into one nostril and proceeded to pick his nose. He pulled something out and looked at it then wiped it on his bare chest. This was the ultimate infraction of his people's fastidiousness. The Osage were a people accustomed to retiring to the sweathouse twice a day. The males especially were driven to high standards of cleanliness to be all the more prepared to die honorably. No civil Osage would dishonor himself by allowing himself to be observed picking his nose. Weeononka could only stare at him she was so shocked. She covered her open mouth with her hand.

"What are you looking at, hog woman?" This expletive referred to the pigs allegedly left behind to become feral by the Spaniards when they had passed this way three generations ago. These wild pigs called razorbacks were known for their downright meanness. Their sows were notorious for brazen and unpredictable attack, as well as unmatched warty ugliness.

She looked quickly away, but not quickly enough. He threw the buffalo cup and what was left of the water at her. But his aim was affected. He hooked it so that it fell sizzling into the fire.

Quickly she dropped to her knees to retrieve at least one coal from the drenching. With her fire stick she found one and tonged it out.

He turned disdainfully from her and began inspecting several deerskin shirts, selecting one for wear.

She knew without doubt why he was grooming. She got the fire going again by scraping away the wet clay of the firepit; it had only been a little water. But she took inordinate care with the task because from here she could watch him further without appearing to do so. She wanted to see more of his symptoms so she could tell the medicine man when he returned. She had a sinking feeling inside, however. From past experience she knew this kind of wound was difficult for the best shaman to heal. It seemed as if a certain kind of wound cut through the body and lacerated the spirit. Sometimes, she reflected, that kind of wound was more destructive than a physical one.

He was clumsily trying to get into a shirt. It was one with incidents of his scalp taking painted in the traditional stick drawings with soot mixed in bear grease. "Help me—" he screeched, tangled in the arms. She scooted over to help him but he became fustrated inside the confiding deerskin and cuffed her wildly.

The blow actually knocked sense into her. This man was gone. There was no way she could help him.

She backed off, staring around, looking for something. In her own way Weeononka was out of control, too, but directed by sudden irreversible insight so that she was so finely in control she couldn't stop herself until this was finished.

There was no thought to her actions as she searched for something. Game Dancer still struggled inside the prison of the shirt. She must hurry. She probably wouldn't have another chance at what she had in mind.

Her eye found what she was looking for. Game Dancer's gun was holstered in an elaborate pouch hanging directly behind him on the pole at the head of his sleeping robe. Still in that state of suspended thought and pure action she managed to get her hands on it and across the lodge toward the flap before he had forced his head into the collar hole of the shirt. He was like a man coming up for air in a cold pond; he gasped.

He only saw the swish of her skirts move past him. But he had some of his old quickness and the skirt was voluminous. He caught a handful of serge and gave her a stout jerk so that she was stopped with a snap and fell to her knees. Already she was scrambling to get away.

He looked at his handful of woven cloth as if seeing it for the first time, which indeed was the case. "What's this?" he screamed. "What is this white man's shit?" He gave the material of her skirt another jerk. The cloth ripped.

She saw that like the lizard who sacrifices his tail she must lose something to be free. She pulled the skirt in her direction, tearing it more.

"My woman doesn't wear white man's trash," he spat, twisting around to protect his stiffened leg. He tried to scoot toward her but her next pull on the skirt jerked him forward along with the cloth.

She gave it one mighty yank. A piece of the skirt ripped off her, whiplashing him backward. He cried out in pain as he rolled in such a way that hurt some broken part of him. But this only made him more angry. He yelled another obscenity at her.

When she had grabbed the weapon, she had also taken the powder horn. She knew enough from watching the whites to load the flintlock pistol. Her secret practice came in handy here as she paused just outside the lodge to pour powder into the gun pan.

"Come back here, hog bitch—"

She grimly set her mouth, her muscles, her bones, all her body for what she must do. She dropped the powder horn and began walking toward the corral just as he emerged dragging his body behind him. He moved forward on his elbow, the only part of him not weakened with some wound. He stirred up dust as he crept along practically foaming at the mouth in his rage.

He had seen her load the gun.

"I'll teach you a lesson you'll never forget!"

She moved with purposeful steps away from the lodge, the gun in her hands. She never quite trusted these things, which she suspected held some ungovernable kind of *wa kon* outside her understanding.

Some old men telling stories over by the council lodge saw her stride out toward the corral. Before long a trail of villagers followed. The air was thickening the way it always did before something terrible and exciting happened.

She went directly to the place where the horse was staked on four taut rawhide ropes. By the time she reached the fence, almost everyone in the village was moving behind her. They could hear Game Dancer screaming as he dragged himself along in everyone's dust, yelling for the bitch to stop.

But Weeononka was way ahead of him; no way he could

catch up with her. She hitched up the tatters of her foreign
skirt and climbed into the corral with the animal. The creature
appeared in as nearly bad shape as Game Dancer. What had
been a beautiful cream colored horse was now a cut,
splotched, and bloodied standing cadaver.

Someone had suggested starving it into submission. It was
gaunt even before its recent struggle opened new wounds. He
leveled one huge eye at the approaching woman and began
snorting at the dust just below his muzzle. His head was as low
as it could get. His ribs bowed as the horse breathed faster in
terror. His eye was bloodshot. Perhaps he couldn't see any
better than the man who had vowed to tame him. Dry blood
caked him haunch and stifle where Game Dancer's Spanish
spurs had torn the flesh.

The eye followed her, widening as she came closer. She saw
a mad glint there identical to the look Game Dancer had
thrown her through the mirror; it was loaded with pure hate
and terror.

That was her first moment of weakness. She stopped,
looking at the animal she once thought was a demon full of *wa
kon*. But it was just an animal after all. Just as the whites were
not spirits but humans like everyone else. She saw an animal
in pain, not a demon possessed of *wa kon*. There was very little
wa kon left in the world, The Blossom had said. Most things,
even strange things, can be explained without it. She wondered what had become of The Blossom.

The horse was very tightly drawn against the four ropes but
his entire body began to tremble under his bonds as if by
shaking he could free himself from the coming torture.

His gaze was sewn on her. This was close enough to shoot
the poor beast. Put it out of its misery, she thought, lifting the
gun with both hands. That eye would not let her go.

Something further in her weakened. The horse must have
sensed it because he lowered his head again, looking about to
fall over but prevented only by stiff pain and the bonds. She
hunkered down, still holding the weapon.

She could feel the many Osage eyes behind her watching,
waiting to see if she would destroy the terrible *wa kon* Game
Dancer had been foolish enough to bring among them.

He reached the perimeter of the corral and was drawing
himself up against the fence rails. It was a grim effort. Several
people saw him and moved aside, not about to help the
madman but not daring to get in his way. He grabbed at loose

dust and stones around the post and impotently threw them at her.

She disregarded him. His hoarse screech called her an obscenity. But it seemed to pass right through her. She could feel the weight of the eyes watching what was going to happen next. They wanted her to do what none of them had dared because it would have unleashed Game Dancer's fury on them.

Suddenly she hated them all more than she pitied Game Dancer or the horse. They would watch and not lift a finger to avert whatever tragedy was being acted out as if for their entertainment.

She looked at the *cabay* over the pistol sight. She could blow his brains out right now and end this terrible contest Game Dancer would otherwise continue to its inevitable conclusion.

Again he called a slurred order, which she ignored.

But what if she did kill the horse? Would that end the contest? Game Dancer would never be the same again. He would hate her for denying him the pleasure of finally besting it. If it were dead, he could always claim he would have tamed it if only she had not snatched his victory. This man's pride was great. He'd never forgive her.

But she knew if she didn't kill the horse here and now, Game Dancer would climb back on it and keep climbing back on it until it killed him. That wouldn't take much more.

Her hand was steady. Even Game Dancer fell quiet as she reached her decision. The intensity was palpable as the assembly waited with her. She was just about to pull the trigger when the horse shook its head and tried to ease a spot on his flank where flies had struck a gaping wound. He couldn't quite reach the itch, but his effort was so pitiful a thing to see, she hesitated.

I have been foolish, she thought, to think that killing this poor animal will change anything. All this flickered in Weeononka's mind faster than it can be told as she gazed into the horse's mournful eye.

"This is your last warning, hog woman!"

She regarded the man draped all alone on his fence. The people had given him a lot of room, nobody wishing to be near him. Weeononka looked back at the horse. She looked at the gun with a sigh that came from deep in her loins and branched out to her chest and arms so that it racked her, leaving her trembling. She dropped the gun and stood from her squatting position and started walking in the tattered skirt toward the opposite side of the corral. She didn't look back as she mounted the fence. She didn't break her stride out of the village, due south, taking the trail she had taken so long ago in that innocent spring with a man named Game Dancer whom she had dearly loved for too long.

Behind her, Game Dancer hobbled into the arena. He was laughing, cackling actually, after her. He said for the audience of villagers that she was a dirty woman who had been stained by white men, only pretending to be a good Osage woman.

He called her another vile name and said this village was fortunate to be rid of such a woman. Personally he was glad she was leaving, always staring at him, getting in the way of a warrior's duty, causing him to spill and break things with her evil eye and bad *wa kon*.

"I was lucky to get rid of you once, arrogant, unfeminine woman, and I am even luckier to get rid of you a second time!"

He called that she was smart to have obeyed him or he'd have had to kill her as he may have to kill this horse right now.

She heard the *cabay*'s terrified scream as Game Dancer approached. She forced herself not to turn around and watch what was going to happen. She must not tarry here.

Someday she would see Crow Sister again. Her joking relative would understand, could easily follow her if she wished. They both knew that The Blossum would take the Osotony Quapaw west to their summer hunting quarters in the shadow of the Lake in the Mountain.

Crow Sister, actually, had been among the first of the Osage villagers to see Weeononka walk out of Game Dancer's lodge with the gun in her hand.

She watched the girl leave by the southern path and stood now looking at the foreign weapon lying at her feet. Game Dancer screamed after Weeononka, laughing at her until she was completely out of sight. Then he turned to see what the horse was doing and beyond spied the gun in the dust. The animal was nervous. He whinnied, stepping quickly to the end of his tethers.

Crow Sister saw the man coming. She hated white men since her experience in the Chickasaw slave camp, and hated anything that smelled of them like this gun here made of carved fancy metal and polished wood. She knew Weeononka had it ready to fire—she'd seen the girl's every move up until the moment she had gone.

She glanced at Game Dancer, who was going around the rear end of the horse to get to the weapon.

Why didn't Weeononka do what she obviously had in mind? Crow Sister saw a chance to rid the village of this menace, maybe even rescue this fine man from his insanity at the same time. She didn't even think about it, she just picked up the gun and pulled the trigger the way Weeononka had begun to do but had stopped. There was a terrible crashing sound, which scared all the people. Children and dogs cried out, women shrieked as they ran for cover with their babies under their shirts.

Game Dancer blinked and shook all over as though it were himself and not the horse who slumped to the dust with a thick whinny and no bones. A bright red flower blossomed between his eyes. He trembled and died without further agony.

It was a very clean shot. Crow Sister had been thrown backward but kept her feet. She stared at the horse still in her sight, then as if the gun had bitten her, she dropped it and wiped her hands. Her ears were ringing so she didn't hear Game Dancer scream as he threw himself at her, hands at her throat.

He rattled her back and forth a few times. Her legs thrashed. She was gone in seconds before any of the stunned villagers knew quite what had happened. He let go of her and she dropped without moving, dead without question beside the horse.

Nobody stirred for a long breath and when they did it was as though underwater. Game Dancer straightened so slowly he could hear his muscles. He blinked again, appearing to wake up.

Some distance into the forest Weeononka heard the shot from the direction she'd come. She hesitated but was not tempted to return. Now she was truly going home; she vowed never to leave again. She was already putting Game Dancer and his misery out of her mind; the noise meant he must have killed the animal at last. She started walking again, keeping on the southern trace, which intersected at a mountain pass nearby with the southwestern route that would take her to the Osotony summer hunting grounds.

If she kept a steady pace and it didn't rain, she'd be at the Lake in the Mountain in four days' time.

IV

ARKANSAS AGAIN

31

Four years later in 1686 when de Tonti started compiling his notes into a journal, he was pleased he'd kept excellent descriptions about the descent of the Mech-a-si-pi. The emotional hardship of losing Weeononka had given him detachment that made him a good reporter and when he finally began his memoirs he was glad his state of mind had aided observation.

Sitting at a desk in a rented room on the waterfront in Quebec, his thoughts floated back to those other days when it had all seemed so hopeful. He was writing the journal in this bleak city room because at the moment he had no other employment, his fortune having taken another strange turn. He hoped the journal could mitigate the bad luck he and La Salle had suffered since the historic trip.

He recalled the descent as though it had happened yesterday instead of four years past. In the flickering sunlight of late summer and without regard for penmanship, he scribbled furiously while he was in the mood to remember the public events that followed his private loss of Weeononka in the wilderness of Arkansas. . . .

"The first day we began to see and kill alligators, which are numerous and can be three times the length of a tall man. When we arrived opposite the village of the Taencas, M. de La Salle desired me to go inform the chief of his arrival. I went with our guides and we had to carry a bark canoe for ten *arpents*, and to launch it on a small lake in which their village was placed. I was surprised to find their cabins made of mud and covered with cane mats. The cabin of the chief was 40 feet square, the wall 10 feet high, a foot thick, and the roof, which was of a dome shape, about 15 feet high. I was not less surprised when, on entering, I saw the chief seated on a camp bed, with three of his wives at his side, surrounded by more than 60 old men, clothed in large white cloaks, which are made by the women out of the bark of the mulberry tree, and are tolerably well worked. The women were clothed in the same manner; and every time the chief spoke to them, before

319

answering him, they cried "—O-o-o-o-o!" to show their respect for him, for their chiefs are held in as much consideration as our kings. No one drinks out of the chief's cup, nor eats out of his plate, and no one passes before him; when he walks they clean the path before him. When he dies they sacrifice his youngest wife to accompany him to the other world."

He stopped the pen and took a sip of wine as he recalled the events behind his knowledge of that custom. He was purposefully leaving out his personal life. After all this was an official report to be read by the king. La Salle assured him that Louis personally read every communication from the New World, the subject being a kind of royal hobby. He knew His Majesty especially liked reports on the habits of the "savages," so playing to his eventual audience, de Tonti continued writing more about the Taencas, much of which he had learned from Handsome Frog. "At the door of the temple is a block of wood on which is a great shell and plaited round with the hair of their enemies in a plait as thick as an arm and about 20 fathoms long. The inside of the temple is naked; there is an altar in the middle, and at the foot of the altar three logs of wood are placed on end, and a fire is kept up day and night by two old priests who are the directors of their worship. These old men showed me a cabinet within the wall, made of mats of cane. Desiring to see what was inside, the old men prevented me, giving me to understand that their God was there. But I have since learned that it is the place where they keep their treasure, such as fine pearls which they fish up in the neighborhood, and European merchandise. At the last quarter of the moon all the cabins make an offering of a dish of the best food they have, which is placed at the door of the temple. The old men take care to carry it away, and to make a good feast of it with their families. Every spring they make a clearing which they name the field of the spirit, when all of them work to the sound of the tambour."

Actually he had gotten this information on the green corn dance from Weeononka. All the tribes enjoyed the ritual he found incredulous; he couldn't imagine such unbridled passion in an entire community and hoped someday to experience it for himself.

"Let us return to the chief," he wrote, thinking that this report would especially please the French Sun King:

"When I was in his cabin he told me with a smiling

countenance the pleasure he felt at the arrival of the French.
. . . His people have a form of worship, and adore the sun.
There is a temple opposite the house of the chief, and similar
to it, except that three eagles are placed on this temple who
look toward the rising sun. The temple is surrounded with
strong mud walls in which are fixed spikes on which they place
the heads of their enemies whom they sacrifice to the sun."

La Salle had asked him to corroborate his own report that
the Louisiana natives were more kindly disposed than those of
Canada to French traders and Catholic missionaries.

"The next day M. de La Salle ordered me to chase a canoe
we saw. I was just on the point of overtaking it, when more
than 100 men appeared on the banks of the river to defend
their people. M. de La Salle shouted out to me to come back,
which I did. We went on and encamped opposite them.
Afterwards, M. de La Salle expressing a wish to meet them
peaceably, I offered to carry to them the calumet, and
embarking, went to them. . . . I convinced the chief men
among them to cross over to M. de La Salle."

That had been another victory for the music box, de Tonti
reflected. The way he'd convinced the highly suspicious
chieftain to visit a white spirit he considered bad medicine was
to dazzle him with the mechanism. By now the melody was
tinny and was out of phase from too much moisture; a couple of
the cylinder teeth were missing but it was still a wonder. It
never failed to get human attention, no matter if that human
being were red or white, cannibal chief or Christian prince.

"M. de La Salle accompanied them to their village three
leagues distant, and passed the night there with some of his
men. The next day he returned with the chief of the village
where he had slept, who was a brother of the great chief of the
Natches; he conducted us to his brother's village, situated on a
hillside near the river at six leagues' distance. We were well
received there. This nation counts more than 300 warriors.
Here the people cultivate the ground, hunt and fish as well as
the Taencas, and their manners are the same. We departed
thence on Good Friday, and after a voyage of 20 leagues,
encamped at the mouth of a large river which runs from the
west."

That was the southwestern boundary of Quapaw territory,
the Red River, which the local people called Nigestai.

"Thirty leagues further on we saw some fishermen on the
bank of the river and went to reconnoiter them. It was the

village of the Quinipissas, who let fly their arrows upon
us. . . ."

La Salle had warned him to be careful when reporting
hostilities. Louis wanted to appear nonthreatening to New
Spain. It was a conceit, of course, but the Canadian had
impressed de Tonti with the politics that might put dangerous
interpretations on their journals, which were bound to be read
someday by the Spanish. With that in mind de Tonti continued
writing: "As M. de La Salle would not fight against any nation,
he made us embark. Twelve leagues from this village on the
left is that of the Tangibaos. Scarcely eight days before, this
village had been totally destroyed by Chickasaw. Dead bodies
were lying on one another and the cabins were burnt."

Remembering the awful scene made de Tonti think of
Weeononka's village. She'd told him the story of the Chickasaw
attack that first night on the island when they shared lovers'
secrets.

At first he'd been able to bury those memories. The further
he was removed in time, though, the more he remembered
those few perfect days with the woman he loved. He didn't
want to think of having her and losing her.

It reminded him that maybe this was punishment for
abandoning Jeanette. Each time he came to Quebec he
thought of her. But he never inquired of her because even at
this moment he was sure she was within a league of him,
anonymously locked away in one of the several stone convents
that were the oldest buildings in the new city.

He finished the wine and resumed the writing: "We
proceeded on our course and after sailing 40 leagues, arrived
at the sea on the 7th of April, 1682. M. de La Salle sent canoes
to inspect the channels; some of the men went to the channel
on the right hand, some to the left, and M. de La Salle chose
the center. In the evening each made his report, that is to say,
that the channels were very fine, wide and deep. We
encamped on the right bank and erected the arms of the
King."

De Tonti sat back, exercising his hand to relieve writer's
cramp. He could hear noises coming up from the Quebec
docks where a ship from France lulled in the harbor, being
readied for docking. Stevadores shouted and winches
squeaked outside the inn where he had taken quarters. From
this window he could only see the masts and upper rigging of
the ship that very well may have brought La Forest back from

France. For weeks now de Tonti had been waiting here, relieved of his command and forbidden to engage in fur trade, hoping there would be encouraging news from France. Within the hour the ship would dock. Very shortly he would go down and see if La Forest was among the passengers. He was anxious and could only fill these last few minutes with work on the journal. His mind was on the uncertain future, but writing about that April day in 1682 recalled some of the emotions he had felt when they'd claimed half the continent for France. He glanced up at the worn parchment map he'd carried and updated since he had left Paris. The Mississippi—that spelling seemed to be favored these days—stretched 800 leagues from New France in the north above the Great Lakes to the Gulf of Mexico.

La Salle's compliment to Colbert in naming the river after him had been long abandoned. De Tonti was secretly glad a variation of the tribal name for the Great River prevailed.

A hundred countries larger than France could be fitted into the territory watered by the river that La Salle claimed that day. He named the Mississippi country *Louisiana* to honor the Sun King and that name appeared to stick, differentiating the southern country from New France in the north.

Such arrogance, de Tonti thought. Not even La Salle knew at the time how much land he was claiming for the Sun King. How much of it would they be able to hold? Very little, de Tonti thought bitterly, especially since the king himself seemed to have only a dilettante's concern about his Mississippi holdings. He was at war again with Spain, so the only importance Louisiana had for him was as a strategy against his perennial enemy.

De Tonti closed his eyes as he remembered the low, flat delta land where the Mississippi fanned in several channels. Its muddy waters mingled with the green Gulf bight that would be called Lake Pontchartrain in honor of the French Minister of Marine after Colbert, who died the year after La Salle claimed Louisiana. There had been a breeze off the larger water. He recalled that it deviled the document in La Salle's hands as he read the words claiming the river, its tributaries, valleys, people, stock, and mines down to the last dogwood blossom and sassafras root for Louis XIV.

The expedition members had stood around him in a circle on the sand where they planted a wooden cross. The fathers had chanted a hymn, which everyone joined in singing. The

Indians with them stood apart, amazed at the ceremony, or
laughing at it; de Tonti never discovered their opinion. He was
sure none of the local people knew that the words La Salle was
reading from the rattling parchment meant they now belonged
to France, nor did they care.

After he read the *procès-verbal*, La Salle had signaled the
musketeers to fire a volley. The noise startled a flock of
seabirds. Like a scattering of black pepper they flared above
the heads of the Europeans and their Indian guides. Handsome Frog muttered a prayer to his manitou; to him the birds
were an omen.

They planted a lead-cast inscription beneath the cross: It
read *Ludovicus Magnus regnat*. Great Louis reigns, indeed.
Everyone French shouted, *"Vive le roi!"* then hurried over to
the brandy barrel that La Forest was monitoring.

In retrospect it seemed melancholy; the handful of wind-
blown, dirty, bedraggled Europeans announcing ownership of
someone else's country. But it was history, de Tonti reminded
himself, picking up his narrative. . . .

"Let us return to the sea coast which, provisions failing, we
were obliged to leave sooner than we wished in order to obtain
provisions in the neighboring villages. We did not know how to
get anything from the village of the Quinipissas, who had so ill
received us as we went down the river. We lived on local roots
like potatoes until six leagues from their village when we saw
smoke. M. de La Salle sent some men to reconnoiter at night.
Our people reported that they had seen some women. We
went on at daybreak, and taking four of the women, encamped
on the opposite bank. One of the women was then sent with
merchandise to prove that we had no evil design and wished
for their alliance and for provisions. We sent back the three
other women, keeping, however, constant guard. They
brought us some provisions in the evening, and the next
morning at dawn, the scoundrels attacked us. We vigorously
repulsed them and by 10 o'clock burnt their canoes, and, but
for fear of our ammunition failing, we should have attacked the
village. We left it in the evening in order to reach the Natches,
where we had left a quantity of grain on passing down. When
we arrived there the chief came out to meet us. M. de La Salle
made them a present of the scalps we had taken from the
Quinipissas. They had already heard the news for they had
resolved to betray and kill us. We went up to their village and
as we saw no women there we had no doubt of their having

some evil design. In a moment we were surrounded by 1,500 men. They brought us something to eat and we ate with our guns in our hands. As they were afraid of firearms they did not dare attack us. The chief begged M. de La Salle to go away as his young men had not much sense. We very willingly did, the game not being equal. We had only 50 men, French and savages. We then went on to the Taencas, where we were all very well received. From thence we came to Fort Prudhomme, where M. de La Salle fell dangerously ill, which obliged him to send me forward on the 6th of May to arrange his affairs at Michillimackinac. M. de La Salle, having recovered, joined us in September. Resolving to go to France to give an account of his voyage at Court, he ordered me to collect together the French to construct the Fort of St. Louis on the Illinois. M. de La Salle departed for France in the month of September, leaving me to command the fort. . . ."

He read over his words, which seemed so simple on the page. Life was much more complicated, he reflected. How to squeeze all the intervening events into mere words? Christ, but he hated this task, which Rob insisted was vital to their interests.

He decided to leave out the fact that he had ordered Sabat to accompany La Salle back to France and then on the second expedition to ascend the Mississippi from the Gulf. The old man had begged to be spared the duty. He confided that he loathed the Canadian and said serving the man would surely kill him. But 'Per was staying in Montreal because of his health and was running La Salle's affairs as his secretary, so de Tonti insisted Sabat take 'Per's place. Sabat could have refused actually, and de Tonti wondered now why he had not.

He felt guilty that he had abused Sabat's loyalty. He'd never forget the last time he saw Sabat with those sad eyes in that creased face. Now de Tonti mourned his absence; his own affairs ran more smoothly with Sabat in charge. He hoped he had not sent the old servant into rheumatism in those southern marshes.

De Tonti sketched a few notes about the war with the Iroquois in which he had played a part. He mulled how to describe how he had left Fort St. Louis because Governor Frontenac had been relieved of his post and his and La Salle's enemies had taken over the government of New France. He, de Tonti, was relieved of his own command by agents of the new administration.

He glanced out the window to see the ship sliding into its berth, humans like insects scuttling over it.

Without his telescope, long ago lost, de Tonti couldn't make out the features of one tall man standing at the railing. It looked like La Forest. His heart beat faster in anticipation. He locked up his notes and went downstairs and across the cobbled docking area. As he expected, there was his old friend and partner. La Forest saw him at the gangplank and waved.

"Great news!" he called, hoping dock gossip would take the message to his creditors over in the business district. "La Salle won his way with the king!"

He spilled out his story as they returned to de Tonti's room. It was imperative they get back to Illinois as quickly as possible to secure the next season's pelts. "His Majesty restored all of La Salle's holdings—we are granted joint command of Fort St. Louis."

The king himself rebuked the former governor for abusing de Tonti and letting La Salle's creditors take his property. There would be a new governor more amenable to an open fur trade.

Better yet, La Salle was successful in convincing the king to start a colony at the mouth of the Mississippi. He was on his way there this moment with four ships, a company of men for de Tonti to command, and La Salle's own brother, a priest, with him to help set up the new colony.

"And would you believe—the king made La Salle viceroy of Louisiana," La Forest said, helping de Tonti pack for the return to Fort St. Louis on the Illinois. "The viceroy of the whole country, answerable only to His Majesty, with virtual autonomous royal powers."

"So he will be a king after all," de Tonti said.

"As close to it as any of us will ever come."

They had de Tonti's few belongings gathered together into six bundles. All that was left was to take them down to the dock. De Tonti took his bedraggled old felt hat off a peg, hefted his share of bundles, and started out of the rented room.

"Here now!" exclaimed La Forest, grabbing the hat.

De Tonti dropped the bundles and started to protest but La Forest moved away so he couldn't take it back. "This thing belongs in a museum, old friend."

"Careful, you're bending the crown—" de Tonti said, not without heat. That old hat was a symbol to him, a symbol of his own survival, maybe, or of what he was unable to save. "François—"

"I'm not going to hurt it."

De Tonti watched as La Forest folded the wide felt crown up in three places. He took stickpins from his own travel bag and secured the new alignment at three points. Then he held out the hat in its new pyramid shape to de Tonti. "What have you done?"

La Forest put it on his friend's head, pulled it at a cocky angle, and swung a window closed so he could see what it looked like. "That's the newest style, my friend." La Forest stood back to judge the angle, himself dressed in a fine new coat of elegant but very simple cut.

He said changes had occurred in gentlemen's attire—gone were the doublet, high boots, flowing hair. Men did not wear as many ribbons and googaws. The king himself was setting the new fashion, complete with braided wigs and this new three-cornered hat.

De Tonti scowled at his image in the glass. "Looks askew no matter where you set the damned thing."

"It's the fashion. You don't want to look like an antique."

"Hmmm." But de Tonti left the hat as La Forest had modified it. He was after all the latest word from Europe.

On the street as they headed toward the waterfront, de Tonti saw two gentlemen who obviously had heard the fashion word: Their hats were pinned up in three places, too. So, though he didn't like it, de Tonti left the hat with La Forest's mark.

After they loaded his things on the next Montreal-bound sloop, they had breakfast in a tavern de Tonti frequented. La Forest used the time to tell his old friend the more personal news from Paris.

La Salle had refused when Alphonse de Tonti tried to sign on the expedition. He didn't know why La Salle rejected him. But he brought mail from de Tonti's younger brother, who was still serving the king as a clerk. Though he was only fourteen, he was to be trusted with editing de Tonti's reports. De Tonti's left-hand script was legendary at the Ministry of Marine, though La Forest spared him this information.

De Tonti recalled the little boy with his name. It didn't seem possible that so much time had passed. Yet, among the letters La Forest brought was a long, intelligent, and highly adult communication from him. In it, the younger Henri explained that Alphonse had bolted from the family business. He was

determined to find his way to the New World despite his
mother's wishes. Apparently Isabelle's objection was the
reason La Salle had decided against signing on de Tonti's
second brother.

La Forest returned to Fort St. Louis with de Tonti, where
they prepared for another trip downriver—La Salle sent
orders for de Tonti to meet him at the river's mouth during the
upcoming spring months.

De Tonti went deeply into debt to Montreal bankers to obey
that order. He would be paying loans off for years with
exorbitant interest on his fur income. He and La Forest set up
a partnership with the idea that New France could be
completely ignored by using the southern route up instead of
down the Mississippi. So it was a good investment for de Tonti
to pay the bills to comply with his patron's order because of the
potential income awaiting them all after La Salle established
his southern colony.

De Tonti took a fair contingent down the river again,
retracing the original expedition's route, and sent scouts thirty
leagues east and west at the mouth of the river.

They didn't find a trace of La Salle. They replanted the cross
he had erected in '82. It was the only evidence of the historic
date when the explorer claimed Louisiana for France. De
Tonti hid one of his last silver *ecus* in a tree trunk near the new
location of the cross to mark his passage there. It had been a
disappointing trip, with all that borrowed money spent
without achieving his main objective. But the trip had some
benefits. De Tonti founded his own small colony, called
Arkansas Post, at the Osotony site he'd first seen with
Handsome Frog, on the north side of the river La Salle had so
blithely named de Tonti.

De Tonti called it the Arkansas River. He did not need such
an inflation of his own personality. It was enough for him to
know the land was his, was there waiting for him whenever he
could leave the service of the king and go claim it as his home.

Home. The word sounded strange rattling around in his
head. Before now, he had used that word only in reference to
Paris. But I'll never return to Paris, he thought.

Home is Arkansas. No, he corrected himself: Home is a
woman called Arkansas. The thought flew into his mind
unbidden. It stung to think of her now, not knowing if she was
dead or alive. "Arkansas," he had playfully called her that lost
spring dawn when she had criticized his pronunciation of her

Quapaw name. For so long he had been able to keep the memory of her in a quiet secret place where it didn't trouble him. His duty, his loyalty to La Salle, his desire to make a fortune in furs—all these practical concerns crowded out the raw wound he was distressed to find still in him going by the name of that woman. That woman I'll never see again, he said to himself, rubbing his eyes. He had not attempted to find her when he went back looking for La Salle. He hadn't even asked the Kappa about the Osotony chief woman who was raised among the Osage. He didn't want to know that she was dead. Surely she was. But he knew that he had not asked about her on purpose. He let practical matters keep him from finding out what had happened to her. As long as I don't know for sure, he thought with stunning clarity, I don't have to accept that she is dead. So, that trip in '86 through Arkansas to find La Salle had been strictly on business.

Several men of his party stayed at Arkansas Post, asking for land of their own. He was glad to give it to them. They collected buffalo skins for eventual shipment back to France, and generally watched out for his interests in that beautiful southern country. He had recently received a forwarded letter from Couture, the factor at Arkansas Post. His little colony looked as though it would survive with the help of Christianized Quapaw. They had a good supply of pelts waiting for shipment, needed more trade merchandise, and were experimenting with a corn crop. D'Arcy, who had been known as De Arcos, asked his patron for permission to marry a Quapaw girl. Thinking of the young man he let slip through the royal net made de Tonti grin with satisfaction. He would like to see D'Arcy again and talk about old times. De Tonti wasn't surprised that some smart Indian girl had seen D'Arcy's worth despite his shyness.

But D'Arcy's request gave de Tonti a bittersweet ache; someone else was succeeding where he had failed. Of course he would write to Couture to grant D'Arcy permission to wed. At least he was asking. Most of the Frenchmen threw off authority as soon as they arrived in the New World. He thought of the several scoundrels who had stolen trade merchandise to take profits for themselves with Indian fur.

But not everyone was a thief. De Tonti prided himself that he had found a few honest men, like D'Arcy and Couture. De Tonti had already given Couture a tract of land in Arkansas. He would give D'Arcy land, too, as a wedding gift. Knowing his retainers were in Arkansas gave de Tonti a good feeling.

When de Tonti returned from the '86 trip, it looked as though the political forces were once again in his favor. But by that time the Iroquois were at renewed war with the Illinois. De Tonti had immediately offered his services fighting for the new government against the infamous Snake-persons. As with all hostilities with the Iroquois this campaign had ended indecisively. There would be other battlegrounds. For now, an unsteady peace prevailed, one the English and the Dutch would have liked to topple permanently.

For de Tonti the ordeal was over. He was on his way with a Shawnee companion back to Fort St. Louis of the Illinois after the brief campaign. They'd camped about a day's journey away on the last night of their trip. While the Shawnee went about some private ritual near the fire, de Tonti was scribbling in the diary that had become a habit for him, writing about the unsuccessful attempt to locate La Salle's second expedition. De Tonti was anxious to return to Fort St. Louis and tend to his business. He was also planning to go south looking for La Salle again come spring. La Forest was off to France, where he was going to plead for royal aid in locating the Canadian and his second expedition. Meanwhile de Tonti and his Shawnee in their lone canoe tomorrow would be back on the Rock, as he fondly thought of Fort St. Louis.

That wavering up and down line of hope was cresting again. All that was left hanging was the whereabouts of La Salle. In Montreal they were betting against him, especially after de Tonti's unsuccessful rescue mission. Their creditors were screaming and wouldn't advance de Tonti any more money until the Canadian showed up.

Where was he?

The next afternoon de Tonti and his Shawnee guide approached the great Illinois camp below the Rock, where he saw villagers and his own men trotting down to the river to greet him.

Close to the makeshift dock now he saw a tall Frenchman among the excited Illinois eagerly waiting to greet their favorite white man, who was surely bringing gifts. The Frenchman stepped more clearly into de Tonti's wobbling line of sight as the canoe bumped into the mossy wood.

It was Rob.

32

Before he cried out his friend's name, he saw that it was not
Rob. The resemblance was uncanny, however, between the
explorer and this man. De Tonti understood immediately even
before introductions that this had to be La Salle's brother,
whom La Forest said had accompanied La Salle on the latest
expedition. De Tonti had to bite his tongue to keep from
blurting out a flood of questions.

"Captain de Tonti, I believe," said the amiable fellow, so
much like Rob in appearance and voice but dressed in the
roughspun field cassock of a Sulpitian priest. He introduced
himself as La Salle's brother, Jean Cavelier, and offered his
right hand, apparently forgetting that de Tonti did not shake
hands. He was unruffled by his *faux pas*.

De Tonti looked over Father Cavelier's shoulder for the
major player in their drama.

"My brother is not with us, sir," replied the priest to de
Tonti's unspoken question. "But I bring good news from him
and his best regards."

That night they sat by the fireside at the huge rough-hewn
table in de Tonti's private quarters; himself, his second in
command Bellefontaine, the priestly Cavelier, and one of the
men who had ascended the Mississippi with him. This was
Joutel, the son of the gardener who tended the ancestral
Cavelier estate back in Normandy.

Cavelier's was a long tale of hardship punctuated by
hostilities. True to form, Robert La Salle had fought with just
about everyone on his expedition. The fighting started at sea
aboard the command ship when he opposed the captain. Then
he tangled with the ship's sailors, who wanted to hold a ritual
equator-crossing ceremony that involved payment to the old
hands. His own men, another rapscallion crew recruited on
the docks, were disgruntled to mutiny a couple of times
because of pay owed to them and the arduous conditions of the
journey.

Once on the Gulf of Mexico the party ran into bad luck in
the form of shipwreck and bad weather as well as loss of
provisions out of sheer stupidity. "Of course, my brother

believed his enemies caused the problems," said Cavelier, a personable man so unlike his brother in everything but looks, who did most of the talking. "But let it be noted that his personality was—and," he added quickly, "remains intractable, to say the least." He laughed lightly in a manner that bespoke years of dealing with that infamous personality.

Joutel, a young light-haired man of serious expression and quiet intelligent demeanor, watched him silently. De Tonti was hungry for detail so the priest continued, "But despite setbacks of every nature, my intrepid brother saw construction of his fort on the Gulf. It's a mean affair, but it is French."

"Buy why didn't he accompany you back here according to our plan?"

"As you know he has a bad stomach. He stayed among the Cenis Indians for their soothing remedies. Of course he kept his Illinois, Nikanape with him."

"And Sabat, the old sergeant. Is he well?"

The priest assured de Tonti that his aide was in fine fettle. "He grumbles at the demands of Monsieur and hates his smoking, but discharges his duties with care. A fine man. Noble of you to part with him."

De Tonti was relieved to hear such a good report. But for some reason he felt edgy, nervous, as though there were something he was missing. He had asked all the right questions. What was it that continued to vex him? A feeling, a predisposition to be cynical he'd learned from La Salle, maybe. It was all too easy somehow. De Tonti felt an urge to rise up in anger and demand to know what was being held back.

But this good priest seemed so cordial, so warm in his desire to answer the slightest question about the events that brought him here to Fort St. Louis on the Illinois. De Tonti pointed questions at Joutel, however, which the brother somehow managed to answer. The younger man was shy, embarrassed, said Cavelier teasingly, at finally meeting the famous Iron Hand. "My brother could not speak highly enough of you, *capitaine.*"

De Tonti nodded his thanks for the compliment, but tried to bring Joutel into the conversation, "I hear you've kept a journal of your adventures, Monsieur. I'd surely like to read it."

Joutel looked disconcerted and mumbled that unfortunately

he had lost his notes somewhere on the Mississippi passing through Arkansas.

"Monsieur Couture was most kind to us," said the priest. "I was never so glad to see the cross as I was the day we stumbled into Arkansas Post. Your people there saved our lives, without a doubt."

Outside a wind with the breath of winter in it whined under cedar shingles. A downdraft hit the flames in the fireplace, sending sparks out onto the unfinished floorboards. Joutel, being closest to the tongs, captured several errant coals while Cavelier continued, "And while you, too, have treated us with utmost civility I feel some reticence on your part."

De Tonti was surprised at the man's forthrightness, so unlike his brother. "Well, you can understand my concern for my patron. This is all a digression from the plans we made before he started this venture."

"The hazards of life in this perilous country . . ." the priest countered with an expansive gesture that implied all of North America.

"And," de Tonti continued assertively but without the offense of interruption, "it's unlike him not to inform me personally. It's also very unlike him to stay behind in a squalid Indian village when he must be fairly dying to get back and report his success to the Court."

"Ah, your doubts have been anticipated. In his wisdom my brother insisted on sending this letter to you." He took a stained document from a pocket and handed it to de Tonti across the table, where their candle was burning low after the long evening of conversation.

Bellefontaine, who had been leaning back on two legs of his bench, let it drop forward with a crack onto the planks.

The letter looked as though it had survived as many ordeals as the men who were delivering it. It had been soaked at least once and probably dried inside a pocket. It was torn in a couple of places. De Tonti unfolded it with care then read silently: "I have asked my brother to go to France to make an accounting to the king of the affairs with which he has charged me. I beg you to give him all he asks for the expense of his voyage, and for those four persons I am sending with him. I also want him to take two Shawnees. Moreover, you will pay him 2,652 *livres* in beaver that I owe him for money he loaned me for my last sailing. If you have not enough beavers, you will supply him with permits to trade at the fort. He will tell you everything."

It was signed with what appeared to be La Salle's signature. It looked quite authentic. De Tonti handed it to Bellefontaine, who read it to himself.

"That's a great deal of money," de Tonti said with a grim smile.

"Indeed. I felt so when I loaned it for your joint enterprises," Cavelier coolly replied.

"I have debts already outstanding for your brother's enterprises. I wonder if I'll ever be repaid, and here I am ordered to loan out even more."

"But surely my brother's intentions are honorable."

"Of course. But I haven't even been paid my salary in all the years I've served him."

"But through his good offices you've made a fortune in the fur business. Just outside I saw a veritable mountain of peltries."

"We have extraordinary expenses you cannot imagine in getting trade merchandise down into this wild country," de Tonti countered. "Our insurance rates on the pelts are astounding because our transporters are sitting ducks to thieves—many of whom are former employees."

Cavelier looked for a moment in this candlelight exactly like his brother. He even groomed himself like Rob; it looked as though he had just shaved. He had Rob's blue chin. The only hairs left on his face were his expressive eyebrows. It was unnerving to de Tonti to have to deal with this go-between who resembled the man to such a degree. But his reply was so unlike Rob it dispelled the illusion of similarity.

He shrugged and touched his crucifix. "At this point, my son, I'm afraid Monsieur Joutel and I are entirely dependent upon your charity." His face fairly shone with innocent supplication. He was very disarming with his noble, earnest features drawn by privation. Only a stone could reject his plea.

De Tonti was thinking, why me? Why did Rob put me into this dilemma?

Bellefontaine, relieved because the letter held no complaints against himself, put it on the table between his commander and the priest.

Joutel was trying to stifle a yawn.

"I too am exhausted," said Cavelier. "I don't know why you aren't falling over with fatigue from your journey, Captain de Tonti."

"I'm well broken in," replied de Tonti languidly, using the French frontiersman's slang word that meant to soften a beaver skin by pounding it with a mallet. De Tonti's feet, propped on a stool, were still in heavy traveling moccasins; he hadn't even bothered to change from his canoe clothes. He regarded the dried river mud encrusting his boots. "Since my first step onto the New World, I haven't stopped walking."

"I'm not so inured," the priest confessed. "I haven't recovered from the trip to this place in the weeks we've been here."

"That's what the word 'tenderfoot' means," the commander replied.

Cavelier uttered his airy laugh. "Perhaps we can continue this conversation in the morning. I want to answer your every question because I empathize with your distress." He stood, catching Joutel's yawn. "Thank you for your time, *capitaine*."

"And you for your detailed report." De Tonti stood with the priest. "I trust you will sleep well—your quarters are comfortable? My men have served you well?"

"Oh, yes. Lieutenant Bellefontaine has treated us like kings."

After they'd gone, de Tonti sat talking softly to his second in command.

"They appeared to be speaking the truth to me, sir," Bellefontaine offered. "I've heard their report twice now and they made no self-contradictions."

De Tonti regarded him silently; there had been reports that this man—Bellefontaine—had not run the fort honestly while de Tonti was away fighting Iroquois. One disturbing dispatch from His Majesty himself concerned "disorders in the woods," which recalled the royal fear that good Frenchmen were going savage. Something to do with Indian girls, of course. He would have to deal with it after he had smoothed out this new wrinkle. He watched the young man toy with the edge of La Salle's stained note.

"And I've seen Monsieur's signature often enough."

The commander nodded.

"This isn't a forgery."

"So it appears. . . ." de Tonti replied idly. He picked up the paper and held it near the candle flame guttering in its socket. Bellefontaine thought de Tonti was going to burn it though such an act was not like his commander, who was scrupulously honest.

De Tonti held the note so that it did not catch fire but only heat from the flame.

"Ah," he said as though something had been cleared up. Bellefontaine, caught by curiosity, leaned forward to see what it was that de Tonti was exclaiming. A symbol was appearing like magic in one corner.

"What—?"

"Piss." De Tonti dropped the note beside the candlestick. Robert La Salle's elaborately stylized signature had appeared a second time in dark brown stain on a corner and upside down to the visible writing.

"See, he wrote it in piss, which is invisible until heated," de Tonti said without any trace of relief or enthusiasm for this intelligence. "It's a trick La Salle taught me."

Bellefontaine unconsciously wiped the hand that had touched the note against the rough tabletop.

De Tonti continued to watch the note as though it might tell him more as he dismissed Bellefontaine, who had early duty. When the lieutenant was gone, the captain continued to look at the apparently forthright communication.

The candle flickered out with a smoky hiss.

The fire on the grate died down to a sizzling bed of red-eye coals. But the captain didn't move for a long time as if watching the note might disclose the reason for his irritation.

Finally, when it was quite late and the fort on the Rock around him was deep in slumber except for the silent guards on the lookout for Iroquois, the captain retired.

He did not sleep. In his mind he still saw the curled and dirty note. He went to sleep thinking about it, trying to decide whether to obey it without question or to obey his gut, which continued to insist that something was terribly wrong.

In the end his respect for La Salle's absent authority overruled his negative instincts. Not long afterward, Cavelier handed over a receipt to de Tonti for "7,072 *livres*, 12 *sols*, 6 *deniers*, for a canoe, provisions and peltries," which in this country without coin was the same as money. De Tonti made sure the priest understood this was all a loan. Cavelier happily agreed. He wasted no time in getting his party out on the river and off to Michillimackinac and points east.

The decision continued to vex de Tonti. But problems connected with the fur business occupied his mind that winter. An Iroquois war party had killed some of his men transporting supplies. He hired a Shawnee troop to go after more lest his men desert in the face of grim winter. The king's concerns about abominations resulted in fewer men stationed at Fort St. Louis. But he and La Forest only hired more *voyageurs* to transport their peltries back to civilization.

The Iroquois continued to harass the transports. Mainly because of his Indian policy the new governor was relieved of his post and Frontenac was reinstated, much to de Tonti's delight. La Salle's old friend could be counted on not to get in the way of business.

The friendly Illinois didn't mind "getting off the blankets" against the Iroquois as long as the French supplied them with guns. But they did little more than slow down the Snake-persons. When Frontenac tried to get more men and money to fight them, he met with little success as the king was fighting Spain again. His Majesty had lost his English ally and had no desire to be distracted by colonial matters when things were heating up in Europe.

De Tonti likewise was unsuccessful in getting money the governor of New France owed to him for the Iroquois campaign. The only answer to his money problems was to open up the southern route free of French politicians, creditors, and Iroquois. This was La Salle's master plan—to transport peltries down the Mech-a-si-pi and out through the Gulf of Mexico—a plan within which he was apparently still embroiled. There was no word from him; only disturbing rumors from trappers coming out of the woods. The Indians carried stories that kept de Tonti from sleeping soundly. It was in this situation de Tonti found himself sitting on his Rock in another autumn, 1689, the day everything changed.

It was a sparkling dusk. The trees were just beginning to turn red and orange but it was still pleasantly warm outside. De Tonti was supervising the implantation of two small cannon on the fortifications. He was sure the guns could ward off an Iroquois attack if he could just secure enough provisions to last a siege. When he heard signal shots, he wandered to the edge of the Rock to see what was going on down on the Illinois River. From this distance he couldn't tell who had arrived, but he could see it was a canoe party of at least one white man and several Indians, though from this distance he was unable to tell from which nation.

He'd been nettled by frustration the past few days. He welcomed any diversion from intermittently troubled thoughts and boredom. Had he not been commander here he would have run down to satisfy his curiosity. But La Salle's admonition to wait to be approached won out. It would take a few minutes for the new arrivals to walk up here to the fort so he delegated the cannon emplacement to his sergeant and went to wash up to receive the visitors and their inevitable news.

He knew when he saw Couture's face that it wasn't good. This was one of his most trusted men, this Couture who was in charge of Arkansas Post. He entered de Tonti's office without ceremony for he was a rough-edged individual. He looked almost like one of the Quapaw who stayed outside, dressed as he was in their style of beaded jacket, leather tube britches, and knee-high moccasins. His wild appearance was furthered by a full untrimmed beard and several long Quapaw-style braids of his grizzled hair, uncut for many years. A hat made of a whole raccoon completed his attire. The long beautifully ringed tail was still attached—a style that was becoming the virtual woodsman uniform.

But Couture was also a shrewd businessman. As factor of the Post he handled both merchandise and pelts—he had opportunity to cheat two ways. The whole system of the fur trade depended on men like him, whom de Tonti had never caught in a lie or with his hand in the sack. But the wilderness had made him shy when he was out of it.

De Tonti offered him brandy but Couture, unlike many of the wild Frenchmen, abstained from alcohol. He took his tobacco by lip, snuff being considered by many to be more noble than imbibing. Lip-stained and leathery, he stood nervously before the commander as though reluctant to bear bad tidings.

"Come on, then," said de Tonti in mounting curiosity, "let's have it."

"La Salle's dead."

De Tonti sat down heavily. He'd known it in his gut, but was still hoping the intuition was wrong. He shook his head. Damnation. He felt needles behind his eyes but he rubbed them before the sensation became tears.

As if this disclosure were a cork removed from an overturned bottle, Couture poured out detail after grim detail.

"You mean he's been dead for two years?" de Tonti asked incredulously after the lengthy report. It took little calculation to figure the explorer was not alive when his brother—the sanctimonious bag of perfidity—had come through here last year. Christ, the gut was right, de Tonti thought with heavy realization. When will I ever learn to trust my intuitions?

Many implications settled on his shoulders. Couture saw him slump further in his chair. "They fooled me, too," he said sympathetically. "But my Quapaw stole this." The Arkansawer offered a small bound book across the table. It looked much like de Tonti's own diary, a common European ledgerbook but a rare oddity in this country where there were as yet neither printers nor binders.

De Tonti reached for it, then hesitated when he saw printed in a precise hand on the canvas cover:

Henri Joutel
(1684–'87)

His heart raced; here, then, was an eyewitness account of what had happened to La Salle. No wonder Joutel was so reticent when the other Cavelier was here. He probably agreed to let the older man, his ancestral manorlord after all, do the talking so there would be no contradictions. Now in retrospect de Tonti realized that he was probably also shamed by the deceit that he most likely would not maintain in his journal.

Calmly, but with his hand on it de Tonti continued to speak with Couture about the situation in Arkansas. The fortifications had been strengthened. The plot of ground set aside for a church had been cleared with the help of converted Quapaw, who had moved from Kappa to Arkansas Post in some numbers, he explained. "They're begging us to send a priest." The Jesuit who had stayed behind from La Salle's first expedition had gone on to other missions. The spot was so remote he hadn't been replaced. A few Kappa had been Christians since Marquette and Joliet's venture into Arkansas, yet now they had no priest.

De Tonti listened to this innocent news of the Quapaw with an odd elation.

Couture stopped talking. The two men eyed each other briefly before he continued in a tone so soft and gentle it was out of character, "She's alive. . . ."

De Tonti looked struck. Sweat broke out on his neck. His body thrilled as if she'd actually touched him. If he'd been standing he would have had to sit down.

The woodsman continued, "Her clan moved west to the Lake in the Mountain. Appears she's very big *wa kon* in those

parts. . . ." His voice trailed off. Actually that exhausted his
store of knowledge about Fleet Woman. He was glad de Tonti
didn't press for more. The captain looked in pain, a mixture of
relief and distress. To be the recipient of such bad news along
with such good would tend to stagger anyone, Couture
reflected as he regarded this man he respected so much. He,
being de Tonti's senior by some dozen years, had watched the
captain mature into the fine man he saw distraught before him.
He was sorry to bring him such conflictions. But at the
mention of the Quapaw woman, he was glad to see de Tonti
brighten to his former fire, which Couture had been distressed
to see dimming over these hard years.

Couture finally begged leave to get some sleep. De Tonti
was glad to be alone with his thoughts. Despite the more
negative parts of this news, he felt hope brightening. Now
with it flooding through him he realized he'd been living in
quiet desperation without it far too long.

In the light of a new candle he sat on his warm Indian
blanket thinking, She's alive, she's alive, she's alive!

When he had dwelled sufficiently on the sublime meditation
of her name, he opened the diary and began reading Joutel's
highly legible notes about the colony La Salle had established
on an unknown Texas river he mistook for the Mississippi:

"The 15th, we held on our journey and found a pleasanter
country than that we had passed through. And Monsieur de la
Salle having in his former Journey hid some Indian wheat and
beans, two or three leagues from that place, and our provisions
beginning to fall short, it was thought far to go to that place.

"Accordingly he ordered the Sieurs Duhaut, Hiens, Liotot
the surgeon, his own Indian, and his footman whose name was
Sabat, who were followed by some natives, to go to the place
he described to them where they found all rotten and quite
spoilt.

"The 16th, in their return, they met with two bullocks,
which Monsieur de la Salle's Indian killed, whereupon they
sent back his footman to give him notice of what they had
killed, that if he would have the flesh dried, he might send
horses for it.

"The 17th, Monsieur de la Salle had the horses taken up,
and ordered the Sieurs Moranget de Lalre and his footman to
go for that meat, and send back a horse load immediately.
Monsieur Moranget, when he came thither, found they had
smoked both the beeves, though they were not dry enough.

They said Sieurs Liotot, Hiens, Duhaut and the rest had laid aside the marrow-bones to roast them, and eat the flesh that remained on them as was usual to do.

"The Sieur Moranget found fault with it, he in a passion seized not only the flesh that was smoked and dried, but also the bones, without giving them any; but on the contrary, threatening they should not eat so much of it, as they had imagined, and that he would manage that flesh after another manner. This passionate behavior, so much out of season and contrary to reason and custom, touched the surgeon Liotot, Hiens and Duhaut to the quick, they having other causes of complaint against Moranget.

"They withdrew, and resolved together upon a bloody revenge; they agreed upon the manner of it and concluded they would murder the Sieur Moranget, Monsieur de la Salle's footman and his Indian because they were very faithful to him.

"They waited all night when those unfortunate creatures had supped and were asleep. Liotot the surgeon was the inhuman executioner. He took an axe being by the Sieur Moranget, giving him many strokes on the head; the same he did by the footman and the Indian, killing them on the spot, while his fellow villains stood upon their guard with their arms to fire upon such as should make any resistance. The Indian and the footman never stirred, but the Sieur Moranget had so much vigour as to sit up but without being able to speak one word and the assassins obliged the Sieur de Marle to make an end of him though he was not in the conspiracy.

"This slaughter had yet satisfied but one part of the revenge of those murderers. To finish it and secure themselves it was requisite to destroy the commander-in-chief. They consulted about the safest method to effect it, and resolved to go together to Monsieur de la Salle to knock out the brains of the most resolute immediately, and then it would be easier to overcome the rest. But the river which was between them and us, being much swollen, the difficulty of passing it made them put it off until the 18th and 19th. On the other hand Monsieur de la Salle was very uneasy on account of their long stay. His impatience made him resolve to go himself to find his people and to know the cause of it.

"This was not done without many previous tokens of concern and apprehension. He seemed to have some presage of his misfortune, enquiring of some whether the Sieurs Liotot, Hiens and Duhaut had not expressed some discontent; and not hearing anything of it he could not forbear setting out on the 20th. With him was Father Anastasius and an Indian, leaving me in command in his absence and charging me from time to time to go the rounds about our camp to prevent being surprised, and to make a smoke for him to direct his way in case of need. When he came near the dwelling of the murderers, looking out sharp to discover something, he observed eagles fluttering about a spot not far from them, which made him believe they had found some carrion about the cabin and he fired a shot, which was the signal of his death and forwarded it.

"The conspirators hearing the shot, concluded it was Monsieur de la Salle who was come to seek them. They made ready their arms and provided to surprise him.

"Duhaut passed the river with Larcheveque. The first of them spying Monsieur de la Salle at a distance as he was coming towards them, advanced and hid himself among the high weeds to wait his passing by, so that Monsieur de la Salle suspected nothing, and having not so much as charged his piece again, saw the aforesaid Larcheveque at a good distance from him and immediately asked for his nephew Moranget to which Larcheveque answered, that he was along the river. At the same time the traitor Duhaut fired his piece and shot Monsieur de La Salle through the head so that he dropped down dead on the spot without speaking one word.

"Father Anastasius, who was then by his side, stood stock still in fright, expecting the same fate and not knowing whether he should go forwards or backwards. The murderer Duhaut put him out of that dread, bidding him not to fear for no hurt was intended him. He confessed that it was despair that had prevailed with him to do what he did. He said he had long desired to be revenged on Moranget because he had designed to ruin him and that he was partly occasion of his uncle's death. This is the exact relation of that murder as it was presently told to me by F. Anastasius.

"Such was the unfortunate end of Monsieur de la Salle's life at a time when he might entertain the greatest hopes as the reward for his labors. He had a capacity and talent to make his enterprise successful.

"His constancy and courage and his extraordinary knowledge in arts and sciences, which rendered him fit for anything . . . made him surmount all difficulties and would have procured a glorious issue to his undertaking, had not all those excellent qualities been counterbalanced by too haughty a behavior which sometimes made him insupportable and by a rigidness towards those under his command which at last drew on him an implacable hatred which was the occasion of his death. The shot which killed Monsieur de la Salle was also a signal of the murder to the assassins for them to draw near. They all repaired to the place where the wretched corpse lay, which they had barbarously striped to the shirt and vented their malice in vile and opprobrious language.

"Liotot said several times in scorn and derision, 'There you lie you brassy bastard, there you lie.' In conclusion they dragged it naked among the bushes, and left it exposed to the ravenous wild beasts."

Joutel went on to recount how he and Father Cavelier were spared along with others in the party. There was later a gunbattle between the murderers in which some were killed; others escaped and as far as he could say still at large.

But it was a very large country to get lost in. Larger than anyone knew or could imagine; de Tonti suspected he and La Salle had erred by thousands of leagues in their calculation of its extent.

Cavelier and Joutel had also calculated how to get from himself what they wanted:

"Monsieur Cavelier the priest had taken care before the death of M. de la Salle, his brother," the damned journal went on to relate, "to get of him a letter of credit, to receive either a sum of money or furs in the country of the Illinois, planning to tender that letter to M. Tonti, who believing M. de la Salle was still alive, would make no difficulty of giving him the needed supplies to get back to civilization." The author's arrogance stung de Tonti, who sat there feeling stupid as he read of those machinations that held himself in such contempt that the man could brag of the deceit in writing.

I played their utter fool, de Tonti rebuked himself.

He felt guilt that his concerns were more for being made a fool than for his lost comrades. It was as though he had already mourned La Salle, however. Since the brother's visit, he instinctively knew that his patron was gone forever.

The gut is always right.

It was for Sabat that he felt slicing sorrow. He hated himself for forcing the old man to go along with a master he disdained. Sabat always gave me good advice, he thought; I should have listened to him in this case. He'd be here living a comfortable

life into a ripe old age. De Tonti had already set aside an
Arkansas farmstead for him; maybe he would have taken an
Indian girl to wife and enjoyed the years left that he deserved.
His death is on my conscience, he thought morosely. And I
never told him I loved him. I never even thanked him for his
loyal service.

From this moment on, nothing was the same. An era was
over; it ended for de Tonti with this grim news, but the way he
felt it that night, in the picture larger than one man's life, was
that the era ended with the last of the visionary explorers,
Robert Cavelier de La Salle. De Tonti had survived to witness
its passing, but there was no further compensation. So much
for playing a part in history. Who in hell cares? he wondered in
the growing chill of midnight.

So, he thought; this is regret. He had even more reason than
remorse and mourning to remain fitfully awake. He calculated
his desperate indebtedness to several Montreal wolves. His
command paid in nothing but worry, but through it he had
license to factor furs, his chief means of livelihood; he
supposed that he could always adopt the raccoon headgear of
the trapper—a lower rung on the fur trade ladder, but an
honest living. He wanted to see more of this country, learn
more about the native people, do some surveying: his diary
notes contained the complete log of the many azimuth
readings from the original Mississippi expedition, but they
were strictly in relation to the river. Inland readings would tell
more about this country. Or he might pick up some more free-
lance work for the governor as an Iroquois fighter; but
whatever he found to pay his usurous debts, it would not be
through the good offices of a formal commission from the
Ministry of Marine. He and La Forest no longer commanded
this or any other French military garrison because whatever
documents legalizing their renewed commissions had suffered
the same fate as La Salle and his effects.

The wind moaned outside, mimicking surf. De Tonti had a
brief unsettling vision of a windswept Gulf beach strewn with
La Salle's bleached rib bones. He could almost hear the shrieks
of gulls and the foreign rattle of mildewed parchment with a
king's seal moldering in the sand. Utterly useless, utterly
wasted.

This dreary imagining chilled him so badly he curled up in
his Illinois blanket of buffalo fleece. Sometimes there was no
more comfort than this; all priorities faded and the only thing
left was a warm blanket against the night.

She had said that.

It had been a long, long time since Henri de Tonti had cried. Everyone near him slept beyond thick log walls so nobody saw or heard. The only man who might have listened for his master's distress in the night was dead without proper burial in the wilderness. Beginning with this night of bitter revelation, de Tonti would suffer greasy-dark but vivid nightmares that forced him to relive the heretofore blessedly forgotten hours after the grenade had taken his hand.

Just as he was about to drift into sleep, he smelled incinerated flour from smoldering hemp bags in the cellar where Sabat had dragged him to hide from Spanish patrols. The vapor of burned bread combined with that of his own charred flesh in a sickening parody of food as Sabat cauterized the stump, Oh no, Sweet Jesus, he heard his own voice beg, his dream eyes unable to watch, and so turned away.

A stranger sat unceremoniously beside him on the littered cellar floor, cross-legged, his rough carpenter's hands wringing canteen water from a kerchief he applied to de Tonti's burning forehead. When the stranger touched him, the fever abated and the pain lessened. He and the stranger spoke for a time— this had been the only part of the experience he'd remembered before now—then in the sudden manner of dreams, he was looking toward Sabat, whose attention was focused on bandaging his master's arm in clean white cloth—every grenadier carried a wad of linen in his kit for just such work— and didn't look up. De Tonti felt tears well in his eyes from gratitude at the sight of the old servant tenderly saving his life in this desolate ruin, waiting for the enemy to come and claim them both for the gravel quarry. De Tonti turned back to remark Sabat's loyalty: "He could have abandoned me—" he started to say, but the stranger with calloused but gentle hands was gone.

There the nightmare would end, only to repeat until a peculiar species of sleep took possession of him, eyes gritty with his own salt.

Sabat wasn't the only one he cried for that night in his ransacked dreams. Memory conjured them all up. His father was there in his prison cell; likewise Isabelle in hers. There was his second brother, Alphy, dying to pitch his innocence against this New World, and his baby brother, Henri, mired in the Old. There was his own innocent self imagining that life would be somehow magically different simply because possibility resided here in this new land. Fool that he was. This land was beyond ancient; it was men who were new.

There was Jeanette's sad, sweet face lurking behind a memory of the song in the music box. He was glad the spring had finally broken. He hated the damned thing and was relieved that rust had silenced its melancholy voice because it had always reminded him of Jeanette, whom he'd given nothing else.

And there was Fleet Woman. Sometime during false dawn he heard his own voice calling her by her many names. Weeononka. *La Vite*. Arkansas. She would always first be that to him—a woman called Arkansas. He woke knowing he was going back.

First he must try to reach any survivors of La Salle's Texas colony. Joutel's diary left doubt about those who remained in that dangerous Spanish territory. He must find the murderers and bring them to justice.

Then he was going home to Arkansas.

33

Once again de Tonti settled into a canoe on the wide bosom of the Mississippi. The river was becoming a habit. This time his party was small—five Frenchmen, a Shawnee, and a couple of Illinois, all he could afford.

It was just after New Year, 1689, but the weather was bright and storm-free when they left the clear green water of the Illinois and entered the muddy channel of the Great River, swiftly descending into warmer regions along its southern banks.

Each time he canoed these waters, he looked for the island he had shared with Weeononka. Once again he squinted at the western bank but the hungry river must have long ago gobbled it.

Information from friendly tribes along the way suggested that remnants of La Salle's company—probably the murderers themselves—were lodged among the Caddo, who lived below the Red River in southern Arkansas.

But the Caddo, though cordial, insisted that no white men had ever lived among them. They'd heard rumors that another tribe eighty leagues west had recently adopted some white men.

"There is no way, monsieur," declared Morant, eldest of de Tonti's Frenchmen, "that I'm going further into the wild western country. Look at my poor feet—" De Tonti could see they were badly swollen. Morant was soaking his toes in warm water that an Indian girl had brought with a smile. "Let me stay here and wait for you."

De Tonti scowled. Time was against him. The governor of New France wished him to join another Iroquois campaign come spring. He owed the governor fealty. If he was going to find La Salle's party, it had to be soon so he could get back to the governor's rendezvous.

"The other men follow you." De Tonti loathed having to beg, but had no recourse. "Don't desert me when I most need you."

Morant shrugged, gesturing at his bunions. "I'm a canoe-man, sir, not a hiker."

De Tonti disgustedly left the hut where the Caddo woman had taken Morant in. He suspected that she was the real reason the crusty old woodsman wished to stay behind. He didn't analyze why this particularly irritated him. Even in this southern clime it was cold out in the wilderness, through the swamps and open prairies they had to cross to get to the village where the murderers might or might not be.

De Tonti walked in the chilly evening between the lodges of the fifty or so families that made up this village. Without a definite plan he approached the hut of the headman, a grizzled, hefty, one-eyed warrior with many tattoos and wives surrounding him inside his smoky quarters.

Small children scampered nakedly between the adults, who fell silent upon entry of the swarthy Frenchman with the metal hand. They'd heard stories about this one; stories and rumors flew with the ravens at great speed in these places. A secret, especially of such distinct foreigners as these Frenchmen, was difficult to keep.

The headman nodded that Iron Hand might approach him. He even offered a pipe, though without the formal ceremony.

De Tonti knew some of their language from his previous travels among their neighbors, who spoke the same tongue. He supplemented with handsign, which the chief found amusing since the metal hand was a strange implement for discourse. But de Tonti was good left-handed and made his wants eloquently known: horses, two guides to take him to the village in question, plus provisions of dried meat and corn in return for a good-sized iron cooking pot and a fathom of blue beads.

The chief looked smug on his lounge surrounded by his women, who eyed the Frenchman with unveiled curiosity.

"I have heard a fantastic report that your hand plays music," said the chief. When he spoke, the lines of blue tattoo on his plump cheeks seemed to puff and writhe with a life of their own independent of the flesh they incised. "If it's the truth I would be pleasured to hear this funny music."

De Tonti sighed with exasperation.

He explained that the mechanism in his hand was broken. It no longer sang. But he opened the watch, which he had taken great care to keep running. He still got it to the Quebec watchmaker as often as possible. He was constantly tinkering with it himself, using a seaman's set of watchmaker's tools he'd bought in Quebec. It had a habit, however, of slowing down in humid weather. No telling how much off it was by now. At least his daily ministrations kept it ticking.

He proffered it to the chief, who chuckled as he listened with his ear close to the strange thing. He imitated the sound with a wide toothless grin, saying his word for "heart" over and over. "I like this little beating heart on the outside of a body."

His women chittered. One scolded him, no doubt warning that to touch the thing might give him bad medicine.

Eventually de Tonti moved the subject of discussion closer to his desires. But the chief continued to give the watch his one eye with flamboyant desire of his own etched between his tattoos.

"Two of your best warriors will achieve great honor by accompanying me on what the mighty Caddo regard as only a short journey."

The fat chief wiggled further into his robes. He jerked a finger at the watch.

There was no doubt what he was proposing. De Tonti adamantly shook his head. "Would you take a father's parting gift to his son?"

The chief simpered, his jowls like jelly. Yes, of course he would. His swift, jerking handsign said, *White man, I've got you by the balls,* so eloquently, de Tonti winced.

De Tonti saw he must part with the watch. But it made him angry at unreasonable fate, bent on stripping him of everything he loved.

"I do, however, need some honest man to hold this little beating heart for me so that it might not perish in your magnificent blue temple." He lifted the timepiece from its bed in his palm and held it in his flesh hand. "I would also like to leave ammunition here if I may so that when I return before the next full moon I can find my belongings have been taken care of by my friends." The way it was worded was crucial, veritably a legal contract.

The chief's face brightened.

"Does the great chief know of a man who could be trusted to keep it dry and return it to me when I come back through here?"

"There are few men worth such an honor in these parts."

"Surely such a fine nation as the Caddo has produced at least one man who would keep it safe."

"Many would keep it safe, but only one man around here can be trusted to give it back," said the chief, straightening proudly. He gestured to his eldest wife to take the wooden box of lead ball and powder to keep safe until Iron Hand returned. De Tonti had slipped a note into the ammunition box that marked this day and place should proof of this journey someday become necessary. The chief himself took possession of the watch, which he promised to defend with his life should such an extreme become necessary.

He left his beautiful timepiece behind in exchange for two hunters and seven horses. He was able to convince the Shawnee and only one of the Frenchmen, Roget, to go with him.

Morant was determined to stay among the Caddo.

The other three Frenchmen and Illinois braves did promise not to let the Caddo know they had disagreed with de Tonti; they left to go to Arkansas Post as if ordered by him to do so.

The chief let de Tonti know that the guides were free to stay with him forever if they wished. The horses were another matter. He expected his *cavali* to be returned in good shape since they were part of his wealth, gained at great cost or thievery from the Spaniards not far away in Texas. He assured Iron Hand that when he got his *cavali* back safe and sound, the chief would return the Frenchman's little beating heart.

"But, honored sir, my little beating heart is faithful to its true master. You will see that soon after I go, it will stop beating and will not beat again until I return and personally touch it."

This amazed the chief who bet de Tonti that it wasn't so. "Whoever loses, white man, must dance the calumet for the other."

De Tonti nodded agreement, adding, "But you must not try to take it apart or otherwise force it to beat again."

The chief nodded, his wattles wobbling.

De Tonti and his reluctant companions were off the next day for the western village. They followed the Red River for a good way, then struck out across the southwestern swamp.

The country was exquisitely beautiful, this being April as near as de Tonti could figure from hashmarks he religiously placed in his diary. Spring touched every branch. Warm fragrant breezes accompanied them through the verdant marshlands marked with bright birds and yellow-flowered islands—oases of dry land where they nightly pitched their camps.

But their luck was bad.

De Tonti had the battle nightmare almost every night, and couldn't get enough sleep. Roget got lost while hunting. He was gone for days, and de Tonti decided one day to give him up for dead. But that afternoon he stumbled back into camp on foot and in a sorry state.

"Please forgive me, *mon capitaine*, but in the river—my horse slipped—I couldn't help it—" He slumped to the squishing sod.

"The powder's gone, then," de Tonti said in resignation. Roget nodded miserably.

They'd agreed not to take the powder out of Roget's saddlebags because finding a dry camp was so difficult. Each man with his own specialized cargo kept his horse saddled at all times to keep their meager stores dry. De Tonti fervently wished he had taken charge of powder instead of food.

He saw now that the precious saddlebag was gone from Roget's equippage, some of which he'd slung over his arm.

De Tonti sat down on a log, unable to summon anger at the terrified boy. Their only powder was his personal damp supply.

This event curtailed his plans greatly. His Caddo guides were nervous traveling here in this damp season because rumor had it the alligator chief was on the prowl. Without shot they couldn't get meat should they lose the services of the Caddo spears, bows, and arrows. He glanced back at the two Indians who sat by themselves on the other side of the fire. The fathomless eyes stared back at him, the message in them unpleasant.

But that night a hunting party joined them from the village where they were headed. The chief among these new Indians spoke some Spanish, which de Tonti understood. But the word was dire. A Spanish troop had followed them to the edge of the great swamp the night before last. As for the Frenchmen, yes, they had been among the tribe for a time, had even fought some Spanish soldiers on behalf of the village. But the chief was vague concerning their present whereabouts. One of his men said they were dead. Something in the chief's manner suggested a lie to de Tonti. This old fox knew about the Frenchmen, perhaps had been instrumental in their demise, which he intended to obscure by fabricating this story.

A woman traveling with this party began to make discouraging noises when de Tonti asked these questions. Her chief warned her to shut up. De Tonti saw she was even more terrified of himself and his metal weapons than her husband. She continued to whimper even when the chief threatened to strike her.

The chief tried to make light of her woman's fears, offering a manly smoke with Iron Hand, whose name was already famous up and down the Great River.

"I don't take the calumet with men who tell me lies," he said, delighted to see the chief squelch fury. It was a gamble but de Tonti's gut told him this man didn't want to offend the famous Iron Hand and possibly the Frenchmen with muskets who came behind him.

De Tonti allowed himself to be mollified. "Perhaps, however, I can forget this unfortunate event by way of some small gift. Some horses and provisions would sweeten my heart."

Among these tribes gifts were often the way scores were settled as opposed to ancient traditions that demanded blood for blood.

De Tonti's little band left the next day with several fine horses, all marked, de Tonti was interested to note, by Spanish brands. The Indians had woven harnesses, saddles, and paddings out of rushes in imitation of the Spanish style of padded battle armor.

He still had hopes of reaching the remnants of La Salle's party, whom the Indians assured him were not more than eighty leagues westward deep in Spanish Texas. But the guides flatly refused to go into Spanish territory because those white men were known to take Indians as slaves they worked to death in deep silver mines in a desert country far away and full of devils. They'd go a ways but no further.

The next day the entire party was strung out on horseback, the pack animals tethered between each rider like beads on a narrow dry strip of sod through the swamp, when the elder Caddo last in line thought he saw the alligator chief behind a log. He leaped to his feet on his makeshift saddle and climbed a tree to get away from this apparition. By the time de Tonti and the others retraced their steps to find him, his horse had gotten tangled in ropes and underbrush. The animal had stopped kicking before they could cut him loose.

De Tonti was furious. On edge from lack of sleep, he'd lost his usual casual diplomacy. Before regaining his composure he made the mistake of rebuking the Caddo in front of the others. That night, having lost face, the hunter ran off.

He was their principal guide, who knew the tangled way back to the Caddo village. The other Caddo was terrified since he was only an apprentice to the elder man. He wouldn't move without him.

"Please lead on," de Tonti said, giving the traditional honor of lead position to his Shawnee, who had remained faithful throughout the dismal trip. At least de Tonti had assumed it was fealty, but when the Shawnee replied, de Tonti saw it had been mere fear to break with Iron Hand that kept this Shawnee loyal.

"This is your business, Iron Hand. I am a stranger here no less than you. The honor is all yours."

So, astride the skittery horse, which took its orders only in Spanish, de Tonti set out with his cringing little band for the Caddo village where Great Fatchief held his watch and some dry ammunition.

Once again he found himself consoling himself with much less than what he wanted. At least he had tried to reach La Salle's party. He'd come back again better provisioned and with more men. Now all he wanted was to get out of these swamps and back to dry ground. But it looked to him like unreasonable fate still opposed him.

They finally had to abandon the horses because the water continued to rise. They could find no dry ground and the horses wouldn't step into the dark swirling current, instinctively afraid to go where they couldn't see.

The creatures had little chance of survival. They speared one that had sprung a leg and feasted on its stringy flesh two

nights. But in the humidity there was no way to smoke the rest
so they left it to rot in the bog. They found no dry places and
were forced to lash logs together on an oozing mudflat to make
camp that night. It started to rain a monotonous gray drizzle.
The water level rose past their ankles, knees, and finally their
armpits. Their skin became wrinkled and sore. The remaining
Caddo started singing his death song and would not shut up
even when de Tonti lost patience, popped the knife, and
threatened to kill him just to get a little peace.

Roget tended to break into hysterical sobs every now and
then. De Tonti had no doubt the man was losing his sanity. The
Indian's keening could drive a statue crazy; much easier a
green young Frenchman.

At night they tried to dry their clothing beside pitiful fires.
Nothing in the swamp was dry enough to burn so they ended
by using fragments of paper tucked in their hats, playing cards,
treasured letters, diary pages, whole chapters of a missal in
Roget's sack.

De Tonti sacrificed the unused half of his diary, secretly
delighted to have an excuse to neglect it. Once hot enough the
fire consumed wetter twigs and finally, blissfully, branches.

They dined on barbequed frogs and fish that the Caddo
speared, cutting off his mournful song for this occupation.

They quite unexpectedly came upon a young bear munching
berries. The Caddo took it with an arrow. At least that night
they had red meat though the greasy flesh was next to raw
because they couldn't get up a big enough blaze and fell on
their supper before it was cooked.

They slept again on tree trunks. That night the water crept
higher so that in the silver dawn it was up into the remaining
baggage.

He woke to the sound of a crow. He sat upright in the lazy
rain, his back and side dripping.

He looked around. There was no sign of Roget or the Caddo,
except for a missing bundle that held the last scraps of dried
meat and corncakes from Old Fatchief's wives.

The crow cawed again, sending chill echoes off ancient
cypress trees.

De Tonti shivered with realization. He was alone.

The gears of his mind slipped immediately into cold tight
mesh. It was automatic. He would do what he must to get out
of this place. Everything else he tossed out of his mind as
though it were a canoe he was preparing to ride down a
cataract.

He simply would not perish here.

Quite methodically he opened the remaining pack and went through it, picking out everything inessential. He pitched these items, including the remaining half of the damned diary, into the dark waters beyond the log.

For some odd reason this gave him raw pleasure. He pissed downstream, stretched, washed his face, and dispassionately stabbed with his built-in blade a small treefrog he had stealthily watched trying to blend into the foliage.

With a surgeon's precision he dressed and cleaned the creature. He meticulously skinned it, determined to retain what civility he could and not fall on it like a ravenous wolf, head, guts, asshole and all. It was only a pink morsel when he finished, barely two dainty bites.

It was delicious.

He drank from what he hoped was upstream current on the other side of the log.

Thus refreshed, he settled down to repack his few essentials.

He tossed away the small metal vial after using the last drops of oil to lubricate the hand's blade. Mansard's workmanship was fine, but even Gallic excellence could not hold out against the inexorable patience of rust.

He also had the two extra blades still bound in paraffin-soaked bandages. These and little else made up his estate. He had: a stone-hard journeycake from Weeononka he'd kept all these years to test its longevity; three lead balls; a leather purse that contained a pewter button and two gold *ecus* remaining from Isabelle's reluctant gift; a flint match and extra flints; a small Illinois calumet of red pipestone; a securing pin of bent tempered wire; a collapsible copper cup; three arm's lengths of white cotton cloth; his pistol; the damp powder in a leather sack; two *toises*, or fathoms, of lightweight hempen cordage; the watchmaker's kit; a little hatchet head; four iron arrowheads; half a core of white thread; two needles; and a small Bible. He looked at this object thinking how useless it was but sat unable to throw it away. He couldn't remember where it had come from. It was a useless thing. He never read it and had no idea why he'd held on to it all these years. It was beyond useless. Except maybe as an item of trade, he reconsidered as he was about to chuck it. He wrapped it in the cloth, then proceeded to pack the rest.

With him still was his hat, aged veteran of his many missions.

When he was through, the briar-laced sky far overhead was a pale blue. The sun was up, but the strange light there made it hard to determine exactly where the sun was in the sky. It was so far away there were no shadows down below. Daytime had no dawn and no dusk in this place. There was only light and darkness, and what light there was, was blue, a slate-gray smoky stain that gave the bayou its Quapaw name, the Blue Temple.

Taking up the pack he began to wade in what he determined after long consultation with the waist-deep water to be north. He knew their last camp on dry ground had been south of the Arkansas River and west of the Mississippi. His own land and Arkansas Post had to be north of his position. But was it northeast or northwest? Surely by heading north where the current appeared to be coming from, he'd encounter the Arkansas. He could lash together logs with the rope, cross the river, and easily determine the location of Arkansas Post, where salvation lay. Elation coursed through him when he considered his prospects alone and unencumbered by faint-hearted companions as he set out through the chill, oddly rippled water.

Elation seeped from him, however, over the next few cycles of light and dark. It grew colder. He no longer bothered to gut and skin the shy frogs, but ate them whole, crouching above his prey.

He looked around. He'd been walking for days, yet where he was now looked no different from the place he'd started. The sky was the same flat silver blue high above his head. Crows still called unseen but near enough to imagine their beaks pecking at lidded eyes.

He stood very still after dropping twigs of straw on the surface of the water. They described lazy circles, then stopped.

He climbed out onto a downed cypress and watched the surface for any sign of the current. There was none. Until he touched it the water was absolutely unmoving with none of the faint ripples like church-window panes on its glassy surface. The current was dead.

If you lose the current for long you're dead. Handsome Frog's voice from long ago seemed to be coming from the cypress tree. *Find a dry place and wait.*

He settled on a mossy arm of the tree. His thoughts moved leisurely through his chances.

The bayou simmered, continuing almost audibly to rot his clothing and rust his metal grommets, buckles, and fittings.

The rain drizzled out, replaced by thin fog. The air hung motionless.

An armada of baby snakes slipped like copper wires through the water. His muscles cramped. He couldn't feel his extremities. A troop of creatures with many orange legs marched off the log and onto the rags of his linen shirt. He watched them without revulsion as they crossed his chest and distributed themselves back onto the log as though he existed only to be part of their geography.

He searched for some reminder that there were still straight lines in the universe. His eye was drawn to the joint of the tree, where it angled into its own reflection. He stared at the water. His yellow eyes looking back at himself were the only bright spots in an otherwise gray smear.

Several moments of looking at his own image reminded him of the humor in his situation. He grinned at his comical appearance—matted beard and hair, leather and linen tatters, prunelike toes at the mildewed seams of his Indian boots. . . .

He settled back, munching the last of Weeononka's journeycake. He had to chew it a long time to swallow each hard bite. But he considered his experiment a success; he'd proved an Indian journeycake could last for years and still remain edible.

What would the Sun King say if he could see his officer like this? A better question, What would His Majesty do if he found his royal self in such a pass as this? A king's toes would turn just as wrinkled as a fallen nobleman's, and the nobleman's the same as a commoner's. Going savage, indeed.

How far away the Court was, how long ago that afternoon he'd stepped onto the marble floor to receive the thanks of his sovereign. Maybe it had never happened at all. Maybe he had gone completely mad in the Sicilian gravel pit, and was still there to this day living a tangle of dream adventures that brought him in imagination to this nightmare swamp.

No, he thought, almost falling off the log. My body hurts too much for this to be imagination.

The water made a perfect mirror but he ignored his own face after that, watching the water only for sign of current. To fall into his own mind was a pit he must avoid. He emptied his thoughts of anything except the desire to get out of here alive.

Wait for the current. Handsome Frog had taught him that wisdom and the further wisdom of fighting the alligator. Was that a green hiss over there? The possibility startled him out of reverie. But evidently it had only been his own fear and not the 'gator chief snorting behind that cypress knee.

His aching body settled into welcome numbness in an unnaturally bent position. He clung on his left to an upright cypress branch that trailed an old man's beard of gray moss in the fatally still water.

A spider spun a web as big as King Louis' tent beside him. The memory of La Salle's outlandish white tent made de Tonti laugh heartily, laugh so hard he almost went overboard again. But he held on to the log, his laughter dying.

Jeweled dragonflies coupled in the steamy air.

A battalion of tiny insects he'd soon know about sensed a new delicacy in his European flesh. Other insects he could see crawled on him.

As though I'm a planet, he mused, reminded of how men crawled across the body of the Earth in search of a New World.

The water ringed beneath the spider's eight fragile legs that looked this close like the scaffolding around the *Griffin*. It was his engineer's turn of mind playing with a last splinter of rationalization. It amused him that this might finally be the last of him after so many travails along the way had failed to kill him.

Little would remain of Henri de Tonti. His right hand dangled close to the water, which held his only portrait. The hand would last awhile, of course, until the river completely rusted it. A marvelous toy, the hand he and Rob had created out of wine and words that Parisian night when the conquest of new worlds and all else seemed possible.

And this is where it ends. Very well. So be it. It had been a grand adventure. That was the final triumph and he wasn't at all sorry that he'd come to the beautiful Arkansas as fine and as fickle as a bitch wolf.

No regrets. He slept for a moment or a day; the light hardly changed. Dazzling blobs of swamp gas danced over the water that presently began to flow southeasterly due to continued upriver rainfall. But he slumped into exhausted sleep. In the manner of those who believe they are shortly going to die, he relived in dreams the peculiarities of life that had brought him to this place.

He felt the blessed current tugging at his hand as he woke in

a daze to the cries of a human baby followed by a splash that
almost swamped him off the log. He couldn't see the screaming
baby but he caught a flash of the living engine that stirred the
swamp, a continuation of nightmare. An alligator twice the
length of a war canoe and already trailing a long wake ignored
him on his log bed and was making for the irritatingly loud
shrieks. The massive, slate-green creature had only one eye.
Protruding from the other was the broken shaft of an arrow
that had collected a snarl of debris. Beyond the alligator's
bulbous nostrils as big as cannonballs and directly in its path
lay a decorated pitch-smeared basket snagged in cypress roots.

A fat little hand appeared clutching the basket edge,
followed by the round tattooed face of a healthy two-year-old
cinnamon-colored child. He stood up naked in the wobbling
little boat holding on for dear life, face puckered by distress.
The 'gator bumped the basket that was festooned with ribbons
and feathers. The little boy sat down, his shriek briefly
interrupted while he took a breath, winding up for another.

The monster circled back.

When it passed below de Tonti's feet, its long face seemed to
grin at him, *After I finish with this hors d'oeuvre, you will be
my entrée.*

When local people had told him a 'gator could get to this size
he had thought they were telling stories to see a Frenchman's
eyes get big. But the reports were true. This thing was at least
the length of three tall men. Its knobbed flesh looked like
another log just under the surface as it leisurely glided beside
de Tonti's perch toward the baby, who had found his scream
again; his large bright eyes saw what was coming.

Without thought de Tonti popped the hidden blade and
leaped on to the living barge.

It'll go to sleep if you can get one on its back, Handsome
Frog had said. *The problem is getting one on its back.*

It was difficult to imagine this armored living boat going to
sleep simply because of a tummy rub. But despite its size it
seemed a sluggish stupid creature. It was so big it was only
now realizing it had a rider.

Without finesse de Tonti started hacking at the forward part
of the body. He thought it would be quick work to simply find a
soft spot on the throat. He was horrified to pull back the
broken stump of his fine dagger. It had snapped on his second
blow against the jade flesh. The child stopped crying, apparently enthralled by the show. De Tonti could see nothing

except the great square bumps of alligator hide like cracked mudflats all around him.

His feet gripped under the stubby front legs, his own legs stretched to extreme by the girth. Incredible strength rippled through the deceptive body. It was trying to rub him off against the tree where he'd slept. His legs were numb in the cold water that turned pinkish where the submerged bark scraped his skin.

The monster got a whiff of blood. He started thrashing ponderously, lifting an awesome tail out of the water to slap at the irritating rider. The creature was moss-slick, hard to hold on to. De Tonti felt himself slide around like a loose saddle. He and the 'gator spun in deadly orbit around each other in the foamy water. With each dunking he swallowed water and came up gasping. What if the creature went to sleep on top of him under the water? Devoured or drowned, did it really matter?

De Tonti poked impotently under the beast's jaws with what was left of his knife. His foolish weapon didn't even scratch the skin. Briefly he was eye to eye with its one glassy orb; he'd swear he saw humor there. Was it just playing with him? How long this jockeying went on de Tonti could not calculate. His muscles screamed beyond endurance. He felt he'd drunk the entire vile swamp; the dashing he received riding the monster made him sick with vertigo. Though he had no doubt he could go on like this for some time, he didn't want to push it. The thing could outlast him. He must find some quick way to dispatch it before he collapsed. The monster must have been thinking similar thoughts because it lashed anew at the man, throwing him forward and sending a stinking hiss into his face.

No thought was attached to de Tonti's reply—he hammered the creature's nose with the metal hand. The fist sank into soft green tissue, hit bone, and bounced back. The reverberation rattled de Tonti all the way back to his teeth and hurt like hell back up his arm and shoulder. But the opponent was in even more pain. The mouth opened in a scream; the nose must be sensitive. De Tonti might have almost stood upright in the red-walled cavity thus revealed. A foul odor of rotten amphibians wafted from the savage innards. It almost knocked him over. From this angle he could see the broken arrow shaft had penetrated at an angle. The Indians usually barbed their arrowheads. That point must be lodged in the tissue of the 'gator's eye rather than through the skull—otherwise the creature would have died. If he could get a grip on the beast, maybe he could drive that arrow deeper. He hooked the metal hand into the corner of the mouth. With this purchase he struggled for a perch on its back. He reached out, grabbed the arrow shaft from behind, and plunged down on it with all his strength.

The beast screamed and thrashed, turning the water to foam. It closed its jaws around Mansard's finely wrought device. The fleshy angle of its jaw settled around the living part of his arm, pinching but not biting because the teeth were further forward grinding into metal. De Tonti looked for all the world as though he were reaching down into the alligator to retrieve something, not unlike the way he had reached around through the halved portal and into Jeanette's cabin long ago.

With his left hand the man held on to the shaft and the beast held on to the arm. The animal, bleeding from eye and nostril, writhed and tried to expel this foreign pest. But it was no use. He only flipped himself over, deadly for the alligator. His weak little legs flailed the air. Presently they stopped kicking. Man and 'gator were locked together as long as Madame Mansard's buckles held out. De Tonti floated half on half off that plated underbelly of the beast for some time until it dawned on him that there was the answer. He unbuckled the straps and slipped free, sacrificing the famous metal hand to the alligator king—the last *homage* the monster would ever swallow.

De Tonti had been stunned by that last tail swipe. He drifted in the water without moving until he felt the log nudge his back. He dragged himself onto its mossy bed and fell like a stone into black slumber.

Presently the little Taencas boy began to whimper.

The sachem's assistant stationed nearby had been told to make sure the chief took the sacrifice. But as the young man stared in wonder, he had seen the strange white man give the king his arm in place of the child—without screaming and without blood. The young sachem-in-training was spellbound. He didn't dare touch anything connected with this scene of mighty *wa kon* but slipped reverently away to find his master, who would know how to deal with this remarkable event.

The priest, a quick-eyed cunning Taencas in his late forties named Stony Owl, returned stealthily with his trembling assistant to see what was going on. It was indeed a scene of mighty *wa kon*, which would live in legend for a long time to come. They found the pitch-swabbed basket empty and drifted against the log where the sacrificial child was curled up asleep like a pup as close to the stranger as he could snuggle. In the sluggish water the 'gator chief lay upside down and dead, de Tonti's ripped-out sleeve trailing between ropy lips. Stony Owl was not as gullible as his helper but he was struck with puzzlement that the man who'd obviously lost an arm didn't bleed. With great care he examined the extremely hairy individual who was obviously some kind of barbarian. The sachem saw no new wound on the stranger's truncated arm but didn't enlighten the assistant. He covered the white man with his own robe and sent the apprentice with the little boy back to get help in carrying this odd person to his village, where the headmen could discuss what to do with him. It was a grave matter, interrupting the sacrifice.

Stony Owl had some time alone to ponder this event's implications for his personal and professional situation. His whole purpose among his people was to intercede on their behalf to the man-eating monster, which had terrified the Taencas and neighboring lowlanders for several winters. With the beast gone the sachem would lose face and power. Maybe the people, stirred up already with news of these white invaders and their metal magic, would have no more use for an aging priest. Worse still, they might give this stranger credit for killing the 'gator chief. As a headman he'd heard rumors and reliable reports from ravens of the famous metal-handed Frenchman. This, no doubt, was he.

Stony Owl poked at the leathery alligator lips with his feathered staff but was unable to pry them open from where he stood. Finally resigned to getting wet if he were to achieve his purpose, the priest set aside his treasured medicine bag and stepped into the water to see if he could get a better purchase on the dead-cold flesh of his erstwhile god. He was determined to see what it was the alligator had half swallowed. Only by further ruining his elaborately feathered costume was he able to lever open the jaws. Inside he found the most amazing thing he'd ever seen, a human hand made of metal, which surely had more *wa kon* than any infirm half-blind alligator. He knew his power was part intimidation, part magic tricks, but the sight of this object filled his cynical old heart with wonder. It seemed to him a direct comment from his manitou.

With drooping feathers Stony Owl dragged himself onto the log and began meticulously cleaning the object. He cut away the leather straps, careful to save the metal buckles. From time to time he glanced at the unconscious barbarian who would demand the return of his magic hand as soon as he woke up. From his medicine bag the sachem took a clam shell held closed with pitch traded at a dear price from some western tribe. He forced it open with his fingernail, extracted a pinch of brown vile-smelling powder then returned the closed shell to the pouch. Using his nail as a spoon he forced the mixture onto the barbarian's tongue. Satisfied that he had administered enough of the powerful narcotic to give himself time to make plans, he settled back to rub the brass hand until it shone like the disk of the sun. Truly this was a gift from the spirit world, the shaman thought with delight that pulled his creased face into a greedy smile. He found a rag of soft leather that brought even more luster to the hand. As he worked, he planned the magnificent ceremony he'd perform to introduce this new and wonderful object of fearful worship to his congregation.

The barbarian mumbled something. The sachem expected an utterly foreign language but was surprised when the stranger repeated the familiar name of the civil chief in the next tribe west of here. Stony Owl decided, as he slipped the metal hand into his medicine bag, to send a raven with this news to Weeononka since it was her name the barbarian muttered a final time before the drug took him down.

34

Weeononka sat with the council under the overhang of the Osotony cave. The afternoon was warm; she would have liked to go back to the lodge she shared with The Blossom and take a nap.

But there was a debate in progress and she had to stay in the council circle. She had to maintain a polite face toward the visitor from the north, who was engaging the councillors at this moment with his eloquent cold voice. She watched Game Dancer pose before the old Quapaw men. Beyond the circle other Osotony stood silently listening to the orator because what he was saying so ardently would affect every man, woman, and child in the band.

". . . and we feel sorrow for our brothers the Osotony Quapaw who lost so many children to the Chickasaw. We were too late to help you and we wish to make that up."

Weeononka knew he was lying. Many times now he'd sent ravens to her personally insisting that she come and share his groundlodge. He refused to accept her rejection and was now trying to win her through political strategy.

The Osotony had been poor ever since the Chickasaw attack and subsequent migration to this mountaintop above the river. His offer was generous—full adoption for the 150 Quapaw. His people must have had a good trading season to take on so many more mouths to feed. Game was scarce this dry spring season when it should be plentiful. Winter-maker was never far away. He was betting that the Osotony would pressure her into taking him as husband so they could benefit from his charity.

"For these reasons and many more of kinship ties it would please our mutual ancestors for the Osage and the Osotony Quapaw to be reunited as one nation, as it was in the days of the great wandering," he said as a sort of conclusion. Weeononka sensed he'd never conclude his proposal; he would go at forcing her the way he'd gone at the horse. Some brave probably bet him I wouldn't return, she thought sourly.

The old men mumbled among themselves and finally Many Trees Talking stood to speak. "We thank you, our Osage brother, but we fear great darkness for the Osotony if their small voice were lost among the many Osage voices."

Weeononka surmised that Game Dancer had prepared every argument, because he answered without reflection, "This honorable council can elect two members to serve with our own council." This was an unprecedented offer; usually the absorbed clan took the identity of the absorbers.

"And our sacred bundle?" the old man queried, so dignified in his ceremonial buffalo horns.

"You may either lodge it with ours with equal honor or honor it with a separate council lodge for as long as even one Osotony lives."

Weeononka thought he was making it too sweet. So far during this council meeting he had not so much as looked her way. But everyone present, Osage and Quapaw, knew she was the deciding factor here. All she had to do was become Game Dancer's wife. He was making this play directly on the council's private motives. One Thunder Turtle and the other headmen on the council worried about Weeononka being manless, a state considered dangerous for any woman but positively hazardous for the entire tribe in the case of a chief woman. The *wa kon* must be balanced.

Nobody except The Blossum seemed to understand or care that she loathed Game Dancer. Before this public ploy she had to finally ask him not to send any more requests to her. She had flatly rejected his suit in front of witnesses. It had infuriated him the last time. He rode off on one of his tamed horses—now he was famous as a horse trader—with several of his men behind him whooping and scaring everyone.

Then, this unannounced overt formal petition to the councillors. She sat there listening to the Osotony elders discuss which of them would sit on the Osage council, wondering how she was going to get out of this one.

For the first time Game Dancer was looking at her. Very pointedly he seemed to be putting the final word to her: He wanted his answer immediately. One by one the councillors turned to watch Weeononka, their arguments trailing off into the smoke.

Her position as chief woman was not as a formal council member. She acted—along with The Blossum, who gave her more and more traditional duties—as an advisor. She was the council's official hostess, the one who usually started and maintained the council fires. She never spoke unless asked for an opinion but she was always asked. In this case nobody had brought up the subject, Game Dancer having been there only since that morning when he had come directly off the trail with his petition to the council. Even the little children knew that it wasn't up to the council to decide this issue.

Everyone was waiting for her decision. She stood and gave herself the luxury of a good, long stretch. They'd been talking all morning and everyone inside and outside the council circle wished to stretch, too. "I think it's time to serve our honored guests some food," she said, gesturing to one of the wives who had been preparing *sagamite* for the council. A kind of informal feast ensued. Everyone was animated at the prospects, and buzzing with speculation about what she'd decide. Those close to Weeononka knew she didn't even like to share food with the northern chief much less consent to be his wife. Others said she was just drawing it out so he'd consider her more valuable. The Blossum knew the truth, that she'd never willingly live with the man. The difficulty was phrasing her rejection in such a way that Game Dancer didn't lose face. The Osage and Quapaw were friendly now but had fought in the past over just this kind of family difficulty. The older councillors remembered and did not want to fight the Osage ever again.

Game Dancer discreetly stayed away from her though she could feel his eyes boring into her when she turned away. She walked with a small bowl among the people, speaking to this one and that, relishing the fine breeze that had come up from the canyon.

Why, she wondered, would anyone want to leave this place? The Osotony had found a perfect sanctuary, a great deep cave open on the south side of an ancient dead volcanic mountain the white people would someday call Petit Jean. The cave was ideally situated above a year-round spring. All their lodges fit under the brow of the cavern while up on the plateau a short distance above them lay plenty of flat land for corn, for a dancing ground, and for a playing field for the men's traditional ball game, a rowdy confused melee where they inflicted large and small wounds on each other with hooped sticks to gain possession of a padded ball.

From either end of the west-east mountain could be seen the verdant river valley and the meandering Arkansas below catching the color of the sky. Near the cave a crater lake brimmed with small fat fish, and the swamps were near enough for parties of hunters to go down from time to time to supplement their larders. The buffalo prairie was within sight on the north face of the mountain, where a lookout could follow the herd's movements from the vantage point of this long, flat bump on the vast rolling prairie. Here on this sacred mountain the Osotony Quapaw healed their wounds and looked with some hope toward the future. As long as there was plentiful rain and the stream held out, the people could survive here in peace and relative seclusion from the encroaching white men who were busy down on the river.

As far as she saw it, there was no need to take the Osage's insulting charity. Weeononka caught The Blossum's glance across the buzzing crowd; she was thinking the same thing.

The Osage warriors who accompanied Game Dancer were beginning a ball game with some of the young Osotony men, so everyone went up to the plateau playing field. The ground was muddy from days of rain but they didn't care—mud made the wild game more interesting.

The contest was well under way when the onlookers' attention was drawn to a Taencas raven who came trotting, sweat-streaked and puffing, into their midst. He ran through the curious throng directly to Weeononka, who had just sat

down in the cottonwood shade with the other women to watch
the sport. The players didn't let the newcomer interrupt the
game but several heads turned, diverted from the play, to see
them in private conversation. "I will walk back with you to the
cavern where you can refresh yourself with food and water,"
she said so that many heard, "and then you can join our men
on the playing field." She walked toward the downhill path
with him. There was speculation about what was important
enough to take her away from the game, but no one followed.
Game Dancer watched from the sideline of play until he
reluctantly allowed himself to be drawn into the game though
his eyes followed Weeononka. Ball was not his game; he
preferred knife and arrow contests. He was playing because he
was expected to do so. When Weeononka didn't return, he
dropped out as soon as he could civilly take leave, after the
long first set. By the time he arrived at the cavern, she was
gone. The Blossum shrugged when Game Dancer demanded
to know what the urgent message was that had prompted the
chief woman to insult him by leaving without a farewell.

"The raven spoke only to Weeononka," The Blossum
replied, seeing Game Dancer's face redden in rage.

"Weeononka begged your forgiveness but felt that since you
are a chieftain you'd understand her devotion to duty."

"Duty to what?" Game Dancer's voice was too loud in
addressing The Blossum, who was an honored person. She
lowered her eyes to chastise him, and he continued in a
softened tone that was almost an unwarrior-like whine, "She
was to give the council an answer."

"She left a private message for you." Her gentle voice
snagged him. He leaned closer, suddenly modest. "She asked
me to say that she would take you as husband if advised to do
so by her joking relative." She was scrupulous in not mention-
ing Crow Sister's name, but watched his face for some emotion
to betray him. They'd been hearing some terrible rumors
about Crow Sister. Nobody from the Osage village would say
anything for fear of Game Dancer. The fact that none would
mention her name, as would be the case if she were dead, had
an ominous implication. It was The Blossum's idea to test him.

Game Dancer was stony cold, as impenetrable as a frozen
lake before the crippled old woman with the twinkling eyes. It
did not show but his instinct was rattled: How much did she
know?

"What Taencas village was that raven from?" he demanded.

"I forgot to ask," The Blossum replied, watching him as he scanned the cavern for the courier.

Game Dancer repressed fury when he found the man had returned to his village with Weeononka. The northern chieftain departed with his men that same day, indignant and without a formal goodbye to the council.

Once again Weeononka was walking the trace, this time with a foreign envoy and an entourage befitting a chief woman: her handsome young son Two Hands, One Thunder Turtle, and seven warriors as bodyguard. She knew what lay ahead; Stony Owl had sent a singing raven, a storyteller, so he gave her much information about the white man whom the Taencas sachem claimed to have saved from the alligator chief. Though she was thoughtfully grave as was fitting, inside her heart was singing after a day and a half on the trail by foot and by bateau down the Nigestai River and southward overland to the Taencas village.

Could it be true that Iron Hand had come to her after all these winters? How many white men of his description could be roaming around in the Blue Temple? Still, she wasn't sure; no mention was made by Stony Owl's raven about the metal hand, so it could well be some other white man waiting for her just ahead in the Taencas village. There was some kind of celebration going on. The Taencas drums, bells, and voices could be heard from here, still some way from the encampment on the edge of the Blue Temple.

One Thunder Turtle and one of his men went ahead to announce their chief woman's arrival to the shaman who had summoned her. Weeononka spread out a buffalo robe and sat down with Two Hands to rest for the encounter. She had been so concerned about her own feelings she hadn't been paying attention to her son's nervous attitude. The boy, long-limbed like herself and golden-eyed like his father, stared at the path where One Thunder Turtle would return.

"Maybe it isn't him," he said when she caught his eye.

"We'll soon know."

"It won't be." He had a serious personality for his nearly seven winters.

She put her arm around him even though she knew he didn't want to be treated like a child with these warriors present. One warrior had gone off to kill an offering of food. The other four men had stationed themselves in a loose circle around their chief woman and were looking outward, adjusting

their feathers and robes, checking the points on their
weapons, speaking softly with their comrades of other things
than a small boy's pride.

"You really want it to be your father, don't you, *Nopa'nom
paa*?" She used his Quapaw name but had proudly taught him
his father's language, too. She ached when she saw evidence of
his longing for the one thing she'd not been able to give him
and loved him all the more that he was trying to be so grown
up about not having it.

"I just want to know him," the boy replied, squinting
because the sun that mild early spring day in Crow Moon was
at about its zenith behind his mother's head. It had been cold,
wet, and rainy until this morning when the sun had broken out
and the earth seemed finally ready to turn green and warm
again.

Presently the war chief returned and so did the hunter with
a still-warm doe across his shoulders. "*Hopo, hopo!*" said the
war chief to everyone as they took up the trail into the village.

Weeononka officially presented the venison to Stony Owl at
the door flap of the council lodge, largest of the dome-shaped
buildings in the Taencas village, and he ushered her inside to
sit in the position of honored guest. The procedure was long
and complicated by protocol but finally Stony Owl, Weeononka, and One Thunder Turtle went alone to observe the
unconscious white man where he lay in the medicine lodge,
attended by a near-blind grandmother of ancient days.

Weeononka steadied herself against a lodgepole. Truly it was
Iron Hand, in a drowning sleep with his lovable smile deep on
his beautiful whiskered face. It was as though she'd never been
away from him. All the old feelings warmed her. Though she
felt her body utter a cry that could be heard all the way to the
Lake in the Mountain, she restrained herself from touching
him or showing any outward emotion. But the old sachem was
observant; he'd seen her eyes dilate with a twinkle reflected off
the cedar fire, which was kept burning to cleanse the sickroom
air. He knew that he had a profitable deal on his hands.

She gave One Thunder Turtle a prearranged signal because
it would have been a breach of etiquette for a woman to
bargain directly with a man. One Thunder Turtle indicated
with a traditional gesture that the matter should be discussed.
The sachem invited them both to accompany him back to the
council chamber, where they found several Taencas elders

waiting for the action to begin. Negotiations started without further ceremony.

The Turtle felt he could have gotten a better deal, but Weeononka was unable to suppress her glow, which even the squinting crone could detect, and Stony Owl was unable to pass up an advantage. He kept upping the ante so the bargain took much conversation.

The upshot of the haggle was this: In return for the barbarian, Weeononka would trade to Stony Owl the glass beads she'd been hoarding since her days among the Iroquois, half the Osotony's store of salt, fourteen of their finest cooking baskets and boiling stones, a bale of winter-kill groundsquirrel pelts, three pots of honey, the clan's only French iron pot given to her uncle-husband by a trapper many winters before, and a bolt of red European cloth The Blossum had managed to hold on to for twenty winters. (Both items she had saved from the Chickasaw attack because of long habit—she had safeguarded them in the corn cache. It was because of her search for those treasures that she had stumbled on to the tribe's sacred bundle where Weeononka had hastily stashed it.)

All this represented a large portion of the Osotony's real and symbolic wealth. The look on One Thunder Turtle's scarred face clearly indicated that he considered Weeononka a rash negotiator, but he proctored her bids anyway. Any husband his chief woman would take was better than none, even this odd French specimen. It warmed his heart to see her light up the way she had for this one after her recent fancy footwork to avoid Game Dancer.

Outside, as it grew dark the Taencas continued their dance of religious celebration. Weeononka was vaguely aware of the shouts and songs but her mind was on the deal so she didn't pay any attention to the content of their chants. Much later, after they had arrived at their bargain, she inadvertently discovered what the Taencas were celebrating.

They were joined by more elders, her Quapaw team, and the boy. The men smoked a finalizing pipe and a light meal was shared by all, then later the men went out to observe the celebration in progress. Weeononka stayed inside the council lodge until Two Hands fell asleep. It had been an exciting day for him and though he was tired he refused as long as he could to give in to slumber. But finally it overtook him. When she was certain he was out, she crept across the lodge toward the door to get some fresh air and relieve herself. But her foot accidentally kicked the Taencas's sacred bundle propped on its pedestal of crossed and bound buffalo bones.

What tumbled out was the tactile history of the Taencas clan, which had occupied these swamps long before the Quapaw had drifted downstream. There were bits of painted shells, coils of hair, a long string of river pearls, nuggets of native copper, desiccated animal skulls, and a gleaming yellow metal hand.

Instinctively Weeononka glanced over her shoulder to see if her sacrilegious stumble had been witnessed, but she was alone with her sleeping child inside the round-ceilinged lodge. Very quickly she stuffed the sacred Taencas objects back into the medicine bundle, but she lingered over the European artifact. Without question it was Iron Hand's, but for some reason she hesitated to touch it. Outside, the celebration swung into a faster tempo and she realized, though incompletely, that the festivities had something to do with this object. Without further thought she grabbed it and hid it inside her own parfleche. She stood to go outside when a thought arrested her: Did she really want her white man to have this thing?

Weeononka stood there in the flickering shadows weighing alternatives. She returned to her parfleche and removed the brass hand, touching it as though it burned her fingers. She didn't breathe until she had put it back in the Taencas's sacred bundle. It would be safer here than anywhere. Stony Owl would protect it with his life.

She stood again, straightened her clothing, and walked out of the council lodge with her head high and her heart pounding.

The next morning she and her people departed with Iron Hand on a litter between four of the warriors, and with Stony Owl's man, who would take back the trade goods. Later Weeononka learned the sachem planned to use their French cooking pot for a helmet. It did rather resemble the metal hats the Spanish wore. Weeononka hoped privately Stony Owl got his head stuck, but it didn't really matter. All that mattered was that Iron Hand had come back to her though she suspected Stony Owl had drugged him heavily. He had no wounds but was out like the dead. She bit her lip pensively as she watched him sleeping. Some of the swampfolk medications could make a grown man stupid forever.

De Tonti came out from under the drug in subdued light a day later, the peaceful sounds of human activity somewhere outside. The first thing he saw was a child playing with a padded leather ball and a looped stick on the buffalo fleece robe beside him. At first he thought it was the child from the basket. But it became obvious when the boy turned his face in de Tonti's hazed direction that this child was older, at least six or seven.

And this one stared frankly with familiar golden eyes. *"Bonjour, mon père."* The French had a familiar accent to it, but the child was up and gone too fast for questions. He returned moments later with a woman. Then there was Weeononka's face before him. She saw that the man on the pallet in her lodge was awake. In the tradition of her people the one awakening from prolonged unconsciousness must be treated with great deference, having just returned from the Country of the Sun. Very seldom did a person return from travels in that place so the event was treated with silent respect. The traveler was allowed to pick up the rope of life at his own speed.

He watched her without expression. Then when he was very sure she was not a dream, when understanding brightened in his eyes that matched the child's beside her, she gently lay down next to him. The boy played quietly as the woman and man found each other with their eyes.

They didn't speak for a long time but lay together communicating in silences, touching with tentative fingers while wonder lingered between them like a glow.

Presently the boy wandered outside where other children laughed, leaving the man and woman to wrap themselves around each other, applying to body and soul the ancient healing *wa kon*–medicine of the blanket. Then they talked, filling in the years life had thrown between them.

35

It was as natural as a sunrise.

He settled into their life without a seam, more serene and soul-satisfied than he had thought it possible to be. His former life seemed a fever dream he'd awakened from that afternoon in Weeononka's lodge. This was simply *home*.

The Osotony, having heard of Iron Hand for years, revered

him as a man of great *wa kon*. Within days he was thinking of
them as his people. Did he not in fact own this entire
province?

He thought of himself exclusively now as Iron Hand, and
the Siouan translation of that phrase was the name the people
knew him by, even without the object that had given the name
to him. Since any metal was spirit to them, they considered
the name meant his missing "spirit" hand. The only metal most
of them had ever seen was their old iron pot and French
hatchets. They wouldn't know brass from gold and would care
less; it was European-influenced Indians such as the Illinois
who had nicknamed him Iron Hand. It continued as his name
here because that was what Weeononka and his reputation
called him before he had come among them.

His old name was not the only fragment he'd lost of his
civilized life. Even the shirt he wore in the swamp was gone,
rotted to tatters Weeononka finally had to burn. She gave him
three beautiful leather suits, however, after they were married
in the simple ceremony of her people: He brought meat he'd
killed and she in turn fed him corncakes. They both felt they'd
truly wed on their Mississippi island, but went through this
ritual for the benefit of the council and the rest of the people.

Nobody so much as spoke Game Dancer's name. The elders
were pleased the problem of the unmated chief woman was
solved without having to move. The women rejoiced. The
spirit of the Mother was said to favor tribes with happily mated
chief women.

Iron Hand was considered a great catch. The Osotony
wanted the iron cooking pots, mirrors, and guns he promised.
They instinctively sensed that this white man could help them
with his fellows when the need arose. They wanted to be
richer than their cousins, the Osage, whom they could now
afford to remember had insulted the Osotony by demanding
charity.

The Blossum particularly approved of this stranger who had
moved into the lodge. Between Weeononka and Iron Hand
she saw a familiar fire.

And Two Hands, the handsome child with golden eyes,
loved him instantly. Weeononka had been telling her son all
his life about his wonderful father, trying to make him proud of
the man in his absence, which she had accepted as permanent
until that night when she bought Iron Hand from the Taencas.
He and his pack cost a great deal. But Iron Hand was worth

any price. From that moment, life started again for her. Before his return she had merely walked around pretending to be alive. Now her heart was home.

He had grieved, much to Weeononka's guilt, when he was told that nobody had thought to retrieve the metal hand from the monster's body, now long drifted away to become food for legends and a square meal for thousands of small stomachs. She bit her lip and held her secret in silence, letting One Thunder Turtle tell him how he was bought from the Taencas shaman, who swore the white man had not been wearing a metal hand when he was found.

Also gone without explanation was his hat. Iron Hand expected eventually to see it on some chief's head. He missed that old hat as much as the hand though he'd come to depend on the hand's hidden blade.

He rarely said anything explicit about wanting the hand, but Weeononka knew it was on his mind. She thought about her silence in the still of a long night, but before dawn, reconfirmed her decision not to tell him about the hand's existence. She was sure they would all lose him if he had the thing back. It never really left her, this feeling that it was wrong to withhold it from him, but it was the only way she knew to keep him.

One morning, it was still on her mind as she went about her beading. From time to time she glanced at him as he went through his parfleche. He was glad the sachem had saved the travel bag when they brought him out of the jungle but he growled when he had seen that the sachem had taken, in addition to his purchase price, an agent's fee from the bag. The fee: the two extra knife blades, a copper cup, and a pistol.

"It's a crooked dealer who profits in both directions," Iron Hand muttered, shuffling the meager reminders of his other life. He'd given her the white cloth, thread, and needles.

"We didn't know what you had in the bag, so we couldn't have bargained for it," Weeononka replied, not looking up from her beading. "Perhaps you can speak to the Taencas sachem someday."

"What do you think he did with that child?" he asked casually as he sniffed the ruined gunpowder then tossed the sack aside.

"The one you saved from the beast?"

He nodded, catching her eye over her work. She smiled, pleasured by the least contact with him. She knew he was

happy here, probably happier than he'd ever been in his life.
These whites pushed so hard against their *aneh*. No wonder
half of them were *windigo*.

"I'm sure he was unfit for further sacrifice."

He gave her an odd look. She never felt this white man
judging her as inferior, a feeling she'd gotten from others of his
color. But sometimes he seemed to be studying her in a way
she couldn't understand, making decisions about her people
from her answers to his questions.

"What does that mean?" He was untangling the rope, using
his hand and the stump to make a coil, sailor-fashion.

"He returned the baby to its mother."

"Disgusting people."

"Yes," she replied with a wry smile, "but I understand since
some barbarian killed the monster, the Taencas don't sacrifice
to the 'gator king anymore."

"Your people don't do that sort of thing, eh?"

"Not in anyone's memory."

"Agh," he replied enigmatically.

She caught the judgmental note in his voice, and felt some
explanation was necessary: "We lost so many on the great
wandering. Someday when Winter-maker walks outside and
it's time to recall, I will tell you the old stories, white man. We
are the Quapaw," she crooned in a ritual chant, "the remnant
who drifted downstream. . . ." Then in a more ordinary voice
she spoke directly to him as though he were any man and not
the one who had her heart. "So many of our children died in
those days. We gave up the practice forever of sacrificing any
human beings for any gods."

Sparks of understanding illuminated his memory of what she
had done to her first baby.

"That little Taencas boy is very lucky," she continued,
starting another row of yellow quills on the moccasin she was
decorating for The Blossum. "Because he was saved by Iron
Hand, he'll grow up with much *wa kon*."

"That's important to you?" He didn't like the idea of being
somebody's diety. Nibbling at him was the prospect that they
might start sacrificing to him.

"*Wa kon* is the most important thing there is."

It melted him to see her smile like that. She was glowing.
She admitted that she had been growing hard and bitter that
so much of her life had been a dangerous disappointment to
her. But since he'd come back to her she'd seen the error of

that path and was once again alive. It pleased him immeasurably to be the agent of her joy. He abandoned the tangled rope and crawled on knees and elbows to lay his head in her lap. "I don't think white people have *wa kon.*"

She lay aside the beading. "You do, Iron Hand. You have more of it than any man I've ever known."

"Even more than your Quapaw husband?"

It felt good for her to be combing out his damp braid with her fingers.

"Your *wa kon* is different from his." She massaged his temples. "He had a flair for knowing the moment to act. You have that but you have even more *wa kon* and it has to do with metal."

He turned over so he could see her face. "Not anymore." He gestured with his right arm. He was long used to the absent weight of the metal hand but it still felt naked. The stump was altogether ugly to him, and though he'd long ago accepted it, he was surprised she showed no disgust.

"But you do, still, don't you see?"

He rolled over, stretched out against her, and leaned on his elbows. "No, I don't see."

"Your name is Iron Hand. You were known here before you came."

Privately she was torn again. The selfish secret burned inside her heart. She knew he would begin to think seriously about returning to his other life if he had that hand. It was bound to remind him of the way things had been for him.

"Someone could say I'm just a crippled Frenchman and not the real Iron Hand."

She ached with seeing how much he longed for his hand, but she hid her feelings behind a shrug, having no answer she wished to share. He was right, of course. Another alternative she had not mentioned violated her own personal code about the sacredness of a person's name. "Maybe your manitou will give you a new name that reflects your new life, beloved husband," she suggested timidly, coming as close as her scruples allowed to the subject. A person's name was so intimate, so wrapped in his *aneh*, it was considered a breach to make such a suggestion. She would never dare to suggest he change his name; that was for the man and his manitou to decide and even a wife could not interfere. She would not have dared to make even that vague comment to a red man or woman but she knew the whites did not hold the same sacred regard for such things. She saw that he thought this a mild joke because he chuckled. I'll never understand these people, she thought, not even this one I love. These thoughts clouded her face, but he misinterpreted. "Did you like me better with the metal hand?" he asked, stroking her cheek with his thumb.

She thought for a moment before answering. "Iron Hand, when I first saw white people, I thought they all must be some kind of spirits with those weapons and suits of metal. But by the time I met you I was disillusioned with their power. I still believed there might have been some kind of inhuman power in your metal hand and I was afraid of it, afraid it would touch me and make me metal, somehow; make me a white woman instead of a red woman. I did not understand, you see, that making metal is an ordinary thing for human beings to do. That's why Two Hands has his name. Until I first saw him I wasn't sure that some part of him might not be metal like his father. I was so happy that he was flesh and blood. This doesn't mean I hated the metal you wore. It just means that I love you, the man, not some part of you."

It was a moving speech that moved him to want to make love. She seemed in a more serious mood so he asked her a serious question: "Do you think the people accept me as Iron Hand?"

"They accept you because I accept you."

Her words gave him cause for reflection. She knew her people better than he did. He wanted to please them, but the truth was he longed to have the hand back. His arm was often cold and he had developed the habit of rubbing or holding the end of it. It was comforting to slip his arms into their opposite sleeves like a mandarin in leather instead of silk. This was a funny image that made him chuckle at the memory of La Salle's route to China.

Chinese person, the king had called the explorer. *Beware the savage call*. Now he understood what that meant. Would the king under similar circumstances have chosen differently? He imagined Louis XIV feathered like an Indian. Was Louis much different from the Iroquois war chief who stooped to touch a barbarian because he needed his services? *La Chine* was a state of mind. He thought, *I have reached my own China*.

Thereafter he kept his bare arm covered in public, where he was more and more frequently seen.

He spent long afternoons in the council lodge discussing terms and items of trade the whites would give in exchange for fur. He would have preferred the higher quality of winter kills but was pleased as the peltry bundles were beginning to stack up in a dry nook in the back of the cave. They had word along the raven network that a French trapper was due to come through these parts before summer was over. The council was debating Iron Hand's suggestion to get a better trade by transporting their pelts via the river to Arkansas Post. Even though they did not invite him to hunt, they took his advice about trapping and packing trade peltries in a manner the whites would approve.

Though they included him concerning trade, it irritated him that he was never invited to join the men when they team-hunted, or in their ball game. It was pleasant to watch the sport, but he'd rather be a player.

In it he recognized the game he'd seen the Iroquois play, what in New France was called *lacrosse*. The northern version was more formalized than this dust-deviling Quapaw free-for-all. But both games were played with a stuffed leather ball batted about by sticks with baskets woven into the end.

The braves would divide into teams and fight each other to get the ball to their respective goals—painted, carved posts decorated with feathers at each end of the long playing ground. One of the more agile of the older men acted as a kind of referee. His duties were signaling the beginning of play, keeping a hash-mark score, and retrieving the ball when it fell out of bounds.

Sometimes everyone in the village would come up for a contest. Little boys from time to time would hang around the sidelines, although this was strictly a man's sport, and the boys played only in their own private games, where they practiced for their manhood. A couple of times his own son crouched watching with him. But often the play continued with himself as the only spectator.

When the ball rolled toward the cottonwood that shaded spectators, he was pleased to pitch it back to the game master with a strong enough serve to prove he could compete, but still none of the players invited him to join. He decided it must be because he had only one hand.

But that had nothing to do with it as he discovered one hot clear day. Because of the dry season, the women were unusually busy hauling water to their corn crop. Ever since hearing of the green corn festival he had been curious about participating in it. Now, seeing some chance to witness this infamous savage dance of the corn, he offered his services toward its cultivation as water carrier.

For his trouble the women snickered at him. He'd considered his offer generous and was offended by their rejection. He'd gone so far as to contemplate a system of ditches and log locks to bring irrigation from the lake to their randomly planted fields. Weeononka and The Blossom could barely contain their laughter when he tried to explain his design to them.

"Don't you know your male *wa kon* will stunt the ears?" The Blossom scolded as she accompanied the workers to the fields for good luck. She and the others, all young women naked except for their short working kilts, smiled shyly at his ignorance as they went on their way. "Go to the ball field like the other men," she laughed over her shoulder.

He had noticed the men never helped with agricultural work, but nobody had explained that his European chivalry was bad for the corn.

Piqued into a bad mood and feeling somewhat useless, he wandered over to the cottonwood tree. After a while, One Thunder Turtle dropped out of the play and approached him with the greeting, *"Tahunsa,"* or "Cousin."

Iron Hand, absorbed in the current play, missed a chance to ask why he was being addressed with that word for the first time.

"I see you like our game," said the war chief as he wiped a smear of bloody sand from his upper lip. "Do the men of the French tribe run screaming at each other bashing heads like this?"

"Only among the Iroquois have I seen such a sport," he answered in sign.

"It's a very old game with special laws." One Thunder Turtle's voice dropped. "A long time ago the winners won the lives of the losers, which they took by slitting their throats with obsidian knives. It was a holy game in those days, played in place of war between nations." He chuckled softly, sizing up the white man to determine what kind of player he might make. "I'm sorry we can't ask you to join us."

"I respect your customs," Iron Hand replied a little stiffly, stung by two rejections in one day. "But I have wondered why."

"You see, you must be a Red or a Black," the Turtle tried to explain, "but since you are neither you cannot play. It's the same with hunting and battle teams. . . ." He shrugged, unable to briefly educate Weeononka's white man in the intricate moiety relationships that structured tribal society.

But without such explanation, it didn't sound reasonable. Iron Hand thought he might have misunderstood as One Thunder Turtle continued, "Would you like to know this game?"

When Iron Hand indicated enthusiastically that he would, the war chief immediately began a detailed analysis of the play in progress, which they could barely follow through the wall of dust. He gave a critical description of the players' performances and added how he would have handled it—he was a Black. His team had just lost possession of the battered ball, which was about the size of a gourd. When it was over and the men wandered away, discussing their bets in pairs and threes, for a dip in the nearby lake, they did not ask him to join them. But later that evening they surprised him. At dusk the warriors gathered in ritual feathers to give him an unexpected ceremony.

"You came to us from the Country of the Sun where the dead ones go," said One Thunder Turtle as he incised a sunburst tattoo on Iron Hand's thigh. "It is only fitting for this new Quapaw to have the sun as his manitou," said the warrior, referring to the unconscious state in which Iron Hand had arrived. He laid aside the tattooing knife and rubbed ashes into the searing design, then helped the initiate in his buffalo robes to stand. They gave him a dog feast, which he survived, and danced the calumet. He parceled out most of his remaining civilized artifacts in the traditional gift-giving that he knew was expected. The entire village chanted and played music until dawn. This initiation moved him deeply; that night under the stars with soot scalding his thigh and a powerful smoke in his lungs he experienced a keen shaft of spiritual enlightenment he'd never felt in any church.

The next afternoon One Thunder Turtle approached him as the day's game was getting under way. "But you aren't ready to play!"

"But you said—"

"That you must be either a Red or a Black. Last night you became a Black." Because the Turtle had sponsored him, the new Osotony took his color. This was appropriate since Iron Hand was mated to a woman of Red moiety, and must have the opposite designation.

Iron Hand took the wispy little wand in his hand. He

swatted it around a few times before One Thunder Turtle commented on his grip. It was an unexpectedly resilient rod about a finger wide, which the players called a "buffalo tail." It was made of a fire-hardened single whip from a young hickory tree, water-bent and tied with rawhide so that it looped on the end. Cross thongs of secured rawhide formed the basket.

He played clumsily left-handed but the players each thanked him politely for joining as though he were a visiting champion. As the game wore on they proceeded to beat him black and blue. He took a few of them, too, and when it was over and they were soaking their bruises in the lake, One Thunder Turtle called, "Woodsman!" to Many Trees Singing. The old headman had been the referee this afternoon so was bathing the dust off with the players.

"Do you think you could make a different kind of buffalo tail for our new cousin here?"

"I've made every kind of wooden object you can imagine, Snapper. Tell me something new." The old man was stretched out in the shallows on his back with his eyes closed enjoying the late sun.

Iron Hand understood what the war chief meant. Left-handed he'd never be good enough to benefit his team or even enjoy the game. "If you could make a similar basket on the other end of a stick, I could wear it like a glove and play right-handed." He lapsed into French to say this. It was a concept beyond Many Trees Singing. Like most tribal people he was ambidextrous. Iron Hand decided it was because they didn't write, and therefore, didn't discriminate between hands. Even so, the woodcarver said he could devise such a ball stick for the new *tahunsa*. A few days later Iron Hand was in fine form on the court, his specially designed buffalo tail the talk of the village. Weeononka and Two Hands watched proudly from the cottonwood as their man helped the Blacks take an easy win. He played whenever possible thereafter, taking quickly to the sport as though he'd been at it a lifetime.

Veterans of the game said he had the most discriminating cut and slash they'd ever encountered. His racket found the ball like a goose finds her egg in the thickest dust or the deepest crunch of fighting bodies. Iron Hand gave credit to his early training with two swords. Any observer could see, however, it was the way he used the racket as though it were an extension of himself that placed him ahead of players who were limited to a mere grip on the wand.

Sometimes talk of the game would spill over into the council chamber, which took several players away from the field these days.

It was a dry season and the council occupied itself with the question of whether to begin the rain dance. Iron Hand listened to their august deliberations. Once begun, the rain dance literally did not stop until it rained. The implication sank into his still-European mind. These people would dance in shifts until it rained, whenever that might be. They were close to deciding to begin.

Only Many Trees Singing, the carpenter, held out. "I hear the trees screaming every night." He made a mournful sound that put chills on Iron Hand's arms. He could imagine this being the scream of a tree going under the saw.

Many Trees Singing continued in a less dramatic voice, "The whites are cutting down trees all around the old river site. My bones tell me they are headed this way." He wanted to pick up everything, the whole tribe, and follow the freshest buffalo trail west. "Despite hostile people in that direction they have red skins like us." He gave Iron Hand a nod. "With all due respect to our newest cousin, red men are nowhere near as bad as the majority of these whites from the east who are cutting down everything in their path."

Iron Hand confirmed that his countrymen would continue to cut down trees. "But the Quapaw can learn many things from them that will make their lives and the lives of their children easier." Unvoiced was growing conflict in him he did not want to confront, that his own and these people might never be able to cohabit. It was a terrible thought he quickly repressed because his own schemes were so hopeful. If they could adapt fast enough, the Quapaw might survive here with the whites, as the Christianized Kappa had done. He was forging a commitment to help them accomplish it and keep the best of the life he'd grown to love among them.

He kept these thoughts to himself, but told them, "It seems to me your best chance is to stay here and pursue the new way of trading with the French. At least one Frenchman is your friend," he said, raising an enthusiastic round of agreement among them.

Many Trees Singing politely joined, but continued his argument for migration. However, he did not carry the majority. The Osotony had not completely settled in this place. Many of their numbers were elderly. They had three pregnant

women with their precious cargoes to think of. All but a
handful of children in the last generation had been taken off by
the Chickasaw. The tribe still mourned.

Despite the fact that lowland tribes thought this mountain
too sacred to live upon, the Quapaw found it to their liking.
Especially with Iron Hand's pelts traded for corn and other
white goods, many believed the mesa would support the clan
without a buffalo hunt this season.

Even in this drought the plateau abounded in all kinds of
small game. This benevolent cavern's open south face let in a
pleasant sunlight, would protect against Winter-maker's big
moccasins, and snared a fair breeze to draft away the smoke of
their firesides.

In short the Quapaw didn't want to pull up stakes right now.
But changing from the old way of the annual buffalo hunt was a
gamble that challenged their traditions. Nobody knew if
there'd be enough game on this mountain in the winter. The
buffalo on whom the tribe had formerly depended for its
subsistence were scattering off the great plain. The hunt had
been postponed too long because the brow lookout had not
seen the telltale dustcloud in more than a moon. Scouts
returned with no sign of a herd. But when it rained, the herd
would return and the ordeal of a migration wouldn't be
necessary.

Iron Hand leaned back on a buffalo robe in the rear ranks of
the council chamber, thinking if they decided to go out for
buffalo, he would of course accompany them. If they decided
to dance for rain, however, he'd take the opportunity to return
to the Caddo. He had an idea. There was no chance of
recovering the watch but he thought he could talk the Caddo
chief out of the ball lead he'd left. If he could get more metal to
add to the lead shot he gave to Weeononka, he could cast
another hand. These thoughts were interrupted by the echoes
of a commotion outside in the cavern that could only mean
visitors. Without moving from his spot, he leaned over to peer
beyond the lodge door flap. It was startling to see more than
three dozen fully armed Osage warriors painted for battle,
silently, ominously sitting their Spanish ponies in a line just
outside the cave.

36

Many Trees Singing exited the lodge behind Iron Hand, then stood in shock for a moment at the Osage arrayed before them. The people were running this way and that, women crying for their children, children whimpering.

Still maintaining great dignity, Many Trees Singing straightened his buffalo horns and approached the white gelding in the center of the Osage line. On it Game Dancer stared straight ahead. When the old councillor addressed him he ignored him completely, his arrowed gaze aimed toward the chief woman's lodge set a few paces inside the cavern.

One Thunder Turtle came up behind Many Trees Singing, about to demand what was the meaning of this, when Weeononka and The Blossum exited the lodge. Game Dancer imperceptibly spurred his mount forward. Its hooves rang on the stone floor. Game Dancer drew the animal up with a jerk, swung him around and beside the woman so close that the horse's sweat stained her shoulder. The rider offered his hand palm up, the command unmistakable: Come with me.

She regarded him with a steady unblinking gaze. He shook his hand impatiently. His horse snorted in the cavern, where all other sounds were being held in by the people. The warriors remained motionless.

Because all eyes were so riveted on Weeononka, Iron Hand was able to signal to One Thunder Turtle, who signed to him the identity of this intruder. The war chief was surprised at Iron Hand's response. This was Iron Hand's play, though, because the woman was his wife. One Thunder Turtle was able to slip quietly behind the council lodge and out the side of the cave to carry out Iron Hand's odd suggestion.

Meanwhile Iron Hand edged closer to the council lodge, melting into the shadows between it and the lodge he lived in with Weeononka. The opening was on the far side, out of the Osage's line of sight had he even been looking in that direction.

Once inside, Iron Hand took off his shirt and splashed his face with water. He jerked his braid askew then smeared dust from the floor on his face and neck. Then he scooped up his

buffalo tail and secured it to his arm. Still hidden by the bulk of
the lodge, he retreated to the spot where One Thunder Turtle
had left the cave.

The scene beyond the lodge was suspended. He could see
Weeononka looking up at the warrior, who hadn't moved
beside her.

Game Dancer reached for her arm just as Iron Hand dashed
into the act as though he'd run down from the plateau. His
sudden movement caught everyone's eye, including Game
Dancer's. He lobbed a glance in that direction, his face twisted
by a scowl.

Iron Hand made a sound of surprise, stopped in his tracks,
his famous racket on his arm. He looked as if he'd just quit the
playing field a moment before. "Wife—" he called in a friendly
but forceful voice, "why didn't you send word to me that our
Osage cousins were visiting?"

It was so unexpected, it even surprised Game Dancer, who
stared at the brown-skinned, black-bearded Quapaw who
spoke Sioux with the strangest accent he'd ever heard. He
knew every man in this village but had never seen this one
before. His eyes narrowed to slits.

Iron Hand casually walked to Weeononka. She watched him
with a look of astonishment and fear, sure that he didn't know
what a terrible line of danger he walked. His return glance
spoke of his love for her. His left arm around her waist was firm
and said, Don't worry; I know what I'm doing.

The moment of surprise was over. Game Dancer with a
flourish that confused his mount flipped out his French-made
scalping knife. His hand moved so fast it was a blur. The blade
struck the packed ground at the toes of Iron Hand's moccasins.
Game Dancer reined in the horse and spat, "You will fight me
for the woman!"

Silent and unmoving until that moment, his warriors
screamed a cheer that rattled off the cavern walls and sent
children to their mother's legs, where they held on, whimpering. When the sound died down Iron Hand looked from the
vibrating knife to the man who had thrown it.

Weeononka let a moan escape her throat. Her hand tried to
push her husband back. She wanted to tell him that whatever
he did he must not touch that knife. To do so would signal the
beginning of a duel that would end only when one of the two
men was dead. She knew who that would be if Iron Hand tried
to fight Game Dancer with a knife.

Iron Hand seemed instinctively to understand this when he said as though the challenge had not been thrown to him, "This must be our cousin, Game Dancer." Casually he loosened and removed the ball racket from his arm, revealing the absence of a hand. "Please," he continued in eloquent handsign, "let us water your horses and serve you some food to ease your long journey."

Game Dancer raised slightly then leaped off the horse in a single motion to stand considerably above the stranger.

"We are not hungry."

"Weeononka, bring our guest a damp cloth so he may wipe the trail dust from his face."

Game Dancer showed his teeth in a dry, predatory smile. It looked like the grin of a skull to Iron Hand, who could see the precise blood-dried gashes under the madman's burning eyes where he'd ritually cut himself in blood vow. Even his smell had a hostile tone as he raised his right hand, made a huge fist so tight it squeaked, and threw it behind his back. There was no doubt he was saying he'd fight with one hand tied behind his back to equalize the match. "It will be a fair fight," he said directly to Iron Hand, "and it will begin now—"

He counted on faking the stranger to lunge for the knife, thinking that he was ignorant of the rule that as long as the challenged did not pick it up, the challenger must hold off attack. Iron Hand was battle-smart if not knowledgeable of Osage custom. He saw Game Dancer tense to take the weapon from him the moment he grabbed it. He heard Weeononka's intake of breath that warned him further.

In the same pleasant voice he continued, all the time exchanging an eyeball-bending stare up at the Osage, "Since you don't want to eat or rest, perhaps you'd like to make a small wager on a ball game."

Every Quapaw in the cave heaved a sigh of relief. The Osage warriors had broken ranks. The horses snorted at lax leads.

Weeononka touched Iron Hand in a wifely way that communicated he was doing exactly the right thing. Of all the moves he could have made, this was the most sensible. She'd never mentioned Game Dancer to him, yet he'd hit upon the man's major flaw.

"A ball game?" Game Dancer repeated, biting off his anger. This was another kind of challenge but it was not unusual for the challenged to choose the weapon of death combat. A ball game threw him off, though. Nobody had ever played such a ball game in anyone's memory.

Almost on cue, One Thunder Turtle returned with several warriors who'd been at the lake after the afternoon's game. Like Iron Hand, they looked as if they'd just come from the playing field—sweaty, dust-streaked, their buffalo tails in hand.

"We will be the Blacks, your team can be the Reds," Iron Hand suggested.

"No!" Game Dancer barked. "Not teams. Only you and I."

Iron Hand demured appeasingly, slipping on his racket and its attached padding, securing it with thongs tightly above his elbow. It was old enough to be worn, a well-broken-in tool that felt as secure and dependable as the wonderful metal hand. In its own way the supple racket was as much a practical work of art as Mansard's bronze.

Game Dancer missed the look of pleasure on the opponent's face, however, as he was nodding curtly to One Thunder Turtle, handsigning that he wished to borrow the war chief's buffalo tail. The war chief smiled to himself as he tossed his racket to the huge Osage. He knew Game Dancer didn't care all that much for the traditional game. He liked blood sports.

It is very good *wa kon*, One Thunder Turtle was thinking, to honor the old ways. This match would remind everyone that a long time ago the game was sacred and always played to the death. He could not wait to see Game Dancer's face when he observed Iron Hand's skill with the buffalo tail. It would be a game of legend.

The air of terror that had held the Osotony since the Osage arrival melted into an anticipatory thrill of entertainment. Even the Osage warriors caught the buoyant mood as they dismounted on Game Dancer's signal and tethered their ponies. They knew many of the Osotony braves and couldn't resist making some wagers, which greatly animated the procession that filed out of the cavern and into the burnished sunlight of the mesa.

Game Dancer insisted his eldest brave officiate the match. Iron Hand agreed. Many Trees Singing would be scorekeeper, a purely ritual position since the winner would not be determined by points as in a regular match. The referee strode in his red and yellow warpaint to the center of the playing field while The Blossum and the council took their positions beneath the cottonwood tree. The others spread out along the edges of the field. Boys ran here and there, the men slapped each other over their bets, and women settled on the sidelines chattering about their own little wagers—not who would win, but how long the play would continue. Weeononka sat behind The Blossum while Two Hands watched from centerfield with the other boys. The only silent humans on the mesa that afternoon were the combatants preparing for ordeal.

One Thunder Turtle hurriedly told Iron Hand the ancient rules for such a duel. They were identical to the regular playing regulations with a single distinction: The men would play until one of them dropped dead.

The referee held the ball high above his head, ready to start the play.

Game Dancer took his position at the Red goal post. Iron Hand, adjusting the ties that held the racket, was ready at the Black. The moment was suspended on the referee's raised hand. He glanced right, then left to catch the ready-sign from the players. Suddenly the ball was sailing high into the bright air. Before it hit the ground, the two men were zeroing in on it, rackets slashing with whooshing sounds, the audience bursting into a cheer.

As One Thunder Turtle anticipated, it was a game that would go down in legend. Iron Hand took the lead with Game Dancer's superior strength and weight dogging him. The first hour the Black goal led with three points. There was no time out, no respites for water, no coaching other than group screams.

Game Dancer perceived very soon what the real game was. He'd supposed this was going to be a quick and easy win. Grimly he saw his error, wondering where and how the Quapaw white man had learned to play such ball. He seemed to be everywhere at once, snatching the ball almost magically from the air before the Red racket. On the run to the Black post Game Dancer might catch up with him but he could not find the ball Iron Hand kept in motion with the flickering racket that worked like an extension of his wiry body. Game Dancer tried every trick cunning could devise. Nothing was a cheat in the game, but even veterans observed some etiquette, such as not striking a downed player. Game Dancer knew no scruple.

By sundown the score was twelve to eleven blood-won points. Both men staggered with exhaustion, bleeding from many gashes and spotted with bruises. Iron Hand had never played so long; the racket chafed; it was glued to his arm by his blood. Game Dancer might have noticed but his right eye was swollen shut where Iron Hand's chiseled heel had caught him when the Red player had tried to bash him in the groin with his polished, plucked head.

The referee caught the ball when Iron Hand bounced it off the Black post and was trotting to centerfield to begin another set. Just as he was about to toss it, Game Dancer reeled and fell over. Only Iron Hand was allowed to touch him and then not with the hand. He gently toed his opponent, who lay unconscious in the dust. There was no response. Iron Hand looked to the referee to see what was to be done. He lowered the ball and handsigned that they must wait for Game Dancer to come around.

It was good to take a rest, Iron Hand thought as he dropped to a crouch to watch Game Dancer breathing a snore in the dust.

The first star winked into existence over on the smoky red western horizon.

During the lull the villagers brought up flaming torches and supper to share with the mingling Osage. Bettors changed their wagers; the odds had shifted even though nobody believed the game was anywhere near over.

Weeononka longed to take Iron Hand a drink of water. He looked about to fall over, crouched above his opponent. A second in advance of his move, she saw Game Dancer was faking. She called out in French that arrested Iron Hand, startling him awake. He heard her as he drifted off, asleep sitting up. The Osage rolled on his shoulders, his legs a knotted whip that would have surrounded Iron Hand's head in a death-vise grip. As long as he didn't use the hands, this was a legal move that brought the audience to its feet with a gasp.

Weeononka's cry gave Iron Hand just enough warning so that he was able to throw himself backward and avoid the pincers of Game Dancer's overdeveloped thighs. The white man rolled to his feet as the referee called the beginning of play and dropped the ball. Iron Hand was on it like a hawk on a mouse, and halfway to his goal before Game Dancer found his feet. He swayed unsteadily and began loping in wide-footed steps to intercept the play. Unable to see straight and bereft of strategy, he let brute force assault the opponent. His left shoulder crashed like an avalanche into the slighter, leaner white man. They rolled together in bone-crunching confusion.

The crowd cheered wildly when Iron Hand sprang up

running, the ball undisturbed in the nest of his racket. He slammed the ball so hard against the post, its binding split. An Osotony quickly produced a new one, which the referee threw in a wide arc that missed the center and technically was a foul, since it benefited the Red.

The Osotony screamed their fury as such favoritism. An Osage warrior and an Osotony exchanged harsh words that would have led to blows except that Iron Hand had somehow managed to magic the whirling sphere away from Game Dancer's awkwardly driven stick. Out of the corner of his eye he saw the red boulder that was Game Dancer's shoulder rolling toward him; fury rose at such boorish play in a game Iron Hand had come to respect as a kind of laborious dance to be respected with graceful participation. He spun without interrupting his own headlong plummet toward the Black post, bringing his heel again to bear in the Osage's twisted, bleeding face. It felt as though he'd kicked embedded stone. Pain burned back along his calf, knee, and thigh bones and pulled a cry from his bloody lips.

But the opponent staggered. He stood, walleyed, mouth slack, bloody drool splattering the smeared paint on his chest. His eyes rolled back above the engorged purple melon that was his nose. It swelled even as Iron Hand stared bleary-eyed, himself about to collapse. He knew he had broken the man's nose, ramming fragments of bone back into the brain. Delivered correctly it was always a fatal blow. As badly as his own foot hurt, he could imagine how it must feel from the Red player's point of view. He fought the empathy, but he felt the old response steal over his aching bones.

Everyone was breathlessly quiet, waiting for Game Dancer to topple. Still he stood though Iron Hand would have sworn he was dead on his feet. The great body wavered as if in a breeze.

Unable to stand it any longer Iron Hand reached with his buffalo tail to push him over. A collective gasp rose from the spectators and he caught himself before the hickory touched the opponent in a dishonorable foul. He pulled back the racket and retreated a step.

He lifted his right foot, looking like a crane about to launch into its mating dance, and ever so gently tapped the Osage on the sternum. The great human tree tottered backward without further sound or motion, his face a hideous mass of pulsating meat. The drop forced a gush of air from him—his last breath.

Iron Hand stood over him swaying. He felt darkness reaching up from the ground and down from the sky to hold him in its arms. He gave in to it without a fight. But he never hit the ground because a wave of Osotony warriors swept over the field and caught him. Screaming and dancing they bore him above their heads around and around the dancing ground, encircling the dead opponent again and again while his Osage companions inspected the body, cursing because they had no grounds for complaint, marveling among themselves over the extraordinary champion.

37

After such an event things must settle down into the boring humdrum of everyday life. The season deepened. The council's debates were punctuated with loud words that sometimes reached hostility as the parties argued their sides.

Weeononka lovingly helped Iron Hand heal from the wounds of his game, telling him the whole story of her relationship with the dead Osage warrior. After his warriors had bundled his body on his war pony, the Osage who'd been referee took Weeononka aside to explain how Crow Sister had died.

"The circle is now closed," Weeononka had remarked to The Blossum. Though Iron Hand tried to play down his celebrity, Weeononka knew his secret: He loved being the center of the tribe's delight.

His former life seemed even more remote than before. But one day the other world intruded abruptly into his Quapaw existence. Again, lost in the world of smoky debate that was the council lodge, he heard sounds that announced something happening out in the cavern.

It was a white man on horseback. Iron Hand of the Osotony, after being among the clean-shaven, mahogany-colored Quapaw, thought, What an odd looking person. Then it hit him who the stranger was.

At first he didn't recognize D'Arcy, who'd grown a heavy beard. A big man already, the whiskers made him look immense on his Spanish jenny mule. As he left the council lodge Iron Hand saw his old comrade was not traveling alone.

There were three other horses behind him—two pack animals, and a third with an unknown rider drawn up just under the overhang of the great cave. In the saddle of the last animal was a French boy of about twelve years. He was so pretty he was ugly with a haughty demeanor apparent even from this angle. He was looking around as if for someone or something. His face was very round, kind of pug, with wide light eyes and a crown of dirty-gold ringlets tumbling from under his tri-cornered hat. He had a smug expression on his face as he appraised the Indians gathering around him.

When he slid from his horse, several Quapaw boys walked over to take a look at him. The child drew back, seeming to Iron Hand's eye to be out of proportion somehow. His head was too big, his forehead too wide. It was suddenly apparent; he was a dwarf. Iron Hand suppressed a shudder of revulsion. He'd been frightened as a child by a dwarf street player. Ever since, his usually tolerant personality shrank from these little people. They seemed somehow malevolent, with good reason to hate normal-sized people whom they surely must envy. Iron Hand didn't consciously think all these things as he stood watching the repulsive fellow, who was now aware that he was being scrutinized.

What did D'Arcy mean, bringing such an unsuitable person here? The boy caught Iron Hand's eye. The captain had the uncomfortable feeling the dwarf knew he'd been looking and knew also Iron Hand's reaction. The boy stared at him now. He felt immediate guilt and tried to hide his revulsion with an insincere smile.

"Look at this savage Frenchman!" D'Arcy was exclaiming through this silent exchange. There had been a time when the Corsican would never have spoken so familiarly to his com-mander. The truth was, D'Arcy was shocked to see the changes in de Tonti, and used *bonhomie* to cover embarrassment. Iron Hand might have thought about his subordinate's change in manner, but was distracted by the odd boy the Corsican had brought along.

The boy glared in a nervy way. Iron Hand didn't know what emotion he saw, but whatever it was, he was predisposed to dislike this fellow, youngster or no. The boy frowned and turned away from Iron Hand as both approached D'Arcy, who was dismounting with a wide benevolent grin showing through his facial hair. He opened his arms and embraced Iron Hand heartily.

"You've gone all the way—" D'Arcy teased him, pulling at the elaborate multiple braids of his old friend's hair tied with feathers and dyed leather bindings. "But where are your tattoos?" He pulled at Iron Hand's shirt, saw he wasn't wearing the metal hand, and backed off politely. "Bit of gray in your beard there, old friend. Never saw an Indian with a beard before."

Iron Hand adjusted the hang of his buffalo robe and tugged on the other's whiskers, even more grizzled than his own.

"I remember you swore you'd never grow one."

"Shaving is a damnable nuisance in this godforsaken wilderness," D'Arcy replied, his arm around Iron Hand's shoulder. The Corsican had sworn never to affect facial hair. Not even de Tonti could have perceived that the choice was a practical one. Bearded, Michel D'Arcy looked too much like the Frenchman's cartoon of a Jew. D'Arcy's surrender to the Gentile persona was that complete. But here in the wilderness, other Frenchmen grew their beards, and so D'Arcy too must take on the custom which coincided so neatly with his former religion. Unbidden, words from the Torah passed through his mind, Jehovah's admonition to devout Jews never to cut the beard. D'Arcy felt torn in two pieces, the one rattled by old memories, the other noting that his captain and the king's boy were not having a comfortable first meeting.

"Ah," said D'Arcy, observing the boy before him, an expectant but not entirely easy look on his face. Iron Hand saw the lad cringe away from the Quapaw hands that reached out to touch him. They sensed something was different about him, and his clothing caught their eyes. He wore a perfectly tailored little greatcoat of brown brocade, matching breeches, and elegant low boots buckled with pewter.

"They won't hurt you, Claud," D'Arcy said. "They're only curious." The boy was less afraid now than disdainful of the people who tried to touch his person.

"Monsieur Henri de Tonti, may I present Monsieur Claud René Fallion."

Iron Hand felt a small jolt at hearing his French name, but it did not show as he turned again to the boy. Claud didn't offer to shake hands; he knew who this was, knew he did not shake hands in the European manner. Instead he gave Iron Hand a crisp little military bow, something like the one La Salle had given Louis years ago. Iron Hand smiled and nodded, but he wished the boy would stop staring at him.

"Claud, mind your manners," D'Arcy said gently.

He snapped out of it. "Monsieur, I've been anticipating this pleasure all the way from Montreal." His voice was thin for a boy's but he was obviously highly intelligent. Now that he stood closer, Iron Hand saw that what he had thought was smugness was really wonder at meeting the legendary Iron Hand.

"What did you tell him about me? That I eat people who wear brocade?"

D'Arcy, advanced in girth since their last meeting, expelled a great guffaw. He slapped Iron Hand on the shoulder and looked at him with a mixture of approbation and condemnation. His thoughts were fairly broadcast. He thought de Tonti had gone completely insane.

"I told him he was about to meet a remarkable man," he said with sudden seriousness. "*Morbleu*, what hell you must have gone through, Henri." It was not the first time D'Arcy had called his commander by his Christian name, but his tone had a peculiar questioning that bespoke judgment and shame that the man he most admired had fallen into savagery.

Iron Hand started to explain the new joy he'd found in life among the Quapaw. But something stopped him. He remembered his own former opinion of Frenchmen going savage. It must look that way to D'Arcy. Anything Iron Hand might add would seem defensive.

"*Nous sommes tous sauvages*," Iron Hand said wryly. We are ourselves all savages. D'Arcy caught the reference; that was what the mutineers had written on the little ship they had left to rot in the ruins of Fort *Crevecoeur*.

D'Arcy philosophically shook his head. With Iron Hand and Claud's help he relieved the horses of their burdens, glad to have this task to do to cover his discomfort. Two Quapaw men led the horses off to be tied with the tribe's small herd outside the cavern.

By now the council members had left their deliberations to see what was happening. The several chieftains stood outside the big lodges, so Iron Hand motioned for D'Arcy to come and meet them.

He was well-received because he brought trade goods for the peltries as Iron Hand had promised. Included in his stores was tobacco especially for the old men; they invited him to enter their chamber for a smoke.

Claud, forgotten by the two men, saw the Indian boys

approach him. He quickly trotted after D'Arcy to avoid dealing with the alien confrontation.

D'Arcy told the council the packs outside held hatchet heads and a good store of dried Illinois corn, which the elders felt was reason to celebrate. Hunters returned with two deer that evening. There were plenty of berries, tubers, and cattail shoots growing nearby. The rock walls echoed with preparations as D'Arcy walked with Iron Hand after the convivial smoke toward his lodge on the other side of the big cave. Weeononka was not in camp right then; she'd gone with some women down to the blackrock pool.

Claud trailed at their heels.

"Why don't you go out and meet those lads," D'Arcy suggested, but it was really an order. Claud looked apprehensively back at the boys.

"It's not too soon to begin, Claud."

"They don't like me."

D'Arcy turned out a deep pocket in his big leather jacket. He found linty chunks of hard sugarcandy there, which he handed over to Claud. "Try this on 'em." The boy smiled. Iron Hand felt rather sorry for him now, sorry he had judged him so harshly before.

The boy took the candy and left the two men outside Iron Hand's lodge. By this time The Blossum had insisted he and Weeononka take a private lodge. Iron Hand was secretly glad. He liked the old woman but felt self-conscious making love to Weeononka when The Blossum was only two blankets away. Two Hands didn't bother him because he slept with childlike innocence like a stone. By custom, firesides lived together in a jumble of generations, but he was glad The Blossum had sensed his European scruple.

So it was into a private spacious lodge that he took his old friend for a long conversation. He suddenly found himself hungry for news of the outside world. He might have just this moment awakened from his swamp ordeal; for the first time he imagined himself re-entering that other world. He hadn't realized his own feelings but in the past few days he'd suffered the irritating mixture of boredom and anxiety he associated with needing a change. Things were almost too serene here. His life needed the spice of challenge and activity.

With greedy anticipation he sat down on his robe and listened to D'Arcy talk for more than an hour. Since they were business partners, much of their conversation centered on how this season of trade was faring. D'Arcy was happy to report that he had a child on the way by his Quapaw wife, who had taken the Catholic faith, much to D'Arcy's private chagrin. Neither he nor de Tonti mentioned D'Arcy's ancestry this time. In this French place, just as in that Spanish place, under the king's orders, being a Jew was a criminal offense, even if this was the hindmost backside of his pure Catholic domain.

Beyond their hillside, a late afternoon wind came up off the river valley far below. It rustled the mulberry trees stationed at the edge of the cave.

The word was out about La Salle. Already a tangle of lies surrounded his demise and even his contribution.

"Some Dutch friar has come out with an account of how *he* was first to discover the mouth of the Mississippi." D'Arcy spat derisively.

"Surely nobody believes him."

"He's the first to publish."

"Poor Robbie, still feeding the wolves."

D'Arcy had little sorrow for him. Though he had been loyal to La Salle, he privately always predicted such an end to the man for his arrogance. To him the explorer's death only meant Iron Hand as second in command was now commander and proprietor of the Canadian's interests. He put it to his captain as earnestly as he could: "Our own interests will be secured by your return."

Iron Hand wouldn't commit himself to anything.

They talked about the deceit of Cavelier the priest and Joutel, the disaster of La Salle's last expedition, and the expiration of his visions.

"The governor sends you his regards and also sends you that boy to be raised among the Quapaw."

"That little snot hasn't got what it takes to be a *mousse*."

"He's extremely bright."

"These people have bad legends about dwarf beings. I don't think they'll accept him." Iron Hand avoided expressing his own feelings because they sounded uncharitable.

"Frontenac regards Claud highly," D'Arcy said, glancing outside, where the lad was standing off to one side of the ball-playing boys but was watching this lodge. "Although I admit he's a bit strange. Practically worships you."

"The governor's mad sending children out to face what mows down grown men."

"Not the governor. The king. He's had good reports from the

boys who live with the Illinois and Sioux. I think it's a dandy idea. Besides, the boys love it."

"That boy doesn't. Did you see the way he drew back when the people touched him?"

"Remember your first experience with Indian hospitality? No, *mon capitaine*, the boy'll do fine. Frontenac wants him here with you. He told me that specifically."

"He knows where I am then."

"There have been many rumors, of course. That you were dead, that you'd gone savage, that you turned traitor selling furs to the English or fighting for the Spaniards."

"That's hardly likely."

D'Arcy didn't have to be reminded that Iron Hand's war experiences had colored his prejudices.

"I figured you were at Arkansas Post, raking in those peltries." A mercantile twinkle flickered in D'Arcy's eye. Despite his rough appearance he was already one of the richest men in New France. Iron Hand had begun as D'Arcy's employer, but now as his partner owed him a small fortune. He had borrowed from him to make his last trip, but he knew D'Arcy wasn't here to collect the debt.

"So you came after me?"

"Well, we've made a good profit this season, so I don't need to drag you back to Montreal's debtors' prison. I came to honor your bones with decent Christian burial." He laughed wickedly at his private joke.

"It's certainly good to know I have a Christian brother looking out for my soul," de Tonti replied, and they both had a good laugh.

"When old Frontenac heard my plans he made me postboy to bring mail and dispatches to our various people down the Mississippi, and to escort a couple of *mousses* according to our sovereign's wishes."

Iron Hand was familiar with the practice of putting boys on ship duty. They were called *mousse*, because veteran mariners considered them froth on a wave, a useless decoration. D'Arcy explained that the Crown was sending bright youths to live among the several tribes as long-term liaisons.

"Utterly foolish business."

"I dropped off another lad among the Chickasaw."

"Don't say that word around here."

"Of course," D'Arcy said, lowering his voice. "There's a new treaty with the buggers."

"They'll eat the king's *mousse,* I'll bet."

"These are new times, Henri. The old days are gone forever. New alliances, new friends."

"But old enemies." His life among the Quapaw had given him their antipathies. Quapaw forever hated Chickasaw.

D'Arcy shrugged and let Iron Hand light his pipe again with a coal from the banked firepit.

"So, tell me what happened to the hand."

The women were angry with the council for putting off the rain dance. The village's many corn patches were suffering up on the plateau. The squash and gourds hardened and dried before they got bigger than a quail's egg.

"Our corn shrivels up without making ears," they moaned to the chieftains as they entered their sanctuary.

"*Mon Dieu,*" D'Arcy said to Iron Hand, "I'd better get going before the flood!" He thought it funny that these ignorant savages actually thought they could make it rain by dancing.

"But you see," Iron Hand explained, "they'll dance until it rains. The old men put off starting because they know it might last a long time. Theoretically it could go on until the last Quapaw drops dead on the dancing ground."

He and D'Arcy were outside the great cave, bent over a small hot fire of hickory wood. When Iron Hand had told his friend he'd travel with him as far as the Caddo to get his ball lead, D'Arcy said he had enough to spare.

Now, down on the creek bed where black sand had piled up in a little beach, they were testing Iron Hand's idea about a sandcast. He had already poured lead into one cavity in the sand, which was in the intaglio shape of D'Arcy's right hand. He said a little speech before he packed the damp grit around his hand then pulled it out slowly. He patted the inside of his wrist, saying that he was honored to be forever the right hand man of the great Iron Hand.

They'd drunk almost a bottle of brandy while melting the lead in D'Arcy's crucible. They finished the brandy while the lead slug remelted, and then they were ready to pour it into a new handprint. But the sides of the mold caved in on the first attempt. D'Arcy was more adept, able to judge from long experience making lead ball, how to fill the mold slowly and at an angle to prevent bubbling.

The lead made a satisfying sizzle as it hit the sand. D'Arcy sat back after filling the mold. Now all they had to do was wait.

It was not a fine impression, and was soft and primitive compared to the magnificent creation of Mansard's forge. But it would serve the purpose after Weeononka had worked it with her artful leather skills.

D'Arcy had concerns about an early winter that could keep him from getting to Montreal for the trading season. Also, he and La Forest were committed to join the new Iroquois campaign, which in de Tonti's absence had gone badly.

"We need your *wa kon*, old friend," said D'Arcy the day he left. He had begged Iron Hand to accompany him, but the captain said he wasn't ready yet to return.

"You know, if the king ever hears about what you've done, he'll never forgive you," D'Arcy warned. "There are already rumors. He'll suspend your license if word of your turning savage ever gets back to him—"

"I haven't turned savage."

"What do you call it? Come back with me, Henri, and undo what you've done."

"Done—what have I done? What every Frenchman does as soon as he hits the wilderness."

"Yes, all Frenchmen love the Indian women, but few have a position as high as you to lose over one of them. Who is now going to be appointed to take La Salle's place? You of course have the best chance of being the king's man in Louisiana, if you don't lose it all because of this foolish escapade. At least bring her back and marry her properly."

"Sometime you sound like Rob himself. Maybe it's you who should take his place."

D'Arcy shot him a disgusted look. He wasn't modest. He knew he far surpassed La Salle as a businessman, though he never did find La Salle's easy way with the Indians.

"I don't know," Iron Hand continued. "All I know is that my time among these people has been the happiest, the most fulfilled in my life."

"Even so," the Corsican replied, giving the community of the cave one last glance, "I believe this is not for you."

D'Arcy had loaded his pack animals with a portion of the Quapaw peltries he'd traded for beads, pots, and blankets. The Quapaw were delighted with their first white deal, though Iron Hand warned them that not all traders would be as fair as D'Arcy. He did not have enough animals to haul out all their peltries, so the councillors were making plans to take the rest downriver as Iron Hand suggested as soon as the weather broke.

The air in the great open-sided cavern was permeated with the burning aromas of sweet sage and cedar. Aromatic smoke drifted around the twenty-odd lodges then up to hover like a small cloud under the cave roof high above their heads. The old men were finally at it inside the council lodge, beginning the first rituals of the rain dance. People were getting ready for the event, which could last a long time. Everyone was wrapping food bundles and getting out their fancy moccasins. Soon all would go up to the plateau to begin the dance under the sky until it opened up with rain.

"You will return to us, Henri. Mark my words," D'Arcy called, his Spanish-accented French syllables ringing off the stone room.

Iron Hand slapped the flank of D'Arcy's horse, saluting him. "Yes," he called, "but this will always be the place I come home to."

D'Arcy waved and pointed his mount and line of pack animals out into the late afternoon sunshine on the path that led to the plateau and off the mountain. He was glad to be away from the smoky cave and what to him were the squalid conditions of the Indian village. The Osotony were so busy getting ready for the rain dance only a few stopped to witness his departure.

Iron Hand saw Claud hanging around near his lodge. He'd begged his old comrade to take the child back but D'Arcy leaned on his duty. He would not disobey the governor.

A day or so later, long after the drums, chants, and foot stamping of the rain dance had begun in earnest, Weeononka entered the lodge with her face etched in concern for Claud.

"They pick on him. I've spoken to Two Hands, but Claud makes himself a target," she remarked.

Claud came running with the boys close on his heels, Two Hands among them. The white boy ducked into the lodge but the others stopped short of entering Iron Hand's home. They yelled outside for the boy to come on and dress for the dance.

"They tried to take off my clothes," Claud whimpered, wiping tears, snot, and dirt from his face. He sat as close to Iron Hand as possible, watching Weeononka with a flat, impervious look on his precious features. He had put away his European togs and was dressed Indian style except for the linen shirt he still affected.

He was extremely shy around the village boys. He treated

Two Hands like the plague and hung around Iron Hand until he became a nuisance.

"I'm sending you back to Montreal," Iron Hand said.

He had really tried to like this boy but could barely look at him he loathed him so much.

"Oh, please, monsieur," Claud blurted. "I do want to stay."

The wind shifted beyond the cave lip, throwing the rainchant down where the community was etched into the wooded canyon wall.

"You don't take to Quapaw ways at all."

"It's just so strange. But I would not change places with the Dauphin of France!"

"You act like the Dauphin, Claud. You don't join in. Are you afraid of getting dirty?"

"Don't tease him," Weeononka said to her husband.

Iron Hand shook his head at this futility.

"I refuse to return," Claud said with the defiance of a nobly bred brat.

"You will do as I say," Iron Hand snapped.

"But surely, my husband," said Weeononka, "it takes a while to grow accustomed to a new home. Give him time."

Weeononka's kindness to the stranger made him ashamed he was being so hard on Claud. Iron Hand considered that maybe the king was right and it was a terrible thing for good Frenchmen to turn savage.

Weeononka reached out to rub Claud's curls. He drew back. His rejection hurt her feelings, though she tried to hide it. "I told The Blossum I'd come and help make corncakes for the dancers," she said hastily. Her duty as chief woman was to be the last Osotony to dance, should it come to that, after all the others had dropped. Until then she would refrain from dancing to serve those who had begun the ritual. She departed immediately, leaving Iron Hand alone with the boy, who watched him intently. Iron Hand was trying to make himself get over his dislike. It seemed so irrational to be so hard on the boy. It had to be difficult growing up so different. Iron Hand swore he'd be kinder.

The boy seemed to gasp.

"Are you all right, lad?"

"Yes, but seeing you like that with your legs crossed, as if you were going to tell a story . . . it reminded me of another time, that's all."

The boy appeared to be waiting for something.

He dropped to his knees before Iron Hand with an extended, expectant manner that implied too many possibilities. It was not a childlike attitude and it made Iron Hand nervous.

"Well?" the boy finally said, staring intently into Iron Hand's eyes.

"Well what?"

"What's wrong with you, boy?" he said with growing annoyance.

"I've been here almost two weeks now."

"So?"

"You don't recognize me, do you?"

Iron Hand looked him over again. He was just a plump, spoiled boy with stubby arms and precocious intensity in his blue eyes.

"Recognize you?"

"You never saw me in daylight, at least not up close."

Iron Hand sat very still, touched by the cold breath of something crucial he had missed. He saw the boy from a new angle where the face did seem oddly familiar. . . .

"Most of our time together was spent in the dark hold of the ship," the boy said in a dreamy voice.

Sweet Jesus. He fought the realization but in the icy moments that followed he knew with knifing certainty whose face this was.

"It can't be—" He touched the round cheek beneath the curly locks, tilting the chin up to catch light from the lodge flap. The boy's dimpled hand curled around his own collar, ripping open the linen shirt and exposing to Iron Hand's astonished view not a boy's chest but the bosom of a girl with breasts the size of demitasse cups.

He drew back as if the sight burned his eyes.

"Henri, my beloved, it's me!" The erstwhile boy flung himself at Iron Hand, hugging his neck with unexpected strength. Iron Hand had to pry the little arms from around his neck. He sat back and took another look at Jeanette.

"It's truly you."

"Surprised?"

"But how?"

"Oh, it's quite a story." She smiled again and threw her arms around him once more, pelting him with wet kisses on his ear and neck. "God, being near you has maddened me—even though you look like a sun-cooked savage."

Unpleasant gooseflesh riddled him.

"And those nasty children trying to undress me." She shivered. "And hearing you with *her* every night—*mon Dieu*—"

He groaned when he felt her hard little breasts against him. It truly was Jeanette, his perfect image of womanhood. How could he forget her? He started, pulling back again as he held her wrist and arm, measuring against unforgettable memories. A blinding pain shot between his eyes.

"I thought you were a child." He leaned back feeling light headed. "I ate myself with guilt because of what I thought I'd done to a child."

"I never said I was a child."

"But you look like—" He stopped himself, unable to say it.

"I'm thirty-one years old," she said softly. She glanced down at her shortened arms, the only malformation of her otherwise perfectly miniature body. "This is as big as I'll ever get."

"But you played the part."

"If you had asked me my age, I would have been honest. The truth is you saw what you wanted to see."

It was difficult for him to admit his senses had lied.

"Do you know how I hated playing the child? That's always the way I've been treated. People think just because I'm small, I'm a cute cuddly little girl. I gave you credit for loving me the way I was. I saw you thought I was beautiful. Am I not still beautiful to you?"

Now in daylight he could see her head was too large for a child's but the curls modified the effect. He was straining to see how he had missed what now appeared so obvious.

"People say I'm the most perfectly formed dwarf they've ever seen," she said defensively in the face of his accusing silence.

He couldn't reply.

"I'm sorry. I won't blame you if you hate me for deceiving you. But you were all the hope I had."

"And I failed to save you from that monstrous woman." His voice was hoarse.

"You gave me hope to save myself. I played along with Madame, pretending to get over my possession. I was the picture of modesty. I read my prayerbook and *Lives of Saints* and said what they wanted me to say and let this depressing converted Iroquois priest say rituals over me. I've been a very very good girl, doing everything they wanted. I joined the order, and gradually worked my way into a position of trust in the infirmary. A year ago I overheard someone talking about the king's boys being sent to live with the Indians. I bided my time and waited for an opportunity. Then it came in the form of three *mousse* who stayed at our school while waiting to be stationed with various tribes. One of the boys fell sick with a terrible illness that made him throw up until he died—"

"Jesus, not cholera?"

"I never heard. But I stole his papers and some of his clothes and ran away. I made it to the governor in Montreal and convinced him to send me with a guide to Monsieur de Tonti. I told him the king wished me to be with you because you were my godfather."

"That old man is hard to convince of something outrageous."

"Please, *mon ami*, know that Louis the Fourteenth's signature will get the governor's immediate attention. Fortunately it would take too much time for him to check me out and as long as my papers were in order he could not refuse. My knowledge of you was the only other credential I needed. I've been with D'Arcy four months trying to find you, following your trail through the different tribes."

She leaned very close to his face as she ran out of words. She lingered in his glance, seemingly trying to plumb the depths of his eyes. He tried to see in her what he had seen before, tried to delve into his own soul to find the love he had felt for this woman, but it was no longer there. His shocked confusion left him speechless and left his true feelings blurred so that Jeanette could read into his face what she wished. "My beloved," she crooned. With great tenderness she touched his furry cheek with her warm tiny hand. "I know I've shocked you senseless but please say you forgive me." She planted a passionate kiss on his lips, drawing him to her with a firm caress, groping for his right arm under the buffalo robe. "Where's the music box?"

"Long story, Jeanette," he said, pushing her away firmly but gently. He glanced over his shoulder beyond the tent flap to see Weeononka talking to The Blossum outside the old woman's lodge. They were silhouetted in the filtered light coming through the trees outside the cavern.

Jeanette saw his anxiety. "Don't worry, I won't get between the two of you. She'll never suspect I'm anything but a little boy. I'm very good at playing the part by now." She was so earnest, so vulnerable.

"This is such a surprise to me," he said, hating himself for being spineless. Self-disgust writhed inside him. "You can understand. There hasn't been a night since those days that I haven't thought of you, God knows, but it's such a shock to see you here in the middle of Arkansas. What determination you've shown!"

She eyed him with a fierce passion, holding his hand firmly. "I would gladly have died to reach you. You've been my reason to go on living. Now that I've found you, I'll never lose you again."

She kissed him, taking advantage of his lack of verbal response to caress his lips with her tongue. For a moment the sheer elemental power of her sensual tongue roused him. The chanting up on the mesa sounded farther away. His head was ringing. He held her arm in his hand again, feeling how small it was, how strangely foreshortened. Her anatomy leaped out at him like a scream. Revulsion rose in him to break the kiss. He quickly stood, feeling his stomach seethe as he looked down on her, a dwarf, a distorted mockery of his ideal. How had he missed it making love all those times? He could only blame it on her shapeless clothing, the darkness of the cabin they shared for such a short time, the circumstances that had brought them together. *And*, he thought, looking down at her now, *my own cupidity*. He felt as if he might throw up so unsettling was this revelation.

Recognition of this on his face twisted her features. She threw herself against his legs, crying, "No, no, don't look at me like that. You must love me, you must love me back as much as I love you." Standing at his knees looking up with her arms embracing his thighs, she pierced him with her intensity. "We were made for each other, don't you see? I knew it the moment I saw you. You understand what it's like to be different, for people to call you a freak. I knew it that first night when you tore through the wall with a hand that played music. Do you know how much I loved you when you bent down and washed my face?" He was paralyzed by her ardency and by his own self-reproach at his response to her. "I must have been hideously filthy to you but you fell on your knees and tenderly washed me. I'll never forget that. It was the single kindest thing anyone ever did for me."

You scum, his conscience was already scalding him; you swived her when you thought she was a child but now that you see she's a freak you spurn her. Hypocritical bastard. There should be an eternal hell just so you can suffer there.

She seemed oblivious of his true reaction as she continued, "Don't worry, beloved, I won't give away who I am. It will be our secret." She embraced his legs while she rubbed her cheek against his thigh, far too near his sex for comfort even through the coarse leather. "I love you so much I'll be your second wife, your secret mistress, your slave forever—any way you want it. Only let me stay with you."

Nausea swept him. He felt the lodge spin as he stumbled, gagging, away from her. Across the way Weeononka and The Blossum looked up as Iron Hand emerged from the lodge and hurried away from the shadow of the cave toward the woods on the plateau. His wife knew he had a spot up there overlooking the river valley where he liked to go when he wanted to be alone.

Weeononka saw Claud dash to follow.

"Stay away from me!" her husband spat, stopping the boy in his tracks, watching after him.

She excused herself from The Blossum and walked toward the boy with a tender word for him when she saw he was crying. How could that good man treat the boy so cruelly? The dancing music swelled through the trees on another shift in the wind. The cavern echoed back the sound of drums, bells, and cries above their heads.

Weeononka saw Claud's shirt ripple open in the breeze.

38

The alligator rain finally came, cutting off debate and easing the growing tension that had brought the Osotony to temper's edge. It crawled in from the west just before sunset on boiling green clouds, violent, spitting lightning hisses all over the mountain. Even beneath the roof of stone on the south side of a protected canyon, Iron Hand thought it was the thunderbird again. But Weeononka explained this was a different kind of storm. After its head came the tail that dragged gray and slow through the countryside for days. Drainage in the big cave was not as good as expected. Seven firesides were drenched. But everyone was happily exhausted from the rain dance so the crowding didn't cause too many squabbles.

After a handful of days the rain slacked off so that by the

sixth afternoon a fine sunset cracked the thunderheads. The corn had been battered by hail that first stormy night, but most of the crop was saved, shimmering green, almost visibly growing with promise of a good harvest. A generally happy buzz came from the Osotony cave as the people settled back into their routines.

But Iron Hand was miserable. Nobody ever mentioned his confrontation with Jeanette. Its disclosures were so shocking they were beyond mere gossip and could only be hinted at. Jeanette accepted Iron Hand's rejection but at the cost of falling into a silent, profound lethargy.

The Blossum, who saw he couldn't bear to look at the unfortunate little woman, took her into her own lodge. Her motives were mixed: She felt sorry for her but was curious to observe up close this first white woman among the Quapaw. The majority of the band judged Jeanette harshly for distressing their white man but no one on the council had the heart to expel her. There was some talk about escorting her to Arkansas Post, where she could stay with the white men. But now that The Blossum sheltered her, they wouldn't dare bring the subject up for debate. Some of the old stories circulated about *wakantake jita*, dwarf spirits who were said to eat little children, but for the most part Jeanette was ignored. Iron Hand, however, couldn't ignore her. Everywhere he looked she seemed to be there, with her wide, pathetic eyes. The more she seemed to want him, the less he could stand to see her. She never made a move toward him, but he was constantly, uncomfortably aware of her. She allowed The Blossum to guide her gently from places where their paths might cross.

Jeanette wasn't Iron Hand's only vexation. The more he thought about it, the more it infuriated him that someone had tried to steal credit for La Salle's Mississippi discovery.

He brooded about it, fantasizing publication of his own memoirs to rebut the lying priest. He'd seen enough of that breed, he thought moodily. Vague plans for various revenges troubled his thoughts. He must avenge his friend. That meant returning to French civilization. However, he decided he didn't want to be one-armed among his countrymen any more than among the Quapaw. So he was somewhat testy because Weeononka wasn't working on the hand fast enough to suit him. She had just entered the lodge with a basket of herbal medicines when he remarked that he'd found a spider web between the thumb and joined fingers of the lead casting. "That spider found a nice quiet place to work," he said in wry French. "No chance of being disturbed, no sir."

She looked at him in a way that said, she had more immediate concerns.

Alerted by her uncharacteristic response to a tease, he asked what was wrong.

She gestured with the large basket as she set it down and joined him. "People are getting sick."

"Colds from the rain."

She shrugged. "I thought so. Now I think it's something worse."

"How many?"

Ten children, thirteen adults, she gestured in handsign: somehow seeing each sick person represented by one finger made the message more real. He was silent as he calculated that was nearly one-sixth of the tribe.

"They just get tired and lie down," she explained. "I thought it was the dancing sickness but people get over that in a day. I have two over on the other side of the cave in bad shape." She concisely described the unpleasant symptoms of cholera.

He was sure of it after making a round of the firesides, where he saw the sick ones. The smell was unmistakable. The only cure was to force the patients to drink massive quantities of water. He explained to her the urgency of not touching their excrement or saliva, and putting everyone sick in one large lodge. Iron Hand knew about the disease, which had ravaged his company during a Mediterranean campaign. He'd been one of those few who never got sick.

Weeononka understood about the bad *wa kon* of refuse, but it was against Quapaw tradition to keep sick people away from their firesides. It was thought the individual personality would flicker and perish without the larger *aneh* of the family.

Jeanette crawled out of The Blossum's lodge for the first time in days. The epidemic had the single benefit of drawing her out of the shell she had climbed into. She stayed on her feet for the next two days assisting Iron Hand. They spoke only out of practical necessity—when he asked for help cleaning someone of their vomit, or to hand him a wet rag for a fevered brow. They rigged the horses with water bags and made countless trips to the lake.

Weeononka and Two Hands were among the stricken. She was strong and fought the disease as though it were a physical

enemy with whom she wrestled for two nights. The boy was
frailer. For a while Iron Hand thought he was gone. The
Blossum fell over giving Weeononka a drink of water. For days
it looked as if everyone in the village was going down. There
weren't enough well persons to care for the sick. Soon persons
in lesser stages were nursing those worse off. Then the sick
began to die.

Many Trees Singing was the first to go. "All the trees are
singing," he said, eyes shining, to Iron Hand just before the
end. "Listen . . . the pines which grow fast are the voices of
those who died as little boys. Hear it—hear it? The dogwood
are the young girls with their high sweet voices. The oaks are
the strong young braves; the hickories are their proud wives.
You heard that—my own sweet woman—so long ago and now
she calls me with the voice of the hickory." He grabbed Iron
Hand's sleeve. "Now I hear the cedars, the old people with
their low ancient songs." His eyes closed. "I can hear them, all
the trees of Arkansas. . . ." He made a sound not unlike an
old stubborn cedar creaking against the wind and breathed no
more.

Iron Hand bent close to his ear and whispered, "Walk
toward the setting sun, Many Trees Singing, and don't look
back."

Others like him found the songs they'd been practicing all
their lives, but many went quietly. The scarred old war chief,
One Thunder Turtle, hovered unconscious for days, but then
rallied. Many did not. There were no places and too few hands
to dig graves. They found a box canyon off the main canyon of
the cave. There they put the dead together under gray lichen-
coated stones.

The awful cairn grew very high. But after an impossible time
when all but Iron Hand and Jeanette lay groaning around
them, the disease abated. He thought he knew the exact
moment when he saw the evil shadow depart by the mulberry
tree. But he was tired and may have imagined it.

In a new light he regarded Jeanette, who was sipping a
buffalo horn of sassafras tea, unmindful of him and faint with
exhaustion. She had been wonderful with the sick people,
especially the children. There would be no more whispers
about evil dwarf spirits. He reflected that this remarkable
woman had enlightened these people.

And me, too, he conceded silently. He meant to tell her he
didn't know what he would have done without her. But he

wasn't sure how to go about it, so he started in a roundabout way. "Only seventy-eight of them are left," he said quietly in French.

They were resting before the single large fire they had kept going in the old Quapaw way, with the ends of three burning logs pointed together, near the line of shadow beyond which one stepped out of the cave and into the forest. It was about noon on a misty day when the sky came all the way down to the ground, settled among the trees, and darkened everything with moisture.

She didn't reply right away. Wrapped in a huge dressed buffalo hide she almost looked like a child again. But her glance was full of old thoughts. "That's the first time you've called them anything but 'us.'"

"Only seventy-eight out of more than a thousand individuals in less than ten years."

"It's a terrible arithmetic," said she who had given much thought to measurements large and small.

"You know one of us brought the cholera."

"Or D'Arcy."

"Whatever. It doesn't matter which white man, the point is we're all death to these people."

"All people die."

Jeanette was beginning to sound like The Blossom and Weeononka. She was more Quapaw than he would ever be, he thought as she continued, "But your son will live. He'll have sons and daughters, and some of them will live. At least you have a child." She was saying she never would. The world's most perfect dwarf would die without issue. "I've always feared it. But it still makes me angry."

He expected hot tears from her but she didn't descend into self-pity. She was *angry*. "All I ever wanted was to be like a normal person. Then I met you and saw you loved me—that is, I thought you loved me the way I was." She looked up, saw the pain her words etched on his face, and added, "It doesn't matter, Henri, because that changed me, even if I misunderstood you, you at least taught me to accept what I am. Since then I realized I can be as normal as I can be—I can love, and marry and have children." Her eyes were rounded in wide-open declaration of whom she would like their father to be.

"There's still time," he said thoughtlessly, wishing he hadn't as soon as the words left his lips. "For you . . . that is, to . . . find someone . . . and . . ." He backed away from finishing the thought as he inwardly evaded her silent plea. But even if she found a husband, how could she carry a normal child to term inside her miniature body?

One of the surviving elders, now the oldest in the tribe, wandered toward them at that point, barefooted, wrapped in his buffalo robe, and so saved Iron Hand from further discomfitting conversation. The five remaining councillors had earlier stumbled into the cold council lodge, roused a woman to get them a fire going, then lit their pipes for a meeting. They'd been at it all morning.

"Aren't your toes cold, old one?" Iron Hand asked.

The elder politely ignored Iron Hand's oversolicitation. "We have decided to adopt you," he said to Jeanette. At first she wasn't even aware she was the object of his address. The people were always deferential to Iron Hand; it was she they usually ignored.

"They want to make you a Quapaw, Jeanette."

"No," said the old man, recognizing a couple of the French words Iron Hand directed to the white woman. "Nobody can pronounce this woman's French name."

"*Me?*" Jeanette said, unsure of the tone she was hearing from this old man, who would have completely ignored her a few days earlier.

"From now on your name will be *Honska'weeon wash tay*." Having said his piece he shuffled back toward the council lodge then remembered something else. "The women will host the ceremony as soon as The Blossum's up to it," he said over his shoulder and moved on.

"What did he say?"

"Your new name," Iron Hand replied in French, then repeated the Quapaw phrase, "*Honska'weeon wash tay*." He chuckled in a way that showed he highly approved its intentional irony.

"What does it mean?"

"Your name's bigger than you are."

"Don't tease me, *Gaucher*," she replied, calling him the nickname La Salle's men had used when they didn't think he could hear. Later, in a contemplative moment he would reflect that his own people had labeled him with a name that implied his loss: *Gaucher*, that is, Lefty. But the Osotony, in naming him Iron Hand, which they associated with their adopted son's skill in the ball game, implied no reference to the hand he'd lost, only to the magical "hand," or unidexterity he displayed at ball. In this revelation lay the source of attraction that bonded him to these people. Thereafter he never again suffered the cold, greasy nightmares that had nettled his sleep since Sabat's death. Continued reflection in years to come gave him comfort long after the events, but at the time he was merely relieved by Jeanette's tease—it meant she accepted his rejection and was growing away from scorning him. He'd noticed she no longer stared at him in that hungry, unnerving manner. Maybe they could at least be *tahunsa,* as the people would say. He translated the Sioux into French for his new cousin: "*Honska'weeon wash tay* means Big Happy Woman."

A few more of the Osotony Quapaw died, mostly old ones and the frailer children. One pregnant women didn't survive. But it looked as though the cholera had run its course. For a long time the cave was silent with many slumbering people. Eventually, babies again cried merely because they were hungry, dogs stirred up dust with their bone quarrels, and life reemerged among the Quapaw.

Before long the young women took up their buffalo hoes and climbed into the sunshine of the cornfields. The surviving eldest among the men conferred with The Blossom.

The fieldwomen returning that warm night confirmed what the stars and moon and old men told the Mother of the village. She held the palest green bud of the grain in its cradle of split leaves, in deep meditation, then suddenly, violently (as a reminder that the corn and all food had to be killed) she wrenched it apart, smelled the mash, and put it in her mouth, slowly chewing, then nodded as she spit out the pulp after sucking all the vitals from it. "It's time for the green corn festival," she formally announced. All the women grinned around her, joining hands in a singing swaying circle, their feet playing on the skin of the earth. Behind them, The Blossum handed Weeononka the crushed cornbud.

"By this taste . . ." the old woman said, deep voiced as she came awake from her trance, "know the exact moment." Weeononka reverently ate the remains of the ear, eyes closed, savoring the green-sweet but, in aftertaste, acrid, morsel; for days The Blossom had set her to privately sampling the crop, testing for that specific ratio of green-to-ripeness, training her as The Blossom's own taste buds had been trained. In this way many generations of women had been able to pass along a way of determining the exact time for the green corn festival.

By now the women's cadence was a chant, their lyric sensuous and mindless, the beat the most ancient rhythm tattooed on the human being—the asynchronous rhyme of heartbeat. The song drew Osotony from all over the compound.

The men out on the playing field heard it first as a faint vibration from the dust beneath their bare feet, followed by the once-a-year melody from the throats of the women. The song ended that afternoon's ball game. The players smiled among themselves, aimed their throng toward the cleansing lake, where all were struck with uncharacteristic shyness.

Iron Hand could get no definite statement from his more experienced cousins about what would happen at the festival. He'd been hearing about this ceremony for years but had never been in any Indian town for its celebration. The tribes were usually all too glad to enlighten white men of their religion and customs. But here the Osotony became reticent, sly and shy at the same time with knowing smiles that infuriated because they shut him out, reminding him that for all of it, he would forever remain an outsider because his mother was not Quapaw born.

"But what am I supposed to do?" he demanded, soaking at the lake edge. A Red behind him cleared his throat; one of his own team members glanced up and shook his head, indicating Iron Hand was wasting his breath with foolish questions.

"The green corn festival is to be lived," said the Red player with an attitude closest to embarrassment he'd seen among them. "That is all."

They usually joked roughly with each other after a game, but this evening they barely spoke as they sand-scrubbed their bodies and rinsed many times. They oiled themselves and attached the brightest feathers and ornaments to hair, ear, and ankle.

"I must know the correct behavior for a warrior during the festival," Iron Hand demanded but was politely ignored by the men as they completed their grooming, all this done with the faraway song of the women as a bewitching accompaniment.

A long spring twilight lingered on the vibrant air. Naked and gleaming, the band of warriors strolled toward the brow of the mountain, picking up a counterpointed melody they chanted back to the women.

"At least give me some idea so I won't dishonor you—"

Still the older warriors pretended not to hear him as they raised their song, but one younger warrior took pity on him.

"It is considered unlucky to ever speak of this night in words," the brave reluctantly whispered behind the others and continued as if imparting the gravest of secrets. "Hold your seed as long as possible—" The white man looked as though he didn't understand.

"It is great *wa kon* to make the pleasure last all night."

"All night?" Iron Hand muttered in French.

"Surely you white people know of this practice," the youth said incredulously as they neared the cornfields. Because this wide flat zone of the plateau had been cleared of trees, the nearby eastern-facing cliffreach offered a spectacular, eye-widening view. The hazy blue countryside rolled away from their mountain for hundreds of leagues to the south, east, and north. Behind them was the west obscured by the length of their forested mountain plateau. Set in the purple east was the moon's first orange shoulder reaching with perceptible motion from the other side of the world. Iron Hand could not remember ever being as conscious of the lunar body hanging out there in space; it seemed to shiver.

Suddenly, he remembered another clear night a lifetime ago around the world's own shoulder, himself a lad peering through his first 'scope, a marvelous collapsing leather-clad contraption. His father had brought back the instrument from a business trip to The Netherlands. This was during the war. The journey had been dangerous, but the old man nevertheless returned laden with gifts for his wife, sons, and houseservants. That night nine-year-old Henri de Tonti saw the moon as a new thing, no longer merely a mysterious light but a spherical object possessing dimension, weight, and texture that a man could cast a shadow upon if he but had the means to cross God-only-knew how many *arpents* of space.

Standing very still among his adopted people on this spring night of his fortieth year he felt a similar jolt of perception. The earth trembled beneath his bare feet. In perfect time with the ancient beat was the drum music of the women stepping in unison onto the path, approaching out of the western cliffside, even more wildly costumed than the waiting warriors. To a woman they had painted themselves with the sacred green earth from upriver Mandan and Dakotah territory. They appeared carrying on their heads and hips clay vessels sloshing with the dark drink that would induce visions. Iron Hand had watched Weeononka gather the various ingredients—a dark stew of dried things, including an ugly mushroom dearly

traded from the southern tribes. She'd intrigued him with
erotic descriptions of its effects, but wouldn't then let him
sample any. Now, offered a potfull, he gulped his portion,
handed it by a winsome girl just into her twelfth spring,
whose nipples were painted as great eyes in colored honey and
ground spices. The drink spilled into his beard and he would
have pulled it away but the womanchild reached on tiptoes to
lift it up and up until the dark bittersweet juice ran down his
neck, chest, groin, thigh, calf, and foot in cool tingling
rivulets.

Now the moon lost its blush and clarified as it loomed higher
up the dark sky, a benediction of light strong enough to
illuminate colors and cast shadows beneath the men and
women merging in a wave of song, bells, and stamping feet.
The tempo increased, the volume heightened. Soon a wide
circle—man, woman, man, woman—ringed the dancing field.
The ring broke somewhere and the circle became a snake. In
the moonlight individual faces passed as the human chain
wound its careful way through the living presences of the
largest cornfield. It was not planted in mathematically precise
European rows, but randomly. Each corn tree had its own
widely trenched declivity and central mound, tended immaculately by one woman, who gave each plant a name, spoke, and
sang to it, and generally treated it as a child.

A woman's voice rose above the others. Iron Hand strained
to see who it was, but the shoulder-high cornstalks blended
with the shapes of painted, dancing people. He thought it was
Weeononka, but couldn't see any particular singer among the
green and swaying bodies. The visions began with twinkling
stars between the cool plants, stars that reflected off the sky in
a woman's eyes; he felt strong masculine hands on his back
pushing him toward a woman apart from the others, a woman
who moved seductively among the leaves and stalks. The
hands gave him to her and soon he didn't need their push. The
female laughed. It was Weeononka. It was The Blossum with
her extraordinary breasts as blue and pale as alabaster in the
moonlight. It was the child who had given the drink to him.
Her costume of freshly cut corn fronds slithered between the
living stalks. He reached out but she eluded him with another
crystalline laugh as sharp as the edges of the corn leaves that
cut if they struck just right. He ran between the plants,
conscious of the feeling that he could smell or hear their
vibrating growth as his skin brushed by. They seemed to

whisper to him in a simple language. The earth was cool and pleasantly damp beneath his toes. He called Weeononka's name, but only the rustling corn leaves answered. One shadow moved over there. Now he appeared to be alone with the elusive woman. He pursued the trace of her scent on the moon-warm breeze.

She laughed a third time; he whirled to see her standing in the glow, waiting only for him. Her bare arms beckoned; it was not Weeononka, not The Blossum nor the girl. She was all of them, yet not any one woman but the incarnation of all, the body of the corn itself with bursting bosoms of grain rising up straight from the fresh earth, nipples as hard and long as the tips of the corn ears and as full of sweet pink milk. He reached for her, and she drew him down into the shimmering shadows.

The loamy earth smelled rich, almost womanly, preserving the illusion that the ancient Earth Mother lifted her loins to receive him.

He plunged into her, uttering a joyous cry the people were waiting to hear. Their song renewed, they clustered near the couple at the heart of the corn forest, cheering Iron Hand on as he stroked again and again into the Corn Maiden.

She screamed and sang in pleasure, her own voice enlarged by the voices of the women who swayed, stamping in time with Iron Hand's pleasured rhythm. He saw then who she was as his seed flowed into her—not his wife, not the girl, nor the Mother of the village, but his perfect image of Woman, *Honska'weeon wash tay*, as she had been in the long ago.

"Sweet Jesus," he cried, impaled by stinging memories, about to withdraw even though it was too late. He had spent his fortune and now only wished to remain inside the warm sweet vault of her, scruples be damned. "I . . . so sorry," he whispered, absorbed by revulsion when he perceived her abnormally short arms, more evident as a dwarf's now that she'd matured. So he wouldn't have to look at her, he buried his face in her curls the color and scent of roasted corn. He would have drunk her and licked the cup if she'd been wine, disgusted with himself all the while like a drunkard who knows his degradation when he sticks his tongue into the bottle to capture the last sheen on the glass. Racked by the conflict between pleasure and disgust, he surrendered the weight of his head to the pillow of her hair and groaned mindlessly.

"Shhh," Jeanette crooned, holding him inside herself a little longer the way The Blossum had taught her. She'd sung all the right songs, repeated the right chants beside the river, and prepared her body the way the elder woman said would attract the spirit of a child.

"I always hurt you. . . ." He would have gone on to apologize.

"No, you've made me very happy."

"But, Jeanette," he choked back a wave of nausea—her head was so large. She seemed far more alien than the copper-skinned Osotony. Though he hated his inability to forget that she was a freak, he couldn't fight the prejudice. Ashamed, he hid behind an excuse, "I love another. . . ."

"Yes." She seemed resigned but without sadness. "I know you'll never love me."

He would have penetrated the enigma of her acceptance; something important resided in her answer, but it eluded him as strong hands on his back pulled him free of her. This time the hands were not the warriors' but the women's, who spun him around to the girl who'd given him the drink. Iron Hand had been spent, but the sight of her and the taste of her spicy breasts warmed him. The men dealt Jeanette out to the boys and the warriors and the old men. As each lover rolled away, he or she joined with another until the warm earth between the corn was alive with writhing, moaning shadows.

The moon hovered at its highest point then began to slide off down the other side. Still the people came together until everyone—man, woman, child large enough to participate, old men, old women, the crippled and the ugly as well as the beautiful and the young—everyone had been swived royally. A runner had been dispatched just after The Blossum had announced the festival. Now the number of adults swelled as clans and neighbors arrived through the night, dropped off the babies with the three old men (and one late-term pregnant woman) on whom celebacy had been precariously enforced. They were the fire tenders, who also tended the babies on this sacred night. But what old man, grumpy because he can't join in the primary ritual, wants to babysit squalling brats? So the babies had their own portions of the drink, and slept, while the old men entertained each other with stories of their glory days.

The night added to itself and lasted to the participants longer than normal. They piled deadfall branches onto a bonfire to kindle sweat lodges already dug for that purpose. Refreshed, many went on to love until dawn, culminating with a favorite or a beloved.

Iron Hand woke in Weeononka's arms. She'd been awake and watching him for some time. Behind her the sky was blue, the sun halfway to meridian.

"So, that is the festival," he said, hoping to draw her out about the Corn Maiden. "Was it really Jeanette?"

"Bad *wa kon to*—"

"—to talk about it, I know, but just answer that one question."

"It was all of us," she whispered. "But it was *Honska'weeon wash tay* who got the first of your seed corn."

On an elbow he looked around. Straight green cornstalks shuddered in a breeze but he could see no other couples.

"We're the last," she said, giggling. Every woman in the field had wanted some of his *wa kon*. She'd never seen such stamina, and now it looked as though he had been thoroughly renewed by his long sleep.

"Our fields are well plowed," she joked, eyes flickering, her hand quick to answer "yes" to his manhood.

"You tricked me, you witch."

"Nobody had to force you, Iron Hand."

39

"I think you deliberately slow down work on my hand," he accused Weeononka. She had cut out the shape of the buffalo leather sleeve to which she'd bind the metal palm with wet rawhide strips. She planned to fill the sleeve with cattail fluff and stitch it directly to his jacket. Iron Hand silently reflected that as a weapon it would be about as useful as a pillow.

He had grave doubts about it working. Besides, the lead casting weighed twice as much as Mansard's; this crude imitation would be as heavy as a small cannon ball.

"I'm ready to go to the lake for cattails," she replied mildly. "Why don't you come with me?"

By this time the Osotony possessed two horses from one of Iron Hand's fur trades. The tribe held them mainly for prestige, while Iron Hand was teaching the men to ride. It would be another generation before any of the tribes became fabled horsemen.

He and Weeononka took the horses out the next morning,

alone together for the first time in too long. They found cattails
in annual explosion in the lake shallows then rode through a
meadow to the mountain's long northern brow. They dismounted and let the horses graze on yellow flowers. The river
valley was resplendent in the hazy afternoon atmosphere far
below them. On the northern horizon a plume of dust marked
a buffalo herd.

"I guess that means a hunting party will go out tomorrow or
the next day," he said, unable to take his feasting eyes from the
horizon-to-horizon expanse of wide open virgin land. He could
imagine smoke curling from a hundred prosperous plantations,
forges, towns, and mills. He could see windmills and diverted
river mill traces, bustling French villages, the crisscross of
possible roads, bridges, and ferry wakes. La Salle's vision
possessed him and made him see all this possibility on the
shimmering air.

"Yes," she replied, shielding her eyes from the sun, feeling
distanced from him by something she didn't understand, "will
you go with the buffalo hunters?"

He shrugged. "Without a pistol I'm useless to those
professionals. But if we can solve this problem"—he gestured
with his arm—"I may travel with them as far as the river."

This remark was pregnant with implication.

"I have bad feelings about your leaving."

He watched the glittering horizon as though it held
solutions to his problems. "How can I stay here knowing that
some Dutch whoreson lied about Rob? There's nobody else to
make amends. You know the law of duty better than anyone."

"It's an excessive law humans can often ignore," she replied,
refusing to fuel his argument.

"The mother buffalo will abandon the calf who can't keep up
with the herd," he countered, quoting her directly. That's how
she'd explained that Indian mothers must, under certain social
conditions, take the lives of their children.

She didn't like it when he used her own voice to contradict
her. But this was a mere spat; what was really bothering her
was that he was going to leave.

He saw in her position the universal female complaint that
men don't stay home enough. He tried to comfort her with sex
but there was only one comfort she'd accept: that he'd relent,
tell her she was right, and not leave.

"It's not only for myself," she said. "It's for the Osotony. Look
how they love you. Stay here and be a king among them."

Instead of the Quapaw phrase for great chief, *chasa on ta pe ka*, she used the French word *roi*.

"I'm no king. The concept sickens me. I'm just a man and all I have is what I am to others."

"No—you have your own *aneh* apart from any other, even me and Two Hands and the Osotony. You said yourself this is where your heart is."

"And I meant it. I'm only going to help the governor, to secure my possessions, and to right the wrong that's been done to my friend."

She didn't reply.

"Warriors must go to war." He was quoting an old Quapaw saying. She was mad at him for saying honorable things. The plain truth was she wanted him to stay with her and forget about honor of either white or red variety. He took advantage of her silence to suggest that she could come with him if she wished.

"Are you crazy, white man? Here I'm somebody. In French places I'm nothing but a stupid squaw." For fear he might laugh at her she kept private her vow never to leave the Quapaw again.

"You will come as my wife," he said gently. "The priest at Arkansas Post can marry us."

"We already are married."

"I mean under my customs. You'll be Madame de Tonti."

"Change my name?" She couldn't believe what he was suggesting. Her manitou had not indicated through dream or omen that she should change her name. What was wrong with this man?

De Tonti missed the nuance, however, in his enthusiasm for his plan. "Come with me, please."

"I left you the first time because I knew I was supposed to live as Quapaw—not a white woman. Besides, they need me here."

He knew she wouldn't leave but he was trying to make a gesture of affection that would soften her. "Anyway, I'm coming home when all that's finished." He took her in his arms. Most of the time he called her *La Vite*, Fleet Woman, or her Quapaw name, Weeononka. But this time he used his special name for her: "This will always be home to me, Arkansas. I may wander far and wide but I'll always come home to you."

She was letting him embrace her but she wasn't hugging back.

"I tell you I have bad feelings. I had a dream . . ."

"You're always having dreams."

"But this one was about you. I think it means if you leave here you can never return."

"Nonsense. I own this country, didn't I tell you? It's all mine. I'm bringing back silkworms to spin among the mulberry leaves, trappers to hunt the buffalo, carpenters to build us a fine house, *habitants* to grow crops—I'm going to make this the most bountiful plantation in His Majesty's domain." He gestured at the panorama spread out below their feet, the heartland of the Arkansas River Valley, fertile and waiting. "This is going to be Paradise."

From Brother Martin she knew the concept. "This already is Paradise," she said, twisting away from him. "Why do you have to own it? What does that mean, own? How can you own the land? The land owns people, not the other way around."

He realized that she'd never understand. None of the Indians would ever understand about property. They truly were savage, he reflected at that moment, looking at this woman he loved so dearly. A savage, for all her beauty and intelligence. She'd never be civilized, even if she did speak French and no longer painted red clay in her partline because he asked her to stop the ugly practice. But she was still boiling their hasty pudding the way her people had boiled food in tight-woven baskets for thousands of years. D'Arcy had given her an iron pot for a wedding present. Instead of putting it over the flame she still boiled food by dropping hot rocks into it. Some of the younger wives were cooking over the flame in the modern way, but Weeononka was holding out. She'd never learn.

"I've accepted the ways of your people," he replied. "You can accept mine."

"But their ways are wrong. You accepted ours because you know in your heart they're right. Now you want to deviate from what's right."

"It's my duty."

"You accepted this as your duty when we mated."

"But that was before I knew about this attack on La Salle's reputation—he was the greatest explorer New France produced. His vision was so large, so ultimately destined to become reality, people couldn't understand him—"

"Robert La Salle was a fool." And far too like another man

she'd known who was unable to carry out his big vision, but she refrained from speaking of the dead Osage chieftain.

"I'm not going to argue with you." He remounted the horse. She saw another tack. She walked to him and leaned against his leg. "I don't mind your taking a second wife, if you desire to."

"That's the last thing on my mind."

"I mean if you want a white woman, I'd understand."

"You mean Jeanette?"

"She loves you—"

His respect for Jeanette was great after her undaunted care during the cholera epidemic. He expected her to be his friend for life, but he had no other feelings for her, despite the charade of the green corn festival. If that ritual pleased the poor woman, very well, then, but it meant little to him. In fact he was ashamed because he felt he'd taken advantage of her again. But the thought of taking her to wife, of taking any woman as a second wife, repelled him. He kneed the horse forward to leave Weeononka standing on her unwarranted assumptions.

But she ran after him as he circled around to meet her. She leaned against him again. He desired her warmth and to reassure her she was the only woman he wanted, so he dismounted, taking off his shirt and loincloth. He slowly undressed her and they made long lazy *wa kon* on his buffalo robe spread in the tall nodding grasses.

They mounted the same horse. The big spotted creature headed for its home corral followed by the riderless bay who tagged behind.

Behind her husband, Weeononka held on with her arms around him, whispering, "I beg you, listen to my words. Some things, sometime, are mighty *wa kon*. This is one of those times."

She could feel him listening.

"The events that brought us together are not of the earth but of the spirit. I believe this vision you shared with me long ago—that we're supposed to parent a mighty nation, the best of my people and the best of yours. You and I together are the *wa kon*. If you separate your half from mine all the magic will be spilled and will seep into the earth, which is jealous of such power in the hands of mere human beings. Please, I beg you. Stay here and help me keep the fire of our *wa kon* alive."

They crossed the meadow. A flock of mergansers settled on the lake. The sky turned pink then orange with sunset.

"Beautiful wife, now you listen to me. We cannot live as though this is the only place on earth. See that horizon?" He tugged on the horse's mane to halt it for a moment, pointing eastward where the sky was already purple and shot with stars. A crescent moon was on the rise. "Over there lies my destiny, my nation's forces—its law and rule. I must go there and let them know I'm alive because I'm part of that. I'm apart of this, too. But even though our mountain looks like an island rising out of the land down there, it's not really isolated.

"We'll die if we try to pretend what's happening down there can't reach up here and hurt us. I can use the law of ownership to secure my claim on this country. That's the best way I know to love and protect the Osotony. If I don't go back and do this thing, others will steal my land from me."

"How? How can men steal the land?" she demanded. "Will they come with big baskets and dig the earth away and throw it in another place? Explain this stealing of land to me that I may go and be a witness to such *wa kon.*"

"On paper. It's all stored on paper far away in a big stone lodge. I've explained all this to you before. You don't want to understand because you want to keep me here."

She regarded the truth of this as the horse's slow movements rocked them. "You really mean to go back no matter what, don't you, Henri de Tonti?"

"As soon as I make a suitable hand."

"No matter what, then, you are going to leave me."

He drew the horse up. "I promise you, I'll always come home to you, Arkansas."

They sat very still with a light westerly wind in their faces, she holding him comfortably around the waist, enjoying the feel of his strong back against her face and body. She saw he was going, whether he had a hand or not. It would mean so much to him to have the marvelous metal hand when he returned to his own people. He was a brave good man, she thought, finally surrendering her secret because she loved him. "My husband, I know where your hand is."

He twisted to look her in the eye as if he thought she might be playing a joke on him.

"It will have to be taken by trickery," she continued. "Maybe we can steal it—"

"Where? Where is it?" He looked as if he might kick the horse into an immediate gallop.

"The Taencas have in it their medicine bundle."

He threw back his head and laughed.

"They worship that hand now that it killed the alligator chief—"

He laughed even harder at such a ludicrous image. What would Mansard say if he knew his handiwork had become a golden calf?

"It's not a laughing matter, husband. That medicine man will kill you if he catches you stealing his god. We've got to think of a plan, ask One Thunder Turtle to organize a raid—"

Mirth remained on his face as he interrupted her. "We'll find a way, I'm sure. You did not have to tell me this. I would never have known. . . ."

"But—"

"Beautiful wife, let me thank you."

Shyly she avoided his eyes, wishing she had told him long ago. Now it seemed small of her to have thought she could hold him like that. But he was kind and understood. She snuggled closer to him. He kneed the horse toward the trail that led back down to the cave. His hand squeezed her own around him and she knew without seeing that his golden eyes were smiling. "Just remember my words, husband," she said, putting her ear against his spine. "When you're out there and can't find your way home, remember I warned you." His flesh was hot and smelled good enough to lick.

He felt her warm breath on his shoulder. His mind was suddenly aflame with schemes but he was also thinking, Thank you, thank you, thank you—someday you'll come to understand how much this means to me.

Weeononka curved to fit herself against Iron Hand's back. She was thinking, We may not see with the same eyes, white man, but at least we are traveling in the same direction.